Edited by Ann Attwood

Dedicated to all the people who have helped me make this dream a reality.

A Midwinter Night's Dream

By Samuel J White

6/8/2023

Prologue

I t's every single nineteen-year-old male's fantasy that on a dull cold winter's day, fate may twist their way and call upon them to save a damsel in distress and finish the night embraced in her naked body. But that's just fantasy. These things don't really happen and definitely not to me... or so I thought.

The lady—whose name was Katarzyna—and I were both naked. We were tightly cuddled up together sheltering from a heavy snowstorm under a haystack. We were squashed into a small gap between the layers of hay bales where two people could barely squeeze. I couldn't see her in the darkness, but our shivering bodies were so close that our chins were resting on each other's shoulders, and I could feel her heart beating against my chest.

She kept apologising for the smell of stale tobacco on her breath, and that she kept coughing and sneezing. I just rubbed her on the back and told her it was okay if it meant she was alive. However, I was grateful that she used a handkerchief.

If we were both going to succumb to hypothermia, it seemed she was more likely to slip away first. I wasn't going to let that happen, so I tried to keep her talking.

I was starting to doubt myself over what was really

going on. I was so cold and tired that I seemed to be drifting in and out of reality myself.

I was no longer sure if I was really there in that haystack with that terrified, shivering, lovely young woman, or if I was there alone and she was a figment of my imagination. What if she was just made up in my head? Or a ghost maybe of a lost soul. Or perhaps the whole thing was just a twisted teenaged dream.

You're probably wondering how two people who had never laid eyes on each other until that evening could end up in such a twisted situation, naked in the middle of a haystack in a cold dark field. Well, this is how it began.

Part 1 Before The Dreams

Chapter 1

A cold winter's night

Things never go according to plan. At the beginning of every day we are alive, we set out our plans only to find that nothing happens in the way we expect. Sometimes the events of that one day can change a person, either for better or for worse. Just a chance meeting with a stranger can change the course of your life forever.

It was a cold evening in mid-December 2008 when I left my job at a hotel on the Norfolk coast. I was nineteen, and I had been working as a fitness instructor. This basically meant I looked after the gym and pool. Sometimes, if I was super lucky, I did some instructing.

I was supposed to be on the morning shift for once and planned to stay after work to work out before going home.

However, things started to look ominous at around 1 pm when my colleague Chloe, the lifeguard who was supposed to be closing up that night, began arguing with the hotel manager over days off.

To be fair to Chloe, she was in the right. The manager, Katherine, was being her usual bitchy self because Chloe wanted to take time off work for her daughter's birthday. Finally, Chloe stormed out and went home, probably getting herself in more trouble. She shouted an apology to me as she left, knowing that I was going to have to close up.

I was used to Katherine behaving like this towards staff. With the attitude she was giving out, I would have turned a blind eye if Chloe had smacked her one. Chloe would later be put on a warning rather than being sacked for leaving, because the rest of the staff pleaded her case. However, that didn't help me that night. To avoid getting on the wrong side of Katherine's vile irrational temper, I didn't protest. She liked to make trouble, and I wanted to get back in her good books, even though she had not been at all grateful for the other twelve times that month I had covered for both shifts.

To me, staying at work that night wasn't such a disastrous prospect considering I was alone. My parents were on holiday and not coming back for two weeks or more, and I didn't have any friends outside of work. As for a love life? Forget it. As a youngster, I never had a problem, but that changed since I started high school.

I'd always been shy. My best friend moved away and left me friendless when I was about ten years old, and I struggled to find more friends. After a bad experience, I had never since had the guts to talk to a girl, let alone ask one out on a date.

It was a slow evening at work. I left at about 10:30 pm, facing Arctic blizzards as I walked out to my car. I didn't know how long the snow had been falling. From the amount that lay on the vehicles, it must have been coming down for hours. I only wore my uniform shorts and jumper, so the snow was stinging my legs.

The journey home in my 1993 Mini City was going to be difficult because there was ice everywhere. To add to that the old-style lock was frozen, but luckily I was ready for it with some warm water.

People laughed at me because I was a 6ft 3in, masculine, well-toned guy driving a car fit for a little old lady. They stopped laughing when I reminded them that physical size had nothing to do with the size of your bank account. Anyway, my Mini was a classic, a stylish car.

I turned the key once, and the car made a chugging noise before going silent. I tried once more, but again the car spluttered and died. I reached down and pulled out the choke as far as I could. (A choke is a pull-out lever used to help start older cars in cold weather. It's something that is automatic in newer cars.)

"Third-time lucky girl," I said to my car, more in hope than in confidence that I would be getting home that night. I turned the key a third time and held it there as the Mini choked and spluttered with more purpose than the previous attempt. Finally, she roared into life.

I got out of the car to clear snow from the windscreen. When I got back in, heat was already firing out into the small space in front of it. I let the engine run for a few minutes to get the car warmed up before leaving. The previous night it had stalled halfway down the hill due to a cold engine.

The headlights were never very bright, but the snow clouded them more than usual. I drove the car slowly up the hill and out of the town onto the A140.

I turned off through Roughton Village, where I stopped for fuel before heading up another hill. From here there were no street lamps to help light the way, and the snow was piling thicker the windscreen. I now had to cover fourteen miles along the dark open road which barely touched the edge of the next town, before heading home between more fields.

As I said before, it was the first winter that I had driven in snow. Although the road had been gritted earlier, the snow was now piling up and causing the car to lose its grip. I was the only driver on the road as I continued into the dazzling flashes of hypnotic snow.

I found it terribly hard not to just gaze into the flakes as they fell towards me in their millions. I squinted and tried to focus on the two small beams of headlights while the radio played Christmas songs, many of which had already been on a hundred times that week.

I was utterly transfixed by the blizzard, when something to my left suddenly caught my eye. A black shape at the side of the road cast a shadow in the headlights. I slammed my foot on the brake, and immediately the car went into a rear end skid. Thankfully I was not going very fast so the car soon came to a standstill albeit facing the side of the road.

Breathing hard, I had the sense to put the car in neutral and leave the engine running. I suddenly saw the shape in front of me again. It seemed to be a man struggling in the snow as he walked towards the car. I sat for a moment not sure what to do. I had heard the rumours about strange people out on dark roads who pulled over cars and robbed the people inside before taking the vehicle. I thought to myself that if they were going to rob me, they should just steal the car and drop me off at home. At least then I could claim it on insurance and get another car. Then again, I loved my old car like a friend, and it had much sentimental value.

The dark hooded figure stood briefly in the headlamps. My heart was thumping, and thoughts were running through my head. I must have died, and the man was the grim reaper on his way to fetch me.

The grim reaper, however, would not fall on the floor in a lifeless heap in the snow.

Chapter 2

The stranger in the snow

I opened the door with caution and approached the figure lying in the snow at the side of the road. The person's head was covered by the hood of their coat, and they were coughing hard.

Not really being the most forward of people, I slowly leaned forward and offered my hand. A soft gloved hand reached up very gingerly and took mine. Although the man was a tiny bit shorter than me, he seemed incredibly heavy. It was only when I got him to his feet that I realised he was carrying a large rucksack.

I heard a muffled thank you from under the hood. "Are you okay?" I shouted above the howling wind. The person nodded vigorously, but it seemed he was unable to speak freely due to the cold air crushing both of our voices. Regardless of what he was doing there, leaving anyone out on that road in those conditions was a death sentence.

"Can I give you a lift anywhere?" I asked, as I took his hand and led him to the side of the car to shelter from the wind. Again, he nodded with enthusiasm, but struggled to speak.

I went around the car to the driver's door, reaching in

to unlock the passenger door before pushing the seat forward to allow the man room to put his bag in the back of the car. Then I let the seat back down, so he could get in. He was shaking from the cold, so I helped him put his seatbelt on.

I pulled the car over to the side of the road and turned on the inside light. The hood of my passenger's thick coat left only his eyes exposed. Although he had tried to shake off the snow, it still lay on him in patches.

"Are you okay?" I asked again, turning all the heat outlets on the Mini's dashboard towards the passenger.

My passenger loosened his hood and reached inside to pull down what seemed to be a shawl that covered his mouth and nose from the snow.

He seemed to be struggling with the change in the air and went into a violent coughing fit, fighting for at least forty seconds to get it under control. Instinctively, I patted him on the back to try and help. After the coughing stopped, it took him several moments to catch his breath. My arm still rested on his back.

"Thank you so much," said a shivery and surprisingly high foreign-sounding voice.

"It's not a problem," I replied, although I was quite irritated by the fact that I had almost crashed my car. However, all thoughts of irritation were forgotten the moment the figure pulled down his scarf. It was dark, but I could just about make out the outline of his face. I was taken aback because what I saw was not a man, but an icy-cold and very frightened lady.

"You're a woman?" I said, not meaning to say it out loud. She nodded, but didn't speak.

From the little I could see, her face was stinging red with cold and her eyes were wide. The poor lady was crying, but managed to give me a weak smile. She wore a woolly hat, from which a lock of darkened-blonde hair hung down onto her chest. From the small parts of her face that were visible, I would have guessed she was in her mid to late thirties, but admittedly I was not good at guessing ages.

Unsure what to say, I waited for her to speak.

Her quiet voice was a little thick. "I no English," she said softly, in a thick, foreign accent.

"Great." I muttered to myself. "Trust me to pick up somebody who can't speak English." My first instinct was to try the little French I remembered from school. "Ça va?" I asked,

"Oui, ça va," she replied, but then added, "Why are we speak French?"

"You just said *I no English*," I reminded her.

"No, no, no," she said in a much lower voice, waving her hand. She cleared her throat. "I mean to say, I KNOW English, but I sometimes am fucking it up." She smiled weakly through her tears.

I struggled not to laugh at her brutal, blunt honesty. She seemed to see the humour as well. Her cheeks rose in a possible attempt at a smile, but fell again as she shivered.

I took my hand away from where I had patted her on the back. She turned and touched me very gently on the shoulder, then looked at me out of what seemed in the darkness like deep blue eyes. She spoke softly and slowly, "Thank you for helping me out of snow." She blinked and continued, "I am v-very so sorry for c-causing you car to skid."

"The main thing is I didn't hit you," I told her.

She nodded. "But I still am sorry, okay? You could have been also hurt."

"There's no need to cry."

She smiled weakly again and spoke through chattering teeth, "I-I w-will try n-no-to b-but f-fucking cold."

Her poor hands were freezing. "Here let me help you warm your hands," I told her, taking both her hands in mine.

"Thank you," she answered quietly, allowing me to take her gloves off and massage her frozen fingers. Although I could tell she was in pain from her fingers thawing out, she turned to me and smiled. "Y-you are k-kind m-man," she said quietly.

"I'm just trying to help," I smiled.

She smiled right back at me and tried to choke back her tears. "My name is K-Kat- arz-yn - na-na," she told me, through chattering teeth. Realising I may not have heard her right, she spelled it out: "K-a-t-a-r-z-y-n-a."

"It's nice to meet you," I replied. "I'm Robert, but call me Rob. I would offer to shake your hand but—"

"Y-you have already got both my hands," she finished for me. Jokingly, she shook both my hands up and down.

I held both of her hands in mine to massage the heat back into them. Suddenly, she recoiled and took a sharp breath before sneezing the most foreign-sounding sneeze I had ever heard.

"*Aaah etrrasshhoooo!*" To her credit, she made a great effort to sneeze into her own shoulder and avoid covering me in mucous. Only the slightest bit of spray hit me.

"Bless you," I told her, gently squeezing her hand which was unintentionally gripping mine.

"Again, I am so sorry," she squeaked, with a horrified look of anguish on her face, as though she expected me to react angrily. "I no mean to sneeze on you."

"It's okay," I reassured her, squeezing her hands once more. Usually it would have irritated me, but the poor girl couldn't help it, and it was partly my fault. Plus, she seemed to be nice enough and in genuine distress.

My head was going through any number of reasons as to how she came to be out there in the cold miles from civilisation. I couldn't let myself cause her to run away and go back out into the snow.

"You are kind man," she said, as she shivered softly and gave my hands the gentlest of squeezes before letting go.

"You're freezing," I told her.

"Yes" she replied, "Outside is brrrrrrr." She folded her arms tightly and shook about as if to demonstrate how cold it was. For the first time, she smiled slightly.

"You are a long way from home," I told her.

"I am," she nodded, "but I am think out of all strange man I could meet on this night, I have found nice one."

I will add at this point that she had a very thick accent and it was taking me a little while to process what she was saying to me. However, after speaking for a few minutes, she somehow became much clearer.

"Well, thanks," I told her. "Where can I take you to?"

"Any distance you are going will be a help to me," she sniffed. "I am grateful, just very, of your kind help."

Her eyes were still streaming with tears. With her hands still too cold to move, she dabbed her wet eyes on her sleeve. "Time do stop crying," she said in a voice that seemed to be talking to herself as much as to me.

"You don't look like you've been having a good evening."

"You could say that," she replied, warming her hands on the heater. "I have fallen in the snow maybe six times tonight, there is not much of me that is dry…" she paused for a moment. "In fact…" she continued, "…only dry thing I have is tobacco, and I no know if that is good thing or no."

"Why's that?" I asked.

As she opened her mouth to answer, she was overcome by another sneeze, but this time she managed to turn away. She coughed several times and took a deep sniff. "Well," she sniffed, "if I choose item not get wet, it would be mobile phone. You no can call a taxi with a cigarette."

"You can use my phone if you want to call someone," I said, offering her my old battered push-button mobile.

"I no know the number," she sniffed, shaking her head. "And anyway, I no need now you been kind enough to help me."

"Well, at least you can have a cigarette now if you want."

She looked at me like I'd sworn at her. "That's rude," she told me bluntly.

"How have I been rude?" I asked, thinking I'd been very generous offering to let her smoke in my car, considering I hated smoking with a passion.

"No," she said with a little smile. "Kind of you offer, but very rude of me to accept, because it no is nice for you. So, I smoke later."

"Okay, but are you sure? I know what smokers are like when they haven' t had one in a while. Plus, it would warm you up."

"Thank you, but I s-still am wait," she said as she shivered.

"I've got a blanket in the back for the dog to sit on. You can put it around you if you want?" I told her.

"I would be very grateful," she replied through quivering lips. "Also," she went on, "there is flask in top of rucksack. In side pocket a pile of clean handkerchiefs. Would you be kind please enough to pass to me?"

I reached over and grabbed the blanket. At the same time, I unfastened the clip on Katarzyna's rucksack. I took out a medium sized thermos flask and passed it to her. Opening the side pocket, I pulled out one of her neatly folded handkerchiefs and gave her that as well. She was struggling to take the lid off the flask, so I took it from her hands and opened it.

"I no could get off myself," she shivered, "because of cold hands." She put the very corner of her handkerchief in her mouth and let it drop so that it unfolded without the use of her fingers, which were still unable to move. Then she very cleverly dropped the hanky onto her left elbow, leaned forward away from me, and blew her nose into it skilfully.

"That is talented improvisation." I congratulated.

She smiled at me and shrugged. "I am well practiced, because sometimes hands are no work after epileptic fit."

"Well, I'm sorry that happens to you," I told her.

"No be sorry Rob," she smiled brightly. "It one of those things, is no like I no got hands or feet. Is temporary, maybe an hour or two on odd days. I no dying. No a big thing when children are starving in Africa. Plus, this time just is cold hands."

As she finished her sentence, she was overcome by another sneeze, which she dealt with in the same way.

When she finished cleaning herself up, I poured her a cup of soup. "What is that?" I asked, looking sceptically at the cup as I passed it to her.

"It's broccoli and Stilton soup. You have some."

"That's okay, no thanks," I told her.

"You have some," she commanded me teasingly. "You too are cold." She looked down at my bare legs, clad only in my work shorts and asked, "Why are da fuck you got dose on?"

"Work and I'm fine," I replied.

"Well, this my mother's family recipe. I make it myself. You must try, or maybe I will cry again and refuse your kind offer of lift to take my chances with the weather."

I wasn't sure at all about this because I'd never really been a fan of broccoli. I poured some soup into the spare cup and gulped the first mouthful. To my surprise, it was creamy and delicious.

"Your mother's recipe is lovely," I smiled.

A playful smile formed on her face just visible above her scarf. She already looked much warmer.

"You bought that shit!" she almost laughed.

"What's funny?"

"Is no my mother recipe. It just some shit I made to use up left over vegetables in fridge before I went on holiday."

"Is that where you are going to with your huge rucksack at this time of night?"

"Work finish for Christmas. Tonight, I stay in hotel airport. Tomorrow early I fly back home for Christmas holiday."

"So where is it you're from?" I asked, realising it would be polite conversation.

With a little smile, she replied, "You no guess from obvious accent."

"Germany," I guessed.

She smiled and shook her head. "I no speak to you anymore," she told me with a frumpy face, then she gave me a little grin to say she was kidding. "It was excellent try though." She smiled, "Wrong, but good enough for half a point."

I listened intently as Katarzyna explained her situation. "It complicated," she said, smiling as she dabbed her nose. "I am born in Czechoslovakia, now Czech Republic, you know where it is?"

"I think I do?" I nodded, thinking I had a vague idea.

"The thing is," she sniffed, "my mother is from Budapest, Hungary. Her father is German, and my father is Czech. But my grandmother is Polish." She broke for a sneeze. "But where I grow up," she sniffed, "I so close to Germany. Erm..." She looked around for something to compare it to, and as she did, she sneezed again. "I so close, I sneeze out of bedroom window and hit a German."

"You so improvised what you were saying," I teased.

"No-oo-oo," she said, smiling. Her tone told me she was lying.

"The airport is twenty miles away!" I explained.

"I know," she nodded, and put her cup down. "Buses no running because of snow. I get taxi. The taxi driver is bastard. I must walk. Now though," she smiled, "my luck is changing when found you, so if you kindly take me as far as you are going, I walk the rest of way."

"I only live two minutes away."

Her face fell and she went silent. "Well, every little helps I suppose," she sighed.

"I'm not Tesco," I laughed, but the joke went over her head. Obviously, she'd not seen the advert for the supermarket Tesco, whose motto is 'Every little helps' (For anyone who's not familiar with England) "Look I'm only teasing," I told her. You're clearly feeling unwell and shouldn't be out in the snow."

"It's just a cold," she replied.

"Well, you're a lovely person and I don't want you walking any further, especially after you gave me soup," I added, "So I'll take you to the airport."

Her jaw dropped open under her scarf. *"Really?* You'd *do* that?" she squealed.

"Why would I not?" I nodded.

"But is this taking you out of your way?" she queried.

I was a little taken aback when she leaned over and kissed me on the cheek. She must have sensed it because she jumped back and put her hand over her mouth. Her face seemed slightly embarrassed as if she thought she'd gone a bit over the top.

"I'm sorry. I hope I didn't pass you my cold," she squeaked.

"No worries," I told her. "I'm honoured. It's rare for me to get kissed, even on the cheek."

"You should feel honoured," she said brightly. "You are the first person I ever did that to."

"Well it's no problem anyway," I told her, continuing the conversation. "It's only a few miles."

"In this weather, you should be going home to bed." She smiled and added, "But I will let you take me to the hotel on condition that I pay you for your trouble." She reached into her pocket and tried to offer me a £20 note from her wallet, which I waved away. Take it," she said quietly, but firmly.

"Where do you work?" I asked her.

Her expression changed to one of puzzlement. "I was team leader in the Crab company, but I hate that place. So my friend gets me jobs cleaning. I am now head cleaner of holiday homes in summer, and I work with maintenance team in winter," she said proudly. "Why this relevant?"

"Because my sister worked in those places for a while and I know you work long hours for little pay. Even the head cleaner gets peanuts. Spend it on yourself."

"I no am no rich, but no am poor but..." She put her hand flat and held it to her midriff.

"Content, or at least managing?" I suggested.

She nodded and stared at me smiling for a second, then all of a sudden, she sneezed into her handkerchief and coughed several times before continuing.

"I am no doing too badly if I can afford naughty luxuries such as Alcohol, cigarettes as well as holidays, so take the money."

"Maybe you should spend it on Lemsip for your cold," I suggested.

She leaned forward and pulled a mock mean face that made me smile. She then took my arm in both hands and pretended to squeeze it. "I want to give you money," she said, almost laughing.

I could hear youthfulness flooding back into her personality as she warmed up. First, I had thought she sounded about forty, but now would place her in her late twenties to early thirties, or maybe even younger. I might have asked her age if I didn't think it was rude to ask a lady. Even in the poor light, it seemed that Katarzyna was not much older than me.

Shock horror – I was actually having a civilised, friendly conversation with a girl close to my age. That was unheard of. *Please, don't clam up and get all silly,* I told myself.

I continued to protest against her attempts to pay me. "But the petrol won't cost me twenty pounds. It will cost five at most," I explained. "I don't want to rip you off."

"Then I shall rip off a quarter." She smiled, pretending to tear a piece off of the £20 note, then she sat back, smiled, withdrew her hand, and said, "I will put it in your pocket when you no are looking."

"You seem to have perked up a lot," I smiled. "That soup you put together must have worked a miracle."

"No," she replied, in a tone that told me the answer was obvious, even though she knew it wasn't. She shook her head and pulled the blanket up to her chest, folding her arms tightly. "I still fucking freezing, just no longer upset, pissed off, and full of snot. Plus, I'm happy that a nice guy has come to my rescue who is no a rapist."

"I'm not that," I reassured her.

"I know that," she said, smiling in the darkness, "but you can't be too careful getting in stranger's cars."

"Well, you have got in a strange person's car," I smiled.

"Strange maybe," she answered, nodding at my bare legs, "but kind."

"If you say so," I replied, with a warm glow in my chest as I wondered if anyone had described me as kind before.

Katarzyna touched me lightly on the shoulder. "Have you eaten tonight?" she asked.

I shook my head.

"Well," she said, "As you no going to let me pay fuel money, would you please let me buy you dinner tonight. Is for thank you."

Even in the low light reflecting off the snow, I could see that the expression in her eyes had changed from overly fake meanness to exaggerated pleading.

Now I was shocked. I had never been offered dinner by a person I knew, let alone a stranger. Besides, she seemed like a really lovely lady, who was attempting to be kind by returning a favour. Hers were the type of eyes you couldn't say no to.

"It would be a pleasure," I heard myself agree.

"The only thing," she said, "only place open this time of night is fucking McDonalds. I would no feed that crap to a dog."

"Me neither," I agreed.

"We shall have to brave it tonight," she grinned. "You must come to my home when I get back from holiday, and I will cook you special thank you dinner."

I wasn't sure. Letting someone buy you McDonald's for helping them was one thing, but making a promise to stay in touch and go to their house for dinner was a big commitment, especially when you've only just met. I wanted to say, "Let's see how things go," but the look on her face was so excited at the idea. I heard myself agree before I'd even thought about it. I immediately felt terrible for considering turning her down. Lacking friends of my own, I wanted to find out more about this lovely, kind, and strange woman who had jumped out at me in the night.

She grinned, still a little weak with cold, and she wiped her nose again. "It will be great," she said with a cough. "I love to cook for people but rarely get the chance."

"Well if it's anything like your soup, it will be amazing," I told her, wondering if this was all just talk, or if I indeed had just agreed to dinner with this unknown seemingly very nice girl.

"Just as friends though," she added.

"Of course," I nodded.

"It no that I no find you attractive," she said quickly as if she thought I might have been upset that it wasn't a date. "It because we barely know each other and want to be friends. I no have many friends, and I already like you a lot."

"I can say the same," I replied, after drinking the remainder of the soup from my cup. The last person I could call a true friend had moved away at short notice the best part of ten years ago. "Shall we get on our way?"

She nodded and downed her remaining soup as I turned off the light and put the car into gear.

I heard her sneeze again as the inside of the car went dark. She spent the next few moments blowing her nose loudly and apologising for doing so. This, however, made her voice much clearer when she spoke again a minute later. "Sorry that so gross," she sniffed.

"It's okay. We all get colds," I told her.

"True," she sniffed. "But I still sorry in advance if you catch from me." There was a brief silence. "You work at hotel fitness club," she said, piping up again.

"How did you know?"

"Observations," she breathed. "Like logo on you t-shirt."

"That would be a giveaway," I laughed. Say what you would about this strange girl who came out of the snow, but she was sharp as a pin.

"You no are catch me in health club, I am afraid," she sighed. "Those places are for people with desk jobs who eat too much chocolate."

"I couldn't agree more."

"In all honesty," she said, sitting back in her seat. "I don't need to work out when I clean twelve hours some days, and I walk everywhere."

"I reckon that would make you fitter than most of my gym members," I agreed, laughing.

"I like to eat healthy too," she sniffed. "Love my fruit and veg, and I like walk on the beach is nice exercise. But on a more disgusting note," she added, "since moving to England, I have picked up an awful cigarette habit, and I usually have a smoke on the go while I am exercising."

I laughed at her honesty.

"So, Mr. Fitness Instructor," she smirked, "Are you going tell me off for smoking?"

"Will it help you stop if I do?" I asked.

"Maybe," she laughed. "I want to stop soon, but no motivation."

"Naughty Katarzyna! Don't smoke," I told her in a very authoritarian tone.

"Did it work?" I asked a moment later.

"I don't think so," she laughed. "I still want a cigarette, but I quit hopefully with patches and gum. I am ashamed of my disgusting habit. Maybe it would help if you smack my bottom and call me a naughty girl," she added, with a smile and an extra cough as if to add to the point.

"I wish," she breathed, "in that moment of weakness when I first put that filth in my mouth, I had hit myself and said *Bad Katarzyna*." With that, the madwoman slapped herself across the face to demonstrate, and then cried out in pain.

"Did that stop you smoking?" I laughed.

"Nope, but it warmed my face and hand up a bit though."

"Did you hurt yourself?" I asked sympathetically.

"Yeah," she replied. "My pride hurts more than my face."

"Well everyone needs one bad habit, and as I said, you guys work bloody hard," I told her.

She looked at me with her head slightly tilted as though she was reading me before choosing her reply. "When you say "You guys", are you referring to foreigners or caravan cleaners?"

Regretting having said that, I thought carefully about my answer. I certainly didn't want to cause her any offence. "Which one would you take less offence at?" I asked nervously.

She gave a little laugh. "Relax," she told me, reaching out and touching my shoulder. She looked me in the eye and spoke softly, "Either choice to me is lovely compliment, considering I am to you a stranger causing you inconvenience. Although I beg differ I always have to tell other cleaners no to be lazy," she laughed, adding that she set stupidly high standards and that she was glad it wasn't any of her colleagues that picked her up. "Day would have left me to die," she joked.

"I think any decent person would have helped you out," I told her as she sighed and leaned back in the seat.

"Bastard taxi driver leave me in farm gateway. Then I try hitchhiking and maybe five hundred cars pass me before you stop."

"Why in the hell would a taxi driver leave you out here?" I asked, in complete confusion as to why anyone could possibly want to leave a person to freeze to death out here.

As I was waiting for her reply, I heard her sneeze again and take another deep breath. Hesitantly, she said, "I no want to say." She waved her hand in a shaky movement as if to gesture that I was moving the conversation to iffy ground.

"I will say only that taxi driver is no a nice man like you."

"I've not been described as nice very often," I said with a smile.

"I never have been called nice," she said quietly.

"Now that I can't believe," I told her. "You seem like a perfectly nice lady to me."

"No," she said, her tone suddenly louder and suggesting that I was completely wrong. "To be honest, I am horrible girl, apparently."

"Wow," I shrugged. "That is honest, I'll give you that. I've never heard anyone call themselves horrible before."

"Well people at work call me ice bitch, because I told

on them to my boss when I caught them watching TV and picking on a girl because she is English. Other staff... they get written warnings. I am having a terrible temper too and say things I am no really mean say and I am rude and nasty. But you go to work to do what you get paid to do, which is clean caravans. No sitting around drinking tea, watch television and picking on people for where they come from or how much they weigh."

I told her my feelings on racism, and how foreign workers should be treated with the respect they deserved for coming and doing the jobs that British were too workshy to do.

"I see both sides," she said, smiling. "I am immigrant. People are racist to me when it's not right. However, I used to be a horrible racist bullying bitch myself. I am growed up though, thank God. I kick myself up bottom. Unlike some others, learned I must respect the country we are living in and people born here. No many people are realising I have growed up and still think I am childish little cow."

"Well," I replied, "you sound like a really decent hard-working lady to me."

"Thank you. I only tell the truth," she shrugged. "I no am sure people who I work with will agree." She took a short breath and gave a tiny high pitch sneeze into her handkerchief. "As for racism," she continued, rubbing her nose. "I just defuse I trying to be nice and show people how wrong it is, but some English people still say I am awkward to work with.

"I'm sure you're not as difficult to work with as my boss," I told her, remembering the unreasonable way in which the general manager had spoken to me in recent days.

"I guess your boss is infamous Katherine McNallty?"

I was taken aback by her knowledge of the cow in charge of the hotel where I had been working for the past year and a half.

"How did you know about her?" I asked, puzzled.

Katarzyna raised her hand in a gesture as if to show that she intended to answer me as she turned away to sneeze again. She composed herself, and this time she blew her nose loudly, then mouthed a brief apology to me. She gave a cough to clear her throat before continuing, "I am live in the town." She smiled. "Most people in are knowing that bitch by her reputation"

"Really?"

"Yes," she replied. "Many English people where I work talk about her. Many of them once worked at hotel. She has wrecked career of many good worker with bright future. I once had the displeasure of meet her myself. She biggest slimy backstabbing bitch in the whole of north Norfolk." She stretched her arms out to emphasise the point, and then quickly pulled her hands in and chuckled at her own over-the-top gesture.

"You don't like her then?"

"Sorry, I no mean to call your boss horrible," she said quietly, as if she was worried it was the wrong thing to say.

"No, I totally agree with you" I laughed. Katherine was a fat lady who smoked like a chimney and never used a gym. She had no clue about the gym or my role in it. With the way, I'd been spoken to and the accusations she had put my way, I certainly had no reason to disbelieve Katarzyna. In the time that I'd worked for Katherine, many people had been driven to find other employment. "It's not only me who can't stand her then?" I asked.

"No," she said, looking around the car subconsciously

as if to check that nobody was listening. "I know a man at work called Charlie. One of the few people who likes me enough to chat over lunch. He used to own that hotel. He paid for it three million pounds and is happy for ten years. Katherine McNallty takes over the running of the place, and in two years, she drives the place into bankruptcy. Yet somehow, new owner keeps her on and she is a manager earning big money while he is forced to sell hotel only for one pound. Now he scrapes living cutting grass for caravan site for minimum wage. The poor man is seventy-five and no can afford to retire"

"Shit!" I exclaimed. I hadn't heard that story. Now I was worried about my job.

"You quit now while you still have a good CV," she croaked hoarsely. "I get you job. You come and work with me." She paused, "On second thought, the head cleaner at caravan site is horrible slavedriver bitch woman."

"Isn't she you?" I asked, baffled at why she continued to abuse herself.

"Yep," she grinned.

"You call yourself a bitch? That's harsh," I told her.

"True-dough," she sniffed. "I no mean to be, but I am. So, I might as well say myself and no pretend people no say it behind my back cos they do."

"Well, I will consider your kind offer," I said, flashing her a smile that said, "Thank you for the offer, but I've worked hard to get the job I've got, and I'm not sure I want to give up on it just yet."

She returned the smile across at me in the dark. "Actually, its probably no good idea if we want to remain friends for more than half hour into first shift," she laughed, "but please give to me your phone number so we can say dank you properly. I would give you but..." She held up her phone. I could barely see it in the darkness, but she was apparently trying to show me it was broken.

I thought about things for a second. An hour ago, I had been on my way to the house where I lived with my mum and dad. I barely ever saw my friends in the last couple of years. I had met this strange girl who I knew hardly anything about. I'd known her less than forty minutes. Now she was asking to be my friend and offering me a job.

Fortunately—or unfortunately—young men of my age always seemed to speak before they thought. I'd already promised to let her make me dinner, so it would be rude not to. In all honesty, she seemed a lovely kind lady despite her self-loathing.

"Of course, you can call me," I heard myself say.

It was the rational decision, of course. You should never decline an offer of friendship, because you might not get any more. A friend gained and lost was better than one never gained. *Plus*, I thought to myself, *maybe it's not strange at all.* She was a genuinely nice lady, a long way from home, who just wanted a friend.

Katarzyna coughed loudly several times and was doubled over. She sat up, composed herself, and banged herself on the chest. "Cough is no good," she said, with a grimace on her face. "I should not swear, but it hurts like a mother."

"Have you seen a doctor?" I asked her.

She shook her head, blowing her nose gently as she did so. "I had a cold, but was no half this bad before I get stuck in snow." She sneezed again.

"Take these," I said, handing her a packet of throat-soothing sweets which I had on the dashboard. She took one, thanked me, then tried to give them back, but I told her to keep them.

"You are very kind man," she said quietly, turning to look out of the windscreen at the road ahead. "But you are strange, too trusting maybe?"

"How do you mean?" I asked.

She sniffed and turned her head to look at me. "You give lift to strange girl, and a smelly snotty one at that—"

"You don't smell," I interrupted, taking a quick sniff just to check. "Actually, you smell quite nice."

In the light that was bouncing from the snow, I saw her raise her finger to her lips to shush me. "I was talking," she told me in a stern voice, although I could see a playful smile on her face. "My point is no many people would be this nice. You have known me half an hour. How you know I am not part of a criminal gang, who drop me off and are waiting at the hotel to beat the shit out of you and steal your car?"

She had an excellent point, and I thought hard for an answer as to why I had been so trusting. "It's unlikely." I replied.

"Why you sink this?" she asked, puzzled. "I know people do that sort of thing."

"You asked me to take you as far as I was going. It was me who said I would take you to the hotel."

She looked at me thoughtfully. "You are clever boy," she said. "You got me. It is one nil to you in game of wind-ups."

"I didn't know we were playing a game of wind-ups," I replied.

"Maybe we are no?" she said, turning away, coughing into her hand. "But if I am no criminal, then why, when you were in the back of car finding flask, did I steal your wallet?"

Instinctively I tapped on my pocket with my hand and was relieved to find that my wallet was still there.

Katarzyna laughed and touched my shoulder gently. "If I was going take something I no would have told you," she whispered in my ear.

"I believe the score in the wind-up game is one all, yeah?" I nodded.

"Point proven. We have now known each other a little while and already is having... what you call? Err... banter?"

"It's good to have a bit of fun," I smiled.

"I think you maybe no have many close friends, no?"

"Is it that easy to see?"

She nodded and coughed. "When you live and work so far from home, and when you work with people in the same position, I see loneliness all of the time, even in large groups. Even the slightest hint of no longer being lonely brings out a certain look in people. I saw that look in you when you smiled."

"You can tell all that from a look?" I asked, as we came to a roundabout on the road.

"I know that look, because I am, myself, very lonely."

"You don't have a boyfriend then?"

She looked me up and down and burst out laughing in the dark as if I'd said something idiotic. "You are silly boy," she grinned, "If I had boyfriend, he would be coming with me to the Czech Republic."

"I suppose," I said with a smile. I should have realised this earlier, because she would hardly have invited me over for dinner without warning me she had a boyfriend.

"No part of my life requires a boyfriend," she continued. "I self-sufficient. I earn my own money. I pay my own bills. I almost fluent several languages. I cook my own food, roll and light my own cigarettes—well at least until I quit the fucking things. I no need a man for any of these things."

"I guess not then" I grinned.

She turned away and coughed some more, but when she cleared her throat, she spoke rather frankly. I listened intently to her words. "I no need man, but there is difference between needing and wanting. My home is cold and empty. I no am ever going to be a housewife, but sometimes when I wake up cold the night, I want a person to snuggle with and tell me I'm no alone."

I could sympathise with what she was saying. However, what she told me next made me see how truly down on herself she was.

"Relationships are all about finding someone you love enough start a family, but I no because no can. No only because I no see a man I like, but I no sure if I want to be a mum. I love children, but no sure if I am fit to be mother with my constant smoking, swearing horrible temper," she breathed. "And lastly," she added, pointing at herself. "Man has to know that I wear the trousers! No, because I am a bossy cow, but because I no am very good at no being in charge of everything."

I could tell from her voice she was smiling, as though she found this funny. It caused me to smile back.

"You know, if you come back with me we are going to have the best sex, right?" My face must have been a picture. Even though I had not yet accepted her offer to stay in her room, I never expected more than to crash on the floor. "Got you," she laughed, tapping my leg. "The score is two one to me. I no quite that much of slut. I am virgin. No sex out of wedlock says my God." I could see the smile in her eyes piercing the darkness as she took out a large silver crucifix from under her top.

"Are you very devout to Christianity?" I asked, in a way that tried not to mock her faith, or let on that I did not believe in God specifically.

"I used to go church early every Sunday as child," she smiled, "but if God is all around, why go to church? With all shit go in world, I no know if he is real, but I keep this on me always. Try to be good girl in case." She touched the cross around her neck. "If any of my family ask," she breathed, "I go every Sunday and confess twice a week... Anyway," she said, going back to the original subject, "You no want to sex with me anyway. Today I no have showered and smell of cigarettes and sweat. I am full of horrible cold germs. No to mention I am no even slightly attractive." She laughed, as if she found the very thought that anyone might want to have sex with her was a massive joke.

"You shouldn't be so horrible to yourself," I soothed. "There are enough horrible people in the world to do that."

"Well," she sighed, "If I tell my self-truth, it no hurt if someone else is saying it. And," she added, "I can be as cruel bitch as I like. Cos some other person says, they are get a big slap and I get in trouble, but am going to hardly slap myself for it."

"So, you didn't slap yourself in the face for smoking and hurt yourself only a few minutes ago?" I teased.

"No-oo-oo," she lied, then confessed, "Was only third time that happens." She paused to laugh before adding, "Today."

"You are a funny one," I smiled.

Part of me by now was wondering what the hell I was doing here. Me making friends and having a laugh with a girl? That was as unlikely as Harry Potter going for a butter beer in The Three Broomsticks with Lord Voldemort.

"So, we get to know each other," she said, as we headed very slowly down the hill away from Aylsham.

"Okay," I agreed.

"Let us guess game about each other."

"Okay," I agreed with her, thinking it might be fun.

"I start," she said. "Let me see... you are young. I say nineteen maybe twenty. You no have a girlfriend, but you would love to have one, and you live at home with your parents. Am I right?"

"You are correct. I'm twenty next March. How did you know all this?"

"It's easy," she said. "Not many nineteen-year-old afford to pay rent for house and have car, so I guessed you still live with parents. You tell me also you are lonely and want to be friends with me. You tell me I am first to kiss you cheek. No man who says that has a girlfriend."

"Very observant," I sighed, looking across the dark car.

"You sad, because you think girls don't like you," she said in a very matter of fact way.

"Got it in one," I sighed.

"That fucking bullshit," she sniffed. "English girls need head examining. They go with guys who treat them like shit and cheat, but ignore nice guys who get rough deal."

"That's how it is," I shrugged.

"Well," she sniffed, "My way thinking is, you no know what is coming. Your turn to do me."

"Okay," I said, taking a deep breath to stall my answer. "You've already said you live alone a long way from home, but you are going home for a visit, so you must love your family. You've already told me you work in caravans cleaning and don't need a boyfriend, but that doesn't mean you don't want one. I think that implies that you've have had several offers, but you are waiting for the right one to come along. At a guess, I'd say you were twenty-five?"

"Other than the age that's accurate. I'm sixteen years old," she told me in an angry tone, as if she was offended.

I wasn't having it, though. It was one thing for a sixteen-year-old to move countries, but if she'd been living in England long enough to have two or three promotions and her own place, she would have to have moved when she was like twelve.

"No," I said, not believing it for a second. "That's another wind-up. You're more like thirty, I'm guessing."

She leaned back and stretched her arms above her head and yawned. "You are correct. The score now is two all." Then she gave my shoulder a playful slap that was hard enough to sting a little, but not hard enough to hurt.

"What was that for?" I asked.

"You called me thirty."

"Oh, I'm sorry," I told her.

"Is okay," she said, rubbing the part of my shoulder she had play-slapped. "I'm last month twenty-one years old, but I forgive your mistake, because you have no seen me in full. Plus, I am full of cold, and I have smokers voice like I'm fifty."

She laughed.

"Did you have a good birthday?" I asked.

"Noo-oo-oo," she replied again, using a tone that suggested it was self-evident.

"Why is that?" I thought that even if she had no family, her colleagues at work might have helped her celebrate her twenty-first.

There was a brief silence then I heard her give a couple of tiny very high-pitched sneezes.

"You really have got it bad haven't you, you poor thing?"

She made a noise in agreement and took a deep sniff. "I forgot," she said, with a hint of amusement.

"Forgot what?"

"My birthday," she replied, in a slightly embarrassed voice.

"How do you forget your birthday?"

"I no know. I was working, you know. I forget."

"You really must work hard if you forget your own birthday." I know I couldn't forget mine, no matter how much I wanted to.

"It easier when you have no friends or family to remind you," she sniffed.

"Considering you've been kind to me, I can't see how you haven't got any friends," I smiled, trying to let her know that she was not disliked by me.

"Well," she sighed, "is not quite true. I do have a friend Jenny. We used to work together at caravan park. If anyone had a bad day, they always take it out on poor Jenny by bullying her."

"So, you stood up for her and became friends?" I asked, thinking that's what she would have done. Although I didn't think I would have had the strength to do that.

"Noo-oo-oo," she replied, using her *isn't it obvious* tone once more. "I am not proud. I was the leader of the bullies. I was horrible nasty girl, but no more. I dink you know Jenny," she sniffed.

"I know a few Jennys," I replied.

"Jenny Hughs. She went to you gym."

I wracked my brains trying to think about Jenny Hughs. Of course, I knew Jenny Hughs. She was a member at the gym. She had a nasty back injury as a child. The medication she was on made her gain weight, so she was a massive girl when we first met. She had resolved to lose the weight and had been well on her way to shedding the fourth stone when she had suddenly stopped coming to the gym.

"She's a big chatty girl, isn't she?" I said. "Very nice lady?"

"Yeah" she nodded. "That's my Jen. I am love that girl."

"She was doing really well with the weight loss before she stopped coming," I told her. "Her weight was coming right down, and she was not comfort-eating."

"I helped," she piped up. "I have banned her from eat chocolate and make sure she comes to my house for dinner for some nice veggies."

"Well done, you," I applauded. It was not often that people's friends gave them the help they needed. This made it clear to me that although she might not have many friends, Katarzyna valued her friendship a great deal.

"Did she tell about the bitch who bullied her at work?" she asked.

"I think she did," I replied carefully, trying to remember. "But I remember her saying they'd made up and become really close friends.

"We are," she sighed. "Because that horrible bitch was me before I sorted myself out." She looked down at the floor, possibly in shame.

She paused and blew her nose again. "I'm guilty of take out my problems by making hell for others. I'm not popular among other migrant workers, because I don't favour them over English workers like they expect. I stand I treat everyone equally, even though English cleaner no like because I'm foreigner and they think one of them should be in charged."

"They think you took their jobs?"

She nodded, "I no did even apply for promotion. My boss is just tell me one. "Katarzyna you are bossiest cow I am ever met, the vacant head cleaner position is yours."

I had to laugh at her blunt honesty. "Being the head of department, you must be stuck in the middle of arguments," I added.

"A few times before we were friends, I sided against her when she in the right. I want to avoid upset migrants because there are more of them," she sniffed. "I no mean to be horrible to Jenny, but would lose job if I don't keep masses satisfied. I thought Jenny realised my position, but one really stressful day, I go over top, and I snap. She burst into tears and ran off. I stopped work and had coffee and smoke while I calm myself down. I think to myself how to say sorry to Jenny. Twenty minutes later, I find in caravan with wrists slashed and blood everywhere." She paused briefly for another sneeze, and continued, "I tied her wrists with bandage and held pressure until paramedic come and take her."

"Fucking hell she never told me that!" was all I could say, followed by, "So, you're a hero."

"No," she scoffed. "Hero doesn't cause problem in first place. Is okay in end though. I visit hospital every day, and when she come home, we go for healthy dinner. I apologise and cuddle her. The poor girl was going through some shit, suffering from depression. I no did know all dis. I would have been nicer if I knew, because am depressed myself. She came back to my flat, and we shared a bottle of vodka and talked through problems. I find that Jenny and I have rather similar personal demons. We had a little cry on each odder shoulders. Well, I had somewhat larger cry. From that day we stick together best buddies, but sticking up for Jenny make me traitor amongst other foreign workers. But who cares? My best friend is okay now."

"I guess it kind of sucks for them that you're the head cleaner then."

"In all honesty," she said, with a hint of a laugh, "I'm fucking terrible at that part of my job. They no sack me because they know however bad I am at people management, standards set are really high and get best reviews, so they no fire me."

That seemed a pretty rough deal, I thought to myself. "So, you don't see her much?"

She was silent for a moment. "We still meet up and get pissed on some Saturday nights, but not so much now. She had a boyfriend, but she dumped his cheating ass because she found she vas only his bit the side and he has a wife."

"Shit! Poor Jenny and the wife," I stammered.

"No," she corrected, "only poor Jenny. Her boyfriend's wife vas a lot to blame. From what he told me his marriage has been dead for years, his wife hits him, and he really worships Jenny. I secretly hope he divorce his wife and get back with . She is pregnant with his daughter."

"So that's why she quit the gym," I said.

Katarzyna went on to explain that Jenny was supposed to drive her to the airport and stay with her that night, but her dad's car, which she had intended to borrow, had broken down. "It was horrible," she told me. "Poor Jenny got so upset that she cried, because she feels she has let me down. But is no her fault car break. Is nice of her to offer in first place."

I thought of her situation and compared it to my own. It was lovely that they had rebuilt their friendship. I barely knew Katarzyna, but I had previously known Jenny through work. I was glad she had a friend to look after her in a rough situation. I told her how I wished I could say the same about my friends, but I never saw them anymore.

"You must stay and get drunk with us when you come for dinner. We will be four grumpy singletons happy together"

"Four?" I questioned, "I thought it was just you and me?"

"I forgot to say that my little sister Ela will be coming to live with me after the holiday. She is my youngest sister. She is lovely. I have two other sisters, too," she informed me. "I think you and my sister get on well. Ela my favourite sister, a very kind, sweet pretty girl, but no tell her I said that. It go to her head. She's an ideal girlfriend for you if you are interested. She is seventeen and she's a good girl, unlike me. She really goes to church and doesn't swear or smoke like I do."

Oddly, it didn't feel odd at all that I was actually looking forward to having dinner with Katarzyna and her sister. Although I doubted dating her sister was likely to happen. I was no longer hoping that it was just a token offer of friendship from a stranger who I would say goodbye to at the end of the journey.

It was as though she had read my mind. "You think this is all just small talk?" she asked, stuffing her handkerchief away in her pocket and taking out her tobacco.

"I'd like to think it's more than that," I replied. "That offer of dinner sounds lovely."

"I will give you my home phone number and address when we get to hotel."

"Cool," I replied.

"Is okay if I roll cigarette so I can smoke as soon as we stop?" she asked quietly. "I no would normally, because is rude, but I have no smoke since I was waiting for bus four hours ago and usually can't go more than two hours."

"Go for it," I told her.

Chapter 3

Stranded in the dark

We were a couple of miles from the turnoff to Noringsham, where I lived with my mum and dad, when things started to go wrong. There were cars queued up along the main road past the village.

"Oh, shit, there must have been accident," Katarzyna said. "I hope everyone okay."

"Let's hope so. We might not even make McDonalds at this rate," I told her.

"I haven't eaten since breakfast," she sighed.

I knew that feeling all too well being in the same situation myself. I didn't want Katarzyna to go hungry, so I did the best thing I could think of.

"Let's take a different route," I said, pulling the car to the far side of the road and overtaking the traffic.

"What the fuck you doing? You maniac!" she shrieked in terror. She put her hand over her mouth, slightly embarrassed, as I pointed out the narrow snow-covered single track lane we were headed for. "Well I feel stupid now," she breathed deeply, beating her chest.

"It's a few extra miles," I told her, "but we might just

get to CrapDonalds before it shuts."

"Thank you. I could eat a McHorse right now, even dough I am vegetarian."

"Actually," I said, "I'm home alone, and I've got food there. Why don't you stop off and have dinner with me? We'll call the hotel and explain that you got held up, and I'll drop you off after dinner."

"That is real sweet. thank you," she said, touching my arm.

I replied, "It's the least I can do for such a nice lady in trouble."

The country lane was even darker than the main road, and the visibility was much worse. The road had not been gritted or used in the last hour, it seemed. We were driving through snow that was about four inches deep. The car was not designed for this and kept slipping and sliding everywhere. Sensing danger, Katarzyna had gone silent so that I could concentrate on driving.

The wind battered us from both sides. As we turned a bend, the car went into a slide down a slope and began to gather speed. This time, Katarzyna didn't shriek. She just gripped my leg in pure fright as we hurtled down the hill into the blinding snow. I tried my best to keep the car in a straight line, hoping it would stop before we hit something.

The road took a sudden turn to the right. With little time to react, I tried to turn the car in an effort to stop the slide and prevent us flying over the bank into the field. Luckily the manoeuvre came off. The Mini came to rest in a passing space at the side of the road. But there had been two loud bangs to my left-hand side that were very worrisome.

Katarzyna was shaking in her seat.

"Are you okay?" I asked her.

"I think so," she replied in a shaky voice. Then she gripped my arm and asked, "Are *you* okay Rob?" I nodded and as I got out to check for damage. She opened her door to follow me.

I got a torch from the boot in order to shine some light on the situation, but the damn batteries had run out. I threw it to the ground in frustration before I felt something tap me on the shoulder.

"Try this," Katarzyna shouted over the wind as she put something in my hand. It was her cigarette lighter. After three or four clicks, it sparked into a flickering ball of light. I struggled to shelter it from the wind.

Hidden under the snow in the passing space was a piece of timber. It had possibly fallen off the back of a lorry or builder's van and had been moved to the side of the road. There were several nails pointing out of it, which had shredded both of the tyres on the left-hand side of my car.

"Oh, fuckin shit, that no look good," Katarzyna said, bending down beside me and putting her arm on my shoulders for balance. Even up close in the light, all I could see was a pair of round gleaming eyes and that same lock of blonde hair. The rest of her face was covered by her hood, which was done up tight against the cold. She had an unlit cigarette poking out of the gap in her shawl where her mouth was.

"No, it's fucking not good," I said in an angry voice, aimed more at the person who had left the piece of timber on the road than anyone. Katarzyna, however, seemed to think I was angry with her and began to apologise profusely, her wide eyes flooding with tears. "I'm not angry with you," I told her softly, squeezing the hand she had on my shoulder.

"It is my fault this has happened," she whispered,

standing up slowly and opening the car door. She sat herself down sideways on the passenger seat with her feet out of the door. Lighting up her cigarette, she blew smoke into the air. "I pay for damage," she said suddenly.

"No, you won't," I soothed, rubbing her shoulder while trying not to breathe in her smoke. She considerately tried to blow it in the opposite direction. We can fix this easily," I told her. "There's one spare tyre in the boot and another at my parents' house a couple of miles away. We'll be back on the road in no time."

As I reached into my pocket for my phone, intending to call my dad and ask him to bring the second spare tyre, I remembered that my parents had gone on holiday. "I'm going to have to walk to my parents' house to get the second spare tyre," I told Katarzyna, over the wind. "You stay here, keep the engine going, and stay warm."

"No," she said sharply, grabbing my arm.

"What do you mean, no?" I asked, confused.

"No!" she replied even more forcefully. "I come with you. Safer together."

"But we've just got you warmed up," I told her.

"I am no care. You no go on you own. I come," she reiterated sternly. "This is my fault. I will no let you go alone."

"Okay," I relented, as I could see that her mind was made up and there was no point in arguing with her. Anyway, she was right. We were safer together.

"Anyway, just before the car slid there was a house," She said, pointing back up the hill with her cigarette. "We could go and ask if the owner could give us a lift."

"Nobody lives there." I sighed. I knew the house well, it was barn conversion with a garden set amongst the barley fields. In my youth, I spent many days playing there. It was the former home of my childhood friend Sally who had long since gone.

"Okay," she frowned, looking down at my bare legs, now covered with goosebumps. "Do you have trousers in the car?"

"I think so," I replied.

"Put them on," she told me bluntly. "If no, I have a pair in my bag are might fit you, but they're pink. I saw a hint of a grin on her face behind her shawl as she said this.

While I found my trousers, she took a couple of deep puffs on her cigarette and blew smoke up in the air. "I wish I not start smoking these bloody things," she sighed, bending down to stub it out in the snow.

I reminded her we wouldn't have the light if she didn't smoke.

"I'll get you to remind me of that in thirty years when I'm dying from cancer," she retorted.

"Fair point," I remarked, nodding as she blew her nose with a honk and stood up.

Katarzyna sat in the car on her own for few moments as she changed into some dry trousers of her own. I turned my back to give her some privacy. As she got out of the car, she re-tied her head scarf, so only her bright eyes were visible.

As we struggled across the fields towards home, I couldn't help thinking that if this had happened to me alone, I wouldn't have been half as calm as I was now. I had to stay calm with Katarzyna there, because the poor girl had already been through enough that night. I hated the idea of her thinking she was to blame for our predicament. If it was anyone's fault it was mine, because I was driving.

Katarzyna insisted that we link arms, so that we didn't lose each other in the vast open fields with the snow driving into our faces. Although it was a good idea, it seemed that we kept bumping into each other. Twice, Katarzyna fell and pulled me over so that I landed on top of her. We ended up walking with our arms tightly around each other's waists and heads pointing down into the snow.

We could barely see a thing. At the boundary between two fields, we walked into some sort of structure with thick metal poles and what sounded like a corrugated plastic roof. Under it was a massive stack of rectangular hay bales about the width of a tennis court and several feet high. We felt our way around it and kept going into the next field in a straight line towards the village.

We'd been walking this way, coughing and breathing hard for about thirty minutes and barely able to speak above the wind. Poor Katarzyna was coughing her guts up so badly that I found myself hugging her tightly and banging on her back to try to help her. Suddenly the ground beneath us cracked.

I heard Katarzyna shriek as her foot disappeared into the ground. Blinded by the snow, we had inadvertently walked across a flood in the field, which had frozen over and covered with snow. The ice was now cracking under our weight.

There was a noise like thunder as it split apart and sent us plunging into icy water. It felt like I was being stabbed from all sides by a thousand knives. Thankfully, the water was only a few feet deep, but I'd fallen on top of Katarzyna. I couldn't see anything, but I felt her face down in the water as I was kicking and blowing bubbles trying my hardest to get off her.

Struggling to breathe, I somehow managed to get away. I reached down to Katarzyna to help her to the surface, where she blew hard with a high pitch. It sounded like she was screaming and crying as she clung to me.

We caught our breath and were able to stand. We waded to the edge of the flood where we both collapsed in a heap in the snow. As I sat up, Katarzyna clung to me again as she coughed and spluttered for several minutes before catching her breath. We-we need," she shivered breathlessly, "t-to g-get m-moving b-before we f-freeze to death."

She was dead right. The icy wind was already blasting us from all sides. As you would probably know, being out in a cold wind was dangerous enough. Add soaking wet to that, and you had a recipe for hypothermia and death. Not only that, but Katarzyna was already full of cold and illness before we got into this situation. I was seriously worried that if we didn't get to shelter quick, she'd die. Standing up, we quickly put our arms around each other and desperately looked for somewhere to protect us from the cold wind.

"S-s-st-ack," she shivered.

"What?" I called into the wind.

"Hay s-stack that way," she pointed behind us. "Sh-shelter."

"Okay," I said, following as Katarzyna charged back towards the haystack.

There was a tiny beam of moonlight shining through the clouds of snow. It illuminated the far side of the stack, where we found that some bales had been removed creating steps. Halfway up the hay stairs was a small alcove. It was perfect for us to shelter inside. I climbed up first and pulled Katarzyna up behind me. Between us we lifted a few bales, which were not the huge round ones but older styled small bales that might well have been stacked by hand. They were about a meter long and cuboid-shaped. We placed them over the gap to create a small roof to shelter us.

Space was small – about three metres long, one metre wide, and one and a half meters in height. There was just enough room for us both to lie down out of the storm. Katarzyna shivered and coughed violently. "T-t-t-take o-off c-clothes," she spluttered.

"W-what?" I shivered.

"Share b-b-b-b-body h-heat," she stammered through chattering teeth.

Of course, I thought to myself. She was a bright girl, working on the logic that it was easier to share body heat via direct contact with bare skin. However, I wasn't sure exactly how appropriate it would be in this awkward predicament. "A-are you s-sure you're c-comfortable being n-naked with a s-stranger?" I asked.

"No, I no f-fucking sure," she snapped, "but it's t-t-the b-best i-idea I h-have."

"O-okay," I told her, starting to remove my clothes. I wasn't comfortable at all with the idea. Not that I didn't like the idea of getting naked with a girl, but these circumstances were different. "Katarzyna, I'm not sure about this," I told her.

"You worried being inappropriate?" she replied, after a heavy cough. I nodded. "I l-l-love and appreciate that you want to be gentleman," she replied shakily, "but now is no the time." Then she sneezed. We were so close that we bumped heads painfully. Quickly, she apologised.

Nothing more was said for a few moments as we fumbled around in the pitch black removing our clothes. Katarzyna was really struggling, so I felt my way, then tried to help her remove her wet shoes and socks. I heard her blow her nose very shakily.

"Come on, lets d-do this," she whispered.

I reached out to touch her gently, not having a clue where my hand was going. In fact, my hand collided briefly with her hand coming the other way. I rested my hand on what I assumed was her abdomen and found the poor girl covered in goosebumps. Her skin was quivering. Without speaking we edged closer to each other until our chins were touching each other's shoulders.

"I sorry I s-snapped at you," she whispered, after a few moments.

"It's okay," I told her. "It's not as though either of us has been in this situation before."

"That true," she mumbled. "I hope you and me s-still be f-friends after this."

"I really don't see why we won't Katarzyna," I told her, rubbing her back gently as I tried to warm her through friction.

"Thank you, that feels nice," she said dreamily, returning the gesture. "And please, Rob, one more favour?"

"Okay, shoot," I shivered.

"No call me Katarzyna. I know it my name, but call me Kat. Is much friendlier."

"Okay, Kat," I told her.

After a few minutes of her coughing and me patting on the back, she suddenly began to sob.

"Are you okay, Kat?" I asked softly.

"No," she sobbed. "I going to miss my flight. I have no seen my family in four years. They think I no want to see them."

"I promise I'll get you on that flight if it's the last thing I do," I told her, stroking her face.

"How we going to d-d-do t-that?" she half-sobbed, half-shivered.

"What time is your flight, my friend?" I asked her gently.

"F-flight from N-Norwich is 10am. Chi-check in is close 9am."

I pressed the light on my digital watch. It lit up showing the time as 12:10 am.

Quickly, I made up a plan of action. The idea was that we were going to stay there in the haystack for a while and get as warm as we could while we waited for the snowstorm to finish.

Once it had passed, I would leave Kat curled up in the hay and jog around the fields on the road, which was half a mile further. I'd get the spare tyre and find Kat some of my sister's old clothes, then I'd meet Kat back at the haystack, so we could walk back to the car together. I'd replace the wheels, take Kat home for some food, run her a bath, and let her rest in my sister's old bed if there was time before taking her to the airport for her flight. The one snag was that Kat was uncomfortable with me leaving her there. Although I didn't doubt her fitness, she sounded more and more unwell.

The best-laid plans of mice and men never worked out.

I kept her talking, to try and keep our brains active enough to try and fight off hypothermia. "Kat sweet-h-heart t-tell me about your family and where you were b-born," I shivered.

"You c-called me s-sweet-t-h-heart," she replied croakily, sounding a little offended.

"Sorry, it was a turn of phrase," I said gently. "You are v-very sweet."

"It's n-nice of you say s-so," she shifted. "Is no true though, so next time you say I have to pull nasty face at you." There was the slightest hint of a laugh in her voice. "I was b-born Severni Lobendava, North Czech Republic close to German border. You have never been no?"

"Nope, never been there," I told her.

"Lovely place," she reminisced dreamily. "If you and I stay friends—which we will—you must come with me when I go back next year." She coughed, and I felt her heart thumping.

"That sounds lovely," I replied.

She took a deep sniff. "Summer it's nice, but winter is fucking cold." She took a rattling breath and sneezed loudly against my ear. "I so sorry," she whispered in my ear, but I rubbed the back of her head to tell her it was okay.

"Your name isn't from there, though, is it?" I asked

"Clever boy," she replied. "Katarzyna is from Poland. I am a quarter Polish from father's mother. I am second of four sisters, and we have one brother. There's Kazia – she is twenty-three, me twenty-one, Dusa nineteen, Ela seventeen, and brother Dowid is fifteen."

"So basically," I said, "your mum and dad kept having children every two years until they got a boy."

"You got it in one." she sighed. "Dusa, Ela, and me, forgotten middle sisters, and it no helps that I the boring one."

"You're not boring," I almost laughed. "You're one of

the most interesting people I've met."

"I twenty-one and I go bed alone, with book and cocoa at 8pm. Tell me that no boring," she breathed, and sneezed heavily again, blowing her nose very gently so as not to hurt my ear.

"It depends on which authors you read," I told her.

She listed a few of them, including Stephen King, James Patterson, and the Harry Potter books. "I'm beginning to like you more and more," I told her, squeezing her tighter. To my surprise, I felt my squeeze returned and felt her jaw move into a smile.

"Are you any warmer?" I asked softly.

I felt her nod. "This hotel is horrible dough," she joked suddenly. "I may be a bit warmer, but this room fucking freezing, the bed itchy, and I hungry. No food, no TV, and nowhere I can have cigarette without burning us alive." Her sudden outburst broke the tension of the situation. The two of us erupted into fits of giggles and rolled around.

Kat somehow ended up on top of me. Barely able to control her giggles, she bent in my ear and whispered, "Is now good dime to say I going to piss myself?"

"At least it would be warm and wet," I laughed.

"Okay here I go." She tensed up, and for a second, I thought she was actually going to piss on me.

"I'm now winning the game of wind-ups," she whispered.

Just then my watch alarm went off. I'd set it to go off every hour to check on the storm. It was already 1 am. I let go of Kat for a moment and wriggled down to the end of our little shelter. I removed one of the four bales I'd placed there and immediately we were blasted with snow.

"We need to stay longer," Kat said, from the far corner with another big chesty cough.

I replaced the bale and lay back down on my side. I felt Kat beside me roll over and as she did, she accidentally shoved her breasts in my face.

"I'm sorry," she said, quickly sliding herself down to rest her chin on my shoulder.

"Relax, it's okay," I said, putting my arm under hers to try and make her more comfortable.

"You don't want my smelly sweaty tits in face even when I have had shower... which I have no today."

"But we did just have an ice bath," I reminded her.

"Still rude of me though," she coughed.

"Relax," I told her again. "It was an honest accident and they don't smell bad."

"So how come you not aroused in the slightest?" she coughed.

"You really want to know?" I asked.

"Uh huh," she nodded against my shoulder.

"Okay," I said. "I keep going over and over in my head, *Margaret Thatcher naked on a cold day, Margaret Thatcher naked on a cold day.*"

She nearly burst out laughing. "Austin Powers. Very clever!"

"You've seen it?" I asked, surprised, thinking that it probably wasn't the sort of thing a straight-laced lady would find funny.

"I love that movie," she said, suddenly sounding slightly sleepy. "I have on DVD box set. When you come for dinner, we will snuggle on chair and watch together if you want. As long as you keep thinking Margaret Thatcher." She yawned. "You no have to snuggle if you no want, we can sit on chair without touching."

I soon realised it was not fear of getting too close too soon. It was the fear that these plans to meet up and be friends when she got home from her holiday were just talk, and we would not see each other again after that night.

"Is no small talk," she told me in a sleepy voice as if she had read my mind again. She stretched her arms and gave a big yawn.

"I could do with coffee," she sniffed.

"What time did you get up for work," I asked.

"4am," she yawned again.

"Try to get some sleep for an hour or so while I keep watch," I told her soothingly.

"Okay, I trust you," she whispered softly, moving up so that she could rest her head on the wall. She blew her nose once more. "But be warned," she told me as I cuddled up to her skinny body to keep her heat in. "I snore like herd of pigs grunting when I have a cold."

"At least I'll know you're alive," I laughed quietly.

"Good night, kind man," she breathed sleepily.

I thought I felt her squeeze my hand as I said, "Good night, lovely lady."

Part 2 Future dreams

Chapter 4

Norwich airport

I was awoken by the roar of engines. I'd been dreaming about that night again. Poor Kat had been so cold that I wasn't quite sure how we made it through that situation. My memories of how we had got the car back on the road and got Kat on her flight were very hazy, but I'm sure we did it as a team.

The poor girl was incredibly dignified about the whole situation. I was worried about her because she had been terrible unwell when she left. However, I could just not recall the circumstances.

She'd given me her parents' phone number in the Czech Republic so that I could phone to confirm her arrival. What I hadn't expected was for her to call me back for a chat every day that she was away.

She was such a lovely, sweet girl. I loved having a good chat with her about how she was enjoying her holiday. She would always ask about work and family too. Despite her sounding still quite unwell down the phone, she insisted she was okay and looking forward to getting to know me a bit better. I'd offered to come and get her and her little sister Ela when she came back to the UK. So, that's why I was sitting in the café at Norwich airport. It was their connecting flight from Holland that had just woken me from my dream about the night in the haystack.

I'd gone straight from work on Friday evening to sit in the arrivals lounge of the airport. I fell asleep with a half-drunk cup of tea while listening to my headphones. The radio was playing a local sports program, which was reflecting on Norwich City's defeats in the previous three matches and how the fans would be calling for the manager's head if they lost tomorrow's game. I smiled as I tried to imagine what would happen if the fans really cut off the manager's head. Calling for that was a bit harsh. Sacking him was a better option.

I had the feeling that there was somebody watching me. I looked around to see who it was, and was surprised to see a lady with long red hair. She wore dark shades over her eyes as though she had just come back from somewhere hot and forgotten to take them off. When she saw that I had seen her looking, she picked up the magazine she had in her hand, and started reading as though she had never been looking at me. I ignored her rudeness assuming, that she was staring at me because I was wearing my work clothes in a place where most people were going on holiday.

I wasn't exactly sure why I wanted to be there to pick up Kat from the airport. Either it was so that I could bring things around to an end and make sure she got home safely, or just because I was doing a friend a favour.

Kat had called me the previous evening, excited to tell me her friend Jenny had gone into labour. As Jenny had been due to pick them up, I found myself offering to step in for her. Kat was incredibly grateful.

Outside the large window, it was already dark when I saw the tail lights of the plane carrying Kat and her sister on the second part of their journey. After the landing, it had disappeared as it turned to taxi to the small terminal area.

I still wasn't sure what it would be like seeing each other again, or how our new friendship would pan out. Although Kat was a lovely lady and I wanted to see her again, I was totally clueless about how to be friends with a girl.

Really, I shouldn't have been, because I had been incredibly close friends with a girl called Sally from the age of around three or four. At ten, she had moved away with her sister and not left any contact details. It was strange that I had suddenly thought of her. I had tried to blank her out, because even though it was never a romance, I was devastated that my best friend never called me after she moved.

I told myself I shouldn't compare the two of them. We were adults not ten-year-olds, and adult male/female friendships were far more complicated than childhood ones.

When the gates opened, I saw Kat before she saw me. She paused to look in her handbag and took one her hankies. She spotted me and gave a warm smile as she pointed me out to Ela, then we made our way towards each other. Kat stayed few feet back blowing her nose, while Ela walked over to me with her hand outstretched in welcome.

I was far from prepared as Ela threw both her arms around me and hugged me like an old friend. Then she turned to Kat and said something in Czech. Kat said something in reply and pushed her playfully away from me.

"Ela would like to thank you for saving her dumb big sister from the snow," she told me with a beaming smile. Putting her used hankie in her pocket, she looked down so that her eyes didn't meet mine. "And Ela's dumb big sister would like to say thank you too."

We stood there, both looking each other up and down, but not really knowing what to say.

"You no repulsed by skinny bony body and horrible yucky nose?" Kat asked. She looked so much better than when I last saw her. She wore jeans and a pink t-shirt with her coat tied around her waist. She looked bright. Her skin was pink as opposed to the bluish grey it had been the last time. Her cheeks were rosy, but her nose was also quite pink like she still had a bit of a cold. She was also taller than I remembered, but you don't always remember people's height when they're lying down in the dark.

"You look much better," I told her, finding my voice.

When she spoke, her voice was much brighter than it had been when I last saw her. Again, she looked up briefly and then back down.

"I much better thank you, but I am still a bit cold."

"Do you want me to take your rucksack, so you can put your coat on?" I asked her awkwardly.

"You very kind, and I will take your offer up, but I mean this cold," she said, pointing at her nose as she swung her rucksack down to me.

Only seconds after she said it, she whipped out her spotted hanky from the pocket she had put it in only thirty seconds ago and stood there breathing sharply. Then she had such a big sneeze that she nearly lost her balance and went flying backwards.

"You've still got your cold?" I asked.

"That is what I mean say," she nodded, almost smiling, but still not looking at me. "No am shivering cold, but having still a sneeze cold and cough." She sniffed, and wiped her nose thoroughly.

"You must have been really sick, you poor thing," I soothed.

She looked up at me, slowly cleaning herself up with her hankie before stuffing it back in her pocket.

Suddenly, she stepped forward and her deep blue eyes were two inches below mine. I could see why she had been hiding her face. It was covered in tears.

"Kat, why are you crying my mate?" I asked, reaching out and wiping the tears away with my finger as they rolled down her cheek.

"I no know, I just being silly," she said, smiling through her tears and giving me a big dopey-eyed look. I couldn't help thinking how adorable she was.

Suddenly she took another step forward and flung her arms around me, kissing me on both cheeks, not once, but twice. I put my arms around her and held her tight.

"I no think you would come to meet us," she said quietly in my ear.

"What on earth made you think that, you daft woman?" I asked, as I rubbed her back. "Especially as I told you I was already here waiting when you phoned me from Holland an hour and a half ago."

"I was giving you time to run away for your life," she whispered, with a hint of a giggle.

"Why would I run away?" I probed, and let her go.

She took a step back and smiled awkwardly, still touching my hand.

"I no know," she whispered, "but you hardly know us and last time we meet, I bring you much trouble. Trouble is following me round like smell these days, and I no want you get hurt."

"You're no trouble Kat," I told her, giving her hand a

squeeze.

"I am blubbering wreck," she said. She took another enormous clean white hanky from her opposite jeans pocket to dab her eyes.

"Wow, how many hankies do you carry?" I teased.

"I am have one in every pocket and several in my handbag, and still I worry it no enough with this cold and now tears," she smiled.

"I might not know you well," I said to her, "but after what we went through, you are the closest thing I've got to a friend."

Her reaction to this surprised me. "Oi, what you mean the closest thing?" She sharply flicked me in the chest with her handkerchief. She narrowed her eyes momentarily with the same fake aggression she had shown when I had refused to take money from her before the car tyres had punctured. She took another step forward and hugged me again. "Rob," she whispered in my ear once more. "You so kind to me, I want to be you friend within twenty seconds of meeting you, but after everything that went on, you always be special friend. No matter where it is takes us. Always."

That was the sweetest thing anyone had ever said to me at that point. As a nineteen-year-old reject, who, until recently, hadn't even plucked up the courage to speak to a girl outside of work until I met Kat two weeks ago, I had no clue how to react. All I wanted to tell her was that she meant the same to me.

"After all the people I've met, I just can't believe that a lovely sweet lady like you exists, let alone wants to be friends with a reject like me," I whispered back in her ear.

She gave a little sob. "Stop being so nice about me, you make me cry even harder. You are no reject. I just some stupid girl whose life you saved."

"If you remember right, it was your quick thinking and humility that saved us. My driving was what got us into a mess," I reminded her. "Plus, if you keep being nice to me, you might make me cry too."

"I hope I never do." She smiled as she stepped away, waving her handkerchief in my face pretending to dry tears.

Ela suddenly made us both jump by piping up. She spoke in Czech, which I did not understand a word of. I think we had both forgotten she was there. Kat turned to her and made her trademark fake-mean look and slapped her playfully on the back with pretend malice. Ela grinned and stuck her tongue out at Kat, who turned to me looking a little red.

"Give me a minute," Kat told me. She dabbed her eyes, then took a deep sniff before rubbing her nose vigorously. After, she gave me an embarrassed grin, took a deep breath, and continued talking. "Ela is saying three things," she told me, going even more red as she tried to compose herself against whatever Ela had said that was making her laugh. "One, she needs toilet. Two, she is very hungry, and three, are you and me kiss? 'Cos if so, she wants a sick bag."

I had absolutely no idea what to say to that. Kat could obviously tell I was lost for words, because she smiled at me awkwardly, and added, "I told her we are good friends, but no kiss friends. She no believes me. She no believes man and lady can be friends."

I laughed and tried to change the subject, "Let's find somewhere for you to have a smoke before we go for dinner."

Being a fitness instructor I didn't condone smoking. Kat was a smoker and already too critical of herself, so she didn't need me to tell her off. It was certainly not my place to stop the enjoyment of her only vice if she wanted one.

However, her answer surprised me. She looked offended at my suggestion.

"You must mistake me for another girl." Then, she grinned and took my arm as I lifted her bag onto my shoulders and started walking. "I have never touch a cigarette in my life," she lied loudly, turning to her sister and starting to walk faster. When we had got a little ahead of Ela, Kat turned to me and lifted the arm of her t-shirt to reveal a large nicotine patch stuck to her shoulder. Then she stuck her tongue out at me and said, "Aaaahh," as though she was showing a doctor her throat, but she was revealing a lump of gum on the end of her tongue.

"Nicotine gum?"

"Uh huh," she nodded.

"Good for you," I told her, trying not to come across as patronising.

"I no did want my family to know I smoked," she said, and smiled. "Is time I got my health back. I no have a cigarette since I sat in you car two weeks ago," she told me with a proud look in her eyes. "I no want to say on phone, because I no want to how you say umm..."

"You didn't want to jinx it?" I asked. She nodded and gave me a big open mouth smile. "Do you feel better for it?"

"After two weeks I'm still gasping for smoke, but yes," she cringed, "Yes, I feel fitter, breathe easier and I smell better, no more stinky fag breath see." In her enthusiasm, she stepped in front of me on her tiptoes and breathed in my face to show me the difference. She took me by surprise, and I bumped into her. I had to grab her to stop her from falling.

Several people nearly walked into us, and there was much grumbling. Kat put her hand over her mouth and rolled her eyes from side to side looking very embarrassed.

"Silly girl," she grinned, lowering her hand. As I lifted her forward, our eyes locked together for a second.

I found myself leaning towards Kat. Her eyes were wide and dopey again. Our lips were just about to touch when we were distracted by poor Ela falling over her suitcase and shouting angrily at us for leaving her behind.

"I don't think I need translate that she a bit upset," Kat smiled, as we went back to help her up.

~~*~*~*

After leaving the airport, we stopped for dinner at a local pub. We ate and chatted away for a good couple of hours. The conversation consisted of what we'd all done over Christmas.

Kat and I sat next to each other while Ela sat on the opposite side of the table. She fired questions at me in Czech for Kat to translate. Ela was excited about her first time in a new country. It was to be expected, but I felt sorry for Kat who was doing her best to eat her vegetables while answering questions in two languages.

I was amazed at how Kat—without being at all rude —used hand signals to control the conversation so that we didn't talk over each other. It also gave her time to translate for Ela and I.

Kat listened intently as I told her about working over Christmas and arguing with my boss about health and safety.

"You should have come work with me," she laughed.

"I'm sure my boss wouldn't have missed me," I said, laughing too.

However, when I asked her if the job was still open, she shook her head vigorously and said, "Nope I no give job to a friend anymore, because the head cleaner is horrible."

"But aren't you the head cleaner?" I asked"

"Yep," she nodded. "I no want to subject a good friend to my temper." She laughed.

The ice broken between us when we met had somewhat refrozen over the two weeks since we'd seen each other. Once we'd got talking, it was like we were smashing it with sledgehammers.

I would not have met up with Kat if I hadn't already known that she was an inwardly beautiful person from the night we'd spent clinging to each other in the haystack. However, I had to remind myself that the night in the hay was irrelevant, because she had invited me to meet up again before the tires blew out.

I made some new observations about my new friend in an environment away from a freezing snow-covered haystack. Despite saying she was an introvert, Kat was such a lovely, enthusiastic, smiley, chatty girl. She had a beautiful beaming open smile. Kat would shrug her shoulders and dip her chin, so that her big dopey blue eyes were looking up at the recipient. She was incredibly funny too. Whether it be her over-the-top expressions, or poking fun at herself, or me and Ela, she encouraged me to poke fun back at her. It was clear too, how much Kat and Ela cared about each other. I couldn't understand what they were saying, but from their tone, they seemed to be poking fun at each other in a good-natured way.

Although she was a looker, it wasn't Kat's beauty that drew me to her. It was that she could make me feel like there was only the two of us in the room. When I was talking to her, she would look at me and listen intently without interruption as though it was just us. She would do the same when Ela was speaking. You could tell she was drinking in everything you said and holding it like a sponge in her head so that she could quote it back.

Kat however, didn't expect everyone to have this ability. When she was talking, she would often get carried away with excitement and babble, so I couldn't understand her. Realising she was talking too fast, she would stop, tap me on the shoulder, apologise, take a deep breath, and smile, before starting again more slowly and in improved, if not perfect, English.

She was extremely polite too, but didn't expect the same standards from everyone else. An excellent example of her politeness was that two or three times when Kat asked me to tell her something, she touched me gently to stop me and, "Scuzyrude,"—her own abbreviation of excuse me for being rude—before blowing her nose with the utmost grace and elegance.

Following that she looked at me with those dopey eyes of hers, took hold of my hand, and said to me, "Forgive me for stopping you. I no want to miss you telling me anything."

"It's quite all right," I said with a smile, and thanked her for listening so keenly. What could I say to that? Nobody had ever wanted to hear to me rabbit on so badly.

Another observation I made very quickly about Kat was that she was doing everything with her right hand. She even used a fork in her right hand and pushed it down on its side to cut her food. While her right hand worked, her left arm hung limp unmoving as though she had injured it.

I was hesitant to ask her about it. However, when I did finally ask her tactfully, I found a lot about her sense of humour as well as her personal health. As she turned to me with a cold look straight into my eyes, she said in a gruff tone, "You are *mind your own fucking business*."

I was taken aback at her sudden change from a quietly spoken polite girl, to swearing at me and telling me to not to be nosey. However, a sudden smile beamed across her face as she laughed, "*Ha ha*, are you thought I was angry, silly boy. No worry me things." She lifted her left arm, put her hand down on mine and smiled. "Can you feel me squeeze hand with all my strength?"

"I can't feel a thing!" I replied, confused.

To which her reply was, "Is because of seizure I had last night, but tomorrow it will health better. Now you see way I am no can use for eating today. But I okay, never worry about me for this."

"Well, sorry this horrible stuff happens to you. If you need help just ask." I soothed, adding on a lighter note, "It's a good job you're not left-handed."

That was obviously the wrong to say, because she then told me in a blunt tone, "I am big ugly girl and I am had this health condition my whole and is not required help. Plus I actually am left-handed, however you concern and help is not required. I am can do anything you can."

I felt awful for asking and I think Kat saw this in my face. However, just when I thought she was grumpy with me, she shot me a dazzling smile, gave me a very obvious wink, then touched me gently with her working hand, adding in her sweeter soft tone. "I am no grumpy for you asking. Concern and help are no needed, but both are apricated more than you understand. I am fine. It is will be okay in a day or so and I no like people worry about me. You are understand?"

I nodded as she smiled back at me. My already high admiration for her had just grown tenfold. Obviously, I knew she was epileptic, but I didn't realise the lasting effect it could have on someone. On top of that, until Ela came to live with her that evening, she had been alone over a thousand miles from her family. She was clearly very independent and strong-willed. When I asked her if it ever stopped her going to work, she just laughed, and announced. "Five years of work and no sick day *ever*!"

So, after that, much of the evening went following like this. Ela would fire questions at me in her language, and poor Kat translated all the questions while she struggled to eat her dinner.

At one point, she looked like she was going to snap at Ela, but then only smiled and said, "My sister is nosey. I am no going to ask that question in public." I just laughed, and she smiled back at me with her dopey eyes. "Plus" she added, "I am hungry, and I no can eat while she wanting translations."

At this point I stepped in and told Kat to tell Ela to calm down and let her finish her dinner before it got cold. When Kat had translated, Ela smiled apologetically and putting her hands up, she kissed her sister on the cheek to say sorry.

Later Kat apologised for eating like a pig after demolishing a pile of vegetables the size of a mountain before going back for seconds and a massive slice of chocolate cake.

"Where did it all go?" I asked, looking down at her flat tummy.

"Magic mouth." she grinned. "Food disappear as soon as it goes in. I eat like a horse and never get fat. I only eat veggies and fruit."

"What about the chocolate cake?" I asked.

"I allow myself to indulge in slice of chocolate cake after my Sunday beach walk," she grinned.

"It's not Sunday," I joked.

"I know!" she beamed at me. "It fun doing something different."

A few moments later when the bill came, Kat lay back in the corner of the pub bench right next to me, sipping her cup of tea and listening to Ela. She wasn't looking, but must have had eyes in the back of her head, because as the waitress handed me the bill, Kat reached and snatched it away from me and thanked the waitress.

When I reached into my wallet and took out my bank card, Kat slapped my hand. She then gripped my finger and put her face close to mine. With narrowed eyes and that same mean face, she threateningly said, "Put your money away, or else."

"Or else what?" I asked, smiling.

"I will stick my tongue out at you threateningly, because I told you I would pay." Then she burst out into a smile and said, "Nice try though."

"But I want to pay," I told her with a laugh. As she tried to stop me taking the bill, she counted out her cash. "What if we go halves?" I asked.

"No," she replied.

"When you stay over at our home," she sniffed, "If you let me pay, you sleep in my bed. I will sleep on chair."

"That's not fair to you. It's your home."

"Shut up, I'm talking," she said, giving me a huge smile. "If you pay," she said, reverting to the mean incarnation of herself, "you still sleep in my bed, but as punishment, you have to share it with me."

"Why's that a punishment?" I asked. "It'll be like a sleepover."

There was no suggestion by either of us that sharing a bed meant anything other than two friends sharing a place to sleep. After all, we'd spent the night together as two naked strangers only weeks earlier, and no there was no suggestion of anything sexual.

"Because," she laughed, "is tiny bed and I am stinky dirty, snotty woman with sneezy cold. *And*, I been eating a lot of sprouts. Extra windy fart bum."

The friendly argument went on for a good few minutes, but I finally got Kat to back down when I reminded her I had no bills to pay, and that she had an extra person to support on her income until Ela got her first payment from work.

When I came back from paying the bill and sat down, I was surprised when Kat put her arms out to me, shuffled close, and gave me a big hug and whispered, "I want to say thank you for such a lovely evening. Sorry for my stubbornness. You are a great friend to Ela and me."

"No, thank you," I told her. "This has been the best evening I've had in a very long time."

"It's no over yet," she said looking at me closely. "There will be many more, but next time I am paying."

We sat back and looked at each other while still touching left hands. Kat sniffed and rubbed her nose with her handkerchief without taking her eyes off mine. The two of us just sat and looked at each other closely. I felt the urge to kiss her. Suddenly Kat did what she'd done earlier in the evening and kissed both my cheeks twice before giving me her open-mouthed shrugging smile.

We all went to the toilet after the meal. On the way out of the gents, someone grabbed my arm.

"Ela," I exclaimed, a little surprised.

"Hello," she said coolly.

"You speak English?" I asked.

"Better than Katarzyna does," she smiled. "I had four years of lessons, and Kat is self-taught, bless her."

"When are you going to tell her you speak perfect English?" I whispered.

"When it stops being funny watching her trying to translate," she grinned." I think she knows anyway, because she tries to catch me out like a game" She laughed.

"I think she planned to match us up," I told Ela, nervously trying not to offend her by saying I saw her as nothing more than a friend.

"Don't worry, but with the greatest respect, I don't fancy you either. I keep telling Kat I like other girls, but she thinks I'm teasing like I always do." She paused. "Did you see how wound up she got when I asked her a naughty question?"

At this point I should have picked up on what Ela said about liking girls.

"What did you ask her that got her so wound up?"

Ela laughed, "I told her to ask you if you wanted to..." She made a motion sliding her fingers in and out of her fist.

"We're just good friends," I protested.

"Sure, you are," she winked. "I'm sorry I spoiled your little moment earlier. You kiss her. You know you want to. I know she wants you to."

"Are you sure?"

"Rob," she said, "Kat phoned you eighteen times in two weeks and spoke for an hour or more. She ran up a big phone bill. She has paid our parents for it, but she won't tell you in case you try to pay her back. She is very proud." Ela smiled.

"I'm glad I paid the bill for dinner," I told her, smiling back. At least I hadn't let Kat pay the bill. Although I was sure she knew what she was doing with her own money, the £40 bill could be a week's food shopping to those two girls.

Ela nodded. "She already told me that she would invite you in for a drink. I am going to suddenly catch her cold and get sick, and have an early night before you show us around tomorrow. I expect you will arrive bright and early if you go at all. Even if you don't kiss," she added smiling, "my sister needs a friend like you, and so do I. Also, you need a friend like her."

She winked at me as Kat came out of the toilet and then faked a big sneeze and sent another wink my way.

Chapter 5

Kat's home

Later, when we got to their flat, I helped Kat and Ela up three flights of spiral stairs with their bags. They had a lovely little flat on the fourth floor of a rather dilapidated, but pretty old building. Kat proudly stated that it was a five-minute walk from the beach, the town centre, the train and bus stations, the supermarket, the bank, the pubs, and the campsite where she worked, but far enough away to be a quiet, peaceful part of town.

I'd never been in a young lady's house before. It smelt clean and fresh, as though she had given the place a good clean before she left for her holiday. Despite this, the flat was clearly lived in. There was a clothes rack in the kitchen with a bra and knickers hanging from it, along with a bandanna and several clean handkerchiefs. There was also Kat's work uniform. It looked like she'd just taken it off and dumped it in the washing basket minutes before leaving. There was a plate on the drying rack, and her hoover was by the door, as though she had cleaned the floor backwards on her way out.

When all the bags were up, Ela yawned and faked another sneeze, and said something to Kat in Czech before hugging her. Then she came to me smiling and laid her head on her hands to signal that she was going to bed. She raised her hand and gave me a high five, then as she passed my ear, she whispered, "Treat her well."

As soon as Ela closed the door, I asked Kat, who was now in the little kitchen trying to light the gas, what time they wanted me to pick them up in the morning for the trip we'd planned around Norfolk.

Kat stopped what she was doing and came trotting over to me. With her arms out, she gave me a massive tight hug, which I returned, still nervous and not knowing what it meant.

"Stay for drink, and I show you my pictures," she grinned, leaning back with her arms still around me. She flashed her lovely wide eyes again, before asking, "Tea, coffee, vodka, wine?"

"I'd love a cup of tea," I told her, smiling.

"Correct choice. I was hope you say that."

"Why's that? I asked.

"Because, you get to know tea is my favourite drink in the whole world," she said with a big sniff. "As long you no mind putting lemon in it there. No milk and milky tea is blaaa!" She stuck out her tongue and made a cringing face. Then she beamed at me. "You stay and watch a movie with me, and I show you where I grew up." Her voice sounded excited. She released me from her grip without taking her eyes off me as she waltzed over to the kitchen area. I followed behind.

"That sounds like a good plan," I said, a little confused about what exactly she was asking.

"You no can say no anyway," she teased, "because I got my arms around you neck would no have let go if you even you want to go. I would have made you drag out of the house kicking and screaming."

I stood back for a minute taking it all in, until Kat asked me why I was so quiet.

"It's just, I don't get out much and don't go to other peoples houses. I've never been invited into anyone's home, so it's a bit of a shock that a gorgeous person invited me to spend to time with her."

I realised that it might have been a bit much to call her gorgeous seeing as it was only the second time we had met. I might add that although Kat could not be considered plain or ugly, I had been referring to her personality.

Kat's face dropped and she looked at the floor for a moment, before saying, "It is shame this other girl is invite you on the same night. If you have go to this 'Gorgeous girl' go, but don't forget about me."

"I was talking about *you*, though!" I grinned.

"Well, then are you need glasses, because I no am gorgeous," she teased, before saying in more serious tone, "That kind of talk is boyfriend and girlfriend talk. You are my friend, no my boyfriend, so please is no talked me like that."

"Sorry," I said awkwardly, wishing I hadn't paid her the compliment.

Kat, however, beamed at me and said, "*Ha!* You thought I was serious. I no mind at all, it just nobody call me gorgeous before. That's was so lovely you. Is wrong, but lovely."

"I bet you're lying," I replied, to which she shook her head. "I am nervous about men. I no am usually talk to boy long enough for them say it."

"So, you are nervous your first time in girl's house and

worry you do or say something wrong?" I nodded. "Well," she teased, "It just like a normal flat. One opened plan lounge/kitchen, two bedrooms, bathroom, smoking area... sorry, fire escape... Only from normal flat is that a girl lives here... and she bites... and live in that room there next to mine." She laughed, pointing with her good hand over at the room where Ela had taken her stuff.

"Is it your first time having a man here?"

She nodded, rubbing her nose with her hanky politely and grinned, "I am more nervous than you are is in case I mess up."

"Well, it's your house, so just be yourself and do what you always do."

She burst out laughing and when I asked what was funny, she told me. "I am usually strip naked and put my clothes in the wash them moment I get the door."

"Well, what do you do after that?" I asked, trying to keep a straight face.

"I used to go out on the balcony for smoke, but I am stopped doing now I healthy girl."

I was unable to control my laughter, "I bet the neighbours loved you smoking in the nude."

She went bright red, "I am meant put night clothes on, then have cigarette." She beamed seeing the funny side.

"Just do something else that you would do if you were here on your own."

"Okay, but no say a I no do warn you."

She turned her back on me, taking a deep breath and blew her nose so long and hard that I almost expected her hanky to blow in the wind like in a cartoon.

"Do you feel better?" I grinned, and she nodded. "Have you been politely waiting to do that since I picked you up?"

She shook her head and smiled, "No. I been dying to do it since I left Lobendava this lunch time. She gave me one of her lovely open-mouthed smiles and turned a little pink. "Can you do me huge favour?"

"Anything," I replied,

"I done really well to last two weeks, but now I am home I am really want a cigarette. I have a pack ready-rolled ones in the bathroom cupboard for when I no can roll them…"

I stopped her by putting my hand up. "Do you really want to start again after such a good attempt to quit?"

"If you let me finish…" she smiled, "…what I was going ask you was if please cut the nasty things up for me while I make the tea, slip in something more comfortable."

"Of course, I will," I said quietly, going off to start the task without question. I realised that it had taken a lot for Kat to admit that she didn't trust herself not to give in to her cravings and light up.

A few minutes later we found ourselves sat together, under the quilt from Kat's bed on her only chair. This was an old and worn, but very comfy reclining armchair, clearly built for one person.

"At least we no get cold," she smiled, adding, "Fucking boiler still broken. Landlady said man came to fix it while away, but is still fucking broken."

"It's not good for your cold though," I told her.

"No suppose is no," she replied, taking a deep sniff and rubbing her nose with a large bright pink handkerchief.

She had changed into a light nightdress under a rainbow dressing gown and taken off her bedcover to put over us. We sat snuggled together.

"You stay as long as you promise no laugh at my green nightdress," she laughed, "and my pink hanky."

"Why would I laugh?" I smiled. "You look lovely in your nightdress."

"Thank you, but these things are for home use only," she said quietly. "I make myself clothes and hankies. Only the good stuff makes it out of flat for public appearance, while the stuff I fuck up stay home. The nightdress was meant be blue dress. This handkerchief meant is to have red spots. They ran in wash and made it look pink, and me look stupid. I keep it close as I do no want to sneeze over you, because might no be my friend long."

"I don't mind if you want to go to bed, because you're not feeling well," I told her, concerned that she might feel better after a good sleep. I didn't want Kat to think that I was trying to find a way out of spending the rest of the evening with her, because I was enjoying our time together. I didn't want it to end.

"Nonsense," she sniffed. "I no let little cold stop me spend time with my friend, but I understand if you no want my germs." She then pulled out a washing line peg and pegged her folded hanky over her nose. I was in stitches laughing, "Hands free sneezestopper, so can do things and sneeze at same time," she said in a heavily muffled voice. "Or my case hand free."

"Did you try that on in the mirror?" I teased.

She nodded so enthusiastically that I could tell she was lying. With a teasing smile, she said, "It sexy, no?" As she giggled, it fell straight off and landed in my lap. She snatched it up with a slightly embarrassed look. "I want to apologise for rudeness," she said suddenly.

"When were you rude?" I asked, somewhat puzzled.

"Rob, did you no notice me sneezing thirty-seven times while we eating dinner?"

"I didn't sit there counting," I told her with a grin, and added that her apology was refused on the grounds that she had nothing to apologise for.

"Do all your friends sit this close on the chair with you?" I asked. I realised how far out of my comfort zone I was, sitting in a small armchair with a near stranger. But, then again, this was Kat. We'd been naked together and remained friends, so it just felt natural that we should be close and not be as nervous as I would with someone else.

"No," she said, "I tell you Jenny, my only friend. Poor girl with her health issues are too fat to share with, so I sit on floor."

Kat told me that Jenny's dad had been feeding her pet Rabbit, Roger—which she pronounced Wogger—and her cat, Charlie, and that Jenny was previously meant to be picking her and Ela up at the airport, but Jenny had gone into labour and had her little girl. Kat wanted to give her a day or so to get used to being a mum before visiting her. She told me she was happy for Jenny and looking forward to helping her with her little girl.

"But, at same time I happy, because my friend, Rob, kindly help us out a second time and I get to spend time with my friend."

"I'm always happy to help when I can," I reassured her.

"You're nice friend, so you welcome here anytime you want," she said, with a quiet and lovely smile.

"Even at three in the morning?" I joked.

I wasn't sure that she realised I was joking, because she smiled and nodded with a little, "Mm-hm," and then said, "I expect it if you stay the night, silly." She gave a small laugh and rubbed her nose with her discoloured handkerchief.

At this point, Kat went rather quiet for the first time that night, and just sat there folding and refolding her hand-kerchief in silence while she kept glancing over at me. When I asked her if she was okay, she smiled and looked at me uneasily.

"Rob, now we alone, I got something ask you," she said, suddenly looking rather serious.

"Ask away," I told her.

"Well," she said, looking a little troubled, "I forget what happened in the haystack. I had a massive seizure when I was away. It is what caused arm and leg to stop working. I forget everything after I went sleep. I wake one morning in bed and I remember you and me in haystack, but nothing of how we got out, or what we did. I just remember you were kind and that you my best friend hero."

"So, there's a big black hole in your memory?" I asked.

She took a deep breath and nodded, "I get them with seizures, but it comes back soon after." Then she frowned. "But dis time no."

I didn't know how to tell her that I wasn't entirely sure about what had happened.

"It's not clear in my mind either," I admitted rather uneasily. "It's like it was all a really long dream. In fact, I was kind of surprised when you called to say you had landed, because I had it in my head that you were just a dream."

"You no have seizures like me?" she said frowning. I

shook my head. "Really odd we both forget. I no call you liar, because I forget too."

"I was going to ask you what happened," I told her. I remembered nothing after Kat went to sleep and had no explanation for that happening.

She smiled and said, "I think we looked after each other. Maybe this why I feel so close and safe with you?"

"It's still scary that we don't know what happened to us," I said, with a frown.

"Maybe we went through adventure like in da movies. We are strangers, but during adventure, we fall in love and kiss at the end of the adventure, but something made us forget everything."

"Why would you want to kiss me?" I laughed, thinking that it was highly unlikely.

"Why would you kiss me?" She grinned back, adding, "Anyway, I think you must have kicked my butt about smoking. I got on plane with no tobacco. Just gum, patches and strange feeling that I no want to smoke anymore. Not that I ever intended get hooked on it. Cravings still are very bad though."

"It's definitely all bizarre," I agreed.

"Something special must have happened," she said softly, "because you and I got on well before what happened. I was going to invite for dinner say thank you for your kind help, but when I called you, I just want to keep talking you. It make me wonder why we are so close friend when this only second time we meet."

"I know exactly what you mean," I said, considering her big blue eyes. "We've become closer than either of us expected."

I did know exactly what she was talking about. In the time that she was away, all I'd think about in the morning was whether she was going to call me or not. She never let me down. I didn't call her, because she was on holiday and out a lot of the time with no mobile, but I would wait for her to call, and then the rest of that evening, all I could think about was the lovely lady on the other end of the phone.

She was like a best mate – the type you could mess about and have a laugh with, watch TV with, or have a few drinks without the pressure of trying. She made it clear she was a single girl and staying that way. I respected that.

"Maybe if we keep spending time together we remember what happened," she grinned.

"I'm up for that. Spending the evening with you is so much better than spending it alone on my Xbox." I laughed.

"I am more fun than Xbox?" She gasped. I nodded, "Well," she smiled, turning to look me in the face, "Next time you lonely in the evening, you come see Ela and me. Bring Xbox and all three of us be lonely together." She laughed and rubbed her nose again.

"I can't imagine you playing me at Fifa," I told her with a giggle.

"I will," she sniffed, sitting up at her full height with her face close to mine and puffing her chest out. "And..." she added, poking me playfully in the chest. "...and, if my other hand is no working, I beat you at it with my one hand."

"Will you?" I laughed, puffing my chest back and poked her playfully on the shoulder.

She nodded confidently behind her handkerchief, turned away and sneezed heavily, then she turned back to me shaking her head and blowing her nose gently. After this, she beamed her smile at me. "I no even know what is Xbox or

Fifa," she said, giving me a mischievous look, "but I still beat you." She laughed, flicking me in the face playfully with the end of her large blonde plait.

Kat was secretly very proud of her hair, which she told me she been growing for seven years now. When I told her how lovely it was, she told me it was long overdue a good wash and cut, and joked that it was probably full of lice. She had plaited it before her seizure, but could not retie with one hand, so it had been left in it's current condition for three days. She tickled my face with the end once more.

"Have you had male friends before?" I asked out of interest.

"No, unless my brother counts, and certainly no get naked with him," she said, and laughed so hard that her face turned a beetroot colour.

"Well, you do live in Norfolk" I teased.

"Heard the rumours" She teased.

For people who don't know, the county of Norfolk where I am from, is known nationally as a place where incest is commonplace. They are, however, just nasty rumours.

"I bet you never been friends with girl like this before no?" she asked me. She smiled awkwardly as if she didn't want to pry. I was sure it was bugging her not knowing if I was in the same situation as her.

"Well, there was this girl a lot of years ago who was my best friend," I explained.

I went on to tell her about my best friend, Sally, who I hadn't seen since I was ten. Sally was the girl who had lived in the house close to where my car had crashed the night I met Kat. She lived with her older sister after her parents died young and my family helped look after her.

Sally and I had spent many summers playing together. However, a little under ten years ago, she had told me she was moving with her sister back to Manchester where her sister was born. She promised to write, but she disappeared overnight without leaving an address.

"Aww how precious," Kat said, putting her hand on her heart. "That's so awful and so sweet at the same time." She said that it was a shame Sally and I had lost touch, because she'd love to meet her.

I explained how I'd even tried to look her up on Facebook, but there was no sign of her or her sister.

"You my friend now though," she said with a smile, before giving me a rather sudden and unexpected one-armed squeeze. "I sure you friend Sally no mean to no tell you where she goes. Odd and sad that she no writes to you. You have me now dough, and I no am losing you, because you are too good to me."

We smiled at each other quietly. "I help you look for your old friend. If we find her, we can tell her my friend now. If she want you back, she will have to share.

It was then that I noticed Kat had put her hanky on the arm of the chair and was holding a different cloth – a purple scarf she grasped very gingerly in her damaged hand, but which seemed to be improving gradually.

"What is that pretty scarf?" I asked.

"Is my angry scarf," she said quietly. "I pull or squeeze it, when angry or stressed, but I no angry with you. It's just... as I say is my evening cigarette time. Even after two weeks I really struggle." She offered me a boiled sweet and explained that she'd been sucking them between lumps of nicotine gum and patches. "Lots of tea helps as well," she breathed. "Even though you got rid of my smoking stuff, the supermarket is open for one more hour. So your job is to hold my hand and stop me running down there for more smokes."

I raised my hand to give Kat an encouraging pat on the back, not only for her efforts in quitting smoking, but for being comfortable with asking me for help.

"You should take up boxing," I told her, putting my hands up. "Whenever you want a cigarette, you should throw a few punches at me."

Kat spontaneously gave me her pretend mean look and started hitting my hands as hard as she could—which was not very hard as she was not overly strong. However, in her eagerness, Kat threw a stray punch and hit my nose. It didn't hurt, but Kat still had a look of horror on her face until she realised I was okay, then we just laughed.

"I kiss it better," she said. Grinning, she leaned my way and kissed me on the end of my nose. I wasn't sure what to do or say to that.

As Kat pulled away, we stared at each other very closely nose to nose. Again, I felt like it was one of those moments when we were about to kiss for real. This time Kat was moving closer to me as though she was actually going to kiss me. Only at the last second, she pulled away and kissed the spot on my nose once more.

"I go to toilet," she said with a smile. "You may want to go first, because I no moving once I come back."

So, I went first while Kat made more tea. Then, I sat on the chair and waited.

When Kat returned, she looked over at me awkwardly. It was as if she was plucking up the courage to do something. This time, instead of sitting next to me, Kat sat across me with her arm around my back. She tucked her head into the crook of my arm and smiled up at me.

She had brought with her an old-style leather-bound photo album. When she opened it, I saw that the first page was a picture of a beautiful little baby in a cot. Underneath it read, *Katarzyna Zofka Bobal 26.11.1987*

"Katarzyna is Polish meaning pure," she said, and smiled brightly. "Zofka means wise, and meaning of Bobal is beans."

"So, you're pure, wise beans," I told her and laughed.

"Yes, that's me," she giggled, rubbing her tummy. "Full of yummy beans. Sister Kazia gave me this album to me as going away present when I leave." She smiled, telling me that it was not just baby pictures, but a montage of her growing up.

She pointed out to me pictures of her as a baby with her big sister and parents. There were pictures of her holding each of her three younger siblings as babies. There were also pictures for her birthdays, each with a cake showing the number right up to sixteen. I liked the pictures of a teenage Kat hard at work on her dad's farm, or messing about with her sisters.

The last picture in the album showed the four sisters in a group hug. They were in a field with the sun shining on mountains behind them. Sixteen-year-old Kat was in the middle with her arms around the shoulders of Kazia and Dusa. Twelve-year-old Ela sat on her shoulders, and ten-year-old Dowid was at her feet. It looked baking hot as they were all in shorts and t-shirts. Kazia, to my uneducated eye, appeared to be rather pregnant.

"You all look so happy," I told her as she closed the album.

"I was."

"So, if it's not personal, what drove you to leave?"

"Freedom," she said simply. "I love my family, but because I was an ill child with my epilepsy, they are protecting me too much even dhough my illness no is that bad compared to other people. To live my life, I need to get away from them."

I found it hard not to laugh at Kat's accent when she said 'other', because she pronounced it 'udder' as though she was milking a cow, not that what she was saying was no joke.

"You're a courageous lady for doing that," I told her.

"No just like stand on my own feet, do what I want and no what I told," she smiled. "For example, they no would approve of us if they knew. They worry I would have seizure and you take advantage of me even dough it no likely to happen."

I reassured Kat that would never happen.

"I know," she said, with wide eyes. "I am trust you, Rob." She smiled, adding, "It like this, I'm twenty-one and this is my first time I dared have a friend snuggle with anyone."

"Me too," I told her.

"I mean…" she continued, raising her voice above the whisper she had used for most of the evening, "My big sister is married at seventeen and is have first baby at eighteen, first little sister is the same. Married and baby at eighteen. Second little sister is seventeen and if that girl is Virgin Mary, then I am baby Jesus's… What is something baby has?"

"Shitty nappies?" I shrugged.

She glared at me and giggled, then went red as she tried to control her laughter in squeaky voice. "You just called me a shitty nappy."

I shrugged, "Do you want me to say sorry?"

"No, is so funny." She grinned.

"I guess you're saying you feel you're old enough and wise enough to spread your legs." I stopped immediately, in horror at what I just accidently said, and corrected myself. "Not legs, wings."

Thankfully she seemed oblivious to the meaning of spreading legs, or she might have slapped me. She rested her head back against my chin.

"I am never feel so relaxed, Rob," she grinned. "I am freezing cold, but you make me warm and snuggly.

"You like it then?" I asked.

She bent her chin forward and gave me her open-mouthed smile. "Do you?" she whispered. My reply was I could not have imagined my first cuddle with a lovelier lady.

It was dark, but we could see each other's faces in the light from the TV. As much as I loved Austin Powers, we were not really watching. We were not getting up to what you might think either. Kat and I just lay there talking quietly, telling each other more about ourselves than we already knew. Kat then picked up her digital camera, which she referred to as her new toy. She showed me pictures of her home. It was beautiful. There were snow-covered mountains and stunning architecture. There were also more pictures of her family members. All four sisters pretty much looked alike, apart from subtle differences. The last one was a re-take of the last picture in the album with Kat in the middle and Ela on her shoulders. The only difference being this time both Kazia and Dusa were pregnant.

Kat was keen to point out that Kazia was having her third baby at just twenty-three, and nineteen-year-old Dusa was already on number two, adding that she was not sure she would ever want a family, because she wouldn't make a good mother.

When I asked her if she planned to put the pictures on her computer and print them out, she looked at me blankly. "Rob," she said, looking rather serious, "I am practical girl. I speak five languages. I play several instruments. I can wire plug. I can totally rebuild broken sewing machine. I can fix TV, video and DVD player. Anything at work breaks and I fix it myself."

"You're a talented lady," I told her.

"Rob," she said, still looking serious. "It 2009, I twenty-one years, one month, one week, one day..." she looked at her watch, "...three hours, thirteen minutes old. I live a thousand miles from where I was born. I stand on own feet, but could you do me one favour?" She paused and smiled awkwardly at me.

"What is it, Kat?" I asked, giving her shoulder a friendly squeeze.

She pulled her sad face at me. "Can you teach to me please how use a computer. I don't have a clue?"

"Wonders never cease," I laughed, and promised not only to teach her, but to give her my old laptop.

"Got you," she laughed, "My wind-up."

I should have known that was coming.

Kat explained that she learned about computers at school but never had the need for one.

Kat showed me a video of her playing with one of her nephews. He was chasing her around until she fell to the floor faking exhaustion. When the little boy caught up with her, Kat jumped up and tickled him until he screamed with delight.

"My sister Kazia's son," she smiled, reminiscently. "He is four. She was pregnant with him when I come to England. He loves his tickles from Aunty Kat."

"Looks like you'd make an awesome mum one day," I told her.

She smiled wistfully. "It no beyond possibility. Maybe there man out there want to make me a mummy, but it hard to find somebody blind and stupid. But like I tell my nephew, I too busy being a world champion tickler of small children."

"I didn't know such a thing existed," I grinned.

"Did you no see it on the news?" she teased.

"I must have been at work," I told her.

"Katarzyna Bobal – world champion of child tickling." She raised her arms in the air and pretended to acknowledge an imaginary crowd, then she stood up, rubbed her nose, and turned her face close to me. "You want me to demonstrate?"

"You're okay, thanks," I said, inching back in the chair as she came forward menacingly. I had bad memories of peeing myself when I was tickled as a child. I didn't want to lose control of my bladder.

"I also champion of child swinging and piggy back race," she teased.

"I call wind-up," I laughed.

"Do you?" she snapped, jumping and kneeling either side of my knees. I nodded in reply, feeling rather nervous at her friendly attack. "I am also queen of stick out tongue at people who no believe me," she said, popping her tongue out at me.

I found myself caught off guard wondering if it was wrong to think that my new friend looked gorgeous when she was pretending to be menacing. In that second of confusion, Kat pounced on me. Her arms were flying everywhere. I tried in vain to defend myself against her lightning reflexes as she tickled every inch of me, laughing playfully as she did.

Suddenly, the reclining chair tipped back. Kat almost fell onto my face, but recovered quickly and pinned my wrists down to the chair, leaving me helpless to move. Again, we were breathlessly staring into each other's eyes, like a scene in a movie where the two lead characters suddenly kissed.

I was powerless to move. What happened next was up to Kat alone. For one rather exhilarating and slightly scary moment, she leaned forward, and I thought—and possibly even hoped—she was going to kiss me. Instead, she slid her arms under me and laid her face down next to mine to give me a squeeze. She made the cutest noise, sort of an, "umm-mummm," and all I could do was squeeze her back. Kat made the noise again and wiggled about. Then she rolled onto her side so that we were face to face as we gazed at each other silently.

After a while, Kat sat up and wiped her nose, then used her hand sanitizer. All the time, she looked at me in silence.

"Are you trying to protect yourself, so you don't catch anything from me?" I joked, nodding at the sanitizer.

"Maybe you should go home now," she said quietly, frowning a little.

"Have I done something wrong?"

Kat shook her head and smiled. "Nope..." she said quietly, "...just it gets late, and I thought you might have had enough of me one evening."

"Is this a kind way of telling me you're tired and ill and you want to go to bed? Have I outstayed my welcome?"

She smiled and shook her head. "I no know why I say. I exhausted, but I really enjoy our evening. I no want it to end yet."

At this, I suggested that we made plans for our trip around Norfolk the next day. Kat smiled and agreed, telling me that she was looking forward to it very much. She insisted on making another pot of tea to keep her awake, so we could sit and plan our journey.

I was right in my guess that Kat didn't know much about the area she lived in, apart from her little part of the town and the few parts of Norwich accessible by bus or train. I felt sorry for her. It seemed she worked so hard at the caravan park that she didn't get much time to travel. When she did, it was terribly hard because she couldn't drive. I tried showing her some of the places we planned to visit. I had to use my poor-quality phone to show pictures, as Kat didn't have internet or a computer. Because it was easier for her to see the screen, Kat sat on my lap. She placed her arms around my shoulders to hold herself up.

By the time, we'd finished, we'd written down several places for the three of us to visit in the coming weeks. All of this depended on our work schedules. Kat and I both worked five days out of seven, but she worked 6am until 2 pm and often much later.

We planned to visit Great Yarmouth, Kings Lynn and the broads, and all the little villages. As Kat was a non-practising Catholic, she was intent on visiting the world famous Catholic shrine at Walsingham. We'd also talked about trips further afield like Cambridge and London.

"Maybe next time you come home with me," Kat said quietly.

"Thanks for the invite," I told her, not quite feeling sure that we had been friends long enough to start planning holidays together just yet.

"Are things better with your family?" I asked hesitantly.

Kat nodded, smiling. "Yeah they are," she said. "Years apart can heal things. I love my country and my family, but I no go back to live, only holiday. I have unfinished in business here. Next time, you come with me and I tell them you, my special friend."

"Special friends is that what we are?" I asked.

Kat sniffed into her hanky and smiled at me. "I no know what we are," she said, "but I say I love sitting with you, and I never enjoy time with anyone so much before. You can come back whenever you want to. I promise I won't be sneezy snot face next time."

"I don't mind if you are, but I never thought I'd end up here tonight," I told her gently.

"It still seems weird that we here together again," she yawned.

"You're telling me," I said. "What's strange is that you're a lady and not only are you're not repulsed by my ugly face, you actually let me in your home." I laughed then, and almost on cue, she had another small sneeze. She mopped her nose and smiled at me. "But you're beautiful," I told her, "and a friend with a bad cold is a million times better than no friend."

"I am no beautiful. I already telled you, you need eye test," she said, forcefully pulling a grumpy face and then showing her beautiful smile. "And you no run yourself down," she added, tapping the tip of my nose playfully. "It just nice to have new friend who treats me like an equal person and no talking down to me because I foreign, or suck up me as people do at work cos I am boss lady of cleaning. You also are no trying to chat me up like some sexual conquest. You say these nice things because you are mean them and no because you want to get me in bed. I already said nobody goes there and you respect my wishes." She held up the crucifix that was still hanging from her neck as it was the night we met.

"That's never going to happen even if you are interested in sex, because I already know you're out of my league," I grinned.

"I know," she said in a rather matter of fact way shaking her head. "We no are playing football, and if we were I be three divisions below you."

"Stop it" I told her.

"I love having you here for tea and special friend cuddle. You can come and sit whenever you want," she said sleepily.

"I love being here with you too," I told her. "It's weird how we seem so close when this is only the second time we've met" I said.

Kat laid her head on mine sleepily, and said, "You welcome for any time." She gave a tired little laugh, then turned and grinned at me so closely that our noses were almost touching. It was just like the moment in the airport where I had thought we had almost kissed.

We hung there for a moment and just smiled at each other. I came to realise that poor Kat was exhausted from the long day she must have had. The reason she was almost leaning her face on mine was because she was barely able to her hold her head up. Kat slid for forward and rested her chin on my shoulder. She put her arms tightly around my waist, and I felt myself doing the same to her.

"Are you sure you're going to stay awake for films?" I

whispered

"I no really am watching," she said, quietly sounding very sleepy. "I just enjoying time with my friend before sleep." She took a deep, tired breath and surprised me by whispering one of the most affectionate and confusing things anyone had ever said, "I love my friend Rob."

I had no idea what on earth to say to that. I made no secret of the fact that I'd quickly grown to care deeply about Katarzyna in the short time we'd been friends, but I was gobsmacked that she had just used the L word.

The best way to respond was to whisper back in her ear, "I love my friend Kat too... Kat," I said gently. "Did we nearly kiss in the airport?"

Kat took a deep breath and answered me with a mumble that I couldn't make out. Then she snored in my ear. I let her lie there sleeping in my arms for about five minutes before deciding that she would be more comfortable in her bed. I lifted her very gently. I was surprised at how light she was, as she wasn't a small girl. However, she was very slim and bony. I carried her slowly into her tiny little bedroom, which was more of a box room.

In her room, she had a second bookcase filled with novels, a stereo, and a rack full of CDs. Her work clothes were on a hanger, along with a pretty white dress marred with a red stain.

Kat had told me that a lot of her furniture came with the flat, and had come from the second-hand shop on the ground floor of the building. The rest of it, including the bed and bookcases, she had made herself from flat packs. She was clearly very handy with a screwdriver and had probably carried a good deal of the stuff up the flights of spiral stairs on her own. It was no mean feat for a lady who wasn't small, but wasn't exactly a mountain of strength.

I laid her down gently on the small single bed covered by a clean red sheet and orange pillowcases. I moved her sewing machine from the middle of the floor where I had left it when getting rid of the spare tobacco under the bed. I didn't want her to trip if she had to go to the toilet in the middle of the night. With the quilt we used earlier, I tucked her into bed. Then I replaced the stagnant glass of water on her bedside table with a fresh one in case she was thirsty when she woke.

I was just about to leave when I realised that Kat left pills in a small medication cup next to her nicotine gum. I didn't know if she'd intended to take them, so I was left with no option but to wake her and check. I touched her cheek gently and said, "Kat, sweetheart, do you need your pills?"

She nodded and in a dreamlike daze, reached out for the pills. She swallowed them and took a mouthful of water without ever opening her eyes. Then she laid her head on her pillow and mumbled, "Thank you."

Still, without opening her eyes, she picked up a clean hanky that had been left on the bedside table and blew her nose again, this time much harder, and mumbled something about it being hard to sleep with blocked nostrils.

In that moment while she was nearly with it, I asked the question again. "Kat, did we nearly kiss earlier?" Her sleepy answer bamboozled me.

She mumbled, "Several times," and then added, "We could be good together. I no want to go out though, you understand? You my good friend."

"That's okay, Kat," I said, gently touching her arm. I knew that there'd only been a slim chance of us getting together anyway. "I'm happy to be special friends, and I'll still take you and Ela sightseeing tomorrow?"

Kat smiled at me and nodded.

"I'm going to go home now, Kat," I told her, "Unless you want me to sleep on the sofa."

Kat shook her head sleepily and mumbled, "No, go home." She reached her hand up and pointed at the door. Then she muttered, "No want you to be my boyfriend." With a tired and rattling breath, she fell asleep.

Chapter 6

Broccoli and Stilton locked out

With mixed feelings, I decided to go home and come back in the morning to take Kat and Ela for their proper tour of Norfolk. It didn't matter that she openly and rather confusingly said she didn't want to be my girlfriend. Though her signals were mixed, I respected her decision and valued her friendship even more for her honesty.

When I crept out, I shut the door gently. Then I nearly jumped to see Ela standing there eating a pack of sausage rolls.

"You want one?" she quietly asked, shoving the packet at me. I shook my head. "Take one," she insisted. "I can't eat them all. Katarzyna is a strict vegetarian. She will kill me if she finds out I brought meat to her house." I took one from her and put it in my pocket. Ela gave me pleading look, and without a word, stuffed another one in my other pocket and grinned.

"I snuck out to the shop while you two were all loved up," she said, laughing. "I walked right past you. I borrowed money from Katarzyna's wallet because I don't have any. Then I went out the front door and went to the supermarket."

"You're very good at English for someone who has not been here before."

Ela thanked me with a grin. "Did you...?" She made a kissing face and laughed, but when I shook my head, she grimaced.

"She just wants to be friends, which is fine," I said.

"She's a liar," Ela scoffed, outraged.

"Really?" I asked.

She nodded. "All through dinner she was asking me if I thought you would mind if she kissed you. She was worried about giving you her cold and putting you off of her."

"Really?"

Ela nodded. "As I say, Kat is self-taught at English. She is an incredibly intelligent lady. If it wasn't for her health, I think she'd be a doctor or a lawyer."

"I realise you two are way out of my league when it comes to intelligence," I laughed.

"Not me," Ela said. "Just her, but she knows she messes up her English and she's very sensitive about it. Because of your accent, she doesn't understand as much of what you say as she wants you to think she does. But she is excellent at making you think she understood when she didn't. Or she thinks she understands when she doesn't. Honestly, I still think you two are made for each other. My sister needs a kick up the backside and so do you." She paused for a moment before adding, "The punishment of sleeping in her bed with her after you paid for dinner against her wishes? You silly boy! That was an invitation."

"Do you think so?" I asked, wondering if Ela was for

real.

She nodded. "She told me she wanted to kiss you in the airport, but she's glad she didn't because it was too soon. She was embarrassed and didn't want to scare you off because she really likes you. She was going to try again tonight, but she must have been too embarrassed. Bless her heart. She never dated anyone before and doesn't know how."

"Are you some sort of dating expert?" I joked.

"I may be young and single, but I am not a pure Virgin Mary like Katarzyna is." She laughed.

"So, she's not making that up then?" With Kat being so comfortable sat in my arms, I thought she might have been bending the truth a little when it came to past experiences.

Ela shook her head. "And you obviously haven't either. I can tell that by your lack of conviction. You're nervous because you really like her and you're scared she won't like you back the same way. It's written on your face."

"Well thanks for the chat," I told her, shaking her hand. "It's been lovely meeting you, and I will be back in the morning."

"Nice meeting you too, future brother-in-law," she said, giving me a high five, "I look forward to being friends too. But you're not going, are you? Kat said she was going to offer the sofa if you didn't want to sleep in her room."

"Kat told me to go home tonight," I told her, "but she said come back in the morning."

"That was quite rude of her." Ela frowned, "Are you sure that's what she meant?"

I nodded.

"Okay see you in the morning." She paused to smile before

adding, "And a warning – Katarzyna likes to get up very early. Like 4am."

A few minutes later, I had crept down the stairs and out of the front door. I'd just gotten in the Mini and started the engine when there was a tap on the door. I was surprised to see Kat standing out in the street barefoot, shivering in only her night gown. The January air was full of snow and the frozen pavement beneath her feet must have been burning them with cold.

"Kat, are you okay?" I asked, hurriedly getting out to meet her. She nodded and smiled at me with the same dopey-eyed look she had given me earlier in the evening. Then her face changed quickly to a pretend scowl.

"Rob, you buy food tonight. That means you are agreed to punishment of sleep in bed with snotty fart woman. You get back inside and go to bed *now!*" she ordered in a hard tone, then a smile burst across her face as she stepped closer to me.

"Thank you very much for being gentleman by tucking me in bed. You so very kind, lovely man." She took my hand and looked at the floor. "But why are going? Ela came running in and ask me why I tell you I go home? I no did tell you go home, did I?"

"Kat, we might have got our wires crossed," I said, putting my arms out to her nervously. "I asked if we nearly kissed, and you said you don't want to go out with me. It's your choice and I respect that. I asked you if you wanted me to stay on the chair or go home, and you told me to go home and that you didn't want me to be your boyfriend."

Kat stood there with her mouth open a little, blinking. She seemed frustrated at herself and went a little red. Then she knocked herself on the forehead with the palm of her hand.

"Sorry my fault. I am fucked up at my speaking," she smiled shivering. She leaned forward and we hugged each other against the cold. Kat leaned back to look at me with those big blue piercing eyes of hers. "I get things wrong, you must understand. No being from this country, sometimes I no am understand or you understand me no, yes?"

"I sort of get you?"

She smiled, but looked as though she was struggling to explain. "When I say no, I no always mean no, yes?"

"I think I get it," I said, and smiled awkwardly. I was completely confused as to what Kat was trying to say.

"I mean say you no go home. As in stay," she breathed. My jaw dropped when she added, "In my bed with me." She paused and looked at me in an awkwardly pleading way. I felt my heart stop beating a split second. I had thought Katarzyna was joking when she suggested us sharing a bed earlier as my punishment for paying for dinner, but she actually meant it.

"It's okay. These things happen "I laughed, more out of shock then anything.

We had a great few hours together, but I wouldn't have thought from that even Kat, who I'd spent the night with naked with, would be so quick to invite me into her bed since we were both virgins and had never shared a bed before. However, thinking about it, it might well have been the trust gained from the night spent together naked that made Kat want to invite me into her bed.

By now poor Kat was shivering from the cold and probably out of her mind. How else could have she have wanted me to go to bed with her? I bent down and gently lifted her up by her bottom. My intention was to lift her over the ice and bring her back inside where it was warm. She was so light I carried her as easily as when I put her to bed. I lifted her, but went nowhere. She stayed in my arms while I looked into her eyes.

"You need to eat more dinner skinny little lady," I laughed.

She stuck her tongue out at me and moaned, "Rob, I am no skinny, I am small boned, and I am five foot ten. I not little. You are what six foot six or more. Almost a fucking giant"

I tried to put her down on the carpet inside the door, but Kat, who had put her arms around my neck to hold on, did not let go. Instead she just looked at me calmly in the eye and said softly, "Broccoli and Stilton soup."

"What?" I laughed. "That was random."

"Something I often make myself for lunch, and we had it the night we met," she smiled.

"What's the relevance?" I asked, keeping my arms around her waist and looking into those deep eyes.

She answered softly, "When we are young, we all hate broccoli, but we grow up to find is very good for you, full of vitamins and taste yummy. Stilton is stinky yucky mouldy cheese, and on its own is..." she put her fingers in her mouth and pretended to gag, "...but put together and blend is make taste magical yummy," she said, as she rubbed her little tummy.

"Very true, but what's your point? It's freezing out here and not good for your cold."

Kat nodded and wiped her nose as though acknowledging my point. Then she put her hand on my shoulder.

"I am Stilton in pretty wrapping," she said bluntly. "I look quite good, but under the wrapping hard is stinky. I'm often overly defensive, spiteful, rude, and if is get on my wrong side can be one horrible nasty woman. Hard outside layer put people off, but once you get through hard bit, there soft and gooey middle. You have already cut through the hard bit and found the real me." Her eyes went gooey as she said this. She paused for breath. "You are broccoli. Like Stilton, taste is not for everyone, but inside full is of goodness and vitamins, minerals make you strong." She sniffed. "What I try to say you and me good together."

"Of course we are." I smiled. "Remember? We're a team." We both raised our hands and gave each other a high five as if it was something natural. Then we both stopped to wonder why. "Did we do that back in the haystack?" I heard myself ask.

"Maybe" Kat shrugged. "But what I mean to say is, you and me, broccoli and Stilton together is, I feel, magic."

"I feel the same," I told her straight. "I'm astonished that you even want to be friends, but I can't get enough of you."

"You ask me if we nearly kissed," she said, not taking her eyes off me.

"Did we?" I asked, with my heart thumping all over the place.

"Several dimes," Kat said nodding. "But I no in the greatest state of kissing health, if you excuse me." She buried her face in her hanky and sneezed, nearly knocking me sideways. "See what I mean?" she grinned. "I no want you to catch my cold. It's no mean I no want to kiss you. I keep thinking maybe too soon, but then I think when I chicken out that you think I no wan to. So I think go for it, but then the moment goes. I know you too scared to try make move, because I say no want a boyfriend and you respecting my wishes. This is huge turn-on by the way, but I no know who I trying convince."

"Neither of us has been here before" I assured her.

"What you mean? This is my home. I been here before. I live here," she said, giving me a confused look, then she got what I meant and banged her head with her palm, and laughed. "You mean something else, what is word?"

"Hypothetically?" I asked, smiling nervously. "Was that what you wanted to say that made you come all the way down here and risk making your cold worse talking about broccoli and stilton?"

She just smiled. "Is no what I want say," she whispered, holding both my hands and sliding out of my arms so she stood on her tip toes. "Is what I want to do, but I no sure you are ready. I know I am no. But I should have done this earlier. Have to do this now, or we chicken out again and pretend no to want it, and never happen."

Without having a clue what to do, I held her with an arm around her tiny waist and another under her bum to stop her from tipping backwards. Then, I lifted her up so that we were nose to nose. She just smiled at me.

"I've never done this before," I told her, shaking more with nerves than with cold.

"Me neither," she said quietly, grinning as her eyes shone brightly under the street lamp.

"Excuse me," she said suddenly. She turned her head and hastily gave her nose a rub and a bit of a blow. She had a little look of embarrassment on her face. I could see she thought it might be a passion killer but I assured her was okay.

"Well, we could wait until I better," she said, dropping back a little, but looking disappointed.

"No" I said sharply, then a little more softly. She leaned towards me again. I started to say, "I'm worried I won't be any g—"

Kat had put her finger on my lips, "I'm nervous too," she smiled, sliding her finger away, "but I want this more than I ever wented anything." Then she gently slid her tongue into my mouth.

I didn't know how long we were there. It could have been a few seconds, or it could have been an hour before we stopped for breath. It was the most exhilarating thing I had ever felt in my life. Kat tasted deliciously of strawberries and cream, with a sharp mint flavour. In hindsight I realised that might have been because she had been sucking a lot of sweets to help calm her urge to have a cigarette. My heart raced in my chest. It was like Kat was a drug and I wanted more and more.

I spun around and sat on the wing of the Mini. I lifted Kat onto my knees, so she didn't get ice on her. "How was that for you?" I asked, a little breathlessly as my heart pounded.

"I no know," she said, quietly breathing hard, rubbing her head against mine and smiling. "Try it again?"

Suddenly our hands were all over each other. I had eyes only for Kat, and for some reason, I'd never know, that lovely crazy girl was just as mad on me.

"Magic," she breathed as we went for a third kiss. After we were finished, she said, "Again, again."

After the fourth kiss, I put Kat down on the warm ground by the open door, while I locked the car and Kat blew her nose.

As I came back to Kat, she said loudly enough so that if anyone had been in the street they could hear, "Do you wanna come and stroke my pussy?"

Already in dreamland after the wondrous events of the last few moments, I nearly choked at the casualness off such an intimate and unexpected question. I burst out laughing when I saw Kat standing in the doorway with the ugliest cat I'd ever seen in her arms.

"Charlie, my pussy cat," she said as she smiled.

"I thought you meant something else for a minute. Hi, Charlie," I said, letting him sniff my hand.

"Everyone loves Charlie," she beamed. "Lady who I get him from says he named after Prince Charles, because of big ears. Even man at work say to me, 'Katarzyna, can I stroke your pussy?' Everyone laughed. I never told him about Charlie. I said he could, but when he meets Charlie, he not very happy."

To be fair Charlie did seem to be a very friendly cat and he was loving Kat profoundly after having not seen her for two weeks. She passed him to me for a cuddle, and he rubbed himself on me lovingly.

"Kat, sweetheart," I asked gently. "Do you realise that man was sexually harassing you when he asked about your pussy?"

"Really?" she sniffed. "Thank you for pointing that out to me, Rob. I no get the meaning of everything. I give him sack next time" She wore a disgusted look. I put Charlie down and he ran inside catching the door with his tail. "Hungry boy! It's way past his supper time," she said, with a look of love that a lady only has for a close pet. "I love my Charlie. He like me. He no helps to be ugly." She looked at Charlie as he ran upstairs with his tail in the air, clearly looking for his food. "Is other reason my friends call me crazy cat lady, other than my name Kat and me crazy lady. Well other than Jenny.

She has four cats."

"You told me you didn't have any other friends apart from Jenny," I laughed.

She stepped forward and almost jumped into my arms. I held her as she put her arms around my neck. "My wabbit Wogger is my friend."

"Did Wogger Wabbit call you crazy cat lady?" I laughed. "That would make you crazy rabbit lady too."

She grinned, but then pretended to frown at me. "Rob," she said. "No laugh at me up fucking of England language. I mean no to do it."

I tried to say, "Sorry, sweetheart, I won't d—"

"Is okay. I kidding you," she interrupted. "If you laugh at me, it makes me want learn better. I only ask you is no correct me in front of other people, cos that make me..." She pulled a very cross-looking face and I nodded in understanding. She gave me her cute smile, and we kissed a fifth time. "Now," she breathed, after a good thirty seconds of kissing, "we need talk about sleeping arrangements and finding you a different punishment for paying of dinner. Sleeping in my bed obviously not punishment, but sleep all it is though for now, okay?"

"That's okay by me," I assured her.

"With lots of kiss and cuddles," she added with a grin. "I will find new punishment."

I let her slip down from my arms, but as we turned to walk hand in hand up the stairs, the door slammed shut in the wind.

"Oh, fuck-balls," she suddenly shouted.

"What's up Kat?" I asked.

She struggled with the door handle for a moment, and then slapped it in frustration.

"The door is on latch," she frowned, "and my keys are on the fucking shitting kitchen table."

"Shh, it's okay," I told her, "we'll just call your phone and get Ela to come down." I lifted her back into my arms to protect her feet while I took out my phone. Kat was so light and scrawny that I could hold her in one arm. "You need to eat more dinner, sweetheart," I said, bouncing her in my arm as I selected her caller ID. I passed her the phone she could speak to Ela.

Kat gave me a pointed look. "I told you I do mean look if you call me sweetie," she said, before grinning, putting the phone to her ear, and leaning forward to kiss me again. "Shit," she said, after a few seconds. "I leave phone switched off after aeroplane. Fucking voicemail."

"No worries," I told her "Let's call your home phone."

She closed her eyes and gave me a weak smile as she started to shiver with cold. "You going to kill me," she said, wrinkling her eyebrows and looking to the floor. She leaned over my shoulder and gave a big cough and little sneeze into the night air.

"Why would I kill you after you've just given me the best moment of my life?" I asked, as I patted her on the back to help her coughing.

She leaned back and gave me her wide-eyed look. "Because..." she said, rubbing her nose with her handkerchief, "...silly woman forgets her home phone number." She looked worried that I was going to be mad at her, but I could never be mad at those eyes.

"Well," I said, putting her down on a dry patch near the door and walking towards the car, "I'm off home. I'll see you bright and early in the morning."

Kat looked utterly shocked at my sudden decision to go. It seemed like she was going to burst into tears. I hurried back and lifted her back into my arms. "What's the wind-up score now?" I asked, as I put her down gently in the passenger seat.

"I dink we have now forty points each," she smiled, "but you had me so worried you can have two for that one. If you walked one step further, it would have been the shortest relationship in history." She laughed, and we kissed again.

Kat wrote a note, which I put through the door for Ela. It explained that we'd be back early in the morning. I took Kat back to my mum and dad's house, stopping briefly on the way to pick her up some extra nicotine gum and patches. I also got a box of man-sized tissues in case the seven hankies she had in her dressing gown pocket were not enough for one evening. She joked that she would need several more boxes and a roll of bin bags with her nose.

Once home, we crept quietly up into my room so as not to wake my parents. We crawled into my single bed together. Kat smiled at me in the light of my bedside table lamp.

"You know," she said, "I never in dreams of wildest dink I end tonight here, but no place I want to be more."

"Hopefully the first of many," I said pulling her close.

"Twenty-one thousand and something if we live sixty more years."

"Wow, that's—"

"Never going to be enough," Kat interrupted.

"I was going to say very quick maths," I said, smiling as she snuggled up to me for another kiss.

Moments later, the lovely Kat had fallen asleep in my arms. She was again gently snoring, but this time with a beaming smile on her face. Just before I closed my eyes, Kat stopped snoring and mumbled, "Rob" with her eyes closed.

"What is it, Kat?" I asked.

"I love you," she murmured.

"I love you too Kat," I managed to say just before I drifted off myself.

Chapter 7

It was all a dream?

When I awoke, I was so close to Kat that I heard her heart beat as she slept. Suddenly, I became aware that I'd fallen asleep on her chest. It was pitch black and we were both freezing cold. We were naked, and the floor was rough and prickly, I could hear the wind howling around us. Wherever we were, it was certainly not my bed.

It was only then that I realised we were still in the haystack. I knew it had all been too good to be true, and that I hadn't really been kissing Kat at all. I was supposed to be helping Kat stay warm while she slept. Instead, I'd fallen asleep on her chest and had a deluded dream that our new-found friendship led to something more special. I woke up to the reality that I'd failed to look after her as promised.

Katarzyna was just an unfortunate lady who I'd tried to help and failed miserably. If we made it out alive, the chances that I'd ever even see her again were slim. She'd probably want to stay away from me forever if I told her the dream I'd had of her.

Kat gave a little sneeze and began to stir gently. I moved so she could sit if she wanted.

"Sorry," she groaned quietly. "How long was I out for?"

I looked at my watch. "Not even forty minutes," I told her, gently rubbing her back to bring back warmth into her. "You get yourself some more sleep, my lovely friend."

"No," she croaked, pulling herself up on my arm in the darkness. "I want to confess something."

"Okay?" I said, wondering what on earth she had done in her sleep that she felt needed to be confessed. I certainly was not going to confess to her that I dreamed about snogging her face off. That was not the sort of thing you told a lady you'd known for a few hours, even if you were entwined in her naked body.

She sat up and leaned away from me before loudly blowing her nose again. She apologised, for which I reminded her that she had no need to do so.

"Are you okay, Kat?" I asked, as we lay back on our sides and reassumed our heat saving position.

"I okay, apart from dying for cigarette," she whispered. "Although I could do with headache tablet, a nice plate of veggie lasagne, with large coffee."

"Do you want tea and chocolate cake for after?" I joked.

"It like you know me or something," she laughed gently.

"I wish I could help you with that, but this hotel is fresh out of food drink and cigarettes, I'm afraid," I told her. This statement caused her to giggle.

"Okay, forget the filthy cigarettes. I need quit those horrible things," she laughed, "but I am love nice clean handkerchief. This is the worst cold I have had in my life."

"Sorry, hotels all out of those too."

"Bollocks. I have to make do." She then pulled me very close, and said, "I had dream. I had very lovely dream where you come to meet my sister Ela and I at the airport."

"I'd love to come and help you out," I said, rubbing her back up and down.

"That's lovely kind offer," she breathed. "It would be pleasure to take you up on if you do not hate me after what I say."

"Carry on," I told her, giving her my full attention.

"In the dream, we went out for food. Then you take as home and we had tickle fight. Then we snuggled up to look at photos and try watch Austin Powers. I fall asleep and you tuck me into bed."

My mouth fell open. Was Kat seriously describing the very same dream from which I'd just woken?

"Kat," I said stopping her in her tracks, "I had the same dream."

"*Noooo.*"

"Yes," I told her.

"No," she said firmly.

"Honestly it's true."

"Okay if it's true," she said, "describe to me my home."

I wracked my brain to see what I could remember about the dream. I also wondered how the hell we could have had the same dream.

"You live in a flat above a furniture shop on the fourth floor. It's very clean and tidy. Your living room and kitchen are joined. You have two bedrooms – a small one where Ela will sleep, and a really small one where you sleep. There is a toilet and bathroom and a fire escape, where I assume you go to smoke, because your flat smells clean."

"Wow," she said, with a deep breath. She was silent for a moment, and then said, "If no know better, I say you been in my flat. And you right about me smoke outside too, cos it smells horrible."

"You hide your emergency tobacco all over the flat."

"And got you to throw it away for me cos my will-power no strong enough," she added. "My addiction is bad. I wish I could stop that easy. Usually, I no am too bad, but recently I been smoking a little more than usual. Need to stop." With that, she coughed heavily.

"It's all really weird," I said, now in even more shock that it was practically confirmed that we had experienced identical dreams.

"Indeed," she agreed.

"So, now you know what I needed to confess," she said, letting go of me and sitting up in the space. She kept her hand on my leg as she seemed to be looking for something.

"Kind of," I said slowly. "Is it that people like stroking your pussy?"

"Stop it," she said, with a little laugh. "You know I no know what it means. I really thought they wanted stroke my cat."

I gave her a quick explanation of what I thought it meant, although I had to admit I wasn't completely sure, as I'd never touched a girl before.

I felt Kat lie back down next to me, but keep her hands away. I had a feeling she was unsure about touching me again. If she had the same dream as me, then she did all the kissing as well. Perhaps she was regretting it, or even disgusted by it.

"Do you no think it wrong to dream of kiss someone you meet only hours ago?"

"Yes" I agreed, "but the circumstances are not exactly ordinary."

"I no realise I was dreaming," she said suddenly.

"I didn't realise either," I told her quietly.

"But what if life really is dream?" she told me, sounding a little scared.

"What do you mean?"

"We were here in this haystack," she said shakily. "Then I woke up on aeroplane with my sister, who said I asleep most of way. Then we have dinner, go home, have amazingly romantic kiss, and get locked out. Then we go you home and go to sleep and now we back here. So maybe this is the dream no?"

"I was asleep at the airport before you landed," I told her.

"Okay, that very odd," she said, taking a deep breath and letting it go.

She shuffled back towards me and slid her arms under mine. This was a relief. I had thought she'd abandoned me after thinking about what we'd done in the dream.

"Of course, no, I just need stretch," was her softly spoken reaction when I told her. "So, you are think maybe this is dream and we are really snuggled asleep in your warm bed?"

"Well, I suppose we could be," I reasoned.

"I wish we were," she yawned. "If I'm honest, it felt like heaven."

"You wish you were in bed with me?" I asked, rather shocked at her admission.

She took a deep breath as though stalling to give herself-time to consider her answer. "I no know," she answered. "Maybe. Dose kisses felt amazing, but cuddles so lovely and cosy, I wish I snuggle up to you every night."

"I know it felt amazing, but have you seen my ugly face?" I asked her, wondering if she actually had seen me. It had been dark since the moment we met.

"Yes, actually, I see you in headlight when you help me out of snow and in the car. You no ugly," she said in a matter of fact voice.

"Did you bang your head when you fell over?"

"No," she laughed, and coughed at the same time. Her cough was getting very deep and heavy. It took her a moment to get it under control. Before I could even ask her if she was okay, she continued the conversation where it left off. "You no saw me though," she said in a matter of fact tone.

"What do you mean?" I asked, just a bit confused. I shouldn't have been, because Kat was absolutely right. As it turned out, she nearly always was.

"Rob, I was wearing scarf and hood. You only see eyes and maybe nose," she croaked, trying hard not to cough.

Of course, I hadn't seen her, because she'd had her face covered by her scarf in the car and she had barely pulled it past her nose when she was talking. Even when she was smoking, the scarf remained. Apart from those lovely eyes of hers, I had only seen the outline of her face in the blackness.

"You're right," I agreed, "but the thing is, why does it matter what you look like? I think you're a lovely person."

"That nice thing of you say," she sighed, "but I no

pretty. I ugly woman."

"You're my friend and that's all that matters," I told her firmly.

"I believe you," she said quietly, "because you nice to me even when you no see my face, but as you no see me, how you know that girl in dream look like me?" she said, holding me even tighter than she had been previously.

"I don't," I said, rubbing her back, which was covered in goose pimples again. "But, you felt like you, sounded like you, and had your eyes."

"But I didn't act like me," she sighed. "That chatty girl in the dream who sit in man's lap and kiss is who I want to be, no who I am."

"Well, what kind of person are you?" I asked gently.

"As I say to you earlier, there is reason why I no have many friends," she sighed. "I really moody, I am rude, bossy, and impatient. I bully people at work. I shout at people and lose temper easy."

"You don't sound like that sort of lady, even before the dream," I reassured her.

"Well, I hardly get a mood with somebody who saves me from freeze to death," she breathed with a cough. "I no mean to take out my stress on others. I much rather be easy-going girl in dream, but the world gets to me a lot." As she finished, she had another couple of heavy sneezes and took a deep sigh.

"If it's who you want to be, perhaps you will be her in the future."

"How I change that much in two weeks?" she sniffed.

"Maybe it's just who you are around me."

"I do feel different with you," she agreed. "I no feel nervous. If you going to hurt me, you would have done already."

"Have people hurt you physically in the past?" I asked instinctively.

Kat took a deep breath and thought about her answer, then she whispered, "Is okay if we talk maybe another day?"

That answer was all I needed to realise that Kat had personal problems that made her act differently to how she wanted and expected of herself. It wasn't for me to ask what happened to her, but her acknowledgement that there was something helped me understand a little about what she was trying to get across to me.

I assured her that I wouldn't ask again, or judge her in any way. Then I explained to her that I was much the same in that I felt like a totally different person in the few hours that I'd known her.

"Perhaps you always were that person, but you need to find someone who needs you to show you who you capable of being."

"You might be onto something there," I told her.

"I no sure if I that person dough," she said. "Is opposite for me."

"What do you mean?" I asked.

"I thought I was Miss Independent. I speak five languages, have own job, rent own flat. At work I am in charge of cleaning. I get to boss people around. Power go to my head and I make other people's lives hell. This why I hate hearing about people like your boss, Katherine McNallty, because I dink what a horrible woman. Then I realise I am well on the way to being just like her. I was starting to think look at me.

I did well for myself. I am head cleaner and soon I will be running whole caravan park, then world domination. I am big cheese. Tonight has shown me that I am no... um, err... how you say?"

"Do you mean you're not infallible?" I concluded.

"Thank you, that is it," she said. "In honest, I pretend I love being single independent woman, but meeting you remind me what it's like to have friend. I realise how much I hate my life. I need friend like you."

"So," I said, "this situation has helped me come out of myself, but it brought you down a peg. We meet in the middle. So, the dream could be the future?"

"Honestly," Kat said quietly in my ear. "I no have a clue about dream or if it true, but I no put it better myself."

"Sounds like we both needed each other tonight," I told her.

"So, true," she yawned, and snuggled into my shoulder.

"If you want to sleep, I can sing you a lullaby," I joked.

"I sing you Czech lullaby if no did I have a cold," she whispered.

"I bet you're a lovely singer," I said, rubbing the goose pimples on the back of her neck.

"I am an awesome singer," Kat told me with a swagger. "I sing at work every day and nobody complains."

"If you sing and people don't complain, you must be good," I replied.

"No," she giggled, "I shut myself in the caravan so nobody can hear me."

I laughed as I imagined Kat dancing around singing *Dancing Queen* at the top of her voice while cleaning caravan toilets.

"Well," I said, "I guess you're looking forward to your holiday."

She sighed, "I no sure."

"Why is that?" I asked. If I'd been in her position and not seen my family for four years, I would have been looking forward to it.

"I look forward to seeing my mum, brother, and sisters, and meet my nephew and nieces." She sniffed, "I no get on with father though, not keen on any of his family. If I honest, they don't like me much."

"Was it your dad who hurt you?" I asked, forgetting I promised not to. Realising my mistake, I apologised to Kat straight away.

"Is okay," she reassured me. "It was no him. I love my father. I no like him, if you get me. He is how you say... a dickhead."

"I can understand that," I reasoned, trying not to laugh at her bluntness. "But, where would you be if not your hometown at Christmas?"

Kat sneezed twice and coughed before answering. "New York, Las Vegas, San Francisco, or maybe Australia?"

"Maybe we'll go to all those places one day," I said dreamily.

"Or," she replied, "maybe you will forget me and take some pretty English girl." She coughed hard and I patted her on the back again.

"I couldn't forget you, Kat," I told her softly.

"I no think I forget if I had to spend night in haystack with naked, yucky stick woman."

"Well you're ill, not yucky," I told her. "And from the pictures, whether that was the dream or this is, you had or will have a great holiday."

"I did," she said softly. "Thank you for remind me that."

Just then, my watch went off on the hour. It was time to check on the snow again.

"Please don't ever let me hear you call yourself yucky again," I told her firmly, as I shuffled to the end to push out the loose bale and check if it was still snowing.

"I have earplugs from work in pocket if you not want to hear me say again," she said with a laugh.

I stuck my head out of the stack. To my horror, the snow was coming down harder. Kat was coughing horribly, then she feebly tried to blow her nose again. It was clear to me, even in the dark, that her coughing was causing her terrible pain.

"Have you still got lozenges?" I asked.

"I think my trouser pocket," she struggled. I felt for her soaking wet trousers, found the lozenges, and gave them to her.

As we lay down again, I suggested to Kat that she try and sleep a little more. Kat, however, thought it should be my turn until I reminded her I'd fallen asleep while I was meant to be looking after her.

"If you no let me look after you, I will pout my cheeks at you angrily," she joked.

"I'm fine," I protested.

"And I am pouting," she replied.

"We could both sleep," I suggested.

"Okay, but what if we sleep too long and I miss aeroplane?"

"Well," I replied, trying to choose my words carefully. "If you miss it, it will be partly my fault..."

"It will no be your fault. It all mine," she huffed.

"We'll try our best to make it," I continued, "but should you miss it, don't worry. We'll sort something."

"How?" she asked. "Insurance no pay if miss plane. It my fault."

I explained to her that I had some savings put away, and as a very last resort, I would help her out if she needed to get on another flight.

"You will give this money to a stranger you know for a few hours?" she asked, after I'd told her this.

"Well, I thought we were going to stay friends," was my reply.

"We are," she said. "You no know my finance situation. How you know I pay you back?"

"I didn't ask you to pay it back."

"I will though," she insisted, "and I will have to cook you several dinners to say thank you."

"If we survive tonight, I look forward to it," I said with a yawn. We propped our heads on the side of the stack to try and sleep.

"I can pay myself really," she admitted. "I just like live within my means. I forget I have savings like you."

As we settled down, I began to realise that we were

both starting to get cold again as the weather closed in. The strengthening wind began to find gaps in the hay. Sleep at this point probably wasn't the best idea now that it was getting colder, but Kat had already begun to snore and mumble in her sleep.

Chapter 8

Meeting The Family

Six weeks ago Kat and I had awoken around 4:30am, the morning after our first kiss. That might seem early, but we would find it normal as two people who often started work at 6 am. I think both of us were surprised, but still over the moon to see each other. We must have lain there in my bed for a half an hour just whispering quietly to each other between kisses.

After a while, we tiptoed downstairs. I told Kat to relax while I made breakfast, but she insisted on doing her bit by making the tea while I made toast. We shared a plate as we sat on the sofa quietly wrapped in a blanket with each other and munched away. We only talked in whispers so as not to wake my mum and dad at this hour.

Poor Kat's cold was bad as ever, but she did an amazing job of silencing her sneezes. We had nearly finished our toast when suddenly the door to the stairs creaked open. A little girl walked right past us, sat on the sofa, and put on a DVD.

The little girl was my four-year-old niece, Jemima. "Uncle Rob!" she yelled, as she came running over to me with arms out. She saw Kat, stopped hesitantly, and stared.

"Hey, you must be Jemima," Kat said, offering her

hand.

Jemima just stared "Are you Uncle Rob's new girlfriend?" Kat nodded and smiled. "I'm sorry about your eyes. How much did he pay you?" Jemima said teasingly.

"What you mean sweetheart?" Kat asked.

"Well, I heard Daddy said the only way Uncle Rob would get a girlfriend is if he paid a blind foreign lady."

"Well you daddy no very nice, is he?"

"No, Mummy called him the C word and said that's why they're getting divorced."

"The word was clown," I added, "but she meant the other C word." I'd explained to Kat that my sister Jeanette had turned up with Jemima a few days earlier, a victim of a Christmas time split. I had told Kat this the night before and I think that was why she felt bad for Jemima and agreed to sit and watch Bambi with her before we left.

"As long as you pass me my box of tissues," Kat asked her nicely. "I always blubber at that film when I was little. I only got three hankies left. I no know if enough for all the tears."

So, Kat claimed that she wouldn't make a good mother, but watching her with Jemima, she was a natural. She even asked my permission to give Jemima some toast and hot chocolate and insisted on doing it herself. When the DVD started, Kat even attempted to explain to Jemima and me why she struggled to understand films and TV in English. She told us that because we spoke clearly and slowly to her she could understand us, but with the pace of movies and TV, she struggled to keep up. Having had a big seizure a few days earlier this had made it worse. This was why she needed German subtitles on films.

"I am not from Germany, but I spoke it since I was your age because I grew near there," she explained. "My home language is called Czech Bohemian, but they no are put that on subtitles because no is a popular."

Kat tried to prevent Jemima getting too close because she didn't want to give the little girl her cold. Jemima ignored her and sat down between us laying her head on Kat's shoulder as Kat in turn laid hers on mine.

"I love you Uncle Rob's girlfriend" Jemima grinned.

"Is she okay call me Aunty Kat?" Kat pleaded, to which I nodded. She put her arm around Jemima and told her. "You and me are gonna be best friends."

~~*~*~*

Kat and I had meant to sneak out quietly, but I must have dozed off. I woke up to the sound of Kat laughing as she sat chatting away with my mum and dad and my big sister Jeanette.

I sat bolt upright. This wasn't in the plan. I was supposed to be awake so that I could have Kat's back in the grilling she was going to get, not only from my parents, but my fiercely over-protective big sister.

"I was telling you mum and dad what happened to us last night and apologising on you behalf that you no calling them," she told me gently as she sat drinking a fresh cup of tea my mum had made her. "I tell them we are staying at my house tonight, but you are call you mummy like a good boy, right?" To which my mum, dad and sister all laughed.

I was much more at ease than I thought I would be. When my mum confided in us that the biggest surprise was I wasn't gay, Kat laughed so hard she spat tea over me.

"I no was sure either," she smiled. "It took him two weeks and all evening to get the hint."

We talked about several things, including how we'd met and Kat's determination to quit smoking, but we left out the bit about the haystack. My parents had only gotten back from their holiday the evening before, so I hadn't told them I was going to meet Kat and Ela.

Kat kissed me and then stood mopping her nose before asking permission to use the toilet.

"No need to ask," I told her, pointing her in the direction.

"Is polite though," she smiled.

As soon as she left the room, my dad high-fived me and asked how the hell I had managed to pull her. Quite honestly, I had no answer.

My sister Jeanette had her usual sense of humour laughing, "Get down on your knees and beg that young lady to marry you as soon as she gets off the loo before she realises you're punching above your weight with her."

"Aunty Kat, can I come with you?" Jemima asked, the second Kat got back from the loo.

Kat immediately bent down to her knees and explained to Jemima that she had to stay with her mum.

Jeanette laughed and told Kat we could take her if we wanted. I told her we were staying overnight, to which she smiled and said, "Even better."

Jemima was supposed to see her dad that afternoon.

"I hate Daddy. I want Aunty Kat and Uncle Rob," she protested.

"Believe me, you no are want to fall out with you

daddy like I fell out with mine." Kat explained.

"Daddy hurt my mummy," Jemima screeched, turning to grab her mum's arm.

I looked Jeanette in the eye. I didn't know why she had split with him, but I knew if he had hurt my lovely big sister he wouldn't live long.

"He's dead" I told her bluntly.

"I will help" Kat added.

"He's awaiting trial and you're not going to get yourselves in trouble." Jeanette told us bluntly as Kat gave her a big hug.

In the end, it was just Kat and I who went back to Cromer. We chatted away about the morning's events and our plans for the day.

"I am love you family," she said smiling. "That little niece of yours – I am love that little girl. I know I used to say no children, but I want one." I looked at her with a shocked smile. "No this soon obviously," she laughed. "Maybe in a year or two if you no have got fed up with Mrs Grumpy Knickers by then."

"I'm sure Ela and I will get on fine," I teased.

"Are you make fun of my sister?" she asked, faking menace again.

"Sorry," I said quickly.

"No, this good you learn to take piss on her. It's fun and make us all family." I went red trying not to burst out laughing at Kat's mistake. "What is it, Rob? You choking on something?" she asked with panic on her face. Only when I broke my silence and explained, Kat nearly wet herself laughing. "Just no tell my sister I tell you to urinate on her."

When we got back to the flat, Ela had opened the bottom door. She'd already been to the supermarket for her breakfast and laughed her head off at us when we came into the flat with Kat still wearing her nightdress.

Kat disappeared into the bedroom and came back out about thirty seconds later wearing a pair of black tracksuit bottoms and sweatshirt. She walked over to the washing machine and chucked in a pile of her home-made hankies.

Standing up from the machine, she turned and grabbed me for a kiss as we made for the door to go out for the day. Ela smiled at the pair of us and made the motion with her fingers she had made the night before. Kat slapped her lightly and dragged her out the door.

"You two really did get it on last night then." Ela beamed at us.

"And you learned English very quickly..." Kat smiled, "...and your sudden illness went away very quickly."

"I meant to say aaaacchhhooo" Ela grinned, to which Kat responded by throwing one her hankies at her.

~~*~*~*

We decided to leave the city for another day and go for a drive around. Kat wasn't overly keen on cities and knew very little about Norwich. She said Jenny had taken her there a few times and she'd been through it on the bus on her way to hospital appointments.

"Norwich City is only a tiny city, but still too many people, and I pity them," she said quietly as we drove. "Many of them go about daily business like soulless robots in suits, with all the life and personality sucked out of them. Then there is the hard worker outside of office, shop workers, the street cleaner, and the like, all working hard all day for little pay with all the fun gone from them. Then there is the chavs on Jobseekers Allowance drunk and smoking weed on street corners. Even I am never touched weed when I smoked."

"Jenny took you to Anglia Square, didn't she?" I asked.

"Hell, of a rundown stinking shithole," Kat nodded.

"I'm sure I can change your mind about Norwich once you've seen all of it," I assured her.

"I like to think you right, but I will wait and see." She smiled, going on to explain that she didn't really do crowds, and even the summer crowds in Cromer drove her into hiding. "That, as well as the pollen count," she added. "You dink my nose bad now? You wait till hay fever season. You might want new girlfriend."

We visited Wroxham first and went for a short walk along the river before touring the small villages and the broads. Then we made our way to our second stop in Great Yarmouth.

Later that afternoon, halfway through our trip, we stopped for lunch in a pub by the harbour.

Kat was wearing dark sunglasses, even though it was winter. She had put them on her forehead while we ate. She later explained to me that she wore them to reduce the chances of having a fit caused by flashing from car lights.

Kat and Ela seemed to have a strange relationship. They would start a discussion in English, but if it got heated, then they would switch to Czech so I couldn't understand and get in each other's faces as though they were really angry, then just laugh and hug each other.

However, when it came deciding when to go the pleasure beach—a fairground theme park—they argued. Ela was desperate to go, but Kat put her foot down firmly and said no. Ela pushed the subject and Kat had lost her cool with her, raising her voice a little, saying, "If you want me to go near flashing near lights and have epileptic seizure, it will be you cleans up the mess."

At this Ela backed down and apologised. When she was in the toilet, I asked Kat if her epilepsy was as bad as that. She nodded, but said, "It should be fine if I take my dark glasses." Then she grinned, "but I no like rides. I worry will piss my knickers."

We made it back to their flat around 6 pm. We munched down a large pot of salad and several pieces of fruit for dinner. Rather than put on the TV, like my family would have done on a Saturday night, Kat put on the kettle and went to the cupboard. From the cupboard, she brought out a beautifully polished and clearly well-looked-after acoustic guitar.

"Look, told you my hand better today." She smiled, stretching her fingers out to prove it as she sat on my knee to make sure it was in perfect tune, then burst into the most beautiful song I had heard in all my days. I didn't know the language or the song, but the sweet passion of Kat's voice, and the beautiful way in which she strummed, blew me away.

"Why on earth are you cleaning caravans for a living when you can sing like that?" I gasped, when she finished.

She shrugged. "I play for fun, no for money. When your hobby become you job, is no fun."

"But have you never dreamed of being famous, or thought of going on the X-Factor?" I asked.

"Yes," she answered, "and I woke up screaming '*No, go away Simon Cowell with your million-pound record deal! I no want to sell my soul to you! I no want photographer following me, or to be on the front cover of Hello! Magazines, with people com-*

menting on my weight and judging my every move!"

"Fair point," I agreed. "Sorry I mentioned it."

"That okay, sweetheart, but it just for friends and family," she said softly, then kissed me and carried on singing a beautiful version of Bob Dylan's *Blowing in the Wind*. Afterwards, she started in on her own hauntingly slow melodic version of Abba's *Dancing Queen*.

"No can sing well with stuffy nose," she smiled, although I begged to differ. "I pass guitar to best singer in the house." She took out her hanky and passed the guitar over to Ela, whose eyes widened as though she had been itching to get her hands on it. To my amazement, Ela was just as good with the guitar as her sister.

"She is the talented one," Kat said, nodding at Ela.

Ela disagreed and said, "I had lessons, but Miss Modest over there..." She nodded at Kat, "...picked up an old beaten guitar from a junk sale and taught herself to play when she was eight, then she taught her sisters."

It soon became apparent that Kat enjoyed teaching musical instruments as well as playing. Later she would teach me to play to a standard which was almost, but never quite at, her level.

Among her collection in the cupboard was an old electric keyboard, a glockenspiel, xylophone, a banjo, a thumb piano, and more. She proudly told me she was looking forward to playing flute and clarinet more now she didn't smoke. She was also looking for a cello and saxophone to add to her collection.

Another thing I was beginning to learn about my new love was that she was good at seeing the funny side of her own misfortune. For example, she was adorable when she laughed at herself and pulled funny faces for confusing her words. After we'd been snuggled on the chair for a while, kissing gently while Ela played, Kat expressed her desire to get some sleep.

She turned to Ela and said something I couldn't understand, then she smiled at me, and said, "I tell her she can keep playing with herself for a while if she wants to."

Ela spat out the glass of Diet Coke she was drinking, spraying it on the floor. She bent over in stitches as she stood up to get a towel. I tried to stop myself from bursting out laughing, because Kat didn't seem to understand what she had said.

"Play guitar to myself," Ela corrected her. "Not play with myself." She pointed her fingers between her legs to demonstrate. Kat laughed her head off and went bright red. She suggested we go to bed before she did anything else to embarrass herself. "This morning I am telling you to a take a piss on my sister, and now am tell her to play with girl bits."

As well as poking fun at herself, Kat was beginning to feel comfortable poking at me too. An example of this was when we went into the bedroom and discussed the house rules.

"My home is you home. Feel free to read my books and play my instruments, as long as you look after them. You can use my hankies as long as you wash them, and wear my clothes... that sort of stuff."

"Wear your clothes?" I laughed

"Just to make sure you was listening," she smiled, "You wear them if you want to, but if you do, I might have to dump you and take you to local gay bar."

"Now listen to the house rules." She told me in a mock authoritarian voice. "I am not your wife and even if I am one day, I work five days out of seven just like you. So I no will have dinner on the table you get home at 6pm." Then she paused and grinned, "Because you no are finish work until 10pm, I put it fridge. On day when is your turn to cook," she teased, "I will cook also. No because I no trust you cooking, but because I am control freak."

She explained her nightly bedtime routine to me. It was very important to her, because she liked to get up early to arrive at work before 6am, which incidentally was the same time I had to start work on morning shifts. She would be up at 4 am having breakfast and making lunch before walking a good mile and a half to work, so she liked to be in bed by 7pm on weeknights and asleep by 8pm, so she could get her full eight hours of sleep.

The fact she had a routine was adorable. She had to have everything set up and in order. Her clean work uniform was laid out and ready. Also, her epilepsy medication had to be laid out in a specific order, along with her nicotine gum and patches and two clean hankies.

"I have ODC." She grinned, as she put everything in place.

"OCD? Is there leeway in your bedtime routine?" I chuckled.

"Of cause is," she smiled. "Sometimes, if my book is good, I allow myself to read until 9pm. If I am feeling really naughty, I allow myself to have a second cup of cocoa."

"You're a bad girl Kat!" I smiled, as we got into bed.

I had better be clear that what happened between Kat and me in bed that night, and for many nights to come, was completely innocent. It was Saturday night, and neither of us had work until Monday. We cuddled up and drank cocoa while Kat read to me from her German copy of a James Patterson novel. We had more fun than you could imagine. She taught me more German in a couple of hours than school ever did in five years, and she wasn't even German.

True to her word, when the clock hit 9pm, Kat took her pills. She leaned over and we kissed for several minutes. Then she apologised for blowing her nose a little loudly before lying on top of me front down. We cuddled each other to sleep in seconds.

Chapter 9

Six weeks later

It was our first Valentine's Day as a couple. I hadn't stayed a night in my own bed since the night I had met Kat at the airport. I was supposed to go home on the Monday, so I didn't disturb Kat's bedtime routine as she had to be up at 4am. She was meant to be in bed asleep at 7pm, but I found her sitting in the hotel reception waiting for me to finish work at 10pm after having walked across town in the dark alone.

"I thought I was supposed to go home." I had said in shock as she jumped up to meet me.

"You are coming home," she grinned, adding, "You live at my house now and no arguing."

So weeks later I had been working the day shift for once and Kat had called me to say she wanted to meet me at the doctor's surgery. I came in very sweaty, having run over a mile to get there on time, seeing as felt it lazy to drive to work now I lived in the town.

Now we sat in the consulting room of the doctor's surgery in town. The doctor was examining Kat thoroughly by checking her temperature and looking at her throat.

"So," said Dr. S. Angel, who was a tall, very young

looking lady doctor with flowing red hair. "Katarzyna, you have been suffering for just over eight weeks. You're on para-cetamol, ibuprofen, and lozenges." Kat nodded, "And has it caused you to take any time off work?"

Kat shook her head saying that she couldn't afford a day off with the credit crunch and she was worried that if she took too much time off she would be replaced.

"Do you think spending a night naked in the snow two months ago might have caused her to get sick?" I probed.

"Yes and I'm not going to ask what that was about… Is your epilepsy under better control?" The doctor asked.

Kat looked at me, and then she said, "I think I had a fit in bed on Christmas Eve, but I was alone so…" She shrugged her shoulders.

"Do you drink alcohol?" The doctor continued.

Once again Kat looked at me again, before answering, "We sometimes get a little tipsy on a Tuesday night." She then added that Wednesday was her regular day off.

"And last time I spoke to you was when we met at the bus stop a couple of months ago when I told you off for smoking. How is that going?"

"I got wrong off, Dr Angel for being a silly girl." Kat smiled.

I laughed at her use of Norfolk dialect, which she probably picked up from me. Got wrong meaning 'Got into trouble with' in Norfolk speak.

"I smacked my face on hand and said no smoking" She laughed, adding, "And this amazing man here made sure I no did it anymore."

"She did it all by herself, before we were together." I

corrected.

"Well Miss Bobal," The doctor said, "There's no infection and nothing showed up on your blood test. It seems like you've had a very nasty virus and your weight is concerning me as your body mass index is very low."

She sent us away with the instructions to put herself on bed rest for a few days.

"Well that's our first Valentine's meal out cancelled." I sighed. I had booked us a place at a posh restaurant in town and paid a deposit which I wouldn't get back.

Kat just rubbed her nose with her hanky and smiled and said, "Rob, no be at mad at me."

"What have you done?" I quizzed.

She gave me a cheeky grin and said, "I already cancelled the reservation this morning and got you full refund."

"You what?" I asked, astounded, but also pleased that she had thought to cancel, knowing she was not well.

"It no is fair on other people who have paid lots of money to go out," she smiled. "No if I going to cough and sneeze all night and put people off their food." She added that she had felt terrible enough being ill the night I had picked her up from the airport. "It no that I no appreciate the gesture though."

She grinned, reaching in her pocket and taking out something which she put in my hand. It was the cash that I paid as the deposit.

"Want to go and get some salad from supermarket, then go home have a chat?" she said quite seriously.

"It sounds important" I responded.

"It is quite," she said quietly.

There wasn't much speaking, although we held hands on the way back. Kat wore dark glasses to prevent the lights of the car triggering her photosensitive epilepsy. Once as a child she had a seizure when a car's headlights shone through railings creating a strobing effect. With these and the fact that it was dark, I could not see the expression on her face.

After going to the salad bar in almost silence, we went straight back to flat. Kat took off her shades and looked at me nervously as we sat in the armchair together.

"Rob this is difficult," she told me, shaking. Then she uttered the words no man wants to hear the love of his say. The words that can bring a relationship to an abrupt end. Only she said them in her way. "It no is you is me."

I sat there looking at Kat gobsmacked. Just like that she was dumping me. That was the real reason who she had cancelled.

"Can I ask why?" I stuttered.

She nodded. "It's because I've no been well, and I think you no have a good time."

"But I love you Kat," I mumbled, feeling like I was about to cry.

Kat sneezed, then rubbing her nose and gave me a tiny. "I love you too and that why I am feel awful about it."

"The only thing about you being ill that matters to me is making you well," I told her standing up. It didn't make sense that she was breaking up with me because she'd been unwell for eight weeks. It had never bothered me once and I just wanted her to feel better, but if she wanted to break up, there was nothing I could do.

"I better get my stuff and leave," I told her turning towards the bedroom.

"Why Rob? What have I done or said?" she whimpered. I could see tears forming in her eyes. "Please don't leave because of it"

"You're splitting up with me, Kat," I told her in a hoarse voice. "We can stay friends, but I can't stay living here."

I'd always thought me being with Kat was too good to be true.

At that moment, Kat jumped up and shouted, "Rob what you talk, silly boy? I am no split up with you!"

"You said, *It no is you is me*," I quoted. "That's what girls say when they end relationships."

Kat looked mortified and threw her arms out. She squeezed herself into me saying, "No, I am love you, silly boy. I was talking about the reason we are still virgins," she said, smiling. "I no want to do it when I am ill, because no think you enjoy it with ill lady."

"So, you're not dumping me?"

"No, never!" she laughed, beaming all over her face. "I want explain why I wait so long to let you make love to me. I no want our first time to be when I all ill." She paused to sneeze and we shared a little giggle at the irony. "I know you not grossed out by me, but even though I not better, I just want to, you know... fuck."

"You want to?" I asked, losing all fear of being dumped.

Of course, I had realised that at some point both of us losing our virginity would come up, but it wasn't something either of us had really talked about. We didn't see it as a priority because our relationship was based on so many other things, like our humour and love for being together. However, now that it *had* come up, I had to admit that I'd wanted to from the start, but on the night when first met Kat she had said she was a devout Catholic and would not have intercourse before marriage.

"But what about all the Catholic no-sex-before-marriage stuff you told me on the night we met?" I asked.

Kat looked like she had swallowed a wasp and she gasped, putting her hand over her mouth and going red. "Oh my god, I did say that didn't I?" She said, going red as a beetroot. "Rob, you sweet, sweet gentleman," she grinned, embracing me. "No listen to me. I change my mind weeks ago. As I said when first we get together, it woman prerogative to change mind. I started the pill right after we start court."

"You want to now?" I stammered.

"Well, the doctor said I had to go to bed," she told me with a cheeky smile, adding, "She no say you couldn't come too." I was already on my way to the bedroom, but Kat turned left towards the bathroom, saying, "Give me two minutes to go toilet, then quick shower and blow my nose... then..." she grinned. "Then we go and take learner plates off bed and ram it into the wall so hard we have repaint it."

~~*~*~*

Suddenly I was awake and could feel my skin burning cold and Kat was pressed against me tightly, breathing.

I was awake, but it was like I was dreaming and sleepy. "Kat did you just dream that?" I asked softly.

She replied almost as though she was still asleep. She took a deep breath between each statement as though she was talking in her sleep. "This is the dream now and that was real," she breathed, "We were in our bedroom... Valentine's day... making love is amazing... I want you twenty times a day... love you, Rob."

"You got to have sex?" I asked, forgetting just how odd it was that we'd shared a second vision. I felt envious that my vision had stopped at the verge of intercourse, when Kat had seemingly gone all the way.

"Did you not?" was her reply.

"No. Perhaps I thought dreaming about sex would have been extremely disrespectful."

"You gentleman, gorgeous gentleman," she breathed. "If it's really our future... you have a lot... to look forward to... sweetheart an I no can wait... to have that experience again."

"I wish," was about all I managed to say before dropping back into the dream.

As the haystack faded, I remembered hearing voices in my head as though there were people all around us.

One of them sounded like my sister Jeanette, saying, "Oh my god, I can't believe I just watched that."

I remembered calling out, "Jeanette is that you, sister? I miss you."

She spoke again but not to me. "Shit, Sally, I think they heard me."

Sally? Did I know a Sally? Yes, I did. My best friend Sally who often stayed with us when I was kid after her mum and dad died. She had lived in the house across the fields from my parents' cottage, close to where my car was now stranded. The same one who moved up north with her sister ten years ago and hadn't spoken to me since. It couldn't have been her, but a voice much like hers replied.

"It's okay, Jeanette. Turn the microphone off and they

will just think they were dreaming."

~~*~*~*

One vision that stuck in my head was Kat playing ABBA's *Dancing Queen* and dancing around the flat like a looney. That was until she thought we were on Strictly Come Dancing and tried to jump into my arms only to knock me off balance. In an effort to catch her, I tripped and fell on her causing her to yell out in pain. When I apologised profusely for hurting her, she denied that I hurt her at all, before squeezing tears from her eyes, saying, "You no did hurt. Stupid girl is hurted my silly self." When I asked what I could to help the pain, she just grinned and said, "Kiss me repeatedly to help forget the pain and do what you wish with me. If my sister is walk in, she can walk out again."

I didn't do as she asked as it soon became clear she was in a lot of pain and bruised herself and her leg quite badly.

~~*~*~*

One evening in early March, I was at work and saw I'd been booked in to do a double gym induction. The person who booked it had written down, Jenifer Whale and Rapunzel Feline, which were clearly not real names, so I wondered if they would even turn up. However, a little before 6 pm, I was just coming out of the men's room having done the half hourly check, when Roy maintenance caught me to say that my inductions had turned up early. Following me through to the gym, he explained that he'd shown them to the office.

Maintenance staff usually went home around 5:30 pm, so he would never have met Kat when she came to meet me from work and probably thought I was single. He grinned to me standing too close to the thin door, not realising the people inside would hear him.

"I've seen the big girl in here before, so you'll know her, but her friend is… shall we say pretty good on the eye, and if she's single, I hope your luck's in."

"Well," I smiled uneasily, "I have an amazing partner at home who I adore and want to spend the rest of my life with, so she's out of luck if she thinks I'm going to take her home and sleep with her."

"Well answered," came a surprising, but familiar voice, "I am bloody well hope you is going to take me home and sleep with me." The door flung open to reveal Kat, and Jenny stood there laughing.

So basically, Kat and Jenny had decided that despite Jenny only giving birth eight weeks earlier, and Kat being close to dangerously unweight, despite me knowing that she ate well, they both wanted to get fit.

Jenny needed the gym as she had mobility issues and had fallen off the wagon when she got pregnant, so current poor diet and weight were not helping her. Kat, however, was walking several miles every day to and from work, and although she was often eating, it was all salad, and fruit and veg. She was painfully skinny. I worried about the effects of exercise on her weight. However, she put my mind at rest by saying firmly. "I no want to lose weight. I want to gain some tone and put some meat on this skinny thing, even if have to eat bucket of pasta for every meal.

I thought it would just be a phase, but Kat really took it seriously. She ate more carbs, and every time I was at work and she wasn't, she would come to the gym, usually with Jenny but sometimes without, and put herself through a tough workout.

One of the harder moments in the early months of our relationship came a few weeks after Kat had joined the gym. Kat wanted to help by giving herself a goal to work towards, and with Jenny have back problems, the activity which caused her the least pain was swimming. So, Kat challenged Jenny to beat her in a swimming race. However, none of us cottoned on to the fact that after working out in the gym, Kat would stand by the side of the pool cheering on her friend. She never got in the pool herself. I thought this might be a deliberate ploy of hers to make the race bit more even by not training for it herself.

So, when it came to the day of their big race, I was on life-guard duty. A much lighter, yet still very big Jenny was on the start line. Kat, however, having got a lift to the pool with her friend, seemed to have vanished. We checked the whole area to see if she'd had an accident or something.

Things got stranger when Jenny checked her phone and found a message from Kat, congratulating her on her weight loss and her victory in the race, and that she had gone home out of embarrassment knowing Jenny was going to kick her backside.

When I got home, Ela caught and told me to be careful with Kat saying, "She's in bed now, but we have had a good old sister to sister to talk and she has something to confess to you. I'm sure you will understand and be kind to her."

When I got into the bedroom, I was shocked to find Kat weeping into one of her hankies. I wondered what I'd done to cause this, but it turned out to be nothing. On seeing me, Kat wiped her eye and nose, opened her arms to me for a cuddle, and promptly denied that she'd been crying.

It turned out that after Kat had got so into supporting her best friend that she neglected to tell us.

"Rob, you know, I like to teach you the things I know, and you are wanted to teach me something you can do, but we no could think of anything." I nodded. "Well next time I go an open my big silly gob and challenge Jenny to swim race, I need to remember two things. Firstly, because I was an ill child with epilepsy, I no was allowed in the pool in case I drown, so although I am under control now, I am no can swim. And secondly, my boyfriend is a lifeguard who wants to teach me something. So please teach me to swim before I embarrass myself further."

So this was a mini montage moment. The very next morning we were both off work, but I was back at work anyway. The pool opened at 6 am and Kat, being ever the early riser, was in the pool sat on a pair of noodles, with a smile on her face at 6:05 am. She really struggled—to begin with, she was useless—but she just wouldn't stop pushing, until late afternoon, exhausted, she squealed with excitement as she splashed her way to a full length of the pool unaided.

"I did it doggy style," she told Ela proudly when we got home.

"I know. I heard you through the wall," was Ela's cheeky reply, "but enough about your sex life. Manage to swim?"

~~*~*~*

Some of the most fun we had in our relationship was on game days. Game days were something we'd invented although I was not saying other couples didn't do it. It was sort of role play, but not in the way you would think. The games usually involved just Kat and me, but if Jenny, Ela, my sister, Jemima, or even Kat's friends from work were around, they played a part. Just to be clear when other people joined in there was nothing sexual about it.

One example was on a day when we were both off work. A little before 6 am, Kat went to the loo and came back dressed in her running kit knowing I wasn't dressed and said quickly.

"Today is the game catches me if you can. Rules are no cars or bicycles." She still couldn't drive or ride a bike at that point due to her health conditions. "You have until nine o'clock this evening to catch, but if I am not home before midnight you also win, because it means I cheated. The boundary is the whole of Norfolk and I have the amount of time it takes you to get dressed to get away, and the train to Norwich leaves in ten minutes."

With that, she slammed the door and disappeared.

I fell for it and flung on my clothes sprinting down the road towards the station and jumped on the train just as the door was shutting, thinking I got her. Then, just as the train was about to pull away there was bang on the window.

I turned to see Kat laughing and waving her hanky like one of the railway children, as she shouted, "Send my love to Norwich loser! Love you, see you tonight."

Her trick got her such a head start that I chased her all day. A few minutes later she texted me a picture of herself on a bus. Later she was having a cup of tea with my sister, then she was sat on the haystack that we'd spent the night in. She was always three steps ahead of me the whole way, so around 7 pm, I messaged her to say I conceded the game. She responded, "Put the kettle on."

I got home to find Kat sat in the recliner wrapped in a cover with a hot water bottle on her tummy. When I asked her what was up, she smiled, "Bad time of the month." Before confessing that she foresaw the fact that this might happen and she didn't want to spoil the game day, so she took the pictures a week earlier, then sent me on a wild goose chase and went back to bed for a bit.

On one game, Kat woke up and took her pills and kissed me and said, "Today's game. I am English upper-class snotty diva bully bitch brat, Princess Perfect, and you my long-suffering personal butler, Carruthers, who I have crush on, which you are pretending not reciprocate, but you love me really. Just remember however nasty I get, I love you. 3... 2... 1... go."

With a click of the fingers, she changed from Czech accent to the funniest impression of a cut-glass English accent, made all the more laughter-inducing by the fact she still got her words muddled.

"Carruthers," she told me, in an *I'm not happy* tone, and she picked up her hanky. "Not only have I woken with the most frightful cold, but it has been five minutes. I see no sign of my breakfast."

"Well, Ma'am," I replied, "It would be prudent to tell me what you would like for breakfast so I can the chief to prepare it for you."

"Very good, Carruthers. Now what would rich snob eat for breakfast? I know caviar on toast, please. Chop chop."

"Ma'am" I replied, "Are you aware that caviar is fish eggs and is not a vegetarian dish?"

"Well get met vegetarian caviar substitute then." She smirked.

"Ma'am," I sighed. "In the very possible event that the kitchen is all out of vegetarian caviar, should I ask chef to prepare you some peanut butter on toast?"

"Oh, yummy, thank you," she smiled, "Oh, I mean which variety of peanut butter?"

"The Morrison's supermarket own brand crunchy variety ma'am."

"Well, tell chief that will do as long as you pick out all of the crunchy bits. Two slices one with and the other kiwi jam, cut into rectangles. I'm also like some cold remedy, paracetamol, ibuprofen, some patches and gum and pot of tea. No skip on the lemon."

"Will there be anything else, Ma'am?" I asked as I reached the door.

She nodded and took a deep breath, then gave her nose three successively snotty blows.

"Feeling a little better, Ma'am." I smiled.

"Rather!" She grinned, throwing her used hanky at me. "Now take that down laundry and fetch me clean one, and be thankful I no did ask to wipe it for me. And while you are there, sack the entire laundry staff, because that washed in the wrong type of detergent."

A few moments later I came back with everything she had asked for and set it down. She glared at me.

"Carruthers, you have no remembered to remove the crunchy bits, and what is this?" She laughed, pulling out the whole lemon I put in her cup.

Basically, you get the gist of this game is that she would bully me in her upper-class tone until I threatened to quit and she would follow me out yelling, "Carruthers, come back. I am sorry. I love you. I always loved you."

We usually ended up in bed.

~~*~*~*

Kat and I had a lovely time together. It was a hot July and we'd both been working the early shift and left work at 2 pm. We left our separate places, walked along the beach to meet each other in the middle. Once there, we stripped to reveal our swimming costumes and got in the water. It was nice to see Kat, who had barely managed a length of the pool at doggy paddle a few months earlier, trying out breast stroke, back stroke, and front crawl in the sea with no fear.

After two hours getting a good work out, we were now home, sat on the recliner together while our tea was cooking. I read to Kat from one of her Czech books while she corrected me on pronunciations and sat there sewing her home-made hankies, which Ela had asked her for.

Kat was teasing Ela saying, "After all the hard work I put into these, you better get a nasty cold."

When I got the end of the chapter in the book, Kat gave me a big grin, whispered in my ear how proud she was that I was trying so hard to learn her language.

I replied "Moje vznášedlo je plné úhořů.,"

She stared at me, then burst out laughing. "You are just said is hovercraft full of eels." Then she came to see the joke. "Oh, Monty Python translations sketch we watched last week. So funny, you and me are so in tune, our relationship is the best."

"You two can't have the best relationship" Ela teased.

"And why is that?" we both asked at once.

Ela shrugged her shoulders, "All the best relationships have big rows and fights, and then you get to have make-up sex. How many arguments have you two actually had in the six months you've been together?"

We both looked at each other and shrugged, knowing that we had never argued in that time. That was right, folks. Never ever, not even once.

"Right then," Kat smirked. "Let us find something to argue over, then are have a real big fight, and we can makeup, and our love will be perfect for ever."

Ela slapped her hand over her face. "You can't pretend to argue, because it's not the same."

"Oh, yes, we can!" Kat and I said at the same time.

"Okay, let's start an argument then." Ela teased. "You two which way up does the toilet roll go."

Both of us agreed that it didn't matter.

"Okay if that doesn't matter," she sighed, "should the toilet seat be up or down?"

Kat replied, "Well, as long as it clean and no wee wee, it no matters."

"Right," Ela continued in an exasperated tone, but winked at me, "I didn't want to cause trouble, but Rob put his hand on my bum yesterday and said I was sexy."

"Well," Kat said, not cottoning on, "He is right you are sexy and... *what?* Wait a minute. *What?*"

"I didn't touch her." I protested.

"I know you no touch her." She smiled, winking at me, "but what a create opportunity to have a big row."

So, that was how we came up with our pretend argument game.

The game from then on would go like this. Ela would give us something to argue about. Kat and I would try not to laugh as we called each other every name under the sun, then Kat would either shut herself in the bedroom and pretend to cry—although I could hear her giggling—or she would go to the cooker and bang pots and pans loudly, telling me she wanted some flowers as an apology.

"But just pretend to get them," she would giggle, because they make me sneeze."

I'd then go and get her a present instead, and she would say. "Rob, I no really angry, you only apposed to pretend you got flower so I can say. *'You think a cheap bunch of flowers from the petrol station is fix our relationship!'* Then I pretend to shove them up your backside, tell you, you are on your final warning. Then we say *'what the hell'* and have the most amazing makeup sex."

That was now how our fun worked, but there was a more serious side to things.

I was getting into trouble at work for no reason. Katherine, my boss, had an agenda of some sort. I thought that she was using her power to control people's lives. I was not the only one who worked there who was falling foul of her scheming ways. I was already on a disciplinary for things I not done when I met Kat. I was one of at least three or four staff in the same position, and despite all the hours I put it and all the extra hours and days, I received a letter stating that I was to attend a second disciplinary interview.

It was with a heavy heart that I showed Kat the letter. I ducked my head, expecting her to get angry. However, she just laughed.

"That woman is desperate, but clever. You're not the problem. Your previous warning is about to run out, and she needs to keep you in trouble, but not enough to get sacked. Then when it you day off and she is short of staff in departments, she has put Lucy, Chloe, or James, Victoria..." these were my colleagues in the leisure centre, "...on cleaning duty and calls you on you day off to cover the leisure centre. Because she has this sham disciplinary over you, so you have to come to work keep her happy."

Luckily the meeting fell on Kat's day off, and because she was a star, she came in as my plus one. Katherine sat there behind her make-up on the other side of the table. Next to her was Lucy, the gym manager, looking a bit awkward.

Kat gave Lucy a wave and a smile and asked her very blatantly if she and her kids had fun the other night when

Kat offered to look after them so Lucy could go on a date with her husband. Kat then berated Katherine for making Lucy come in on her day off to take part in the meeting.

Katherine leered at us both with her frog-faced smile. We listened to a barrage of petty and silly accusations that were being made such as constantly being late for work, leaving work too late, not emptying the bins, not hoovering the swimming pool when it had been full of people all week.

Kat and I listened intently, then when she finished before I could say anything, Kat excused herself, then blew her nose and cleared throat. She then explained about her being a head of department herself and having experience of disciplining staff. She went on to point out politely that all of the times I was accused of being late were days I was due to be off and that I hadn't been contacted until ten minutes before the shift was due to start.

"Also how is it possible for someone to watch the swimming pool and hoover the gym in another room at the same time? He is hoover the gym after the pool closes, which is why he goes home. And if you question his ability as a gym instructor," she said, pulling up the t-shirt to reveal her abs, "Look what he helped me do."

You get the gist. She pulled Katherine apart and got Lucy on her side. Then she dropped a bombshell that even I didn't expect. She told them I'd been offered a job in the leisure pool at the caravan park where she worked. When Katherine questioned, I lied that it was true, and suddenly, her tone changed.

By the end, even Lucy had turned against Katherine, and she stood up for me and said what a good member of staff I was and that she didn't want me to go anywhere. The disciplinary was put on hold for now.

~~*~*~*

In late September, I had just got back from working and was cooking dinner. Kat was out with Jenny and Ela and a couple of mates from work. They went to see Evita at the Theatre Royal, and they would be back soon. However, Ela called me with some urgency and told me Jenny's car had broken down.

"Just please come and us," she asked frantically, "I'm really worried about Kat, but I'll let her explain."

I jumped in the Mini and zoomed down to the BP station on the outskirts of Norwich. Kat, Ela and my sister Jeanette were lying out on the grass. Kat was wearing a white top and trousers, her sunglasses covered her eyes as though she was sunbathing optimistically in the fading rays of sunlight. She wore the shades for her epilepsy to prevent flashing lights. As she saw me, she jumped up and downed the dregs of her takeaway coffee and came jogging over, with her plait now so long she had doubled it up, but it still swung around her waist as she jogged.

Passing me without a word, she took the fuel pump and started fuelling the car. I started to walk towards the shop to pay. She dragged me back with one hand and hugged me. She whispered in my ear. "This my fault sort of so I pay for fuel out of my own money."

Jeanette and Ela didn't want to tell me what had upset Kat, but Jeanette said, "Don't be hard on that poor girl or I'll kick you in the balls."

Kat did not look happy as she came back carrying drinks. With Ela and Jeanette now in the back, Kat jumped in the passenger side and told me to pull into the parking space and stop for a drink, because she had something to tell me.

Whatever it was, I didn't like it. She took her shades off. Her eyes were damp as though she'd been crying, but she grinned and told me. "Hay-fever," then added quietly, "and a little bit of crying."

She sat for a second and mopped her eyes and blew her nose yet again before talking.

"You know when I do stupid things?" She smiled weakly.

"You're not stupid" I assured her.

"Well," she huffed, "I done something so stupid, that when the next edition of the dictionary comes out, the word *stupid* will have a picture of me. Also, I'm worried that some men in white coats might come along and take me away and put me in the London Zoo and charge people to see the stupidest person."

"What did you do?" I grinned.

"I got wrong." She huffed. Wrong being Norfolk slang for getting in trouble or told off. "From a nice pole-ice man."

"A what man?"

"You know flashy blue light."

"You mean a policeman."

She nodded, "Nice policeman, because I no am in prison."

"Why would you go to prison?"

"Because," she sobbed, "Jenny has weed in my knickers."

"I don't know what you girls like to get up to when you're out. I'm concerned that Jenny pissed on you. *Very* concerned."

Jeanette was cracking up in the back of the car. "Sweetie let me explain it to him." She grinned. "Jenny has a bad back injury, and as you know, she smokes marijuana for the pain. She's been caught twice and could have her daughter taken into care if she's caught again. Jenny stopped to get some marijuana on the way back. Then her car broke down, and a lovely policeman stopped for us. Kat grabbed the weed to stop Jenny from losing her daughter. She shoved it down her knickers, but she dropped it, and the policeman saw it and slapped her on the wrist." Medical marijuana being illegal in England.

Kat looked mortified at Jeanette, "He no did hit me, he was nice man doing his job."

We then had to explain that a slap on the wrist did not mean he hit.

"So," Jeanette giggled, "Jenny has 'weed' in her knickers. No urine involved. Plus we need to get out of here before anything else happens, because she's still got most of it."

"No funny though, Jeanette," Kat told her over my shoulder. "I am the first person ever in my family to get in trouble with a policeman. The shame I will bring on my family."

"Well, we won't tell them," I assured her, to show her how proud I was of her.

"I will," Ela piped up. Kat's eye widened as if she was about to snap at Ela, who quickly added, "I'm going to tell them what a kind brave thing you did to help stop your best friend getting into trouble." Ela then added, "By the way, you are not the first one in the family to be told off by a policeman. When I told you I stayed with a friend the other night, I was in a police cell for being drunk."

Kat then flipped at Ela.

A week later, I was surprised to find myself speaking to Helen, who was the manager of the caravan park where Kat worked. I didn't realise to start with that she was teasing me.

"What have you done with Kat?" She asked.

"Well, nothing." I replied, "I thought she was at work?"

"She's here slogging away with a smile on her face as usual. The thing is," she continued, "Kat has always been an excellent cleaner, but we had reservations about making her head of department, because of her temper and social issues, and things didn't work well at all in first year."

When I asked, "What does it have to do with me?" she laughed pleasantly.

"Well, you see, since you two have been dating, she has been a breath of fresh air. All the people who had a problem with her now love her to bits, we've got a whole load of reviews on Trip Advisor naming Kat as a person who has gone out of their way to make sure that families had a good holiday. We just let you know that it's time for our annual staff awards. Well, the caravan owners and staff both vote for their employee of the year."

"Okay," I replied.

"Are you working Friday night or are you free?"

"I should be free?" I told her.

"Oh good," She replied, "Our award ceremony will be held in the show bar at 7:30 pm and I know how Kat hates crowds, but drag her there even if she kicks and screams, because we can't have awards night without the winner.

In fact, I had no trouble getting Kat to go along. The first thing she said to me when she came to the gym later that evening was that she would like me to go with her on Friday to support her friends. No kicking and screaming needed, but she didn't dress up.

So, Kat was shocked and embarrassed when she was the most improved member of staff from last year. In true Kat form, nothing went smoothly. In shock at her surprise award, she had a few drinks to celebrate.

We were were sat at a big table in the back of the room, near the bar, with a mixture of some of Kat's cleaning team and some of the receptionist. Early in the evening, Kat's friend Kelly who had a drink or two, tried to re-enact the time Kat tried to resign and she tipped coffee over her resignation letter. Only this time she tipped a bottle of tomato ketchup over the table.

Kat laughed out loud and used her spare hankie to mop up the mess. Nobody thought anything of it at the time. That was until just seconds before the winner of the staff members' employee of the year was announced. Kat was cheering her friend Milly, who got second place, and she choked on her beer. Instinctively, she picked up her hankie to avoid spraying people. So, seconds later, when the announcement was made, and the spotlight found her, the place fell silent. Her face was splattered in ketchup.

I knew she didn't feel comfortable accepting the award, but deep down, she would feel immense pride. Again, in true Kat style, she seemed to take it in her stride. She walked up to the stage very quietly with no fuss and tried to hand the award back to her boss. Then she went very quietly up to the microphone and said quietly, pointing at her tomato-covered face and said to a packed bar, "What is wrong with you lot? An employee of the year is very serious award. Firstly, you voted for the wrong person, and secondly, I look silly! Laugh at me."

Finally, the room burst out into fits laughter. She went on to list quite a few people saying, "And that just the first list of people who deserve this award more than me."

She proceeded to try to give the award away to everyone she could.

,*~*~*~*~*

Suddenly just a stark reminder that none of this was real, the dark and the cold hit us once more. I woke, although Kat stirred, she did not sit up or open her eyes. I shook her a little to check she was still alive.

"You okay, hum?" She murmured.

"We're hay again," I sighed.

"No. No, we are no there" She moaned grumpily. "This is a bad dream. I am home in bed with my real Rob. You are a dream."

"I wish it was." I breathed.

"Is true." she snorted. "Now if you no mind, get out of my sleep. It is my birthday, and I feel really ill and want to be rested because my real boyfriend has planned a surprise for me. I need rest in case he is taking somewhat tiring. I am hoping he is going to give me a ring because I want to marry him. So kindly fuck and let me sleep."

"Charming." I scoffed, knowing she didn't mean what she was saying. "I'd better fuck off then."

"Okay, then night, sweetheart. You still sound like my boyfriend, so you are still a sweetheart. Oh and just in case this is really, I sorry am said fuck off."

Chapter 10

Kat's birthday

I opened my eyes to find Kat's eyes looking right into mine. In the dim light her eyes looked like I felt. Vacant and sleepy like she'd just woken from the same intense dream I'd just had. It was strangely common for Kat and I to have these dreams on the same night. In these dreams we would revisit our night in the haystack almost like we were still there. These dreams had become so regular that we had started to right them down and compare notes.

At this point as we gazed at each other sleepily I felt it necessary to say that a lot more things happened before this point.

A lot of romances had a honeymoon period and once it was over and normal life kicked in, people became bored and they argued and found they were not going to last. I feared this would happen with Kat and myself, but somehow we always found a way to make each day fresh and new

Here is a brief list of the many things which happened in the months that passed since Valentine's Day.

I felt like these were happening like a montage in a movie.

So, Kat and Ela working together at the caravan park

didn't last long. Kat applied for a job at a local care home, but she lost out on the position to none other than Ela, who had applied for it in secret. Kat had applied thinking she was going to fall out with people at her current job. But instead, after making her peace with the colleagues she worked with, she returned with big grin her face. She even took me in in meet her team who turned out to be a lovely bunch of girls, who had become very close friends after apparently more than a year of constant arguments prior to Kat and I getting together.

Ela passed her driving test, insured herself to drive my car then took it on a two-hundred-mile drive without telling us. When she got found out, we punished her by making her do the dishes for a week.

Other things happened obviously.

As mentioned in the montage, Kat took back the things she said and admitted she rather enjoyed the gym and getting her once frail and skinny body into shape. She was brightening the place up with her smile most days, as she ripped up the club record for women on every piece of cardiovascular equipment. All this despite her constantly having a cold and many times still suffering from the effects of her seizures

Kat and I liked to travel, and we used our days off to do this once or twice a month. We often camped to keep the cost down, and Ela and Jenny joined us sometimes, and even my sister and her new boyfriend on one trip and they brought Jemima.

When not camping our days off were spent hiking along the cliff, or relaxing in the park, or on the beach if it was too hot.

On cold rainy days and dark evenings, we'd sit in the armchair together and play instruments, or read a book, or even play Xbox. It didn't matter what we did as long as it was together.

So, by now it was understood that Kat and I were a permanent thing and not just a passing obsession. Kat was *the one*. At home away from the stress of our jobs there was nothing more important than to make each other smile.

Opening my eyes on that dark November morning I gazed across at Kat. Her big blue eyes were already open, and she was calmly looking into my own.

"Good morning, honey," she whispered softly, rubbing my leg.

"Morning, beautiful lady," I said, rubbing her back with my hand. "Did you sleep well?"

Kat replied in a croaky voice which sounded like she was wearing a nose plug. She often woke up like that when she had a cold, which seemed to be always.

"Who you talking to?" she asked. "There no beautiful lady here in this bed, just grumpy one."

"That smile doesn't look grumpy, birthday girl?"

"I am now twenty-two. That means I am nearly thirty," she told me, turning her smile into a fake frown. "I getting old and grumpy." As she said this she took of her top to reveal her perfectly toned athletic twenty-two-year-old body.

"Do you want me to get your walking frame and take you to the toilet?" I teased.

"Yes, please, if you are no mind." She grinned, lying back down beside me and inching closer as though she was going to kiss me.

Just as our lips were about to touch, she pulled away

teasingly, saying, "I no can kiss you now, my old person morning breath is maybe kill you."

With that she blew a breath in my face as if to prove it, but there was absolutely nothing wrong with it.

She had a stretch and big deep cough and reached clumsily towards the bedside table where her pills were, but lost her grip and fell so her breast landed in my face.

I calmly lifted her off me and put her back down on her side of the bed, then passed her what she called her waking-up kit, which was her pills, a glass of water, smoking patches and gum and two clean hankies.

She thanked me and downed the pills with her right hand as I put the patch on her left arm. She then berated herself for still needing the patches and gum almost a year on from her last cigarette.

"I no does help when in my dreams I am smoke more than a coal-fuelled power station."

Kat rolled and laid herself on top of me on her front, with her elbows by my sides and held her chin in her hands so she could look me in the eye.

"Bad dreams again?" I soothed, wrapping my legs around hers.

"The one about the haystack?"

"I guessing you know it was, because you are there too. And I told *Fuck off.* I sorry, love you." She said quietly before trying to change the subject by showing me the large words she had embroidered into her homemade hankie.

The big bright green letters stitched into the white cloth read LOOK OUT! SHE'S ABOUT TO BLOW.

"You like it?" she croaked, sounding really quite emotional.

"I love it." I smiled. This summed up Kat's sense of humour down to a tee.

She proceeded to lie there on my chest, blowing her nose with what looked like a huge effort. Then she looked up at me with her *I'm sorry I just did that* face knowing that I couldn't be annoyed at her.

Part of the of fun of being with Kat was her pushing personal boundaries, then apologising after the act. What worried me was that Kat's cold had been ever present. In the eleven months I had known her, it was very rare for Kat not to be suffering from a cold. I just worried about her because I adored her and wanted her to enjoy her life not be ill all the time.

Back to that later though. What Kat said next concerned me.

"It is weird," she said, with a slightly troubled voice, "I'm starting to think that this dream of haystack may well have happened in some other life."

"But it did happen," I told her. "But we're here safe now."

"Hmm, yes it did," she nodded. "It just so real I wonder if this now is just a dream. I mean we still no know how we got out, so how we know this is no the dream?"

"What happens if this is just a dream?" I teased.

She grinned and kissed me. "I no want to wake up ever again, but anyway, it is no the dreams of the haystack that terrify me," she sighed. "In the haystack and cold and ill, but you there with me keeping me safe. If I never met you that scare the fuck out of me."

When I asked Kat if she wanted to talk about the

dreams and why they scared her, she shook her head so hard that she whipped her plait.

"No want to ruin my birthday talking about that shit. Anyways…" she continued, stretching. "I no can laze around in bed just because it my birthday. I have to go work."

"You're not going to work today, sweetheart." I grinned.

Kat looked at me a bit funny as if she wondered what I was implying. Then she opened her mouth in shock remembering.

"Of course! I no go work today because I am *sick* and no because it's my birthday. You planned a treat for me." She must have forgotten in the confusion of waking, but she knew full well that she'd been planning to pull a sick day, so we could spend her birthday together.

A lot of people took sick days when they were not really ill. The difference with Kat was that she was the opposite. She would go into work even if she was feeling very ill. Taking an unplanned day off for illness was like a sin to Kat. That was why I was surprised that she agreed to pull a sicky when she had no paid holiday left. It actually worked in our favour because of the amount of times Kat had turned up to work unwell. They would think she must be seriously sick to ask for a day off. What she didn't know was that I planned to take her to London for the evening to see Mamma Mia, which had been a long-term dream of hers.

"Nope," she said, making a sad face with big sad eyes and sniffing. "I am got the flu," she said in a very dramatic voice as she pretended to cry. "Well, that's what I'm going to tell my boss, anyway." She smiled, picking up her mobile phone and dialling her work number, and waited for the answerphone to kick in. Then she spoke in a terrible rough voice. "Ello is Kat, *cough* Katarzyna, *cough*." She smiled deviously as she took it. "A so sorry," she croaked, "a think am too sick to..." She faked a sneeze into the phone and coughed hard. "Too sick to come to work today."

I showed her two fingers to suggest she took a couple of days, to make it sound less suspicious that she was pulling a sicky. She faked another sneeze. "I my no be back till next week," she sniffed, giving me a cheeky smile and thumbs up. Then, she blew her nose loudly next to the phone before giving croaky instructions for the staff she was in charge of and apologising again.

"You were awesome," I smiled, you even had me convinced it was the flu."

"I no am sure I sure no have got it," she told me, stretching her arms. Then she snuggled up to me with her chin on the pillow by my head, where she convinced me that she actually didn't feel well at all. "I am no let it ruin my best birthday ever though." She smiled weakly.

I was intrigued to know why Kat said it was her best birthday despite her feeling ill. She had told me a lot about her past when she lived in the Czech Republic and I believed she hadn't had good birthdays as a child.

"You must have had some shocking birthdays if being ill is your best one." I soothed, rubbing her gently as she laid on me.

"Marajina." She said suddenly.

"What did you just say marijuana for?"

"No marijuana, Marajina." She corrected.

Kat hadn't told me much at all about her time in England before meeting me, other than she had not found it easy.

"Marajina was Lithuanian lady who I shared my bedroom with in farmwork accommodation when I first came here."

I listened in shock as Kat told me the story. It was a long one, so I settled down to listen.

Sixteen-year-old Kat had a job in south Norfolk where she and other migrants would travel to different farms. Their job was to pick and sort whichever fruit or veg was in season and could not be done by machine.

They lived in accommodation rented from the employer, which meant Kat had been forced to share a room with a twenty-year-old Lithuanian woman called Marajina.

Marajina was a bully and a thief, who made Kat's life hell. She would pretend to be Kat's best friend while bullying her, stealing her possessions and money. She had got Kat into smoking seemingly for the purpose of stealing her tobacco.

On her seventeenth birthday, Kat had phoned her mum and got very upset because she was missing home. Marajina had secretly filmed her crying while on the phone and showed it to everyone in the house.

"Then," Kat sighed, pausing to sip her tea, she got on her computer and uploaded her 'My face' or 'Space book' or some computer interweb thing. She didn't really do social media. Kat had left the home and job in tears and had to move to a B&B while taking the first the first job that came her way.

Her birthdays after that had not been much better. After moving to the flat Kat had spent her eighteenth alone reading a book because she had no friends.

Her nineteenth was spent at the hospital with her new friend, Jenny, who had recently tried to kill herself.

Her twentieth, she and Jenny had gone clubbing before realising they both hated clubs. They left after twenty minutes when a fight broke out. Kat told me she had also been forced to kick two drunk men in the balls after they attempted to grope her.

"Getting groped after what happened when I was teenager made cry." She breathed, "Well, afterwards when I got home."

This was far from the first time she had mentioned some kind of sexual abuse when she was a teenager. However, when I pressed her to talk about it she began to cough and splutter even louder than she had been, with a look that said, "I'm coughing louder because I don't want to talk."

So on her twenty-first birthday, she went to work and did nothing to celebrate.

I was shocked at how utterly miserable Kat had been in those years.

She finished by saying, "Since I met you my life has been so great, even if do spend the day in bed with flu it will still be my best birthday, because you are here."

I didn't know what to say to that statement.

"I became as bad as Marajina, if not worse." She added. "Before I met you I was in trouble at work, because I am shout and bully people. Now look at me." She pointed at the certificate framed on the bedroom wall which read, "Clifftop Caravan Park employee of the year Katarzyna Bobal."

"See…" She grinned, "…being with you made me back into a person people like. Can you think of the last time I was rude anyone."

The timing couldn't have been anymore comedic because my mobile phone rang on the bedside table. Kat seeing that caller ID said *Work,* picked up the phone and instead of giving it to me she answered it abruptly.

"Katherine it is Rob's day off, you no should be calling. He has already worked five extra shifts for you this month. It is my birthday. He is not coming to work so go fuck yourself."

She put the phone down and looked at me sheepishly and said, "That job offer at the caravan is open again. I may have just got you fired."

"She'll get over it." I grinned. "So," I teased, "if you are so ill, you won't be up for seeing Mamma Mia in London tonight."

Her face dropped. "I'm better *already*." She shrieked.

"But you're too ill for work so you can't possibly go to the theatre."

"I no am ill I just made it up," she said in her *isn't it obvious* tone, but this seemed more like a little white lie. This lie was immediately rumbled by a heavy sneeze.

"Do you want to change your answer?" I laughed, giving her a squeeze. She nodded reluctantly and made a pretend angry noise.

"Not funny," she said, almost laughing at her own misfortune. "I no want to sneeze and be ill on my birthday." She pretended to sob, and then she smiled and said, "I guess it what I deserve for planning to fake it." She grinned, then she added. "You know this was all a laugh and my boss Helen and all the girls knew I was gonna be sick today."

I nodded, knowing full well that Helen knew Kat was going to be *ill* on that day, because I had asked if she could give Kat an extra couple of days holiday and she had suggested that she pull a sicky.

"We can make this better though," she smiled weakly. "Ibuprofen, paracetamol, lots of tea, with kisses, cuddles and lovemaking from Doctor Rob, and I will on fine form. I'll be there and I'll be dancing in the aisles."

"I wouldn't," I teased, "I may have asked you if you'd be well enough to go to Mamma Mia, but I got us tickets to Shakespeare."

Her face dropped again in disappointment. "Well I do enjoy Shakespeare too," she said, a little deflated.

"Well, it's a good job I got us tickets for both and a hotel then." I grinned. "Should I go and get you some breakfast in bed?"

Kat shook her head smiling and told me she had already made breakfast for us both when she woke up in the night, before coming back to bed. I told her it was my job to spoil her, but what she said made sense. Making breakfast was her present to herself, because she never had anyone to make it for her on past birthdays.

"Before we eat, I have set you a task." She grinned, removing her PJs slowly.

"Tell me my task, mistress." I smiled.

"I am turned off my sister's alarm clock." She smirked, "If she no wake up she is late for work and get fired. You task is to wake her by touching nothing but me. I want you make me scream."

"Okay," I chirped, then I rolled her onto the bed and tickled her until she cried out in delight as the scene faded.

Chapter 11

<u>Anniversary confusion</u>

A few weeks had passed and yet I remembered everything that happened. Kat tried her best considering how unwell she was feeling on her birthday. Kat just thought it was one of her colds and would not have gone out to a crowded theatre if she thought she was infectious. However, after watching her become too exhausted, I had to give her a piggyback through Central London to the hotel. With plans to go sightseeing the next day cancelled, I took her straight home on the next train and to the doctor.

It was later confirmed that she really had the flu, which she generously shared with me. So, we did in fact get to spend more than a few days in bed together.

Ela thought this was hilarious and taunted us, because she had got the flu jab at work. "It's only a diddy little prick."

To which Kat's retort was, "I hear you are had enough of those to know they are like."

This made Ela spray the tea she was drinking all over her work clothes, before confessing it was true, adding, "The last person I slept with didn't have one."

What she just said should have been a major clue as to

where things were leading for Ela.

To give El due credit, as far as girlfriends, sisters, or housemates went, she was top class. She looked after both of us when we had the flu. She did the shopping and the cooking and kept us dosed up all while having her own job to go to.

We were both much better a few weeks later when it came to celebrating our first anniversary. There had been a question as to whether it should be a year from the night we first kissed, or the night we met. Kat told me it was her opinion that although we'd not been officially together for two weeks, she felt we'd been a couple from the moment we met, so who was I to argue?

It was the afternoon, and I was about to meet Kat's vicious temper for the first time. To be fair, in the circumstances that followed, I did not blame her for being angry, even though her anger was misguided.

Kat had always been honest with me about her temper. She told me that when she was upset or angry she would fly into a blind rage at the drop of a hat, but I'd never seen it. In the year that I'd known her, Kat had never shown even a hint of her anger.

I was about to learn about it.

I came home in the best mood I could have been in and was happy to could start cooking dinner for Kat.

I was off work for the day. Both Ela and I had things to do in the city and seeing as she didn't yet have her own car. I'd dropped her off to get her hair cut while I went to the bank. Later, we met up to take care of some other business before popping to the supermarket.

The business that Ela and I were attending to was so secret, that I had to tell Kat I was working that morning, meaning we would both be 6am to 2pm. I planned to be home by the time she got back to cook her favourite vegetable lasagne and celebrate our one-year anniversary together.

She thought I'd forgotten that it was our anniversary, but I wanted to make her feel as special as she was to me.

At the top of the stairs, Ela told me she'd left her phone in the car. I gave her the keys to go back and look.

It all changed when I opened the door. I was expecting Kat to be at work, but she was sat in the armchair stroking Roger, her beautiful white rabbit, and staring at the blank wall.

"I wasn't expecting you to be home, sweetheart," I said as I passed her with the shopping. Kat didn't respond, she just continued stroking Roger. This was completely out of character for her. She'd usually jump up and give me a hug, but not today.

I saw that she had packed luggage and left it next to the door and wondered what was going.

"Been having fun?" she asked. Her voice was cold and completely out of character.

"How come you're not at work?" I replied. I hoped my short answer wouldn't give away where I'd been and what I'd been doing.

"I could ask you the same question," she replied moodily. She'd never spoken to me like that before.

"I can explain," I said, sitting down beside her. She stood up to put Roger back in his cage and moved away from me to sit on the arm of the chair. Instead of cuddling up to me as she normally would have done, she sat looking away from me, wiping her eyes.

Kat had clearly been crying.

"Have I upset you somehow darling?" I asked, bemused.

"Yes," she said stiffly, nodding at the luggage. "Those are yours. Take them and fuck off and no come back here ever."

"What is it Kat? What have I done?" I tried to put my arm around her, but she pushed me away.

She turned to me with an angry look. "I got to leave work early," she said in a hard-spitting voice. "I decided to cook dinner for man I love, because it our anniversary and he is still at work."

She took a deep breath, but before I could speak continued in her icy tone.

"I came home and found the car gone when all three of us worked to work today. I thought maybe Ela took it again, but then I got a call on the landline. Then I cried my eyes out while pack you bag and you can leave now."

"Who was the call from?" I asked, wondering exactly what kind of phone call could upset Kat and why on earth it was my fault. Whatever it was, I'd never seen sweet and lovely Kat so cold and angry.

"Mr. Johnson of Johnson's Jewellers," she said coolly. "He said you gave our home number as back up. He couldn't get you on your mobile, and that lovely black-haired girl you bought the ring for left her phone in his shop."

"Shit," I said under my breath, but before I could explain, she burst with anger.

"I loved you!" she screamed, aiming slaps at my head. Thankfully, she kept narrowly missing. "I thought we were forever. I wanted to marry you, and have you children. How can you do this to me? How you do this to us? I know there was good reason stayed single. Men are always doing this woman. I'm terrified that I'm not good enough for you, and I'm terrified that other girls want steal you from me, but I never thought you let them." Her face was red with anger like I'd never seen.

I tried to find the words to explain what had happened, but she threw herself at me again with her hands around my neck, screaming, "Get the fuck out of my home." Then she took out one of her large hankies and covered her face, before crumbling on the floor in a flood of hysterical tears.

"Kat, look, I can explain," I stumbled, putting my hand on her shoulders as she sat with her head between her knees.

"Fuck off and *leave me alone!*" she screamed, banging her head on the floor.

"But Kat..."

"How you do this to us after everything?" she wailed.

She stood up, shoving me toward the door with a sort of strength that made me regret having given her such a heavy workout plan. My instincts told me not to defend myself physically, because I didn't want Kat to get hurt.

Grabbing my ear and twisting it till it bled, she opened the door to the flat with other hand. She pulled me by the ear out of the door, dragging a suitcase in the other hand yelling. "If you are no going to leave I throw you fuck out shit out myself."

With that she lobbed the hard suitcase down the spiral stairs, unaware that Ela was on her way up.

Kat was still ranting with fire in her eyes and spitting flames, when Ela, sporting her new shorter hair, now black instead her natural blonde, came up the stairs spitting fire herself.

"Who the fuck threw a fucking suitcase down the stairs when I was coming up? You cut me you fucking morons."

"Ela, I sorry." Kat cried, grabbing her sister, "It's Rob's fault. He is leaving."

Ela looked at her as if to say *are you serious* and then tried to crack a joke by saying. "Bloody hell, Katarzyna, you sound so American when you're angry."

"I no do." She screamed back at Ela, "I am Czech. I am proud of it. Once this asshole has gone, I am packing my stuff going back there with or without you."

"Well, I think I have left my phone at the jewellers, so can I at least use his car to go and get it before you throw him out?"

Kat looked at Ela confused, and then to me. "She knows," I told Ela quietly, "but she got it wrong."

Kat stopped crying and looked up at Ela, hiding her eyes from me. Obviously, Ela had not told her she was getting her hair cut that morning.

"You!" Kat breathed, "You are cheating on me with my little sister."

It was Ela's turn to look confused at the pair of us, and I managed just in time to get between them to block Kat from slapping her sister.

"Kat, *stop it!*" Ela screamed. "Think about it. I am your sister. First of all, I'm gay and second, if I wasn't I wouldn't cheat with your boyfriend who has just bought you a very expensive engagement ring."

Kat looked from me to Ela. Then she hid her face and ran back into the flat.

"I had to tell her." Ela sobbed, holding her arm with tears in her eyes. I wasn't sure if Ela was crying because of the accusations, or because she was scared of Kat. In truth she might have been crying because Kat had really hurt her with the suitcase and her arm was bleeding heavily.

Kat was lying face down in the chair in floods of tears. She lay there motionless, sobbing for as long as it took to get the first aid kit and dress Ela's arm.

Kat sat up slowly on the chair and looked at us both, then she got up slowly, hugged her sister and spoke in Czech. Kat was apologising to Ela for everything she said and for hurting her with the suitcase.

"We need to wash and bandage this arm." Kat told me, tugging Ela in the direction of the bathroom. She stopped at the bathroom door and smiled weakly. "You need to go and get that suitcase. It is up to you if you want unpack it or run away from the monster you just saw."

I wasn't going anywhere and when I got back upstairs, that was not monster, that was passionate lady who thought she had just had her heart ripped out. If she cared about me that much, then I knew I had made the right choice to do the thing I did next.

After retrieving the suitcase, I waited for the ladies to emerge from the bathroom. They were smiling as though they had made up. Ela had accepted Kat's apology. As the three of us sat down, Kat and I on the chair and Ela on the floor by the chair, Ela put her hand on Kat's and compared their finger size.

Kat then turned to me, nervously facing me as she blew her nose gently. Then stuffing her hankie in the pocket, she said quietly. "I have got one hell of an apology dinner to cook now you seen my bad side."

"You're scary when you're angry," I grinned.

"And incredibly embarrassed by my behaviour and overreaction." She sighed.

"It was a misunderstanding" I soothed. "And it was passionate."

"But should have let you speak, and now you know what a raging angry monster inside me."

"True," I replied, "but it proved one thing to me."

"That I am raging psychopath." She smiled weakly.

"That our love is as important to you as it is to me."

"And I went and broke it by pushing you out." She sobbed.

At this point I reached over to pick Kat up and put her on my lap. She was a bit heavier than she had once been now she was more toned.

I sat there for several minutes, just holding her while she sobbed and telling her she had no reason to cry. Kat, however, said that her confused outburst gave me more than enough reason to walk out on her. She took a lot of convincing that there was no quarrel between us, and her outburst had been understandable in the circumstances.

"So," she sniffed, "you got my sister to help get the ring size right so you could ask me marry you?" I nodded. "So, you gonna ask me or make we wait?" She smiled, with a look that told me the old Kat was back.

My life had been leading to this moment and I was flowing with emotion as I slid off the chair and down onto one knee.

"Wait, Rob, stop." She said, looking nervously at me. "I have to confess something before you asked me in case you want to change you mind."

"Okay, go ahead." I told her nervously. I was terrified that it was something really big, like Kat was going to say she had cheated on me. She looked incredibly guilty and worried about what my reaction would be.

"Rob." She trembled, "After I told you quit smoking on my first day back at work, I had a rollup, but I felt so guilty for lying, I put it out after one puff and never smoked again."

"What's the big confection then, sweetheart?" I asked her.

She rolled her eyes at me and smiled awkwardly. "That was the confession. I was really naughty. I was really worried you'd find out what I did."

"I love you Kat." I smirked, before looking down at her feet.

"Katarzyna Zophia Bobal, would you do me the honour of becoming my wife?"

There was a moment's silence when nothing was said until I looked up and saw Kat sticking her tongue out at me and shaking her head.

I hadn't prepared for her to say no. I was crushed at her answer, but then was grinning all over her face and bending down to meet me with a kiss.

"Rob," she grinned, putting her arms around me, "I wasn't done confessing. I no was done confessing. No at work today either, work finish for Christmas yesterday."

So, the gist of what she told me was that at 6am she went to Jenny's and pretended to be at work before going on a girly shopping trip.

"We talked," she grinned, "about whether or not it was okay for a girl to propose to her man on their anniversary and I decided it was. So, I went to a rather cheaper jewellers called Argos. Rob, will you marry me."

I was dumbstruck. I did not see that coming ten minutes earlier. Kat never failed to surprise.

The pair of us just stared at each other, grinning nervously, just stuck in the moment.

I heard Ela standing beside us in tears say, "Come on, one of you say yes before we all die of old age."

That was until Kat leaned over and whispered in my ear.

"If you no are say yes in ten seconds, I throw another hissy fit. I will cry and I throw you other bags down stairs."

"Yes." I said quickly, leaning towards her adding, "Please don't throw another hissy fit."

As I was about to kiss her, Kat put her finger on my nose to stop me. "No finished yet." She teased, "My answer to you question is also yes. However," she continued in a cool calm voice, "There is one more thing I must ask before we go to the bedroom." She pointed up at her sister. "Why the fuck are you let my idiot sister get such silly haircut?"

We spent the next few moments wrapping our tongues around each other's before Kat pulled away, and solemnly announced, "Now that I got my man always wanted, there is more one thing I have to get off my chest."

"What is it, sweetheart?" I asked uneasily, trying to smile.

Kat looked down, and then smiled up at me with a gleam in her eyes. "My bra," she whispered, loud enough for Ela to hear as she turned and tugged me towards the bedroom. I vaguely remembered hearing Ela as the door shut, shouting something about going to the pub if anyone remembered who she was.

Chapter 12

The dark and the cold

Suddenly, it was cold and dark. The wind was howling all around the haystack. It seemed even colder than before, and there was ice forming on my body. It took me a few moments to wake up before I realised there was something seriously wrong with Kat. A moment ago, I'd been having a lovely, but far from realistic dream, where we had proposed to each other, but now I was back awake.

I couldn't hear her heart beating or feel her breathing. "Kat wake up!" I shouted, but there was no response from her whatsoever. We shouldn't have gone to sleep at the same time. She might well be dead. If I ran for help, I would leave her with no chance of survival if her heart had truly stopped.

I knew from my first aid training there was very little chance of me being able to bring her back, but I had to try. This poor lovely girl didn't deserve to die out here in the dark, away from her family. I felt for her mouth and gave her two rescue breaths, but felt no response.

I felt for the left side of her chest and started pumping down on it. "Come on Kat!" I yelled. "Don't leave me! You have to live for our future."

I carried on for several cycles, but there was nothing there.

"Come on, wake up!" I yelled, with tears rolling down my face. "Come on you sweet gorgeous lady!" I screamed. "Don't leave me."

Suddenly, there was a voice that seemed to come out of the walls of the haystack. It was a long wail that whispered on the wind as it drove a shiver down my spine.

"Rob," it called.

"Katarzyna?" I responded.

"Rob," it wailed. "Rob stop it!"

"What?" I called.

There was a cold hard slap across my face. "Rob," I heard in my ear, "Rob wake up."

"Kat?" I said into the darkness.

"Rob," she said breathlessly, "You awake! I sorry I hit you, but you are dreaming. I no dead, but you do sleep CPR on my tummy."

"Kat, you're alive?" I called, reaching out and hugging her. "I thought I'd lost you."

"Is okay," she said. "You have nightmare."

"But before that, you had that same dream, didn't you?" I asked.

She nodded. "Can we talk about dream in minute?" she groaned.

"What's up?" I asked, panicking.

"You no can see, but I'm pulling my I'm really, really sorry face," she breathed. "I need toilet really badly.

"It's okay," I told her. "Just let it go. It will run down in the hay."

"That would be a good idea but..." she whispered in my ear with embarrassment. "We just got warmer, and I going to have to go outside again."

I was still too sleepy to get quite what she was trying to say, "But why do you have to...?"

I heard her stomach make an ominous rumbling noise. "I'm sorry," she squeaked. "I need a big poo."

"Okay, I'm sorry for that," I breathed. I was happy for Kat to piss on me in these exceptional circumstances, but the thought of being in a small space with my own shit, let alone someone else's – even if she was a lovely person, was wrong. So, I helped Kat up and slipped on her soaking wet shoes. I put mine on too and helped her slide out of the hole in the wall of hay. Right away, we encountered a blast of icy wind.

She kept saying how sorry she was. "It's all right," I kept telling her, as the wind burned our skin. I tried to go with her, but she let go of my hand, and shouted, "I am a big girl. Been go to toilet on my own since I was two. You stay warm. I will need a cuddle when I am get back."

"Are you sure?" I called in the dark.

"I fine," she shouted back. "You stay there, so I can follow you voice back."

I realised I was kneeling on Kat's packet of rolling tobacco. It had fallen out of her coat pocket, and by some miracle had stayed dry with a lighter inside it. I sparked up the lighter and the hole in the haystack filled with light. While Kat was out in the cold, I rolled her a cigarette to help her warm up and calm her down when she got back. I heard her coughing her guts up in the corner of the haystack, and thought maybe it might be better to let her believe the tobacco was wet, because it might only make her cough worse.

She seems to be gone for ages. As the minutes ticked by, I readied myself to go find her in the snow. Finally, she called out to me.

"*Rob!*" I heard her shout. "Which way are you, sweetheart?"

I clicked the lighter on. "This way," I called, trying the best I could to light her way.

She reached up her hands, shaking with cold as I pulled her in. Having put the lighter down, I didn't see her face.

"Ello," she shivered, pulling the bale back across the gap.

"Did you have a good poo?" I asked, rather stupidly.

"The en-suite bathroom was a bit itchy and there was bit of draught." She shivered as she pushed the haybale back in the hole to seal the shelter. She pulled off her wet clothes and threw her shivering body around me. "The toilet didn't flush either."

"You're not going to give this haystack a good review on tripadvisor.com, then?" I laughed.

"I no have computer, but I guess that's some internet thingy?" she laughed, through chattering teeth. "I think I am must of passed out for a while," she said, shuddering suddenly.

"What happened?" I asked, concerned.

"Well," she answered, "vas dreaming again, but this time of home and no us, just me. I was warm and snuggly in bed. I stretch and blew nose really well, and then I went to toilet."

"Okay, too much information," I joked. "Did you do

anything else?"

"Only normal waking up in the night things," she laughed. "I made myself big cup of tea. I roll myself cigarette and sit on fire escape and had a good old smoke, then went back to bed. That was when I am wake up sitting on a hay-bale."

"That is bloody odd," I agreed, "but at least you're alive and back here."

"You are telling me," she laughed nervously.

"You wake up in the night to smoke and drink tea?"

"Rob, please don't judge when you hardly know me," she said, sounding annoyed and poking me in the back.

"I'm sorry I didn't mean to—" I tried to say, but she interrupted in a very grumpy tone.

"If you and me going to remain friend..." she paused and sneezed, then gave a little laugh, "Then you have to get used to me teasing you."

"You're not angry for judging me then?"

"No, I should be angry be because it is rude to judge, but I no can be, because you are telling truth."

"Talking of that, I found your spare lighter, and it's working," I told her, rubbing her all over trying to get rid of her goose pimples.

"I saw," she shivered. "We should get good look at each other and see if we are look as in dreams."

"Okay, moment of truth," I said, pulling back slightly. I took out the lighter between us and clicked it.

The light fell on Kat just a few inches from me, and I almost jumped.

"Hello sexy," she grinned. "I bet I no am what you were expecting."

I knew a little of what she looked like, but I was expecting her to look a lot different from the girl I dreamed about when it came to reality. However, there she was – her lovely deep expressive eyes shone, her long blonde hair was not as shiny, but still in a plait twisted around her shoulders just like in the dream.

The Kat from the dream had been painfully skinny when we first met, but she'd gained a little weight since she quit smoking and started the gym, and looked all the better for it. Kat in reality was still painfully thin, and her dirty face was red from the stinging wind.

"You're definitely the Kat in my dreams," I told her with a smile. As I said it, she turned and sneezed, but she recovered herself quickly, and grinned at me with her shy dazzling smile. "Am I your Rob then?" I asked quietly.

"No, you are no the same," she answered, and then she smiled and said cheekily, "You even more handsome." With that comment, I felt a little warm feeling inside me. She blew her nose heavily, "Sorry, that's yucky," she said, tossing her handkerchief into her drenched handbag. She then took something out and put it in my hand. "Smelly candles. I was going to light these and have relaxing bath at hotel, but you find lighter we use them. Plus," she added, "I just realised I'm stupid because you can't light candles in a hotel for the same reason you can't smoke."

"Good thinking," I told her, taking the flame and holding it to the wick. As the candle wick was soaked, it took a moment or two before a tiny flickering light took hold and created a little heat between us.

"Just two. We must save the others," Kat said, passing me a second candle. When it was lit, we could see each other perfectly. "I forgot my extreme emergency spare handkerchief," she said, taking a large blue handkerchief out of a pocket in her handbag. "It is a little bit soggy from water, but at least I won't sneeze on you." She laughed. "I know I no can help it, but I feel terrible for giving you my germs."

"How on earth many hankies do you have?" I joked. "Never enough when for this cold," she replied, ironically sneezing seconds later.

"You know me." She grinned. "I love embroidery, so I find making hankies fun, as well as the fact it good for environment. "I make them really so easy to keep my germs to myself," she added. She looked at me as though she was expecting a response. "I told you I was most boring woman in the world," she whispered in my ear.

"I'd say unique is a more accurate word," I whispered back. "In a nice way."

"Thank you," she replied quietly. "Seriously though," she told me, "I am also make head scarves, sweatbands for work, knit cardigans, and jumper for myself." She coughed so hard that she nearly fell over and grabbed me for support. "I do all these things in the dream. Did you know?"

I nodded, remembering just how amazingly skilful she had been at making clothes. "I admire you trying to look after our planet," I told her once she steadied herself.

"I do my bit," she said. "I recycle and I no drive car, that because epilepsy." She let go of me and shook her body mimicking a fit. "I should no laugh," she said. "I lucky my epilepsy is a bit more than mild, but in Czech, medication is expensive. Here, I get medical exemption on NHS. Which," she added, "my taxes pay for."

"Too right," I nodded, agreeing that the NHS was badly stretched. Anyone who worked paid into it, so she had as much right to medical exemption as anyone else with epilepsy.

"My neurologist helped cut down, but still I am having them at night sometimes. I know when it happens, but they hurt me afterwards. Muscles pulled, and sometimes I lose memory forget where I live and stuff."

"That must be horrible," I breathed, wondering how frightening it must be to wake up alone in your house.

She sniffed and nodded and cuddled up to me again. "Last summer I fitted and not know where I was. Broken wrist, forgot English, and my hands are no working. Also, I can no feel my legs."

"That's terrible," I told her, shaking my head.

"Thank God it was Wednesday morning and my Jenny vas there help me get myself out," she sighed. "I love that lady."

"You didn't have any fits in the dream," I commented.

Kat's answer to that was, because it was a dream. Although she could go from weeks to months fit free, they would always happen sooner or later. When they did, they would come in clusters that could go on for days.

"If was no for the pills, I would be having in the daytime too and probably tonight," she sighed.

She told me that although her neurologist was good, she felt he should be helping by increasing the medication to get rid of the remaining fits. If he couldn't do that, then at least decrease them, so that she could have a restricted driving license, but he refused to do further tests.

"I rolled this if you want it," I said, holding out the cigarette.

"Oh, I love you! I am dying for smoke," she said, her eyes lighting up as she took it and leaned forward to kiss me on the cheek. "That's for being considerate of my filthy, yucky, horrible addiction." She smiled, and was about to light it from the candle. But she stopped, put it down, and looked at me smiling and shaking her head. "You know," she said, seemingly reminiscing as she shuffled over on her knees, put her shivering body against mine, and resumed cuddling into me. "In Czech Republic, I was five times long distance running race champion of school."

"Well done you." I told her. "It makes my thirty-second place in the area cross country look even more pathetic than it was. I did fall over and get trampled by forty-odd people though," I added.

She smiled. "It was only out of thirty girls at my school year, but my legs were slightly longer and lighter than other girls."

"You're not as short as you first seem, are you?"

"No, and I got to national championship for my age," she laughed. "People think I small because I narrow, skinny, dainty girl, with stick woman limbs and a small head. But you are what? Six foot six?"

"About that," I nodded.

"You're big gorgeous man," she teased, "but I can kiss on tip toes. So, I no giantess, but I no little Katarzyna that people treat me like."

"I didn't say you were," was my reply.

"You did no, did you? I sorry," she breathed, and then sneezed and rubbed her nose.

"How did you do at the nationals?" I asked out of pure interest. I was quite shocked that it seemed we had a mutual interest, despite Kat saying she did not exercise.

"Did you no see me running the marathon in the Beijing Olympics last summer?" she grinned. I shook my head, and she laughed. "Is because I was never quite took it seriously enough to make the grade at nationals."

"Still bloody good though."

"Anyway," she continued, "My point is used to be healthy runner. Five times school running to five time cigarette before work each morning." She sighed. "I only start because I try to make friend with that Marajina and her cronies. Silly girl get myself hooked. No could get myself to stop and it been four years. Smoking is first thing I do in morning and last thing at night. It was just few time a day. Now I lost count, but more than twenty a day sometimes. It rules my fucking life. Plus, I gave up running too because of work."

"You're not the heaviest smoker I've met," I told her. "My boss smokes forty a day – more smoking than working."

"And no want to get that bad," she sniffed. "Is why I want to stop now. In that dream I feel so much better when I no smoke. I was running and fit and healthy, but I no know if I really have willpower to quit." She looked at the time on my watch. "No cigarette in three hours. Only one in eight hours," she breathed. "Fuck it I can do this. Thank you for your consideration, but I am done with smoking." She smiled and then ripped up the cigarette. She pulled the pack of tobacco out of her coat, ripped it open, and tipped it out on the hay.

"Was that wise?" I asked.

"I no know" she said. "It was very considerate of you, but I need stop. When I thought I could no smoke, I was okay with it. But when it was there, I want to. Now is I no can have, I am being fine."

I told her it was a very hard and brave thing to do.

"In dream, I say I have no cigarette since in your car. I already smoked in your car so that was my last one. We get gum and patches at airport. I will do it." She coughed heavily.

"That's a good logic, and attitude," I agreed.

"For now," she smiled. "I think they call it cold turkey."

"Don't talk about cold turkey," I laughed, rubbing her goose pimpled arms. "You're making me hungry."

"No cold turkey. I'm vegetarian," she laughed.

"I remembered you were in the dream," I said. "Have you always been?"

"No-oo-oo," she grinned again as if it was obvious. "Only since I come to England. In Czech Republic I had to eat what I was given or starve. I no mind other people eat meat, but is no for me anymore."

"Good on you," I said, still rubbing her up and down as she knelt there shaking.

"I so hungry I eat mountain of veggies," she said, closing her eyes to imagine a plate piled high. "Potato, carrots, cauliflower, broccoli, parsnip, swede, butternut squash, sprouts. Wash down with lemon tea and choccy cake." She licked her lips in a circle, then opened her eyes and gave me a massive grin, which made it look like she was having a sort of food orgasm. She saw me cracking up at her face, and she started to laugh so much I thought she might cry.

As we were settling down to embrace each other for body heat again, I hit my leg on something that hurt like hell and made me shout. Kat bent over, and to my amazement, she picked up her flask of soup.

"All this time you had more soup?" I asked her, feeling

not angry, but confused that she had brought the rest of the soup. We had been freezing to death, and she hadn't said a word about it.

She just stared at it perplexed. "I honestly thought I leaved it in your car, and it was empty." she told me shakily.

"Well don't worry how it got here. Let's just get it open and get you warmed up."

Minutes later, we were sipping Kat's amazing broccoli and Stilton soup. It warmed through both of us like warm nectar.

I suddenly realised what was wrong about this living version of Kat. As she licked soup from her lips, I saw there were blood stains on the side of her mouth. Her lip was blue, and there was a tooth missing from her top row. "Kat sweetheart," I asked firmly, "who on earth has punched you tonight?"

She said nothing and cuddled up to me again. "Who hit you?" I repeated.

Kat drew a huge breath and sneezed again. Then she took a deep sniff. "Taxi driver," she sighed. "I no want to talk about it, but he come off worse."

"Did he try to rape you?" I asked, suddenly grasping the seriousness of what she had just said. "Why didn't you tell me earlier?"

"*I said I no want talk about it*," she said firmly, but her face softened. "I know you ask because you care about me. He no rape me, but he did try force me to give him blow job, which still sexual assault."

"What the fuck?" I said, feeling the anger coursing through me. I wanted to hunt the guy for what he'd done to my friend, or any woman for that matter.

"He didn't get one from me," she said, almost with a laugh.

"What is funny about that?" I asked, a little shocked at her attitude.

"He's probably in hospital having surgery on his penis after what I did."

"What did you do?" I asked, purely out of shock of what she was telling me.

"He pulls car off road, and he says give to me blow job or get out."

"Bastard" I cringed.

"I pretend I'm going to do it." She gave me a twisted smile. "Then I bit off is tiny willy, spat it at him. As he was screaming, I stole my money back from him." She went on to explain that in her hurry to grab her rucksack and get away she had knocked out her own tooth on the door of the taxi. The driver had driven off—presumably to go to the hospital as Kat had said his private parts were hanging off by a thread —leaving Kat in the snow.

"I wonder how he explained it to the nurses" I said almost smiling, even though I shouldn't...

"You think that's bad," Kat smiled, adding, "Do you want be fly on wall when he has to explain to his wife where what happened his cock."

"You should go to the police" I told her firmly.

"I will call them if and when we get to the airport," she nodded. She told me she would not continue if it prevented her from going on holiday and that she was sure she had stopped him from ever trying it on with another poor woman.

I could have thought a lot of things at that point, but the overriding thought was that I should never do anything to piss her off. I told her that and she laughed and told me I had nothing to fear as long as I behaved myself.

"You're a brave lady," I said quietly, rubbing her skinny ice-cold arms.

"I've had worse stuff happen to me," she said glumly.

"You want to tell me about it?" I asked gently.

"No know," she sighed. "I tell you over a few drinks when I get home."

"Okay," I nodded.

"I just want to snuggle my friend and get more sleep maybe dream about this wedding we going to have."

"Are you wishing like me that these dreams were real?" I asked softly.

"Maybe they are real," she said quietly, nodding. "What if this is the dream?"

"I'd love that future to be true," I said, as we lay down together.

"No quite that exact future though," she said with a little laugh.

"What would you change about it?" I asked, as we wrapped our legs around each other for warmth.

"I no think I could wait six weeks to make love this time," she smiled.

"Maybe not." I told her, returning the smile.

"Like you say," she breathed heavily, "I not the girl in the dream, but in two weeks I might well be her." With that she kissed my cheek again. To my surprise, I found myself kissing her back...   on the cheek, of course.

"I wasn't going to call you," she said suddenly.

"What do you mean?" I asked gently.

"Tonight, after you drop me off, I would let you stay in my room. I would take your phone number, but I no call you" she said, a little sadly.

"It was just small talk then?" I said, looking away and thinking she had meant the normal *I'll call but I won't really.* "That's typical of what women do," I said bitterly, "once they've got what they want. Then you never hear from them again."

Kat, however, looked rather upset at that statement. She squeezed me and grabbed my shoulder. "No-oo-oo," she said, pulling a sad face, "Please, no think I that sort. I would want to call. I would sit by phone try to get courage. I cry with frustration, but I'd be too scared to call in case you no want me. I get freezing toes."

"Do you mean cold feet?" I asked.

"I might mean that," she smiled, and nodded. "I no think I good enough for you."

"Kat," I told her firmly, "I realised within a few minutes of meeting you that you were one of the nicest people I've met in a long time. I would have cried if you didn't call me."

I saw her smile in the dim light. Suddenly, she sat up and took something from her coat pocket. She put it in my wet trainer, sneezed again, gave her nose another wipe, and then lay back down with me.

"What was that all about?" I asked.

"Well there's no way I chicken out of calling now. I

give you only key to my home."

Seriously? Giving me the key to her home as a guarantee that she would make herself call was a sure-fire sign that she was desperate to stay in contact.

When I asked what would happen if she was unable to get a new phone, she just told me the date and time of her return and asked me to pick her up if I wasn't working.

"I write it down. If you no there, I assume you have work and come find you," she said and smiled. "Jenny is supposed to pick me and Ela up in her dad's car, but this is no confirmed. Also, her baby is due soon, so she may not be around. Jenny is used to come to mine all the time when were both single." she reminisced. "She still comes over to get drunk on Tuesday night. Is just me drinking the vodka since she gets pregnant, and now she going to be single mum, we are best buddies again."

"Look at you getting drunk on a Tuesday night. And I thought you were boring," I laughed. I knew Kat got a little drunk on Tuesdays, because in her job Wednesday and Thursday was her weekend.

"Maybe no when I'm tipsy, but only on days off work," she said, and grinned. "You can help me finish bottle so no give myself liver damage."

"Do you ever go out to the pub?" I asked.

She shook her head. "I prefer stay home. I went on my own to pub few times before meet Jenny and again since I see less of her. I never felt so alone in room full of people."

"I know how you feel," I empathised. Having lost touch with most of my friends, I told her about the times I'd tried to socialise by going out to bars. I found them a terribly lonely place, when you saw other people in groups with long-term friends, while I felt invisible and nobody else was as lonely as me.

Kat had been nodding as I spoke. "That's no as bad as me," she said ruefully. "I told you in dream, Jenny and I went a club in Norwich. We spend loads of money on taxi and entry and I got groped twice. We stay one drink, and hate it so much we come home."

"That's horrible. I hate clubs," I groaned. "I'd take a night at the local pub or a night in over that any day, if I had someone with me."

"Well if these dreams are right," she smiled, "we going to have each other and maybe Ela and Jenny."

"I'd like that," I told her.

"No more going alone," she grinned. "In 2007, I try to watch England football at pub on my own while Jenny was with her boyfriend. I get dolled up in makeup and put on my nice dress, which I made myself. I hoped England win and I was going to make some friends."

She told me almost tearfully how her handmade dress had been ruined by a drunken idiot who threw his wife's glass of wine when the opposition scored.

"He thought because I am foreigner that I was support other team."

I felt empathy for her. It must have been so horrible trying so hard to make friends in a foreign country. Then for your night to end early with something created lovingly being destroyed... I felt heartbroken for her. I imagined her walking home alone, dejected, head down, and crying. Maybe she had makeup running, and she was probably puffing on one of her cigarettes to calm herself. I wished I could have been there to put an arm around her and tell her everything would be okay. I realised we'd been doing that for each other all night, holding each other and making promises of a better future.

"You poor lady," I said soothingly, still rubbing her, though her shivering had stopped a little. "It's horrible that this world can do things to make people feel so alone."

"There are plenty worse things it does," she sniffed, "like child starve in Africa while rich fat politicians let them. Anyway, I no feel alone now," she whispered.

"Neither do I," I smiled.

"I am glad all this shit happened tonight, because it means I meet you," she said sleepily. "Apart from falling in fucking water and I still so cold I probably going to die." She laughed. "But then where we be if we had no?"

"Well" I said, "if things had gone to plan, you'd be in a warm hotel room with a full tummy, sleeping peacefully."

"Or," she said, "I be sat there with my stress scarf and crying because shit scared of aeroplane crash. I come here on boat, so is my first time on plane and I terrified."

"That's understandable," I soothed, remembering the first time I went on a plane. I thought I was going to die from fright. "Your stress scarf?" I asked. "Is that what you hold in your hand in the dreams?"

"It comfort thing," she nodded. "Like stress ball when at work to try and calm my temper. So, when I want to rip someone head, off I do this." She leaned back a little to show me how she took her handkerchief in both hands and pretended to pull it from either side.

"You know the other reason I use it?" she smiled.

"Because they add to your cute look?" I heard myself say, with disbelief that I'd just summoned up the courage to tell a girl she was cute. However, this was Kat I was talking to. Of course, I thought she was my fiancée whose home I lived in. The girl who I adored with all my heart. However, she wasn't that at all. She was just someone I met that night, someone I barely knew.

Or maybe she wasn't. Maybe this here was the dream, and we really had been together for some time. This was us looking backwards from the future, not forward from the present. I wasn't sure what the hell was going on anymore, but the one and only thing that linked both time zones was the lovely Katarzyna.

"Oi," she said in my ear. "I no am cute." Then she smiled. "I use stress scarf as comforter, because although I pretend I big grown woman, I am twenty-one-year-old toddler."

"I leave in your car though," she sighed. "Poor baby Kat misses her comfort scarf," she laughed with a little embarrassed grin. "Poor baby. Waaaaa."

"You're pretty funny Kat," I told her.

"I know," she said, her eyes wide as if it was obvious. "And no always in good way. More often stupid baby way."

We looked at each other and laughed. "We must be getting so cold and delirious if my jokes are getting funny," she laughed.

"Maybe we should live in a freezer," I teased. "Then my jokes would be funny too." Kat burst out laughing "What's so funny?" I asked.

"Because I do live in freezer," she giggled. "Heating broken in flat. Is freezing. That why I catch cold. Is why I been coughing and blow my nose all week." She laughed hysterically. We looked at each other and laughed.

"My landlord and lady is fix it while I'm away though," she sniffed and grinned. "This morning is so cold I have to boil water for tea in saucepan because kettle froze in the night."

"How are you feeling now?" I asked softly.

She coughed and sneezed before answering, "Still fucking cold and ill, even dough we have soup." She coughed again. "But I don't think I going to die with you fight my corner. I want you no die either."

"We make a good team," I said, as she turned her face upwards to blow her nose again. When she finished, she raised her hand in the air.

"Teamwork!" she said, and we high-fived each other.

"Now," I said, "Let's go to sleep and see if we can dream ourselves up a nice wedding."

Chapter 13

My 21st birthday party

We had a great Christmas that year. Kat, Ela, and I had been invited to stay the two weeks that Kat's job was shut down for Christmas, with their parents in the Czech Republic. In fairness, we could have scraped the money together. However, Ela and I couldn't get the time off work.

Kat could have gone, and I told her she could go without me. She didn't want to leave either me or Ela, saying, "We are go as three or no at all." I was glad she said that, because although I would never have stopped her going, I would have missed her like hell.

I didn't think either of the ladies was that bothered that the trip didn't happen. We were already saving money for our honeymoon. The three of us all got along so well, the banter was electric. Anyone who didn't know Kat and Ela as I did might have thought they actually hated each other, but their insults of each other were all for fun.

The day after we got engaged, Kat started her two-week Christmas break. She was in the toilet when Ela passed me on her way out to work. I said, "Have a good day at work El."

"I won't," she replied. Then she spoke up, so Kat could hear her, and said laughing, "Tell my smelly ugly sister to enjoy her two weeks of being a fat lazy bitch."

"Fuck you, honey. Have a good day wiping old people's shitty bottoms," Kat called back.

"I will, enjoy sitting on yours while it gets fat," Ela smiled.

"Is no as fat and spotty as yours, cow bag," Kat replied.

"Good to see the sisterly love flowing," I laughed.

"We wouldn't take the piss if we didn't love each other," Ela said and smiled.

"I love you pig face," Kat called to her as she got to the door.

"Love you too you gorgeous spotty, smelly, fartface cow bitch," Ela grinned.

Although I didn't get any extra time off from work over Christmas, including the day itself, it still felt like I had two weeks off because I got to spend lots of quality time with Kat. We'd have a lie in until 5:00 am on the few days I was working early and until about 9:30 pm on late shifts. We usually got up at 4:00 am when Kat was at work.

When we weren't chilling in bed, we were in the cinema or in the swimming pool—the local fun pool and not the crap one where I worked. Instead of going to the gym before work like I usually did, Kat and I enjoyed jogging together every afternoon on the beach. With all the gym workouts she'd been doing and the road races we had both run that year, she had made the transition from a heavy smoker back to a very talented athlete in a short time.

Sometimes Ela or Jenny and her daughter, Amy, joined in what we were doing, and sometimes all of them.

Several times, my sister brought my niece, Jemima, round, and Kat would love to babysit while Jeanette went out on a date with her new man.

Jenny, her dad, and Amy joined us for Christmas Day. Ela and I both had to work a few hours in the morning. Kat and Jenny made an amazing dinner vegetarian style with cake, Christmas pudding, mince pies, and trifle.

Ela called Kat from work to ask a favour, which I heard on speakerphone as I arrived. She was asking if it would be possible for a relative of one of the old people in her care, whom she had become friends with, to have dinner with us, because she was a long way from home at Christmas. "I no can set your friend a place at the table," Kat said firmly.

Ela sounded a little disappointed because she couldn't see Kat's grin, but Kat continued, "We no have a bloody table. Tell her she has to sit on the floor with the rest of us. We have way too much food anyway."

I never did see why we had invited everyone to our flat. Jenny and her dad had a house with a table. Going there made
more sense than sitting on the floor with food.

Ela's new friend was a lovely youngish woman called Katie who had been visiting her grandmother in the home Ela worked in. Katie lived alone in Colchester. She was a very lovely young lady, and she seemed to enjoy our company as much as we enjoyed hers. She even kindly offered to pay for her food. Kat and I, of course, refused to take her money, but thanked her for her company.

We all ate so much that even Kat, Ela and Katie, who were all very slim ladies, looked slightly pregnant after dinner. So did I. We chipped in with washing up, and then sat watching all the Christmas TV shows. We put the Freeview music channel on, and all sang along with the Christmas songs. Kat played her guitar beautifully in time with the TV, despite being tipsy. Everyone stayed over in the end. Jenny and her dad slept on the chairs, while Katie slept on Ela's bedroom floor.

Earlier in the year, Kat had a rather upsetting appointment with her neurologist. There she was told that her epilepsy was still not stable enough for him to give her clearance to apply for a driver's license. Kat had gotten her hopes up, but she appeared to take the judgement on the chin. However, the tear stains on her face when she came out of the hospital toilet gave away her true feelings.

This hadn't been helped by Ela who had just bought herself a cheap second-hand scooter to get about town. The scooter would have been something Kat would love.

It was for this reason that my Christmas present to Kat was a second-hand racing bike with a detachable motor fitted. It was meant to help soften the blow of having her driving hopes dashed.
A motorised pushbike was the closest she would get to her dream of riding a scooter or driving for the time being.

"I am love it, but am never learned to ride because after seizure my left hand is no can grip the brakes." She sobbed when I gave it to her. That was until I showed her that I'd adapted the bike so that both brakes were in her right hand. Then she cried, because she said it was nicest thing anyone had ever done.

Teaching her was hard work, because even as a child she had never learned, and teaching her was hard work, but a lot of fun. There were crashes and cut knees, but unlike a child Kat did not cry when she hurt herself. She bounced back up even if she was bleeding and got back on.

From then on, she enjoyed zooming about town on her speedy racer, and we went for lots of long romantic rides together in the countryside. The motor rarely got used.

I was loving life with Kat and whoever we were with, wherever we were, and whatever we were doing. Whether it was driving in the car, food shopping, working out, riding our bikes relaxing on the beach, or helping Kat with her creative hobbies, we were always laughing and poking fun at each other. We were so in love that I barely remembered my life before this wonderful lady came into it.

The one thing in my life that scared me was the fact that I thought I wasn't good enough for Kat. She wasn't just a dumb damsel in distress who fell in love with the first man who showed kindness. She wasn't just some former factory worker turned caravan cleaner.

She was a very intelligent lady who had only been stuck where she was because she never had the opportunities as a youngster that other children had. She was a talented girl and sharp as a pin. If she'd had the chance to go to university, she could have been a doctor or a lawyer, but I thought with a little more self-belief, she would have made an awesome teacher or fashion designer.

She was fluent in Hungarian, Polish, French, German, English, and of course her native Czech. She read books in each of these languages to keep them in her mind. She was easily capable of teaching all of them. She loved her guitar and her flute, but there wasn't a musical instrument that she couldn't get a tune out of.

She was always looking to add new ones to her collections. She also loved to draw, and her talent for making clothes was nothing short of exquisite. Things that Kat couldn't do better than me were on a very short list, and that only included driving because her epilepsy stopped her.

Kat was an excellent teacher. On our days off, we went travelling on trains on our mini breaks. When we had spare time together, we'd cuddle up to each other, and she would teach me languages. At home, she would give me guitar lessons or combine music and language.

I wracked my brains to think of something that Kat didn't know that I could teach her, to give her something back for her effort.

I was just a lowly gym instructor of low to average intelligence. There was nothing I could teach that didn't involve sports. Not that Kat wasn't into sports. I already said she was a good runner. In fact, she regularly kicked my arse at tennis on the Nintendo Wii, and she pushed me all the way with our running and cycling workouts, despite her often being unwell and having a blocked nose. In fact, I felt inferior to Kat in every way and was terrified that some powerful intellectual with a good job would one day sweep her off her feet and take her away from me.

It was the last Friday in March and the day before my twenty-first birthday. We'd planned to go to Alton Towers for the weekend along with Jenny, Ela, and her lovely friend Katie, who had visited us several times since Christmas.

Kat hadn't been so well. She had started having mild shaking fits in the night. They affected her memory a little. Her arms were left weak, and sometimes she struggled to move her hands for an hour or so afterwards. She told me that the effects were not as bad as the bigger fits, but they left her stiff, aching, and run down.

It was the first time in a long time that Kat and I had both worked early shifts, and we wanted to make the most of our evening together while Ela was at work.

I always loved the days when we got to cook together. We were supposed to take turns, but we never did if we were both home. We always worked together at everything. As we prepared dinner, I talked to Kat about my fears that I wasn't good enough. Kat, being the lovely lady, she was, had made me feel so much better about things once I told her how I felt.

"Rob," she moaned, pulling a sad but cute smile. She threw her arms around me. "Why you say this? You know we are love always. Just because you no learn as much as me yet, it no mean you no as intelligent." She paused for a moment, but then continued. "You know, you just need help your confidence and that my job. You know who gives me new found self-confidence to express myself?"

"Ela?" I replied.

Kat had picked up a teatowel and she used it to whip me playfully in the face as punishment for my incorrect answer. "My broccoli, you daft sweetie," she said, placing the tea cloth on the drying rack. She then stood on tiptoes and kissed me. "And," she added, "You no listen to your boss Katherine either. Only two things that plastic, backstabbing cow bitch do better than us is wear makeup and get paid to screw with lives of her staff."

Kat was rarely nasty about anyone, but as you might well have realised already, deputy hotel manager Katherine was top of her worst enemy list.

I could never forget the time Katherine had come into the gym accusing me of arriving ten minutes late, when if she'd looked at the rota she would have seen that I had actually arrived nearly two hours early to work out. Katherine had not been able to understand why I couldn't keep a straight face as she was telling off in her overly sweetened voice. The reason was that Kat and Jenny were working out on the bikes behind her, and both were pulling face and sticking their middle fingers up at her.

"Anyway" she continued, "Do you no think that I worry that with you being so sexy and working in the gym that some hot blonde with an athletic body will steal your heart."

"One already did" I teased.

"What? Where is she? I'll kill her?" Kat replied with laughter all over her face, knowing I was winding her up. "She's in the bathroom mirror." I smiled.

We finished preparing dinner, neither of us was actually hungry, so we put it in the oven ready to heat up later. Unfortunately, we were both feeling a bit under the weather and run down. Once we'd stripped our uniforms off and put them in the washer for next week, we both took a couple of paracetamol and ibuprofen and cuddled up naked under our duvet on the armchair. We drank tea as we watched TV.

"Paracetamol and ibuprofen fix everything," Kat

smiled sleepily and a little sarcastically.

"Remind me of that in sixty years when I'm on my death bed," I laughed.

"No-oo-oo," she moaned, "I will be dead then."

"How do you know that?" I asked, as I rubbed a hand up and down her back to help her relax.

"Because I am going to die first," she said with a little grin.

"But how do you know?" I asked again. She sat and smiled at me with her open mouth.

"One," she grinned playfully, "because I eighteen months older than you. Two, because is ladies first. Three, because I said so and four..." She paused suddenly and sneezed before continuing. Then she laid her head next to my ear and continued in a sleep whisper, "Rob I love you so much that I can no spend another second of my life with you no in it."

I didn't remember anything more being said. Kat and I lay there gently kissing each other. I rubbed Kat's back and could feel how stiff and tired her muscles were after suffering through her fit. Without saying a word, Kat sat forward on my knees and sipped her tea. I continued to press my hands in circles up and down her spine to try and relieve some of the tension. After a few moments, she turned to me and gave me a lovely grin.

Quietly through her stuffy nose, she said, "Thank you, sweetheart. I love you, and love it when you do massage for me."

"It's my pleasure," I told her quietly in her ear as I did little circles. I was trained in sports massage, but it wasn't part of my job at the hotel.

Without a word, Kat stood up very stiffly and shakily. She walked over to the gas fire to put it on, and then she lay down on the hearth rug where I joined her. I helped her stretch her muscles out. Stretching and massaging was something we often did together to help Kat unwind when she was tired and stressed from work, or suffering from the effects of one of her fits like she had the night before.

We talked about our separate days at work and how we hated our jobs while I helped Kat stretch her legs and core muscles. "You an amazing husband, Rob," Kat told me in a relaxed voice.

"Stop it," I told her. "I just want to help you feel better."

"Exactly," she said, "you no think you good enough for me or anything you can help me with, but you doing it now. Most husband, if their wife no feel well, would stay away and make them go to bed with painkillers, but you just want to help me feel better because you love me, and I love you."

"I'm not your husband until we're married," I responded.

"I know," she smiled, trying to look up at me sideways. "But wedding is just piece of paper, words, rings, and a silly expensive dress. Lovemaking," she continued, "is an amazing, exhilarating recreational activity which I intend to take part in a lot of this weekend. But what we doing now, together..." She twisted her torso so she could face me. "This is what real love all about."

I bent over and kissed her gently. She grinned and

made a little-satisfied noise.

"I take it we won't be buying a wedding dress?" I laughed, knowing that Kat would never spend lots of money on something like a dress.

"No, fuck that," she sniffed as I went back to rubbing her back. "I make my own dress, or failing that wear jeans and t-shirt or tracksuit from Primark."

We both stopped and laughed, knowing that it was exactly the kind of thing Kat would do.

"I love it when it's just you and me," I said, as I pressed my fingers into her spine.

"Nice of Ela to give us some space," she smiled up at me.

"I really like Ela." I told Kat. "She's the best sister-in-law I could have asked for."

Kat nodded. "She is very good sister. I love her to bits."

"We need to afford her the same privacy she gives us when she finally meets someone," I told Kat as I ran my hands up and down her arms.

"No-oo-oo," Kat laughed. "Is my name on tenancy. She gets boyfriend, she can go and live with boyfriend, so we get more alone together time."

She cracked me up. I knew Kat was too protective of Ela ever to throw her out, and we were also very grateful for her third of the rent and bills, because it helped us save money towards our regular mini-holidays.

"Anyway," she smiled, as I rolled her onto her front and started to work on her stiff skinny legs, "I dink Ela have secret boyfriend."

"Is this sister's intuition?" I laughed.

"Nooo," she replied, rolling onto her side and looking up. "Let me tell you story in old lady talk." Kat loved to spend time with old people, and we often visited my grandparents together. She liked to pretend she was an annoying old lady because she knew it made us crack up. I found her anything but old or boring. She was hilarious when she did her old lady impression.

She sat up and blew her nose before clearing her throat. She put on her old lady voice and told me the story of how she had come to her suspicions about Ela. "Yesterday I come from playing bingo with the girls," she had been at work. "You at work still, so I change into woolly jumper and grey slippers, make myself a cup of tea, and put some classical music on. Then I put on reading glasses and settle in the armchair by the fire to read Pride and Prejudice for the Twelfth time. I had just blown my nose. I put feet on a pouffe and lit my reading pipe for a good old smoke, when blow me down with a feather! There was the rudest noise of tomfoolery coming from Ela's bedroom!"

"I call wind-up," I said bluntly, moving on to her other leg as I continued the massage.

"Really? Why you no believe me?" she smirked.

"Well," I said, "I don't believe you'd be smoking a pipe after you've done so well to quit cigarettes. I don't believe Ela was having sex, and you've read Pride and Prejudice more than twelve times. But the tea, the jumper, the slippers, the granny glasses, the armchair, and pouffe are all true."

"I think one point each," she grinned "I was no smoking, my slippers are pink, and I only read Pride and Prejudice..." She paused and counted on her fingers. "Seven times, first time in English. But seriously though, whoever it was they were banging away like..." She paused.

"Like what?" I asked.

"Well," she said sheepishly, "like we do."

"Seriously?" I asked. Kat nodded. "Good for her," I added. Kat laughed and went back to her moaning old lady voice. "I was most affronted by this act of foolishness," she sniffed, pulling an exaggerated offended face. "But then I feel guilty cos I remember," she paused, as her offended face turned into her sneeze face and she picked up her handkerchief and nipped her nose. She gave a couple of high pitched little sneezes and continued as though nothing had happened. "I remembered we do that to her a lot, and she must get pissed off with us."

"Should we stop doing it then?" I laughed.

"No-oo-oo, do more," she grinned, mischievously. "Piss her off more, and she move out and leave us alone."

"Is that what you want?" I asked, rubbing my hands up and down her neck as she lay on her front again.

"No really," she sniffed. "She my favourite sister. I love her, and I know she your friend too. She is really nice girl, and I love having her around."

"So why do you want her out?"

Kat twisted her face upwards and looked at me with serious eyes. "I don't want Ela out," she said and smiled. "I just have dream that maybe one day soon we have our own place, just us."

"That sounds lovely," I told her. I bent down to kiss her bare bum. She squealed as I moved on to her shoulders.

"Plus," she said, "this place is no big enough for bring up children, with Ela living in next room."

"Children?" I asked, wondering why she was mentioning children at this point. Kat and I had both been clear with each other that we wanted to be parents at some point. However, the topic of when had never come up. We both worked so much and treasured our alone time. I thought I better ask. "Sweetheart, is there something you're not telling me?"

At that question, she rolled over, sat up, and took a deep sniff. "I no pregnant," she smiled. "I good girl and take my pills, but I get bit maternal when I see Jenny with her little Amy, and Jemima is so lovely."

"I know the feeling. They're cute little girls," I smiled.

"We no ready for baby though," she said rubbing her nose with her hanky. "This my plan. We get married. We save up two, maybe three years for big holiday or together – America, Australia or somewhere." She paused for another couple of sneezes and took another deep sniff. "Then," she continued, "we come home to Cromer or somewhere near and rent out a little house. You be twenty-four, I be twenty-five or twenty-six. Perfect age to start being mummy and daddy."

"Sounds like a great plan. I'm loving it!" I said, sitting beside her and putting my arms around her. We stared into each other's eyes. Our noses were almost touching, and I was about to kiss her passionately, but she put her hand up and stopped me.

"One moment, stay right there," she said with a little laugh, then pulled a comedy-twisted face and sneezed. "I sorry that was disgusting," she said, going a little red.

"You wouldn't be you if you weren't disgusting at least twice a day," I teased, as she cleaned herself without taking her eyes off me. Then she pulled her pretend angry face and kissed me.

When the massage was done, and the tea was drunk, Kat and I, who were both tired, decided to snuggle up and have a little snooze on the chair together around 4 pm. Around half an hour later, we were cuddled up naked under the covers snoozing away when I was awakened by Kat having a convulsion. I let her finish her fitting and cuddled her until she opened her eyes. It wasn't a severe fit, but was enough to leave her in a lot of pain.

When she came around, I asked her how she felt. Kat told me she was feeling a little exhausted and wanted a cup of tea and another nap to sleep off the second attack. I went to make her a fresh pot of tea, planning to cuddle up in the chair for a bit longer, when there was a knock at the door. We both looked at each other as we weren't expecting anyone, and we were both naked, having put our clothes in the washer.

"It's probably Ela forget her phone or keys again. She had seen me naked a million times," Kat laughed, standing uneasily from the painful attack and walking stiffly to the door as I quickly put a towel around me.

Kat picked up Ela's keys and phone from the mantelpiece above the fire. She then clicked the latch on the door and flung it open, expecting Ela to be on the other side. Paying attention to making tea, I didn't see exactly what happened, but I heard poor Kat screaming at the top of her lungs. I turned around to see her running towards the bedroom where she slammed the door shut.   I opened the door and followed her in.

"What the hell's wrong Kat?" I asked.

She grabbed me and buried her face in my arms as she shook. "Is no Ela at the door," she squealed through hard breaths. Her face was red as a beetroot, and the look on her face was one of major embarrassment. It seemed that any second, she would burst out crying.

"If it's not Ela, then who just saw you naked at the door?" I said, trying not to laugh at Kat's little calamity. She screwed her face up so much that she looked like a shrivelled tomato. Quietly, she said, "You mum and dad, and your Grans and Granddad." She breathed again, looking again like she didn't know whether to laugh or cry. Then she added, "And your Great Nan and your sister, her boyfriend, and Jemima. Oh, and Jenny, her dad, and Amy.

"My God, what are they all doing here?" I asked, panicking. It was weird that they all just turned up.

"I invited them for your birthday. We go out for dinner," she breathed, trying to remain calm. "It was mean to be a surprise, so I no tell you, but..." She paused. "Oh God, today is Friday."

"Yes, it is Friday," I agreed.

She sighed heavily. "Last night's fit must have screwed my brain, because I thought it was still Thursday. I no have even got my dress ready."

She crumpled to the floor by the bed crying. It was only when I bent down and put my arm on her shoulders to comfort her that I realised she wasn't crying from sadness or embarrassment, but with hysterical laughter. I laughed too and shook my head despairingly as she tried to compose herself.

"Deep breaths," I told her trying not to laugh too much myself. We crouched by the bed looking at each other. She took my advice, and after a few seconds seemed to have calmed down.

"You no going to let me forget this, ever are you?" she squealed through her tears.

"You know I won't," I smiled.

"Good, please no let me," she said, her face creasing with laughter, "cos it so funny." Her beautiful blue eyes widened as she struggled to keep her composure again. "Your granddad's false teeth fell out when he saw my boobies."

"I love you, you special, gorgeous lady," I told her, finally bursting out laughing.

Kat kissed my head and said, "I be out in minute. You get your guests drinks. Ten shots of vodka and three or four triple expressos for me," she grinned.

"Would you like a slice of humble pie with that?" I chuckled.

Kat creased up with laughter again. "No," she squeaked, and held up her fingers. "Can I have two or three pieces please?"

"Of course, you can sweetheart." I chuckled as I quickly pulled my clothes on and went out to see our guests. I shook hands, gave hugs and collected drink orders. I felt honoured that Kat had thought to invite my family for my birthday. However, I was more than a little worried that she had forgotten about doing so. Kat told me that forgetting things had been part of her epilepsy before she had been put on her current medication. In her opinion, the levels of it needed to be increased. I let her deal with it, but I worried about her because I loved her so much.

It was a total surprise to me because it wasn't my birthday until Saturday. Kat had apparently booked a day early as we were going away to Alton Towers in the morning.

When I went to switch on the kettle, Kat quietly snuck up behind me and nestled her head up under my arm. She was wearing a beautiful knee-length blue dress that she had made herself over Christmas but not yet worn. She was squeezing her pretty scarf in her left hand.

She'd untied her plait, and combed her long, gorgeous golden hair and tied back her fringe. I have no idea how she did it so quickly with all that hair to brush, but she had gone from beautiful to amazing in a matter of moments without even a scrap of makeup.

"Fuck me," I said out loud.

"Rob, not now," she smiled, "later if I have energy, but I don't think you family want us to make love in front of them."

I couldn't believe she thought I meant it literally. Kat went bright red again realising her misunderstanding. "You look amazing darling," I told her quietly.

"Thank you, honey," she whispered, with a little smile. "I wish I felt it dough." Almost immediately, the poor girl had a big sneeze. She hid herself behind my arm while she wiped her nose. She was trying to make an effort to disguise it, so people didn't realise she was unwell. That was an impossible to do seeing poor Kat had seemed to have a cold ever since I met her. She looked at me sadly and then leaned her head on mine for a second before we shared a kiss.

Having a cold was one thing though and having just suffered a minor seizure was different. "Are you sure you're well enough to go out darling?" I asked, cuddling her into me.

She glanced up and nodded, "I so tired. I be happy to go bed now with cuddles and cocoa, but of course I come," she breathed. "I no think my cold is contagious either, is just cos I run down." She smiled wearily. "Remember what I told you. Ibuprofen, paracetamol and bucket of strong coffee will fix me good as new. Just say sorry for me if I go to sleep when we are out." She laughed and embraced me tightly as I told her how much I loved her. "Time for me apologise," she said quietly as I kissed her forehead. "Wish me luck honey." She giggled nervously as we turned to face my family together arm in arm.

With Jenny, her dad, and Amy added to the family, there were at least eighteen people crammed into the tiny flat. Poor Kat still had a slight fear of large groups of people. There was a stony silence, and we both looked at each other, not sure who should speak. Jenny was sat against the wall and gave Kat a look of empathy. Eventually it was Kat who spoke.

"Hey everyone," she said nervously. "You all saw what

happen just now and if you no see me, I sure you all know what happened. I want to say sorry, everyone."

"It's okay to love," my great nan told her. She was eighty-four, and she and Kat got on very well. "Rob's great granddad and I got up to all sorts when we were your age."

"That was only last week then, Maggie," Kat smiled, hugging my nan.

"Last week sixty-two years ago."

"I bet you no go nude in front door though," Kat said, with a nervous smile as my nan sat down.

"We had eight of us living in one room," she laughed. Kat explained about her mini fit and how she'd forgotten they were coming and thought it was Ela at the door.

"So, everyone, thanks for coming," she added, "and I am going to eat a big fucking slice of humble pie." There was another shocked silence. Kat turned to me with a gob-smacked look of shock on her face and said slowly, turning a shade of red. "I just say fuck in front of your whole family, including grandparents." The whole room was laughing by this point and Kat, despite her embarrassment had a huge smile on her face.

"Twice honey," I added, showing her two fingers.

Kat was slightly pink and gave me an embarrassed smile, which I returned. She mouthed a little, "Sorry," at me laughing, she turned back and took a big sniff as she prepared to apologise some more. "I will be eating humble pie for dinner two days in a row," she added, much to the amusement of most people who gave her a big clap.

Kat finished by telling people she was out of body

spray and didn't usually wear makeup, so she didn't have any to wear to the pub. Then she added that it was okay, because she had an ugly smelly sister to steal from. Kat was unaware that Ela had just stepped out of her bedroom behind her. Ela was wearing the pretty red dress Kat had made her for Christmas and dolled up for a night out. She looked like a million dollars. Next to her was Katie, now a regular visitor. Ela tapped Kat on the shoulder, making her jump, and gave her a fierce look.

"Which sister is that then?" Ela said sternly, and then she broke out into a smile. "Go on, help yourself, big sis," she laughed, giving Kat a friendly slap on the back.

"Sorry," she continued, "I mean to say I borrow from my beautiful sister and pay for it."

"Weren't you meant to be at work?" I asked Ela.

"I swapped shifts," she smiled. "You think Katie and I would miss an excuse for a piss up?"

Kat said something to Ela in Czech. I picked it up as being an apology for calling her ugly and smelly. The two of them hugged each other afterwards.

"I just told her we go to cash and carry and get year's supply of humble pie when we get home next week," she laughed, dabbing the tears that formed in the corners of her eyes with her stress scarf.

Several of my family came and hugged her and told her not to worry about it. The consensus among them was that Kat was brave for admitting she wasn't well. They applauded her for the effort she'd made to get everyone together.

My sister hugged Kat, and then slapped her own boy-friend for saying he enjoyed the show. He spent the rest of the night in the doghouse.

Kat and Ela went off into the bedroom to get her made up while I made her a big strong cup of coffee.

After the shock at the beginning, the night went really well. I was so grateful for what Kat had done even if the poor love had forgotten. Obviously, we couldn't cater for all those people. I think Kat, with her fantastic cooking, might well have tried if we weren't so pushed for space in the tiny flat. Thankfully, she suddenly remembered the room she had booked a hundred people at the pub in the next street. That's right one hundred – there were another eighty or so guests invited, including cousins, my aunts and uncles, colleagues from work –not Katherine—and even the odd school friend I hadn't seen in years. I was amazed and overwhelmed by the effort she and others had gone to for my surprise party.

Kat had hired out a big room. It was decorated with balloons, and a big sign displayed Kat and Ela's sense of humour, "HAPPY 21st BIRTHDAY WOBERT BWOWNLOW." That was how she pronounced my name in her accent.

There was a vast buffet laid on with the usual options –sausage rolls, crisps, and cheese and pineapple pizza. There were also lots of vegetarian options, such as carrot sticks and apple slices. Kat later told me that she had genuinely for-gotten about the party even though she arranged it all with my mum and dad and grandparents.

I had to explain that when Kat had mini seizures, she often lost huge chunks of her memory in the short term. She had suffered a least two of them that day, which accounted for the fact that had made dinner when she should have known we had a buffet.

I'd never seen Kat so sociable as she went around mingling with all the guests with a smile, but it was clear to everyone that she was not well and running on empty. Trying to mingle with different people to make everyone welcome, we passed each other like ships in the night. Sometimes we grabbed a quick cuddle as we spun each other around to go off in opposite directions.

On a couple of occasions, Kat ducked under my jacket to use her handkerchief discreetly, because she didn't want people to realise how unwell she was feeling. There were black bags under her eyes by the time we joined the line for food. She leaned on my shoulder, coughing into her stress scarf as sweat dripped from her brow.

Nobody talked about Kat's little embarrassing moment, not in front of us anyway. The talk consisted of the usual how people couldn't believe that little baby had grown into me and how people couldn't believe I was twenty-one, because it seemed like only yesterday I was born.

It was little things like family get-togethers that you take for granted as a child, but when you reach your twenties, and people are older, you treasure every moment with your family members. You never know when the last time will be that you're all in the same room together.

I felt even worse when I thought of Kat and Ela and the efforts they had put forth to make sure my family was all there for my birthday. Neither of those lovely women got to share these kinds of moments with their family over one thousand miles away, and I felt bad that we never got to go at Christmas. They didn't get to see their parents, grandparents, or their nieces and nephews, all of whom were growing older.

It made me appreciate Kat and Ela even more than ever.
When I asked Kat how she felt about it, she took me to another seat away from the others and sat down on my lap. She was very ill and tired, but she was smiling brightly as she blew her nose and took a big gulp of my beer. She shrugged, saying she knew what choice she was making when she moved to England and that I shouldn't worry myself.

"Thank you for doing all this," I said in her ear.

Her reply moved me to tears. "This is my thank you to you," she smiled, snuggling into me.

"Thank you for what?" I smiled.

"Is for making a lonely, plain, ordinary, shy girl like me feel loved and wanted every day of her life. Also for asking her to become part of such a lovely family. No just you, but you parents, you sister, Jemima, you great-nanna, and all you family are my family and Ela's family too."

The conversation, unfortunately, stopped when Jemima came running up to tell us that the cake was ready to cut. She wanted a cuddle with her aunty and uncle, which she duly received.

It wasn't too late when we got back to the flat. A lot of my family had to travel to Norwich, and my parents had to give lifts. It was an excellent job, because poor Kat was so exhausted after her fit and a long week at work. She needed an arm around her to help her climb the spiral stairs to the flat. Usually on a Friday if I wasn't working, Kat, Jenny, and

I would be up drinking in the lounge until midnight. We'd often be joined by Ela and now her friend Katie, but tonight we had an early start, so we all went straight to bed.

Kat was so tired, in fact she barely had the energy to talk. She didn't even take off her dress. After popping her pills, she just put her arms around me, and whispered, "I love you, Rob," and was asleep in my arms before her head hit the pillow.

Chapter 14

Gifts and revelations

Neither of us dreamed of the haystack that night. Instead, it was like the alarm went almost straight away at 5:30 am, which was a lie-in for us these days.

Kat, Jenny and I borrowed my dad's car to drive the long trip across country to Alton Towers theme park, where we were spending my birthday weekend. With a lot of luggage to take, Ela and her best friend Katie drove separately in Katie's car.

Kat had been very sceptical about the idea of going to a theme park for the weekend. She'd never been to one before and wasn't keen on the idea of rides. However, the trip was partly to celebrate Ela's nineteenth birthday too, and she had her heart set on it.

It was surprising to me that Kat actually overcame her fears and her illness and had whale of a time and ran around the park from ride to ride like a child, while Ela, on the other hand, didn't seem herself. The surprise life and soul of the party turned out to be Katie who was quite the comedienne as we spent the evening in the hotel bar.

We got home late on the Sunday night.

Kat and I were sat opening my birthday cards as we waited for Ela and Katie who were worryingly late, seeing as we left at the same time. There was a huge shock when I opened a card containing several cheques payable not only to myself, but Kat Ela and Jenny. The letter with them explained that my nanna wanted us all to spend the money on our wedding and taking Ela and Jenny on the holiday of a lifetime.

In the card were some very personal letters to myself and Kat from my nanna. Considering that Kat had been very wary of my Gran and her casual racism when they first met, it had surprised me that they had become so close. The lovely old lady gave us £5000 towards the wedding and £2500 each for Kat, Ela, Jenny and myself.

I would have typed the letters out here, but they were very long.

Kat was in tears after reading her letter and immediately started thinking of ways to approach the subject of returning the money to my gran, thinking that she did did not deserve it.

After a few minutes where we both sat that there deep breathing in shock, Kat had begun to cry quietly for a while. This was natural, because I think it hit home to her how loved she was, not just by me, but by my family. Plus, it was a generous amount of money just for being her grandson let alone an almost granddaughter-in-law, and Ela and Jenny too. That was just generosity gone crazy.

Jenny was in the room with us, but had fallen asleep on the sofa before we opened the cards and Kat didn't want to wake her until morning. Ela and Katie must have stopped off for a drink somewhere, because they were an hour behind us, even though we had met up for dinner halfway home. Kat had made the point we never saw Katie's car and that maybe it was old and slow, and she was embarrassed by it, and that was why they were so late.

Standing up and mopping her eyes, she turned, smiled and pointed at the door, then at the bowl full of cat food which she had recently laid out for Charlie, then at Ela's room and back to the door that led to the stairs, then at Jenny sleeping, then she did a very over the top mime of blowing her nose very loudly and grinned trying not to laugh at her silliness. This was one of the random things I loved about being with Kat. We didn't do normal, and I think life would have been a lot less colourful if we always spoke to each other sensibly. However, I got the gist of it – she was stepping outside to blow her nose loudly, so she didn't wake Jenny, and at the same time, she was going to get the cat in and look out for Ela and Katie.

However, once she got to the landing, something caught her eye. Instead of shutting the door, she beckoned me to come out there. As I followed, she put her finger to her lips and put an arm around me. Silently, she pointed at something behind the door as she wiped her nose rather than blowing, to keep the silence.

On the landing, to the left of the door, two people stood kissing rather passionately. It was very dark, but one of them was clearly Ela. The other couldn't be seen clearly, because they wore a hood, but their clothes seemed familiar.

"Told you Ela is have a secret lover," she whispered. "Shall we leave them to it, or tell them we are knowing?"

"She's your sister, so it's your choice," I whispered.

Kat grinned, and we tiptoed towards them. Kat tapped Ela on the shoulder and said, "Hey ladies, it cold out here. Would you like a cup of tea?" Then she turned to me and smiled her cute open-mouthed smile with big eyes. "Ela been kissing Katie," she explained, as though I hadn't just seen it for myself. I was stunned as they shot apart and stared at us side by side. Ela went white as a sheet and Katie as red as a tomato.

Kat and I continued down the stairs and went out to find Charlie. Nothing was mentioned about what had just happened until we came upstairs with Charlie, the cat. Kat stopped outside and grabbed me for a kiss, then whispered in my ear, "Shall we have fun with them?" I nodded and grinned.

Ela and Katie were on opposite sides of the living room looking sheepish. Jenny had woken and just sat there watching the situation sleepily.

For the record, I have never had a problem with anybody's sexuality and was ninety-nine per cent sure that Kat didn't either, but it must have been a shock for her to find out her sister liked kissing ladies. I wasn't sure how she would react. However, the fact that she had mentioned fun suggested she was looking forward to winding them both up.

Kat turned, grinned at me and winked, and then put on a face like thunder and turned to Ela and Katie who were both pale and exchanging nervous glances. "What was going on there?" She asked them, rather sternly looking from one to the other. Ela just stood there looking pale while Katie stared at her feet like a naughty schoolgirl.

"We were erm..." Katie muttered.

"Erm, what?" Kat said, in a harsh tone.

"K-kissing," Katie mumbled.

"Why?" Kat demanded in an authoritarian tone.

At this point, Ela found her voice and stepped in saying something to Kat in Czech.

"Ela say it because you love each other and you no need my permission. Is this true?" Kat said harshly, but turned to me and grinned. Katie nodded sheepishly. "Well I am afraid you do need my permission as I am the only one on the tenancy agreement for this flat and I could throw you both out for being gay," she raged. Looking away from them, she winked at me with a big grin.

"What she said," I added, trying not to laugh as Kat came over to me for a cuddle. Jenny watched on, bemused. Kat then turned to Ela and Katie and said, "Rob and I love each other, and we kiss and cuddle in front of you all the time. This your home too, Ela. whoever you want to kiss in here is up to you, sweetheart, and we have no problem."

"Fine whatever," Ela said moodily. "I'm staying at Katie's tonight." She stormed towards her room, clearly having not understood what Kat was trying to say, or maybe she just hadn't listened.

"El," I said sharply, putting my arm out to stop her, "listen to what your sister just said."

Ela stopped and looked. It was Kat who spoke to her in Czech for several seconds. Ela smiled uneasily. Then Kat went over to Katie. She shook her hand, gave her a big hug, and said something in Czech. Ela continued her uneasy smile while Jenny just sat and watched on, confused.

"Katarzyna says welcome to the family," Ela told us with a little grin.

Kat came trotting back across the room and hugged Ela. Then she came back and stood arm in arm with me.

"Why didn't you tell us?" I asked Ela.

She shrugged and looked at Katie, and said, "Well I kind of did tell you I like girls quite a few times."

She then relayed to us several of the occasions on which she had told us about her sexuality. This included the night I had picked the ladies up at the airport, and the time Kat had tried to set her up with a guy she worked with among other times. I thought we both felt guilty that we had thought she was joking.

It was Katie who smiled and said, "We're st... we're still trying to get our heads around it."

"That's a pretty fair answer," I told her, "but we're happy for you. Very surprised, but very happy."

"Thanks guys," Katie said with a nervous smile. "We thought you might not be too comfortable."

"I am no you mother," Kat said, taking Ela by the arm and leading her back over to Katie who stood by the door. "You my favourite little sister and can kiss whoever you like, as long as it no my fiancé." At that, she gently pushed the pair of them together and strode across the room to me. Then she announced that we were tired and going to bed and would see them in the morning.

~~*~*~*

"I no think Ela's very happy that they got caught," Kat smiled a few minutes later when we snuggled into bed with our cups of cocoa. We were still shocked at that evening's events.

"As long as they're happy together," I replied.

"I really hope they are," she smiled. "Honestly, I love my sis and Katie's a lovely girl. I want her to be happy like I am, no matter who she loves. I am hope it's forever."

"When did you figure it out?" I asked.

"Weekend," she grinned. "After we spoke about it yesterday, I realise Ela is always text to her secret lover, but this weekend she is no texting all the time. So, I think to myself on way home that secret lover may well have been there all the time."

"Good detective work, Sherlock," I smiled.

"I was going tell you," she grinned excitedly, "but then we got shock with money from you Nana and it get lost in my head."

"It's still a shock, though isn't it?" I asked. Kat looked like she was about to agree, but then she gave me a thoughtful look and changed her mind.

"I would agree, but looking back, no really," she breathed sleepily. "Ela is pretty girl, but she never interested in having boyfriend."

I laughed. "I could have said the same about you before that night we spent in the haystack."

"You no could," she said, tapping me gently on the nose with pretend malice on her face. "One, I no pretty, and two, because we no even know. We still no can remember what happened in the haystack."

It had been a year and a half and even wracking both our brains, we couldn't remember what happened that night.

"I wonder if it even matters what happened as long as we're together," I told her sceptically.

"You are right, of course," she said, stretching across me to reach her cocoa. "But I still wonder about these dreams we keep having together and what they are mean."

"You're not the only one," I agreed, as Kat took a sip of her cocoa and then leaned over me to put the cup on the bedside table.

Ever since we had been together, we kept having these odd dreams that we were back in the cold haystack on the first night we met, comforting each other and talking about our real lives as if we had just dreamed it. What's more, as we told each other everything, it became clear that we were both having the same dreams.

"The question," Kat would tell me, "is are we here in spring of 2010 dreaming of that night in winter of 2008? Or are we on the winter night in 2008 dreaming of a possible future 2010?"

"Which one would you prefer?" I asked honestly.

"Well, I have to give that some tough consideration," she teased making a confused expression. "Horrible freezing haystack with a nasty cold and empty tummy, or a nice warm snuggly bed full of love."

"You've still got a cold though," I teased, knowing that even Kat liked to poke fun at her seemingly never-ending cold.

"No, I told you, Rob. I no have a cold. I just like to sneeze a lot to show off my home-made handkerchiefs," she smiled, and then ironically blew her nose heavily.

This was Kat's way of making light of her illness. She always likes to look on the bright side and always had a big grin on her face these days.

"Anyway," she grinned, "let's finish the weekend with some naughty fun of our own." She grabbed her guitar from the side of the bed and gently used it to nudge the cat off before drifting into her own version of Bryan Adam's Summer of '69. At the end of the first verse, she disappeared face down under the cover and slid her legs around my neck.

Chapter 15

Holidays

I remembered dreaming about the haystack again that night, going back to that time where we were cold and taking small sips of broccoli and Stilton soup to keep warm. I kept thinking and wondering exactly how the soup got there when Kat was sure the flask had been left in the car. It always seemed to be full, no matter how much we drank as we talked about our trip to Alton Towers and finding Ela and Katie kissing.

A few more months after that night, Kat's health had settled again. She had been to the doctor the next day, and was found to have a bit of a chest infection. It was nothing serious, but enough to prevent her medication working fully. Her mini fits calmed down once she got onto antibiotics. However, her never-ending cold remained.

As well as that, people outside of our relationship still found Kat's English very hard to understand. I, however, was now so used to her heavy accent and muddling of words that I no longer noticed them. Kat on the other hand often got frustrated that in her opinion her English barely improved despite living in England for nearly seven years.

We spoke to my Nan at length about her wishes for the money, and she had remarked that Kat was a girl after her own heart in not wanting to accept help or spend too much on the wedding. Kat and I booked a cheap wedding at the registry office for the next spring and put the rest of the money away in savings. We intended that she and I would both use it for online university classes that we planned to start in the autumn.

As for the money that was given to Kat, Ela, Jenny, and myself for holidays, Ela thought we were winding her up. Jenny was so grateful, and she sobbed her eyes out so much, Kat had to lend her a hanky. Both came with Kat and I to my Nan's to personally thank her for her generosity.

What resulted undoubtedly hadn't been the outcome I was expecting. In fact, I was surprised that Kat and Ela got on with my Nan at all. The reason for this was because my Nanna had a reputation for having a few negative opinions when it came to people from other countries coming to find work in the UK.

"Bloody foreigners," she would tell her customers at work. She was eighty-five years old and ran a small corner shop on Aylsham road in Norwich. "Coming over here, taking jobs off hardworking English people and robbing them of their rights to work till they die."

Even before I met Kat and Ela, I would tell her, "You mean those people who travel away from home to find work, because even the worst jobs in this country are better then what they get at home? And those that come to do jobs that English people don't want or are too lazy to do?"

"Yep, them's the ones," she'd say.

Back when Kat and I had first got together, it had taken me a while to decide when it was time for her to meet my Nan. I loved them both and was a little afraid that there might be some conflict between them.

My way of dealing with it was not to tell her that Kat was from abroad until they met. When I talked about Kat to my Nan and gave her a glowing reference, I assumed my Nan had thought her name was short for Katherine.

However, Kat had an excellent and mature attitude towards the whole situation. "It no your Nana's fault that she thinks these things. She listens to hearsay and is ill-informed. I guess set in her ways," Kat had told me on the way to meet her for the first time. "I will no hold it against her, because in some cases she is right, but no about Ela and me. I will just show her who I am and that I love you and hope that is enough. And if is no enough, she can go fuck herself."

After all that, they really did get on very well. In fact, my Nan had gone on to change her mind completely. Now she told people, "Poor foreigners, coming over here, working their backsides off, far from home, for little pay in rubbish jobs."

It turned out that Kat and my Nan had a lot in common. They were both one of five, both second eldest, and both had three sisters and one brother.

It wasn't just that though, it was work ethics. My Nan still worked way into her eighties running her various rental properties. She also could often be found behind the till of the paper shop she owned on Aylsham Road.

She saw Kat as someone with the same work ethic. Nan worked in factories as a teenager during the war, as Kat had done before she moved on to cleaning caravans. Kat told us in her old factory job she had often had to work seven-day weeks in the run-up to Christmas and sometimes had to do overtime.

However, on the day when I was working, and she wasn't, Kat would often go to the city for the afternoon with Jenny and her little daughter Amy. Sometimes Ela would come as well. When they did this, Kat would often make the time to go and visit my Nanna while they were there.

This was not because she wanted anything from Nan. Kat was just being her lovely self and wanted to make sure Nan was okay. They enjoyed having a cup of tea and a good natter. It was on these occasions that they had got together arranged my twenty-first birthday party and talked wedding arrangements and our holiday.

The short of it was that Nan had given us the money for the holiday so that we didn't have to save up for as long. She did this because she was a genuine kind lady, who loved her family and wanted us to have fun while she was still here to see it.

The following September, a year or two earlier than planned, Kat and I, along with Jenny, Ela, and Katie, had booked just over two weeks off of work and taken a once in a lifetime trip to the USA.

Katie hadn't been given a cheque. The main reason was that my Nanna hadn't met her before the night of the party. However, we had all offered to chip in for her ticket, because we all really liked her, and it was not fair for Ela to leave her girlfriend at home while we all had fun.

Katie, however, was a mystery. She just smiled and waved away our offer, telling us to enjoy our own money. She said she was more than rich enough to pay for it and didn't want to steal our amazing gift from my Nanna. It turned out that Katie had a very high-paying job. She and Ela had always been secretive over what job she did. She was away a lot but stayed over two or three nights a week. Ela would often disappear to where Katie was working.

While we were all on holiday together, the idea was to fit in as many places and sights as we could in the two weeks. We decided that there was the possibility of coming back for a more relaxed holiday in another couple of years. We lived out of backpacks, staying in youth hostels and cheap hotels. Often, we shared a room between the five of us to cut the cost. We also slept on buses and trains between places of interest.

We flew overnight on a Friday after work to save us from using a day for travel. The first week was spent on the east coast. We spent three days in New York seeing sights such as the Empire State Building, Times Square, and The Statue of Liberty. We took no end of selfies and group pictures.

After a half day spent in Washington DC to see The White House and The Senate Building, we caught an evening flight across the country to Las Vegas.

After Christmas, when we were first talking about wedding plans, Kat had said she wanted it small and intimate. In a moment of longing, she told me, "I wish we could just piss off to Las Vegas and have our own little ceremony without all the fuss." So that's exactly what we were doing. Because my Nan had given us the money and wanted to see us married, we had booked the registry office for the next spring to keep the family happy. This, however, would be our wedding. Ela would give Kat away, and Jenny would be the bridesmaid. This left Katie as the next best thing to a best man.

What we had planned was very similar to what we had been discussing as far back as that day before my birthday when I'd massaged Kat in front of the fire and she'd said she didn't want a dress or a reception. So, we had booked a few weeks ahead, and for the first time in eighteen months, Kat and I followed tradition and slept in separate rooms.

I was made to stay the night with Jenny. According to Ela and Katie, they had to hold Kat down to the bed to stop her sneaking out. Neither attempt was successful. Kat and I both managed to escape once the others had fallen asleep. We went for a romantic walk along the Las Vegas strip before heading back to bed to pretend we'd been there all the time.

Early on the morning of Thursday the 9th September 2010, we turned up at the cheapest side room of a casino wedding venue in the whole of Las Vegas, if not the world.

When I asked Kat why she was so set on a small, cheap wedding, she said, "It because it about taking vows of love. It no matter how much it costs, or what you wear, or who is there to witness. All that matter is that we mean our promises to each other. So why spend money that could be put to better use?"

We wrote our own vows with themes of love, laughter, and the light-hearted banter shared between us. As planned, I stood at the altar in my old trainers and cargo shorts. Kat wore her favourite pair of cut-off jeans and a lovely purple top which she had made herself. They didn't go together at all, but that was why she wore them. She'd let her beautiful hair down, so it draped almost to her knees. Her long fringe was tied away from her face, on which she did not wear a scrap of makeup. This was done so that I was marrying her with nothing to hide.

As I was the only man involved in the whole operation, we had to break with tradition. Ela gave Kat away. Rather than a slow walk, Kat came trotting down the aisle. We threw our arms around each other and kissed before a word was said. The minister in charge of the service, stood there looking a bit awkward and cleared his throat. We finally stood apart once Ela and Jenny had caught up.

Then she looked at me and flashed her amazing smile. "We need something old," she said. Then she turned to Jenny and laughed, "You're nearly thirty. You'll do." Jenny, who was only twenty-five, just laughed along with her. Even when Katie put her hand up quietly and confessed to being slightly older that Jenny, which was odd, because we thought she was the same age as Ela who was not twenty for another six months, but it turned out she was almost seven years older.

"Something new," she touched her ears to show me that she had some shiny new studs.

"Lovely," I told her.

"Something borrowed," she said, suddenly seeming to realise that she didn't have anything borrowed. She looked around for something to borrow and she reached out to Ela, whose hair was tied in a bun. She pulled out the band and Ela's hair fell down in a twisted mess. Kat quickly hugged her and apologised. Ela smiled back at her, telling her it was okay that one time.

Kat turned to me and as she looked, she screwed up her eyes. I realised, in true style for Kat, she was making a face she made when she sneezed. She reached into her pocket and pulled out what seemed to be one of her hankies and stood with her eyes closed hands to her face, about to sneeze.

All of a sudden, she opened her eyes and smiled. She pulled her hands apart to reveal the pretty patterned, home-made blue handkerchief she had used several times on the night we first met.

"Something blue," she laughed, reaching over and placing it in the pocket of my shorts. As she did, she whispered in my ear, "Got you, one more point to me," and we grinned at each other. "I have washed it several times." She added that she hoped she would not need it during the vows. We both giggled, knowing her that was the sort of thing that would happen.

"Shall we begin?" said the reverend in a deep booming middle American accent. Kat and I both smiled at each other.

He was an old grey-haired minister, dressed in his traditional robes, dog collar, and glasses. Kat turned to look at him, smiled back at me and mouthed, "He looks like Stephen King." Our favourite author.

The reverend began, "We are gathered here today in the presence of God to witness the…" He stopped and looked a little awkward. I realised that Kat had raised her hand.

"Sorry," she said, quickly turning to the reverend, "I just want to ask, are you Stephen King?"

I heard Jenny and Katie burst out laughing behind, while Ela screwed up her eyes and thumped her forehead several times with the palm of her hand. I tried hard to keep a straight face as Kat just stood there smiling kindly at the reverend and his assistant.

"Erm, no ma'am, I'm Reverend Stephan Trumly," he replied.

"Stephan is almost Stephen," she said. Then she laughed, reached forward and touched the reverend on the arm. Smiling, she whispered, "Thank you for marrying us."

"You're welcome, ma'am," he smiled, still looking a little nervous. He cleared his throat. "We are gathered here today in the presence of God to witness the unity between Robert Andrew Brownlow and Katarzyna Zofka Bobal. I believe you two lovely people have written your own vows?"

We both gazed at each other lovingly. Kat gave me that gorgeous smile that I'd come to realise was only for me and nobody else. "Ladies first," I said quietly.

"Go on then, ladyboy," she laughed quietly.

"No, you first," I said.

"No you," she replied. Then we just stared at each other stubbornly for about a minute with the reverend looking bewildered, until Katie, the voice of reason, said, "Why don't you do rock paper scissors?"

We both laughed and nodded. Then we put our hands behind our backs, counted to three, and balled our hands into fists.

"Draw," I smiled.

"No, I win," Kat said shaking her head. "I was playing with the other hand." She took her other hand from behind her back and wrapped it around mine.

"You cheat," I laughed, and just stood there looking at her lovely eyes. I thought I was going to be nervous, but you can't be when you're with the person you wish to spend the rest of your life with. When I looked at Kat, everyone else disappeared from the room. There was just us and I knew I could say anything. I knew our love would not change. Even if I called her a poo face, she would laugh and kiss me.

"Katarzyna," I said putting both my hands on her little waist. "I've never met anyone like you, and hope I never do again."

"Thanks, I think," she grinned. "Because there's only one Katarzyna. It a common name, especially in Polska." She laughed and added, "I shut up now."

"I never knew a person like you existed. In a room full of people, you make me feel like we're the only two there. You're like the Duracell bunny. You're cute and cuddly and you just keep going and going. All you do is for the good of your family and friends. You're also the best cook ever and the maker of the best fruit smoothies the world will ever see. Your cups of tea and sympathy keep the fair-trade tea industry and the supermarket's home-baking aisle in good shape, even if it's Jenny, Ela and Katie who eat the cakes and not you."

At this point, Kat took a sniff and looked down, then back up at me with tears in her eyes.

I continued, "My only fear is that one day you'll realise you're so much more than me, because, lovely lady, I love you more than I ever thought I could love a person. I am in utter disbelief that such a kind, thoughtful, smart, hilarious, beautiful lady would even give me the time of day, let alone stand here and vow to become my wife. I love you Kat, more than I can express in words. If I can spend the rest of eternity with you beyond death doing us part, I will."

I could have left it there, but decided to go on and finish what I wanted to say. "Kat my love," I continued after a deep breath, "on the night when we met, the car spun in the snow and I thought I was dead. When I saw you coming out of the snow in your hooded coat with your hand reaching out to me, I thought you were the grim reaper coming to take me away."

Kat looked up very briefly. She bared her teeth at me and made her hands into a claw shape as she pretended to reach out to me with a death touch. Then she smiled and looked down at the floor.

"My theory," I continued, "is that maybe I did die that night, because ever since I met you, I've been in heaven every day. If it is heaven, I'll happily do eternity with you."

There was a minute where nobody spoke. Kat looked up at me slowly. Her face was dripping with tears. But her eyes were narrow, and her cheeks were pouting. She pointed at Ela who was choking back tears, and Katie was the same. Jenny had just dissolved into tears.

"You naughty boy you made us all cry," she said in her pretend angry voice, "and you make me snot monster."

Kat smiled through her tears. She leaned forward and took the blue handkerchief she'd put in my pocket. "I think Jenny need it," she said, and quickly turned to pass the handkerchief to Jenny. She hugged her best friend tightly, and I heard her say, "We love you Jenny." Then she turned and hugged Ela and then Katie. Finally, she threw her arms around me. She whispered, "That was so lovely darling. I hope I can do as well as you."

"You'll do better as always," I smiled, running my fingers through her beautiful hair while she sobbed into my shoulder.

Kat then stood back and took a deep sniff. She reached into her pocket and took out several of her home-made handkerchiefs. She passed one to Ela and one to Katie. She stood there quickly cleaning herself up and apologised to the reverend, who nodded and smiled.

"Rob, I was lost in many ways. I was no quite on the road to self-destruct, but at crossroad looking the right way. I was in worse place than I ever dared admit to you. I was lost and dying, but from the moment I touched your hand, something deep in my heart told me everything going to be okay." Kat took my hand and put it on her heart, which was beating almost out of her chest. "I was lost, and you help me find myself again. You made me smile like I no done in a long time. Before you, I scream and shout and lash out at people, but now I just want to be a calm and gentle person I wanted to be all along. I thought I never want anyone. I was always to be single woman for the protection of humankind from me, but being with you made me remember how to love. The first time we touch, you make me feel all scared, but given how I was and what happened that night, I no want to say, but could no let you go. It like I mentally ill, and you're the medication that makes me all better. Without you, I go to pieces."

She stepped forward with her handkerchief. I wondered for a second what she was doing. Then I realised that I'd been concentrating so hard on her that I hadn't noticed that I had started to cry silently. She wiped my face, smiling through her own tears as she mouthed, "I love you." Then she stood back and started rocking from heel to toe as she laughed at herself.

"Look at me," she smiled, "I so excited to be your wife I can no contain it. I can no wait to say *I do*, so we can get on with rest of our lives and have a little family with a home and a doggy. If we can live beyond death, you be stuck with me forever, because I never want to spend a second of my existence without you."

We both leaned forward and hugged for a long time until Kat rubbed on my t-shirt and whispered, "Time for some fun."   She stepped back and wiped her nose. As I looked around, I saw Ela and Katie doing the same, but Jenny now looked perfectly composed.

"Who gives this woman to be with this man?" asked the reverend.

"Oh, that would be me," Ela said, stepping forward.

"And does the best... erm, man have the rings?" he asked, looking sceptically at Katie.

"I have," she smiled.

"I believe you have written your own vows," the reverend continued.

"Me first, then you," Kat said, as we each pulled out a piece of paper with the vows we'd written.

"Rob," she said smiling, "Do you promise to keep leaving dirty socks on our bedroom floor, so I can pretend to be angry about picking them up?"

"I do," I said.

"Kat, do you promise to stop doing the washing up when it's my turn?"

Kat screwed up her eyes and pulled her angry face. Nope," she said, pretending to snap, but quickly added, "I'll try as long as you let me dry."

"Rob, do you promise to stop trying to help with ironing? I no want to hurt your feeling, but you no good at it sweetheart. But neither am I," she added quickly.

"I don't," I laughed.

"Kat, do you promise to try harder not to kick me in the balls while we're asleep?" I asked, trying not to laugh.

Ela and Katie burst out laughing and poor Kat just went red. Finally, she laughed and said, "Do you want me to kiss it better?" while pretending she was going to bend down.

"Not here," I smiled, and Ela, Katie, and Jenny hid their faces behind their hands sniggering.

Kat mouthed a little apology, laughed, and said, "Nope, because I love sleepy snuggly cuddles."

"Fair enough," I smiled.

At that moment, Kat turned away and sneezed. When she turned back, she laughed, rubbed her nose, and said, "I knew that would happen."

Then came the moment that we put our hands on each other's waists and stared into each other's eyes. Kat rubbed her nose again.

"Robert Andrew Brownlow. do you promise to love me, honour me, and protect me for rich or for poor, in sickness, in the sunshine and in the rain, and until the earth stops spinning and there is no more sky for stars to shine?"

"I do," I said, trembling as my heart beat almost out of my chest. "Katarzyna Zofka Bobal, do you promise to love me, honour and protect me, for richer or poorer, in sickness and in health, in the sunshine and in the snow in our case, until the earth stops spinning and the stars go out, and our souls are floating on the wind?"

"Nope" she smiled cheekily.

"Can I ask why?" I said, rather taken by this surprising news and guessing there was a joke there somewhere that only Kat new.

"Rob, I want to love you longer than that," she wailed pulling me closer. "But for purpose of this wedding, I do."

"Thank God," I heard Ela say behind me as we took each other's hands, and slid the rings on in perfect harmony. Before the reverend even permitted us, we were kissing.

After many minutes we were walking as a group back down the aisle towards the exit when Katie pointed to the back row of seats and said. 'Look you guys are so sweet you even made a stranger cry." Both of us looked over to where she was pointing and saw that she was right. Over on the back row in the far corner, there was a lady with red hair dabbing tears from her eyes with big spotted hanky. We waved at her, and she smiled. She was clearly somebody who was either left from the previous wedding or waiting for the next couple to come in, but still it was nice to have an audience, and we both felt very touched that woman had cried. However, as we went approached her to say hello, she stood up and left through a side door.

Chapter 16

Kat's Big seizure

We left Vegas the next day. We'd spent a lovely evening, but we didn't get much sleep, as we ran around sightseeing most of the night. While Ela, Katie, and Jenny drank every cocktail they could get their hands on, Kat seemed oddly content to drink ice tea. Although the cocktails looked amazing, it seemed only right that we both kept our heads clear to remember our special day.

With our stuff already packed, we stayed out most of the night. After only a few hours' sleep, it was Kat and I who took great pleasure in waking up Ela, Katie, and Jenny in time to have breakfast, before jumping on the bus to LA.

Kat didn't seem herself that morning. She was on the toilet longer than usual, and she was very quiet at breakfast.

It was one of those cheap *all you can eat* breakfast spreads that casinos sold to get people to come in and gamble their hard cash. There were plates full of sausages, bacon, and hash browns. Thankfully there was huge selection of vegetarian food, and Kat piled her plate with fruit doughnuts, grapefruit, apples, olives, grapes, cheese and a large slice of quiche, as well as her usual bowl of muesli. Katie was also a vegetarian, and she sat with Kat and me at breakfast rather than sit with Ela and Jenny who piled their plates with bacon, sausages, chicken and so on. Although I wasn't a vegetarian, I had made a promise never to eat meat in front of Kat, despite her telling me it was fine outside of our home.

Though she was skinny, Kat always ate quite well at meal times. She mainly ate salad, vegetables, or soup. Not because she was on a diet, but because they were her favourite foods. She rarely ate snacks, and when she did, it was always fruit. I was happy that Kat seemed to have put on a little weight during our holiday. She looked good for it. She remarked that we'd only been married a day and her jeans were a little tight. She told me I should be proud of her, which I was for finally putting some meat on her bones.

"I going to be a big fat wife now," she laughed. "Let myself go now I am married woman."

It surprised me when Kat piled her plate full, took one bite of her quiche, and then put it to the side of her plate saying it tasted odd. She proceeded to do the same with her fruit doughnuts. She picked at her food, eating only grapes and cheese and saying that everything else tasted off. In fact, she went for more grapes and cheese twice.

After a while, she looked at Katie and wrinkled her nose a little. She moved farther away from her. Katie looked a little affronted until Kat told her it wasn't personal, but she could smell cigarettes. Kat, being a former smoker, now couldn't stand the smell. I was surprised that Kat could detect the scent. I couldn't smell anything. Katie was a light and very considerate smoker.

When we got on the Greyhound bus, she put on her neck pillow and her pair of headphones. She gave one ear of the headphones to me, and we listened to a mix of Simon and Garfunkel, with Bob Dylan and some lovely Czech folk music. Kat, however, didn't hear much of the music. Soon after putting on her dark shades, sitting on my lap, and cuddling up very tightly, she whispered, "I loved you," and was asleep before the bus left the station.

Ela and Katie apparently hadn't had much sleep the night before. After about an hour of talking, Jenny also fell sound asleep. It was about then that Kat stirred a little from her deep sleep. She opened her eyes, shuffled her bottom, and retightened her hold on me. She also encouraged me to lean my head on her breasts. Suddenly, I began to feel sleepy myself and just as my eyes were closing, I heard Kat whisper, "I love you."

Suddenly everything had gone cold. I was dreaming about that haystack again. Was it dreaming? Or was it real? I didn't know anymore. The candles were still burning and didn't seem to have burned down at all. Kat turned her head away, and I heard her blow her nose gently. "Are you okay?" I asked.

"Were you California dreaming too?" she asked softly.

"I was," I told her."

"It was most amazing," she smiled. "We are get married Las Vegas. It was perfect – no silly dress, just us and friends."

"It was amazing," I told her, "just how I want it to be too."

"I no know what was wrong me at breakfast," she frowned, "Cheese and grapes? And I was rude to Katie. I do hope I say sorry. I hardly one to lecture on smoking, but vas really stinky."

"I love the fact that you want to apologise to somebody you never met when we don't know if she even exists."

I laughed a little, thinking how strange it was that we'd not yet met someone who we considered to be a great friend. In fact, I'd never even met Ela, who seemed to have been around forever, and Katarzyna, who I loved with all my soul was just a stranger I'd encountered that evening. We were back in that damn haystack again, in the cold, shut off from any-where. We still had to get out, get the car fixed, get some clothes, and get Kat on her flight.

I think Kat could see what I was thinking. "What is the time?" she asked, "You say we need to try to be out of here by 4 am, but I no look forward to putting wet clothes back on."

"Me neither, but I don't want to be naked in the snow."

"Good point," she added.

I looked at my watch. "It's two is," I told her, a little confused. "We have two hours more for California dream-ing."

She smiled. I couldn't settle back down as something was nagging at me. "What is it, Rob?" Kat asked.

"We don't know where these dreams are coming from," I told her bluntly, "and the crazy thing that's getting me is that it was already 2 am last time we woke up. No time has passed."

She coughed. Her expression conveyed utter shock. Kat looked at me wide-eyed and scared, and said shakily, "What the actual fuck is going on?" The look in her eyes was one of absolute terror, and I thought the fear was going to swallow me up. Suddenly, she was pulling at my shoulder. Whatever had caused us to have these dreams had the power to stop time itself, and we were powerless to stop it.

Something still pulled at my shoulder. I turned, full of fear, to see what the hell it was. My mouth fell open.

It was Katie. The scene had changed, and we were suddenly back on the bus. "Wake up sleepyheads," she smiled. "Lunch stop. You guys are going to hate it as much as I do."

Kat stirred sleepily and opened her eyes. She said what I knew to be a Czech swear word quite loudly when she saw the big yellow M out of the window causing Ela to smile.

"I know there was a reason I stole us some fruit at breakfast," she smiled sleepily.

She put her arms out to Katie and apologised in case she offended her with her earlier comments about her smelling of cigarettes.

Katie laughed it off, and said, "It's all right. I needed telling off." She smiled and hugged Kat before adding, "I want to stop, but you have no idea how hard it is. Your sense of smell is something else, though."

"I hardly am one to preach," Kat told her quietly. She gave Katie a little wink and lifted the sleeve of her t-shirt to reveal a nicotine patch stuck to her arm. "No cigarette in nearly two years, but I no can get off of gum and patches."

Katie looked at her, shocked. "You have just spoiled my image of you as Miss Goody Two Shoes," she said with a laugh. "But I'll forgive you because you brought fruit."

Kat, being the thoughtful, resourceful lady, she was, had secretly stuffed food from the breakfast buffet at the casino into a carrier bag. There was only enough for the three of us who were not eating meat, but it didn't matter because Jenny and Ela loved McDonald's.

Kat remained quiet for the rest of the journey. She sat on my lap with her back to the others, looking out of the window. She'd taken out her sketch pad, and sat there quietly drawing her beautiful sketches. She had a natural talent. I was astounded that she was not a professional artist.

At the moment, she was working on an incredible picture of our wedding.

We spent a few days living in a lovely little hostel just off of Hollywood Boulevard. We went on one of those trips to see houses in Beverly Hills where the big celebrities supposedly lived. Kat was back to herself, laughing, joking, and saying that the film stars probably had a good laugh at the people who paid money for these tours. The closest we came to seeing a celebrity in LA was a drunk man in the hostel telling us he was sure he had seen Elvis Presley in a corner shop.

The group of us spent our last night in Los Angeles walking along the beach at Santa Monica. Then, we rode the big wheel several times in the dark. Kat and I got a lovely picture of ourselves with the lights of Hollywood behind us. It was a night that I would remember for the rest of my life.

I was glad that we took those pictures and videos of that night. Neither of us knew it, but the part of our wedding vows that promised fidelity in sickness and in health were about to be tested.

It was around 8:30 the next morning that we were due to leave LA for our last stop in San Francisco before flying home. That night, Kat and I had gone for a little walk along the boulevard on our own, leaving Jenny drinking in a bar called The Cat and Fiddle with some Australians, while Ela and Katie walked off the other way.

Once we got back, we sat up late in the corner of the dining room drinking tea and talking about plans for when we got home. Kat was due to start her course in business studies after Christmas. She wanted to keep working for her own pride and to bolster our joint income. I told her I would support her if she wanted to be a full-time student, because I knew how she was growing tired of her job.

"We could defer it and stay here a few months," I

laughed, showing her a leaflet which depicted a bunch of happy people at work in the sunshine and read, "Work California."

"And leave shit jobs for even shitter ones and lose our home?" she laughed, brushing my suggestion aside. "They no get to spend time having fun when they work low pay factory work." She smiled, pointing at the people in the picture lying on the beach, or playing volleyball, or hiking in the mountains. And I miss my pussycat," she added.

I laughed out loud and she grinned. "I have the best holiday ever, and we come back many times before we old. Maybe bring our children," she smiled. "But I love my husband and our little nest back home."

Even the mention of children told me that it would be a long time before we made it back to LA if we ever did. None of that mattered, because wherever Kat was, that's where I wanted to be. Whether we were living it up in New York or sleeping on a park bench in Ipswich, all I wanted was to be by my wife's side. I'd take that back – Ipswich would be a bit much too handle. I was sure there are better park benches closer to home.

When we got back to the room, Jenny was already asleep. As were Ela and Katie, who were tightly cuddled up in their single bunk, both of them snoring.

"Bless their hearts," Kat smiled. "I had my doubts if Ela was really gay, but they really are as in love as we are."

"I know. They're both lovely girls, and I'm glad they had the courage to come out," I told her, as she pulled a cover over them, so they didn't get cold. Ela stirred slightly, but without waking up, she tightened her grip and kissed Katie.

After murmuring long into the night, Kat expressed a desire to make love even though we were in a bunk bed underneath Jenny. It was a little insensitive, but it was the naughtiness that made it extra fun. Kat fell asleep lying on top of me naked, much like the night we first met, only in a warm bed full of love.

I was dreaming of that cruel, yet magical, night. We'd been wrapped around each other in the dark, drinking soup again. My watch still read 2 am. We had decided that we would make a break for the house soon, in case the time on my watch was wrong. However, Kat had drifted off to sleep in my arms again.

All of a sudden Kat let out a horrifying scream. She started to shake and thrash about. "Fuck! She's having a terrible fit," I thought to myself, but as I awoke, there wasn't enough time to think about the fact that Kat might have forgotten what happened that night because she had had a fit.

I was awoken suddenly by that same blood-curdling scream right in my face, and a hell of a thump as Kat's head smashed into my chest. I was suddenly flashing back to the haystack in which Kat was also having a massive fit. Whichever world was real it didn't matter, because she was fitting in both of them.

I only saw flashes of the haystack, and it was the hostel in California where most of it took place. It took me seconds to realise that she was not just having one of her small, occasional fits. This was a full-blown epileptic seizure, the size of which I'd never known her to have. I was being kicked and hit all over with a tirade of flying knees and elbows. I was headbutted in the face and covered in piss and shit as her bowels lost control.

If you had never experienced seeing someone you loved thrashing about convulsing and screaming, it was an experience you would never want to have. It was good that the five of us had booked a small dormitory, so that there were only our little group and no strangers. When the light flicked on, everyone was awake. Kat and I had fallen from the bed. We were on the floor naked, as we had ripped through our sleeping bag. Kat was thrashing about screaming with her eyes rolling in the back of her head and her face and body splattered with blood.

Since we'd been together, Kat had often had smaller fits where she had shaken for a while. Usually, she'd then gone back to sleep and woken up suffering from memory loss, tiredness, and a stiff back, but nothing like this.

My heart was pounding with fright. I'd never seen her this bad. What if she really hurt herself? What if it killed her? All the first aid training I'd had told me to keep back and let her finish, but I couldn't help wanting to intervene as I pulled myself out from under her thrashing body. Even Katie, who had once been a nurse and must have seen quite a few people have fits, just stood there in shock with tears in her eyes.

I tried to go back to Kat, but I felt a hand on me. It was Ela, and she was yelling at me to stay where I was and putting her arms out to block me. It must have been awful for her seeing her sister in such a state, but Ela was calm.

"Stay back," she said calmly. "Katarzyna used to do this often when we were girls. I know it's horrible, but she will be okay."

Even as she said it, Kat suddenly stopped shaking and lay flat on her face. The four of us quickly rushed to help and put her in the recovery position.

Kat's breathing was slow and laboured. She'd fallen into a deep sleep. While we quickly went about checking Kat for injuries, Jenny went to the hostel reception as quick as she could to get a first aid kit.

Once we'd assured ourselves that Kat hadn't broken any bones, Katie turned to me and pushed down onto the bed saying, "Your turn." I didn't know what she meant until I looked down and saw that I was bleeding from several places where Kat's movements had injured me.

It didn't matter that she'd pissed and shit on me, or that I was bleeding. I only cared about Kat. My whole life was lying there, unresponsive, crumpled on the floor, battered and bleeding. Helping her was all that mattered.

I sat there for an hour cleaning her with a warm wet flannel, while the others kindly helped clean up the mess. After a while, the other ladies went back to bed leaving Kat on the floor, so we didn't cause her any pain from moving her. We slid a spare quilt under her to keep her comfortable, and I lay on the floor holding her hand, so I was there when she came around. I put my arms around Kat, and stayed there all night in case she woke and needed me.

I must have dozed off because when I awoke a few hours later, there was light. Kat had moved closer to me. She was awake, but there was a look of pure terror in her eyes.

"How are you sweetheart?" I asked her gently. She didn't reply. She just looked at me funny. After a while, she shakily spoke in Czech and then looked confused at me. She seemed to be saying something along the lines of, "What the fuck just happened?"

Again, she spoke, but it was in Czech, and I didn't comprehend her native language well enough to understand what she was saying. Also, her voice was slurred. Kat didn't seem to get that, and just looked at me weird for a moment as if thinking, "Why can't you understand?"

By now Ela had woken. She came over to us, knelt, and spoke to Kat gently in Czech. Kat replied weakly and was looking from me to Ela as the pair of them spoke to each other.

After a while, Ela turned and spoke to me softly. She said that Kat's fit had been very bad, and it had not only affected her physically but mentally. "She can't remember how to communicate in English," she told me in a rather shaky voice, "and she asks where is Ela?"

"But you're right here," I told her, now seriously confused.

"The brain does funny things with epilepsy," she said sadly, "like sending her back in time, so she thinks she is fifteen. She remembers her husband, but not how to speak English, and she thinks her favourite sister is a tiny little girl and not a grown woman."

This revelation shook me a little, even though Kat had warned me that this might happen one day. It wasn't only Kat I felt sorry for, but Ela must have been heartbroken with her own sister not even recognising her at all.

Kat's face was beaten black and blue with bruises and a cut down the right side. She gasped in pain as she tried to stand, so I put my arm out to help her.

"Where does it hurt?" I tried to ask her in Czech, but she couldn't understand and looked at me blankly. Ela asked her the same question and Kat answered slowly.

"She says everywhere, but mainly her head and back," Ela said quietly. "She asks if we could help her get clean?"

Ela looked at me funny. "Is there something you two haven't told us?" she asked.

"Not that I know of," I answered.

"Strange," she replied.

"What's strange?" I asked.

"She's not pregnant, is she?"

"Not that she's told me," I said.

"Hmm," she said looking puzzled. "Katarzyna has just asked me if God took her baby again."

"She must be confused," I replied.

"Probably" Ela concluded.

If Kat had been honest with me, she had never been with another man or been pregnant, so it had to be down to confusion from the fit. However, if there had been somebody else before me, it wouldn't matter. The Kat I loved and cherished would have had a very good reason if she was hiding something and fibbing about me being her first love like she was mine.

As I was getting Kat some clean clothes to get into once I'd helped her shower, I discreetly asked Ela, "Not that it will change anything, but did Kat ever get with anyone and get pregnant before she was with me?"

Ela looked at me with a sincere expression on her face. "What she said just now sounded really bad but..." she put both hands on her heart and said firmly, "To my knowledge, Katarzyna never even took as much as a second look at a man before you."

Jenny backed Ela by saying she'd never known Kat to be with anyone before me.

What Kat had said about a baby and God taking it for a second time must have been due to the fit. Ela and I sat with her while Jenny and Katie went to reception to explain the situation and ask permission to put one of the hostels outdoor plastic chairs in the shower for Kat to sit on.

After she was helped into a sitting position on the bed between Ela and I, Kat gave me a little smile. She nodded her head towards a tattoo of a half a heart on my right leg with her name in it. Kat had the other half of the heart on her leg. I lifted her gently onto my lap so that the halves met together. To anyone looking at us it said, "Katarzyna & Robert". Under my name on Kat's leg, it read, "Always together and in love forever."

As we pressed the tattoo together, Kat tried to speak. She looked at me with her eyes full of pain, but she couldn't find the words, so she sat in silence.

Kat couldn't lift her arms at all. She kept sniffing, and it sounded like she was getting uptight with herself, because she detested sniffling. Like teaching a child, I picked up one of her clean hankies and put it to her face and gave her a good wipe over. After that, she turned and gave me a little smile of thanks to tell me that was what she had wanted me to help her with.

When Jenny and Katie returned with a chair, I carried Kat to the shower. She clung to me as well as she could. She had tried to walk herself, but really struggled due to all the pain she was in. She looked like she wanted to speak, but didn't know how, and instead, looked rather sadly at me as if she was fighting herself not to cry.

She held off crying, but never said a word the whole way. She communicated through facial expressions and started to smile a little as she became cleaner.

She obviously remembered the trust she had in me, because she just sat silently as I stripped her down and washed her all over. I even undid her plait and then washed and combed her hair to clean bodily fluids out of it. It was so long that I had to be careful not to let it go down the drain.

After drying her, I helped Kat to stand and put her clothes on. I had just slipped her hooded jacket over her when she tried to say something. I waited patiently to see if she could find the words, but she struggled. In the end, she said what she wanted by touching our wedding rings together and smiling. Then all of a sudden, she slowly put her arms around me and burst into tears.

When we left for San Francisco later that morning, I carried Kat the quarter of a mile to the bus stop and left her with Ela and Katie while Jenny and I went back to the hostel to collect our rucksacks. We popped into a pharmacy and got Kat the strongest painkillers available. Kat spent the whole of the nine-hour journey without speaking. She just slept tightly in my arms, waking every now and then. The most energetic thing she managed was to dab at her nose after a sneeze, before falling straight back to sleep.

Ela said that was normal behaviour for Kat after such a bad fit. Her brain was healing itself like a computer rebooting. However, we were both worried as it should not have happened with the level of medication she was on.

Kat finally got her English back towards the end of the journey. She whispered quietly that she loved me and tried to say sorry for the fuss she'd caused. I wouldn't let her apologise.

Still, things were not quite right with Kat. In all of the languages she tried speaking, her speech was noticeably slow and slurred as though she had suffered a stroke.

It later became apparent that her brain was not the only thing that hadn't recovered. A look in her mouth revealed a horrible gash in her tongue.

Usually, we would have walked from the bus stop to the place where we were staying, but it was four miles, and Kat was in no state to do it. Even though the use of her arms and legs came back in a limited capacity, she was apparently in a lot of pain.

While we were waiting for a taxi to take us to our hostel, Katie stepped away from the group and lit up a cigarette. Kat started feeling in her pockets and in her handbag. She looked a little confused and said, "R-rob, d-did I leave my t-t-tobacco on the bus? I must have dropped it. Can we get some more p-please?"

"I finally got you. I knew you used to smoke before I moved in with you," Ela teased.

Kat just looked blankly at her and replied, "I still am smoke do, do I no?"

"You stopped nearly two years ago, Honeybun," I reminded her gently.

"Really?" she said, and smiled as I nodded. "Okay, but I no can remember that. Are you sure h-ad power of will?" she said pulling a puzzled face.

"You certainly turned your health around," I assured her. "You go to the gym five days a week now."

"Of cour-se I do, silly me," she smiled lightly. "Fit made me forget what a good girl I am these days. Anyway, I very happy I no smoke now. Terrible thing in my condition. Di-d I s-shit and piss on you?" she asked rather sombrely, "when I am was fitting?"

"I wasn't going to mention it," I replied calmly.

"I am so sorry," she told me with tears in her eyes as the taxi turned up.

As the taxi pulled to a stop, a little of the lady I loved showed herself when Kat looked at Ela and asked me who she was. When Ela frowned, Kat grinned the best she could and said, "Only joking." She gave Ela a heartfelt apology for forgetting who she was and cuddled her little sister for the whole journey to the hostel.

Little things like this happened over the next couple of days, but Kat quickly regained her memory. Despite our injuries, we had a lovely last few days of our holiday. Kat stayed very close to me as though she was scared to be apart.

We took a trip on a boat to Alcatraz, and when Kat felt up to it, we walked over the Golden Gate bridge and took selfies. We spent the last night in the San Francisco hills looking down as the sun set over the bay. We took pictures of each other as couples and one of all five friends with the red sun at our backs as it disappeared beyond the horizon. As we descended the steps, we promised ourselves we would all go back there someday soon.

However, just as Kat seemed to be back to herself, Kat and I took a private walk to the hills to look down on the city. Just like before, we returned to find the others asleep, and minutes after falling asleep, Kat had a second massive fit.

The journey home was horrible. Customs almost refused to let Kat trave,l because she was confused after her fit and couldn't answer questions. We had to push her through the airport in a wheelchair we hired. She got very upset when Ela explained that people were asking how she got bruises on her face. The poor lady just wanted to get on the plane and sleep. Despite this she insisted it had been the best holiday ever.

Arriving home late on Sunday night, both of us had to work at 6 am Monday morning. Kat tried to say she was going to work, although she could barely move due to the pain she was in.

I called her work and left a message for her boss with the overnight security guard who answered, explaining the situation and that I was going to call the doctors as soon as they opened. The member of staff I spoke to was lovely and had nothing but good things to say about Kat. He wished us luck at the doctor.

When I called my work to say the same thing, the reaction of Dave the security guard—who knew Kat and wished her well—was to warn us both that Katherine McNallty was on my case. He added that my not going into work, even for an emergency, would only give her more fuel for her fire.

Kat told me to go, because she didn't want me fired. So, I left her in bed with breakfast and a pot of tea. I phoned the doctors from work and made her an appointment for the afternoon.

Katherine caught me using the phone on CCTV and despite the situation, decided to give me a verbal warning because she chose not to believe my explanation. She also made me to stay at work an extra hour with a threat of further disciplinary action. However, we both knew it was because she was an evil cow that she was trying to stop me getting Kat to the doctors.

Kat's appointment was at 3:30 pm. I had planned to drive her there, so she didn't have to walk in pain. However, Katherine's decision to keep me an extra hour meant she had to walk to the surgery herself.

I left work at 3:15. With only fifteen minutes, I ran all the way to the surgery, but Kat had gone in when I got there.

She was in the appointment for a reasonable amount more than the allotted time. When I saw her coming out, she was barely recognisable. She wore a thick pair of track-suit bottoms and a hooded top. She had tied a scarf over the bruises on her face, leaving only her eye and nose open to the air.

When I went to meet her, she gave me a quick hug and kiss. Then she told me she had to do a urine sample and go back to the doctor, but she'd be out soon. She also asked me not to apologise for her having to walk, because she knew what Katherine had done.

Five minutes later, Kat reappeared in the waiting room. What was visible of her face was white as a sheet. "Let's go home," she said quietly, taking my arm as we walked out.

"What did the doctor say?" I asked gently.

"I'm so hungry. Can we go out for dinner?" she piped up suddenly.

"That's a strange answer," I laughed, "but of course we can."

"I tell you what doctor said when we get home," she smiled, "but right now, we go pub for carvery."

We walked slowly arm in arm down the road to a local pub, which served all day carvery. It was Kat's decision to go there, which I thought was a little strange considering she was vegetarian. Kat, despite being an amazing cook, was never a big eater, hence her stick woman figure. However, she filled her plate with sprouts, carrots, cauliflower, peas, and parsnips, washed it down with a pint of orange juice, and went back for seconds and thirds.

"Kat, are you okay, sweetheart?" I asked, as she came back with her third helping of veg.

She nodded at me with wide eyes and hastily finished her mouthful. "I'm so hungry," she told me. Then she excitedly asked, "Can I have chocolate cake and a pot of tea?"

"You know you don't have to ask," I told her before saying, "If I didn't know better I might think you'd been smoking wacky backy and got the munchies." It was all in jest because I knew she never would.

"As if," she giggled. "After how hard it vas to give up those bloody horrible cigarettes, I need healthy lungs. I kiss you to prove it." She smiled, leaning across the corner seat where we sat, and we kissed, tongues and all. She tasted amazing and her breath was clean and fresh. She had definitely not been smoking anything.

"Mmmm, love you, sweetheart," she grinned.

"I love you too," I breathed.

Feeling inquisitive, I asked, "Has all this eating got something to do with what the doctor told you?"

"Yeah it has," she replied, flicking her shiny plait out of her face, which was dripping with sweat. She reached out and squeezed my arm so that I looked into her eyes. "No worry." she smiled, "I am okay."

As we walked back to the flat, Kat was so full of food that she struggled. She was still in a lot of pain, making the walk somewhat leisurely. Once in the flat, Kat flopped down on the chair.

"I would love another cup of tea," she said, mopping streams of sweat from her forehead with her purple scarf.

"Of course, sweetheart," I told her, flicking the switch on the kettle and wondering how much more tea she could drink, considering she drank four cups at the pub. Asking me to do something like make tea was unlike Kat, because although I always pulled my weight around the house, Kat liked to be the one who made hot drinks. I passed her a clean handkerchief and sat thoughtfully rubbing away the stream of sweat while I made the tea.

"Thank you, Honeybun," she said quietly, when I brought her tea. Then she blew her nose loudly, apologised unnecessarily for doing so, and said, "You know I never ask you for helping me with things unless I really no feel well."

She had taken her lovely blonde hair out of her usual plait and was combing it through so that it spread everywhere. As I sat down next to Kat, she smiled and shuffled so that she was on my lap before cuddling up to me.

"So, what did the doctor say about the seizures?" I asked tenderly.

"I have tomorrow afternoon emergency appointment at the hospital to see new neurologist, Dr Staunton." She gave her nose a little rub and continued, "They think it is changed in hormones, because maybe infection stops medication working. They treat with antibiotics, but there is no water infection."

"Then what does the doctor think is wrong?" I continued, probing her for an answer.

Kat shook her hair and fluffed it up so that it covered us both. Her hair was now so long that she had to pin the bottom end of her plait to the top to avoid tripping over it. This despite her daily claims that she hated her hair and was getting it cut next week.

"I am going to have to take time off work," she said suddenly.

"What? Why darling?" I asked her, but she shushed me.

"I so sorry Rob. I know how much you love your car. I love your car too, but we have to get a different car."

"I do love my car, but what has my Mini got to do with you being unwell, sweetheart?" I asked her, now very confused about what the hell was going on.

Kat took my hand in hers, but she looked away and put her other hand in her trouser pocket as she reached for something. "I love your silly old broken rubbish car and really wish I could drive it," she repeated, still looking away and rummaging in her pocket.

Then suddenly she found what she was looking for and looked up at me with the brightest smile I had ever seen beaming across her face.

"But the boot is too small," she said.

"Why are we talking about the car?" I laughed.

"Because you no can fit a pushchair in it, daddy."

I was speechless. Had I just heard right? Pushchair... daddy... did that mean? No? Yes? What?

Kat knew I wanted to have children with her one day, and she'd always wanted to be a mum, but it came as an utter shock. Kat and I had been at it like rabbits for eighteen months, ever since our relationship became sexual, but Kat took the pill religiously, because we were planning to wait another year.

"I know it sooner than we planned, but the doctor said the pill failed because I had tummy bug before the holiday," Kat said, looking at me with a broad smile on her face and passed me the thing she had been trying to get out of her pocket. "Is it sinking in now? The doctor took a blood test, is going to confirm it with a scan, but I already had my suspicions." She smiled, nodding down at the thing she passed, adding, "so I pissed on this earlier this morning."

I looked down at the thing she passed me. It was a pregnancy test clearly showing two blue lines.

Still speechless, I took hold of Kat around the shoulders and embraced her excitedly. After about ten seconds, Kat pushed me back a little and looked right at me with wide eyes. Her voice was squeaking with excitement, she squealed, "We going to be mummy and daddy."

Even though she was in pain, she stood up and took my hands, pulling me with her. Barely able to contain her excitement, her exhaustion from her fit all momentarily disappeared as she jumped up and down like an excited child.

My heart was thumping all over the place. All I could do was take Kat in my arms and hold her close to me. Finding my voice, I was able to breathe the words, "I love you, Katarzyna Bobal Brownlow."

Chapter 17

A very scary day

So happy were we that it seemed like we'd daydreamed our way through the next few months. 2011 was upon us all too soon. It was almost as though we were in a movie with yet another montage or novel that skipped a passage of time within two paragraphs. There had been so much to do with both of us working full time, preparing for the coming of our baby, and our second wedding.

With the registry office booked for 10th May nearly a year earlier. We hadn't accounted for the patter of little feet. Our little one was due on 5th May just five days before big day number two.

The months seemed to go by so fast. Kat and I were so excited about becoming parents that we spent little time thinking about anything else while we weren't working.

Most people were happy that we were bringing our little bundle of joy into the world.

My parents couldn't wait to become grandparents for the second time, and Ela was so happy at the thought of becoming an aunty that Kat had to remind her that they were both already aunties to their other sister's children.

"But I get to be more hands on this time, and this is my favourite sister's first baby," Ela had protested.

"You no tell Kazia or Dusa that I'm your favourite," Kat had laughed.

Even Kat's boss at work was happy for us and made sure that Kat could keep her job while sticking to light duties, because of both her pregnancy and her health struggles.

She had a couple more fits, but the neurologist seemed to have done a great job in helping her keep them to a minimum.

When we woke together on the 4th May, we were all ready for the birth and the second wedding plans were all sorted.

Kat insisted on walking to work with me at 5:30 in the morning, telling me that she would go batshit crazy if she had to spend all day in the flat alone now she was on maternity leave.

The most beautiful sight I'd seen in my whole life was Kat walking barefoot along the beach on that warm May morning. The sun rose behind us. Kat rolled up her tracksuit bottoms, so she could cool her feet in the sea. I warned her against wetting her feet, because she still had a bit of a cold, but she laughed and said, "When do I not have a cold?"

The baby bump made Kat look like she had swallowed a football, but she was happy and smiling as we messed about, kicking water at each other.

Seeing my pregnant wife standing in the sea with the sun rising behind her and the most prominent smile on her face was an image that would never leave my mind. It was times like these that I thought to myself I must be the luckiest man alive.

Unfortunately, I had to go to work to spoil the day.

"Now," she said, as we reached the hotel carpark, "remember I no coming to meet you after work today."

Of course, I remembered she wasn't coming to meet me. She was taking Jenny out for a girly day to see Dirty Dancing the musical in Norwich.

"Enjoy your Patrick Swayze lookalike," I laughed, squeezing her.

"I will clean flat and make dinner before we go," she smiled.

"No," I told her, "you'll look after yourself, have a nice warm bath, and watch the TV."

"I do that as well," she added.

"Stop pushing yourself too hard," I told her gently.

"I feel lazy," she sighed. "I have worked my whole life since the day I leave school, and now husband go to work, and I am fat, lazy stay-at-home wife."

"You don't like your job, and you've been on maternity leave for all of one day," I laughed.

"I know, and I so bored. Yesterday," she sniffed, digging in her pocket as we walked arm in arm through the car park, "I am clean flat, I am done washing and ironing, and dinner ready for cooking all by 9:30 in the morning."

"Have you tried going back to bed for a while?" I smiled.

"I no sleep without my husband," she grinned.

"What about watching TV?"

"Rob, you know I no like watch like TV in the daytime. It lazy," she moaned, "Although, I did watch a program with Ela. This man gets a lot of ugly people with no teeth to shout at each other for entertainment. I no sure if it plain dumb or genius. It called Jeremy Kyle show."

I laughed but didn't tell Kat that I'd been watching Jeremy Kyle when I worked evenings in case she thought I was lazy too.

"You know I might watch it today, but I got to hoover the stairs before Jenny comes over," she added.

I stopped in my tracks at the sudden thought that Kat was even considering hoovering the spiral stairs that led up to the flat.

"You're not seriously going to do that in your condition?"

She looked at me with her pretend angry face and said sharply, "No tell me what to do. I no want to be wrapped in cotton wool."

"I just think it's dangerous," I told her. "What if you fall?"

"I just want it clean for baby, and you at work I need do something," she protested.

"You are doing too much," I told her. "I'll do it when I get home."

"Okay," she sighed, looking a little frustrated, "but I get to cook dinner before I go instead, because I refuse to be lazy."

All of a sudden, she took her arm away from me and held her tummy under the baby. For a moment, the expression on her face was one of pain. I thought she was having a contraction, but suddenly, she whipped out her hanky and sneezed so heavily that I had to grab her to stop her falling.

When Kat composed herself, she stood there grinning. "What's the grin for?" I asked smiling back.

She stepped forward and put my hand on her bump. "Baby no like it when mummy sneeze. She needs daddy to say is okay."

"She? Is there something you know that I don't?" I asked, rubbing the bump gently, knowing full well that we had both decided not to find out at the scans.

"Mother intuition. I feel it in my bones," she smiled. As we started walking again, she put her hand on her tummy. "Keep your phone handy," she added a little breathless. "I might curse having another cold, but one more sneeze like that may mean baby come out this morning."

We chatted happily as we climbed the hill to the hotel reception. I told her to enjoy herself at the theatre and not to run off with the Patrick Swayze lookalike, while she protested that she had no interest in any man apart from me. Kat joked that her pregnancy would come in handy by giving her extra weight should she need to stop Jenny from running onto the stage.

I had to convince her that just because she was going to be a mum soon, this wasn't the last time she would get to go out for a girly day. I was willing to stay home with the baby and do my fair share. Kat, however, was at pains to point out that she wanted to stay at home and be family.

We kissed passionately on the steps of the hotel, and Kat smiled at me as she turned to go home. When I got upstairs, I watched her from the window as she made her way down the hill with her lovely plaited hair swishing in the breeze. She paused and blew her nose. Then took out her phone and started texting somebody as she walked. *Probably Jenny*, I thought, but it was 5.45 am. Jenny might not be too pleased.

However, when Kat got to the bottom of the hill, she turned to look up at me and pressed a button on her phone.

A couple of seconds later, a message came through to my phone. It read, *"Stop being such a hopeless romantic and get to work, love Kat and baby xxxxx."* I blew her a kiss out of the window, and she blew one back and smiled before turning on her heels and drifting out of sight.

Just then, there was a sight I dreaded. It was Katherine McNallty driving up the slope in her BMW. I wouldn't have blamed Kat if she'd given my boss the one-fingered salute as she passed. We hated her, and she hated us. She was looking for a reason to fire me, but was so far without success.

Kat often wondered aloud why I still worked with that cow bag. In truth, so did I. The main reason was it was close to home, and if I'd not come to live with Kat, I'd have walked out of the job much earlier. I had looked for other jobs in the area, but with the credit crunch hitting hard there hadn't been much around. Clinging to my current job was a must now that I was supporting our little family.

My boss Katherine was one of those people who were fake, and two-faced to the last. I couldn't say what I thought of her for fear of losing my job. Kat, however, made her feelings clear, because she told me that an employment tribunal would laugh Katherine out of the building if she sacked me for not liking my choice of wife.

The dislike between Katherine and Kat was apparent, no matter how hard they tried to be civil to each other. When we told her about the baby, Katherine's happiness was so fake that I thought her exaggerated smile was going to crack her face. Kat returned the smile, but there was none of her usual beaming happiness. It was more like she was reading my boss with her piercing eyes, trying to see what was going on behind the tonne of cheap makeup.

Kat had left me at work to go and spend that Sunday evening with Jenny and Amy, before walking home with me later. I was just signing in when I got a text from her that made me smile, asking if Katherine had finished putting her face back on after her smile had cracked it.

Unfortunately, I hadn't realised Katherine had been walking through reception at the time. She was on the way back from having a cigarette by the stink of her, and she saw the text over my shoulder. Despite me not having to start work for another five minutes, she told me that if I were ever seen with my phone during work time again, she would put me on a third disciplinary. In short terms, this meant she was looking for an excuse to fire me.

Later she came down to the gym to discuss arrangements for paternity leave, but put it in the meanest way possible. "I suppose you'll be wanting time off when the little monster gets here?" When I nodded, she continued with, "I can't believe you of all people are playing happy families." She had looked down her nose at me and added, "It just shows that there is somebody for everyone if you scrape the barrel low enough."

There's still hope for you yet if that's the case," I told her, looking away. "That's the last time you'll speak about my wife like that."

"But if you'd set your sights a little higher, you could have been as lucky as my husband is to have me," she smirked.

"You've got a husband?" I asked in shock.

"My personal life is none of your business, Rob," she said in a harsh tone.

"It's as much business as my life is yours," I told her.

I loved Kat's analysis of the whole situation when I told her later. "I feel sorry for her husband," she laughed when I told her how horrible Katherine had been. "She is jealous of us because we have love and baby on the way. Nobody wants horrible dried up bitch like her. I am sure her husband no love her as mine loves me and I love him."

Kat's text message and the lovely smile she gave me as she turned away for home would keep me warm inside through a tough long day.

We knew our lives would be changing forever with the coming of our first child, but that morning, neither of us knew how much our lives would change before we saw each other again. The reason I saved that particular smile in my mind was that it was the last time I would see her smile like that in a long time.

I tried to avoid Katherine as she was always out to get me, she liked to pick on people who worked in departments she didn't understand – the gym and pool being two of them.

As an overweight woman who smoked like a chimney, she knew nothing about such places, yet tried to stick her nose in because she could. She was always trying to fix things that were not broken, or move staff to other departments like cleaning. This left the gym and pool short-staffed, which endangered customers. She blamed others for this.

Before I met Kat, Katherine was always calling me into work on my days off.

If anyone from any department was off sick, she would replace them with whoever was working in the gym. This would result in her calling whoever was on their day off to come into work, meaning that I rarely got a day off. I practically ran the department myself from 6 am to 10 pm, when the gym manager was off sick for three weeks, but I got nothing but moaning from Katherine.

When I got together with Kat, I wanted to spend my

days off with her. So, I exercised my right not to come into work every single time Katherine called me. That was when I became next on her disciplinary list. From then on, she knew that Kat worked in the mornings and she had made sure I was on the rota for as many evenings as possible.

I guess she hoped that Kat and I would argue and split up, so I would work days off again. When that failed, she tried to put me on disciplinary warnings for every little thing I did. Examples were not hoovering the gym when there were people in it, and then for hoovering the gym when there were people in it because she told me to.

She also scolded me for using my phone at work even when I was on my break, not coming into work when Kat and I were away in Cambridge running a half marathon, for which I had booked annual leave, and a whole load of stupid things.

I wasn't the only member of staff she targeted. The worst thing was, that she did all this in a way that made her seem as though she was helping staff to better themselves. She told people off in a sugar-coated voice in order to hide the threatening undertone.

In her sweet tone, she'd call me up and say things like, "Oh my God, how many hours have you spent cleaning the gym? I can see a speck of dust in the corner. Don't you think you'd better stay an extra hour and do it all again?" Then there was her most recent one, phoning the gym from her office to say, "Hello, Rob, it's meee. Can you pop down to my office? I've got a letter for you to put in your bag and read at home. It's nothing to worry about." This happened twice, and the letter was far from friendly as it was giving me notice of disciplinary action.

Kat was angry at Katherine when I showed her the letter, but it was Katie who took it from me, read it and told me not to worry. Katie never explained why though.

However, on the second occasion, Ela kindly came with me for support and secretly recorded the meeting. It did not go well, and I was on my last chance, even though I'd done nothing wrong.

That morning, Katherine had come straight up to the gym and demanded to know why my wife had been on the hotel grounds. When I challenged her to give me a reason why my wife could not walk to work with me and asked what exactly Kat had done to be banned from the hotel, she was lost for an explanation of either.

Instead of even bothering to give a reason, she just put her hand out to me and said in her sweetest domineering tone, "Give me your mobile phone, and I'll pop it in my office drawer until your shift ends."

"I need to stay in contact with my wife," I told her bluntly.

Her reply made me want to punch her in the face. "Are you sure you're actually married, sweetie cheeks? I heard you weren't getting married until next week."

"We got married abroad, and this is the second wedding for friends and family," I told her through clenched teeth.

"Well," she said in her sugar-coated tone, "I am sure my wedding invite got lost in the post. Didn't it, my lovely?"

"I assure you that it didn't," I replied.

"Well in that case," she said in a slightly harder tone, "as a paying member of the gym, I can't ban her from the site until there are complaints about her, which I'm quite sure I can fabricate a few of. Until I see evidence that she is married to you, you will have no permission to have leave if she is unwell. Also, there will be no paternity leave until I see evidence that the child she is carrying is yours."

"What happened in your life to make you such a cow and feel you can talk about my wife in that horrible way?"

"Well, before you met her you were a good employee," she smiled. "Now look at all these disciplinary warnings you've had. You need to ditch her and get a wriggle on with your work."

"You never once told me that I was a good employee," I countered.

"Well, you were average," she said spitefully. "But since you met that girl, you want stuff like days off and holidays, and you're not showing your full commitment to the company. That makes me sad. I mean, considering she's just a dirty foreigner using you to get a visa."

"That's not really your problem, is it? Or are you too stupid to know the EU doesn't work like that?" I told her, finally snapping. "You're jealous because you have no love in your marriage, and you're married to your job. You don't and never will have a real family. If you treat your husband like your employees, then I wouldn't blame him if he found someone else."

She stopped and stared at me in the face. Then the real Katherine McNallty came to life as she raised her voice. "How dare you bring my personal life up at work again, you little..."

"Little what?" I asked, puffing my chest out and showing her I was a foot and a half taller than her. "How dare you bring up everyone else's family life?"

"Fortunately for you," she retorted, "the customers seem to like you. The area manager at head office has a different opinion of you than mine and has decided to remove the disciplinary action against you against my advice. Otherwise, you would be picking up your P45, if you know what that is. And if you don't put that phone in your locker this instant, you will get one."

We looked at each other with evil stares as I wondered who on earth at the head office had saved me from the chop, considering I didn't know anybody there. "They saw sense," I told her calmly.

"By the way," she said sweetly "It's 6:02. I believe you were due to start work two minutes ago, so for that you can stay for an extra hour unpaid."

With that, she put a cigarette in her mouth and headed for the door. I was really pushing my luck, but I followed and said to her in a calm voice, "I do believe that you were also supposed to start at 6 am, so I am afraid you are also two minutes late for work, so there's no time to smoke because you are a professional boss who doesn't break rules."

She tried to ignore me and walked off as I protested that Kat was due to give birth any day and I needed to be reachable. Katherine retorted that if Kat went into labour, she could phone the main hotel number, and it would be up to the reception staff if they chose to inform me or not. She left me with the threat of further disciplinary action before leaving.

She stopped at the door and smiled, so that her makeup cracked. In her patronising tone, she said, "Do have a lovely day, sweetie."

Chloe, the lifeguard, was passing on her way to open the pool—the same one who walked out on the night I met Kat. She'd been having similar problems with Katherine in the past and was also on her final warning, even though she hadn't anything to deserve it. Chloe knew Kat and me well. Her partner Mike also worked at the hotel in maintenance, and they were forbidden from speaking to each other at work despite having two children together. She had heard everything.

"If I didn't have a family to provide for, I'd slap that bitch for you," she said quietly.

"You'd have to join the queue," I laughed.

Chloe took a swing at the punching bag as she passed, leaving it swinging wildly. "I like to pretend it's her head," she laughed.

The day went smoothly after my encounter with Katherine. I was keeping my head down and working hard with clients. At the start of another assessment, the door flung open with a bang.

It was the last person I expected to see. Ela came storming into the gym with a look of thunder on her face and tear stains on her cheeks. "Ela what the hell...?"

"Why the fuck haven't you been answering your phone? I left you twenty messages." She looked like she was going to throttle me, but all of a sudden, she threw her arms around me tightly and burst into tears again.

"What's happened? Is the baby on the way?" I asked in a panic.

Then suddenly Katie was in the doorway "Rob, you need to come with us now," she said urgently.

"Where's Kat?" I asked, terrified at what the answer might be.

"We'll explain on the way," Katie told me as Ela pulled me towards the door.

"Katarzyna has had a terrible accident," Ela sobbed.

"What kind of accident?" I breathed as we walked

quickly down the stairs to reception.

"She has fallen on the stairs," Ela sobbed. "Jenny found her and called me. We both tried to call you, but you didn't answer. When we called the hotel, they said all calls to you were being ignored and slammed the phone down."

"Katherine made me put my phone in my locker," I told her.

"She what?" Katie snarled angrily.

It was all taking time to sink in. My pregnant wife had fallen down the stairs, and my boss had tried to stop me getting calls.

"Jenny went with Kat in the ambulance," Katie told me hurriedly. "They're taking her to Addenbrooke's in Cambridge. We've got the hospital bag she already packed. I'm driving you there now."

"That's eighty miles away," I yelled.

"Don't worry about that. They went in a helicopter, and they may already have landed," Katie told me calmly.

My heart was thudding all over the place, and I didn't know what to do. I just wanted to be with Kat and our unborn child so that I could hold her hand, cuddle her, tell her I loved her and it was all going to be okay. But she was miles away in God only knows what state, if even still alive.

When we reached reception, Katherine was stood right in the middle of the room waiting for us. "Oh, my God, Rob, are you wanting to get fired sweetie?" she smirked. "First, you're texting that freaky double Dutch speaking thing you call a wife, and now bringing her freaky sister into work? Ooh, I'm going to enjoy seeing you in my office. Right now," she added, tilting her head towards the door while raising her cheeks in a smile and rubbing her hands together at the prospect of finding a reason to give me the sack.

"You will get the fuck out of the way. You pick up your own stuff and leave now," Katie screamed at her, stepping out from behind me. The look they gave each other suggested they knew each other, but there was no reason I knew of for this to be the case.

"*You!*" Ela screamed, suddenly turning on Katherine, "You were the one who kept putting the phone down while my sister is probably dying." Ela tore at her, and it took Katie and me to hold her back. "Let me hit her, let me hit her," Ela was screaming. We held her back, carrying on down the steps and ignoring Katherine's threats as we made our way outdoors.

A crowd of staff, guests, and gym members were gathering on the steps to see what all the shouting was about.

"Rob, you are on duty. You are going nowhere," Katherine continued in her patronising tone. "Am I to take it that you're going to ignore my instructions and leave? Your P45 will be in the post."

"My wife and child could be dying!" I yelled at her.

"Is this another one of your tall tales you're making up to get time off?" she smirked. "Next time, could you ask them to do it while you're not at work?"

That was the last straw. I flew at her with all the rage of years of torment, backhanded comments, and pure hatred. I tore away from Ela and Katie and was about to smash Katherine's face when two of the maintenance workers grabbed me, one of them shouting, "She's not worth going to prison for."

Suddenly, it was Katie who stepped up towards her. She pushed Katherine back so that she fell onto the steps.

"Don't worry Kathy, I won't hit you," Katie said, stepping forward menacingly.

"Get away from me, you filthy dyke," Katherine retorted, causing Ela to come at her again.

However, Katie turned, grabbed Ela, and cuddled her, saying "It's okay, sweetheart. Let me deal with her."

"Oh, this precious," Katherine laughed, "so you're in love with a freaky Dutch woman too?" Katherine smirked, slipping on the steps as she tried to get up.

"She's from the Czech Republic, and I love her," Katie said fiercely, turning towards Katherine again. I would have cheered at what happened next if I hadn't been so full of worry of what had happened to Kat and the baby.

With a look of loathing in her eye that I had never seen from happy smiley Katie, she walked up the steps towards Katherine, who was still sliding as she tried to stand up. "I said I wasn't going to hit you, you bitch," she smiled sweetly as she drew back her right foot and brought it crashing into Katherine's face with a sickening crunch. Katherine howled in pain as Katie kicked her again and again and blood spurted all from her nose head and ran down onto her dress.

The next thing I knew, we were running, and Katie jumped into a red soft-top sports car with the top down. "Who the hell's car is this?" I asked, thinking it looked expensive.

"It's Katie's," Ela told me quietly.

"But what happened to the beaten-up Ford?"

"You know that sign in the back that says my other car is a Ferrari?" Katie smiled awkwardly. I seemed to remember her having a joke sign in the back of her Ford. "Well, it's not really a joke, because this is that Ferrari."

Gobsmacked at the news Katie really did have a Ferrari, I spun my head around at the sound of cheering. We looked up to see that many people had followed us, wanting to shake Katie's hand, but we were in a hurry to leave. As I got in the back, I looked in the mirror and saw Chloe walk up the steps as if to help Katherine, who sat there alone. Instead of helping her, Chloe drew back her hand and gave her the best right hook I'd ever seen, knocking her back to the floor to the cheers of the crowd.

As Katie turned the car around and put the top up, I saw several people punching and slapping Katherine as they passed her on the way back into work. Some were cheering while others were in shock.

As we were about to speed off down the hill, there was a bang on the window. It was Chloe. I wound the window down, and she threw something in. "The bitch stole it from your locker and had it in her pocket the whole time," she shouted to me. Lying there on the seat was my mobile phone with more than forty missed calls from Jenny, Katie, and Ela. There was also, heartbreakingly, another smiley, "we love you" text from Kat and baby, sent only minutes before she must have fallen.

There were tears in my eyes as I thanked Chloe and congratulated her on finally punching Katherine. She smiled and said she'd see me at the Job Centre and probably see Katie at the police station. She asked me to send Kat love from her and Mike.

"Nobody's getting fired, apart from her," Katie told her stony-eyed. She put her foot down without another word and sped through the town, stopping only at the fuel station where she refused to take my money.

She filled up the car and bought drinks for us all. For herself, she bought a pack of cigarettes, one of which she lit up as soon as we got going. It caused both Ela and I to choke. "I'm so sorry. I just had to smoke after that. I will quit again after this pack," she told us in a hurried voice.

Ela sat in the back with me, still crying with shock at the whole situation. She was too upset to be angry at Katie, who had quit smoking in the New Year, but obviously been driven back to it by the stress of the situation.

Kat's hospital bag was slung in the back. I saw her favourite pair of PJs hanging out of the top, and my heart raced. I just wanted some news on what had happened to her, but Ela was crying too hard and didn't seem in any mood to talk.

I reached into Kat's bag, which we had packed together a few days earlier, and took out one of her handkerchiefs. I gave it to Ela, who was sobbing. She took it and continued to cry into it.

Katie reached back, touched Ela on the leg, and said softly, "Love you, El."

Ela reached forward and touched her on the shoulder and sobbed, "I love you too K, and you too Rob."

"I'm sure Kat will be fine," I told Ela, rubbing her on the shoulder with my arm around her. I didn't know who I was trying to convince – her or me. Those spiral stairs were very high and went up four floors. Kat was always so careful with her footing and... "She was hoovering the stairs, wasn't she?" I'd told her to leave it, but she was too pig-headed and independent.

"I don't know. I was at work, and Katie just happened to be there visiting her Nanna when Jenny called, screaming that she couldn't get hold of you," Ela sobbed. "I told Katie, and we ran home straight away."

"Thank you both of you for coming," I said gently.

"Rob," Katie said, "When I was eighteen, before I got my current job, I trained to be a nurse. Trust me, Kat's in excellent hands, but there's always a chance that…"

"What?" I pleaded.

"They don't call the air ambulance unless it's nasty, and well," she paused, "she was in a terrible state. She was unconscious and bleeding. It's only fair that we should tell you in case… in case we lose her… or the baby."

"Or both," I added quietly. Katie and Ela nodded at the same time.

I couldn't cry, because Kat would want me to stay strong for Ela, but I didn't want to talk about it. I wanted to think of Kat in my arms, sleeping safe and sound as she often did, and not fighting for her life in a helicopter somewhere above Cambridgeshire. Neither did I want to talk about what just happened at work, but I saw a police car come racing in the opposite direction, followed by a paramedic.

"Do you think that was for us?" I asked quietly.

"Not for you guys. Just for me, but she wouldn't dare press charges," Katie said.

"How can you be so sure?" I asked.

"Don't worry about that now," Katie said quite offhand. "Let's just say I know people in high places, and nobody is getting fired or charged with assault today, apart from maybe Kathy."

"Plus," she added, "It felt so good. I've been wanting my whole life to kick my half-sister in the face."

"She's your half-sister?" Ela shrieked, before I could ask, "Why did you not say?"

"Would either of you want to be associated with

her?" Katie replied.

"I see what you mean," Ela sniffed, wiping her eyes, "but none of us would have judged you on it, and I love you no matter who your family is."

"You can't choose your family," I added.

"It's all right," Katie said firmly. "If she knew that Rob and I were friends, she would have caused more trouble. Never mind now. Let's just keep our hopes up for news on Kat."

Katie had put her phone on hands-free mode and made a call to someone.

She was very friendly, but spoke with an abrupt tone. She said to the person, "Whatever you're doing, it can wait. Get up to Cromer and take charge of the hotel. There's been a bit of a situation. I've got a family emergency, so I'll meet you back there when I can. It might not be until tomorrow or later, so take one of the empty rooms. Your first task is to suspend Katherine McNallty and take charge."

"What is she on about?" I asked Ela, confused as Katie seemed to be running the hotel.

"You better tell him. He was going to find out sooner or later," Katie told her.

"Katie is the European head of HR for Aricot International," Ela told me tearfully.

Aricot International was the hotel chain which had taken over the Cromer Hotel where I worked. They'd taken control not too long before I met Kat.

"So, you're like my boss's boss's boss?" I asked, bemused.

"Yep, that sums it up," she said, with a weak smile. "I

didn't want to say, because you're under enough pressure at work without having your big boss living in the same house as you."

"So, you got me off those disciplinary warnings?" I said, stunned.

"Along with all the other people she gave them to who didn't deserve them," she said bluntly. "If you had done all that stuff she said you did, then I'd have let her fire you," she added with a smile.

"How on earth did you land that job?" I asked her, stunned.

"Not what you know, it's who you know," she told us, lighting up another cigarette. "I was a nurse on the night-shift, but I went back to college during the day and studied hotel management. Years ago when I was a teenager, I was covering first aid at an event, and there was a big train crash nearby. I helped this young woman with no legs. Her name was Georgie. We stayed friends, and now she's my brother's wife. It turns out when her dad died, she inherited the company as a teenager, but she didn't want it. So, when she heard I had a little experience, she offered me this job. That's all of it, and we are not talking about it anymore."

We drove for nearly forty-five minutes in silence, breaking every speed limit. Katie seemed to know the road and dodged every speed camera with skill. Ela and I clung to each other, both out of fear for any news the phone might bring us about Kat and for our own lives in case Katie's driving killed us all. She dodged in and out of traffic at over 100mph while talking on the hands-free kit.

We were on the A11, heading towards Cambridge when Ela's phone rang. "It's Jenny," she screeched. "Something must have happened. I don't want to answer it," she said, panicking as she pressed to answer.

"Hello," she said, breathing hard. I could feel her heart pumping as she squeezed my hand. Jenny sounded panicked on the other end. Although I couldn't hear what she was saying, I could tell from Ela's face that things were serious.

Ela took fast, hard breaths of panic as tears rolled down her face. She gave a sudden wailing scream of pure terror, which was so horrible and blood curdling that Katie pulled the car off into a lay-by.

Ela jumped out of the car onto the verge, still clutching her phone. She got violently sick and vomited into the grass verge. Katie and I held exchanged worried looks over her head. As Ela fell to the ground screaming, she threw her phone into the road where it smashed to pieces under a passing car.

Katie and I both bent next to Ela. I was breathing hard, but my heart had stopped beating in my chest. Neither of us needed to ask what Ela had just been told by Jenny on the phone.

We didn't need to talk, as the look on Ela's face said it all. Her tears ran everywhere, and she grabbed both of us, shaking as she finally produced the words that I was dreading to hear.

"Katarzyna is dead."

Chapter 18

The Hospital

My heart didn't want to beat anymore. My wife and soulmate, along with our unborn child, had been taken from us somewhere in the skies over Cambridgeshire.

Nobody spoke or knew what to do. I thought my heart had given up on me, but if it hadn't, then I wished it would. I hoped the ground would open up and swallow me or shoot me into the stars, so I could be with Kat and our baby wherever the gods had taken them.

I wanted to fall to my knees and cry like Ela was doing, but it was like in the movies where only one person could cry loudly while the others suffered silently, looking on speechless with grief.

I didn't know how long it was that Katie and I held Ela as she howled. When we finally got her back into the car, she flopped down in her seat. Katie had quietly suggested that we find Jenny at the hospital, as she must have been terrified and all alone, having just lost her best friend. We needed to get her back to her daughter.

Before getting back into the driver's seat, Katie threw

her arms around me, but couldn't think of any words to comfort a man who has just lost everything. None of us spoke for the remainder of the journey. It was the longest half hour of my life. Ela clung to me, but nobody spoke. Katie slowed her driving, and I could see in the mirror that she was crying silently.

When we pulled into Addenbrooke's Hospital, I tried to summon the guts to phone Jenny, but my phone was dead. Katie tried too, but swore when she realised her phone was also dead from making calls and she left her charger in her other car.

I had to be with Kat, no matter if she was stone cold. I just had to be with her. My grief made me do the most selfish thing I'd ever done in my life. I jumped out of the car, leaving Ela and Katie behind, and ran for the hospital reception.

I'd never been there before. It was such a busy hospital. I stood there in the middle of the reception jumping up and down as I queued to speak to someone. I almost fell onto the desk with my numb legs.

"I need to see my wife," I stammered to the older man on reception.

"Could you tell me your wife's name, mate?" he replied.

"Katarzyna Brownlow," I told him and spelt out her name to ensure he had the right person. "She erm," I heard myself say it as though it was somebody else, "she died in the air ambulance."

"Oh, my lad I'm sorry," he said looking at his screen. "I'm sorry," he said, "can you confirm your wife's name?"

I spelt out her name again, but told him that she could still have been registered as Bobal rather than Brownlow. It didn't matter now she was stone cold dead.

All I wanted to do was to put my arms around my dead wife and our child, and lie with them until I joined them in heaven or wherever she went. Being alive right now was hell.

The old man was taking so much time to find her, I wasn't sure what he was doing. "That's not a common name," he said. "You're sure your wife passed away?"

I nodded as the tears started to form in my eyes with the realisation of what I was confirming.

The man called a passing nurse over and showed her the screen. They spoke quietly, and the old man smiled at something. What on earth could make him smile when my Katarzyna was dead? How did anyone in the world dare smile?

The nurse, a kind looking lady in her mid-thirties, grinned at me and asked me to follow. I wondered again how she could dare smile at my pain.

"Robert Brownlow," she grinned, "my name's Colleen. I'm one of the nurses. I can take you where you need to be. Could you follow me please?"

I followed her blindly as she quickly walked down a long corridor and up two flights of stairs. I couldn't speak.

All manner of things were going through my head. Of course, the shock hadn't quite hit me. I'd never thought about how I would be in a situation where Katarzyna was taken from me, because we were so young.

I thought we had another sixty years together. I had never lost a family member before, and not for one moment did I stop to think that I could lose my twenty-three-year-old soulmate before my eighty-five-year-old grandmother.

Only that morning, I was thinking how fortunate I was to wake up every morning with a woman that I loved with all my heart. I didn't know it would be the last time. It was impossible to describe the feeling of suddenly having everything you loved taken from you in an instant.

My heart was thumping with fear. I kept saying to myself over and over that I should not be scared. I told myself that a dead body couldn't harm me, especially when it was the body I snuggled up to in bed every night and made very passionate love to only that morning. I wasn't taking in anything the nurse told me as we walked. Her voice just a blur as I followed like a sheep.

On the one hand, I was feeling terrible and selfish that I had run off ahead of Ela and Katie. I felt maybe it was better that they were left to comfort each other. I needed to find Jenny too, as someone needed to hug her and thank her for being there with Kat at the end.

Colleen was still talking about Kat's injuries, but it all just buzzed past my head. Why did she need to tell me about the injuries Kat had sustained in the fall? It wasn't as if they were going to heal now.

I suddenly realised that we were in a ward at the end of a corridor, and all around me were babies. What kind of sick joke was this? My wife and child had passed away, and she was taking me to a place full of babies?

I was about to get angry when suddenly I heard my name shouted from behind me. Next came the sound of breathless running along the corridor. I turned to see Ela running down the hall. When she got to me, she stopped and threw her arms around me. She was breathing so hard I thought she was going to pass out.

"I'm so sorry," she breathed. "I... must... join... your gym... and stop... eating... Katarzyna's... yummy cakes... I'm so sorry. I fucked up."

"And I've got to stop smoking again," Katie panted, as she caught Ela up. Jenny walked along behind her.

"Fucked up what?" I stammered, rubbing her back calmly.

"I misunderstood," she breathed. "Katarzyna and baby are still alive."

"What?" I breathed. Was this all some kind of joke? I was stuck somewhere in the middle of sadness, shock, and elation. I wondered if this whole thing was one of those screwed-up dreams I kept having where I woke up, back in my own bed, having never met Kat on that stormy night.

Hopefully, I'd wake up, and all would be well. I'd have my pathetic job back as well as Kat. She wouldn't even be hurt, let alone dead, or as it turned out, not dead.

Kat was hurt, and very badly too, but she was alive. Colleen replayed everything she had just told me that I had ignored thinking Kat had passed away.

Ela cuddled me and told me how sorry she was for her misunderstanding before going back to hug Katie. Katie, along with Jenny, was still looking very choked up.

"Mr Brownlow, I need to tell you that although I'm happy to confirm that Katarzyna was still with us when I last saw her, your wife still is a very sick young lady." I nodded slowly as she continued to tell me that when Kat tripped, her first thoughts had been our unborn child.

"Your wife must have instinctively curled herself into a ball as she fell, using herself as a human shield around the baby. Kat had multiple fractures to both arms and legs. She also had head trauma, plus internal bleeding.

What Ela had mistaken when Jenny was on the phone

was that Kat's heart had stopped in the helicopter. That was true, but the paramedics had also managed to shock her back to life quickly enough to save her and our little one. However, Ela had only heard the part where Kat died and had screamed so loudly that she never heard Jenny tell her the rest.

Kat had been taken straight from the helicopter into the theatre to stop the internal bleeding.

We followed Colleen as she continued talking. "Your wife is still in theatre," she said, as we came to an open cubical, "but this little bundle of joy was delivered to us here about an hour ago."

She drew back the curtain to reveal one of her colleagues—a nurse with long red hair—feeding a baby from a bottle.

"It's a baby," I said blankly, looking from Colleen and the baby to Ela, Katie, and Jenny. They all seemed to have got what was going on, but I was still in the dark. "But I don't get it," I told Colleen.

"Rob's been under a lot of pressure," Katie said to Colleen. "What with losing his job and not losing his job, and his wife dying and then not dying. He's only male and his brain can't think of more than two things at once." She winked at me.

"Rob," Ela said with wide eyes that reminded me so much of her sister, "this baby is yours and Katarzyna's."

"Born via C section at 13:20 this afternoon at 9lbs 2oz," said the young female nurse. She then whispered to the baby, "By the look of your daddy, no wonder you're a big girl. I wouldn't want to have given birth to one that size."

How random it was that the nurse who had looked after our gorgeous little girl, was the sister of the rather young looking red-headed doctor from our local surgery.

As the nurse stood and passed the baby to me, I couldn't help but think I'd seen her somewhere before with her shocking red hair. When I asked her if we'd met before she smiled and shook her head, but said, "No, but I look like my sister, and I think you might know her, because I've read your wife's notes and my sister is your wife's GP."

Another hour, possibly three passed. Jenny's dad had turned up to take her home with her little daughter Amy. I promised that we'd call her as soon as there was any news. My parents had come as soon as they got the message.

After a frantic and rather emotional call to her mother in the Czech Republic via the hospital payphone, Ela had taken Katie to get food.

They told me to come with them, but nothing on this earth was going to get me to leave our little girl. Kat had been right all along that our baby was a girl. She was a very big baby girl, and had her mum's eyes and little bits of blonde hair.

She was asleep in my arms when a kind male doctor came to tell me that Kat was out of theatre.

I had to leave our baby in the baby care unit for safety, as they were still concerned that she needed close monitoring after a traumatic birth. Ela and Katie found me on the way up to intensive care. When we were shown to her room, Kat looked terrible.

She was covered up to her face, her head was bandaged, and there were tubes going in and out of her hand. Under the covers, she had casts on both arms and legs and a brace on her upper body. The nurse who was looking after her told us that she had seen car crash victims in a better state.

The doctor told us that Kat had some swelling to the brain where she hit her head and was in an induced coma which was to help her recovery. He believed it wouldn't cause any lasting damage with the treatment she was getting.

He also explained to me how Kat's cardiac arrest had been brought on by the trauma of her injuries, which included double fractures to both arms and legs, a broken collarbone, and seven fractured ribs. There were thirty-eight fractures in all with damage to several vital organs.

As he left to see his next patient, he assured us that the induced coma was only a very temporary measure. He believed that Kat was a tough cookie, and given a lot of time and support, she would make a full recovery.

Ela looked as horrified as I felt. Kat was breathing on her own, but the drugs they were pumping into her were keeping her asleep. I kissed her hand gently and told her I loved her as Ela looked her over from top to bottom.

"Rob, just a little warning," she said quietly. "What's the only thing about Kat's appearance that she actually likes?"

"Her amazing hair that she's been growing nearly half her life," I said, quietly holding Kat's hand.

"She's going to be very upset," Ela told me, peeling back the bandage on Kat's head very slightly to reveal a heavily stitched cut. It had clearly been bad enough that the doctors had felt it necessary to shave off all her beautiful hair.

~~*~*~*

Kat wasn't due to be woken from her coma for two days.

I spent the next night and day swapping places between Kat and our little girl. Late in the afternoon of the second day, I was permitted to take our little girl upstairs to be with her mother.

On the second full day, Jeanette and Jemima visited to spend time with Kat, the baby and me.

However, Ela and Katie were noticeably absent. It was about tea time before they suddenly turned up. With them, to my shock, were four faces I'd only ever seen on a computer screen. Kazia, Dusa, Dowid and Kat's mum all filed into the room. I stood up, and each of them hugged me and the baby very briefly.

"How?" I said quietly to Ela. "I thought they couldn't afford to fly over for the wedding."

"They were always coming," she said. She smiled and explained that it had always been the plan to surprise us for the wedding. They were staying at the hotel where I worked, as Katie had got them free rooms. "They brought bridesmaids' dresses just in case," she grinned.

I had forgotten all about the second wedding. With Kat lying there still not awake, there was no way she was going to make it down the aisle for a second time in just a couple of days.

I stayed back to give them space and watched as the four of them sat around talking gently with tears in their eyes. It was Kat's seventeen-year-old brother Dowid who was the first to come to me and offer his hand for me to shake. He was followed by Kazia and Dusa, whom I had never met before in person, but both of them wanted a tearful hug.

Kat's mum and siblings stayed a few hours before Katie and Ela took them home. Before they left, I asked Ela quietly why her father wasn't there.

"Well," she shrugged, "as you know, Katarzyna and our father don't get on. They love each other but... He didn't want to spoil her big day by showing up uninvited."

"But he was invited," I told her.

"I know," she shrugged.

Never having met Kat's dad, I couldn't be sure if their dislike for each other was overhyped in a way. Although Kat made it clear that they didn't get on at the best of times, she had told me she wished he could be there.

When I laid our daughter down next to her unconscious mother, I swear I saw a flicker of a smile form on Kat's face as she slept.

I fell asleep that evening in the chair with one hand holding my wife's and other in the cot with our little daughter.

When I awoke, everything was cold and prickly. Kat was cuddled up with me so that we were nose to nose, and it took me several moments to realise that we were back in that cold, damp haystack.

The candles were still alight as though they were never-ending. My watch still said 2 am.

"What did you see sweetheart?" Kat said, rather urgently. She looked rather scared. Obviously, she would if she had just dreamed what I had dreamed from her own perspective. The poor lady must have had a horrifying experience.

"Are you okay, Kat?" I asked, rubbing her gently.

"I no think so. I scared," she sobbed, cuddling into me. "I lied to you, because I say I no hoover stairs, but I can no help myself, because I just want to make everything right for baby."

"It's okay," I reassured her, "It's just a bad dream."

"But I no think it is all dream," she said, moving back and giving me a serious look in the candlelight. "You tell me what happened to you and we see if my theory is right."

"Okay," I told her.

Kat listened intently and held me close as I told her of the events that had happened in the dream. I started when she left me at the hotel, moved onto Katie kicking my boss and revealing that they were sisters, and then to thinking Kat was dead and holding our little girl.

"Okay, Rob, my theory is this," Kat sniffed, sitting when I'd finished. "I think this here is dream," she said brightly. "I am in a coma, and this is sort of limbo."

"Go on," I told her.

"I am in coma, and my life is resetting. I am in limbo, and these visions are my brain resetting itself."

"That's one hell of a theory, but it's better than anything I've got," I added.

"I think these dreams no are dreams, because it's my memories coming back," she sniffed. "You picked me up when I was walking down the road, you take me to hotel, and we make friends. Then you come pick me up, and we decide we like each other. But you nearly went home, and I came running after you, and we kissed and got locked out." I nodded, and she went on. "This here in hay, this did no happen, but everything else did. Your birthday, Ela and Katie, our lovely holiday, those horrible fits I had, and our lovely little baby," she breathed. "So, I've remembered, and now I ready to wake up."

I couldn't argue with her point of view. The only place it all came unstuck for me was that if it was only Kat's dream, how I come I was here? Undoubtedly if it was just her dream, there was no reason why was I having these dreams.

"Maybe you are no dream," she said, when I pointed this out. "Maybe you just part of my dream. This is reason that we feel so easy together because we did this before. Maybe deep down I remembered when I met you that you are not some stranger. You are my husband who I am loved for years, coming to guide me home to meet our little baby after my stupid accident. Have you noticed anything unusual about me in these dreams?" she asked when she had finished.

"Apart from the fact that you're an exceptional lady and you married a nobody like me?" I replied with a smile. Kat gave me that look she always gave me in the dreams when she thought I was running myself down too much, and she picked up her handkerchief.

"Example," she said pointing, "have you no notice in dreams I always have a yucky cold? I am always snot monster."

"I wasn't going to mention it because it doesn't matter. In the dreams, it doesn't affect my love for you anyway. So why would it if it was real?"

Kat put her head on the side, gave me a lovely smile, and told me that I was too sweet about it.

"My point though," she sniffed, "is that in real life, I very rarely am having a cold. These handkerchiefs are for my horrible hay fever, which is different story, but I don't get a cold very often." I nodded in reply, unsure what she was trying to get at. "I maybe have one each winter, but I no have a nasty cold often, except maybe two or three times in my whole life. But two of the worst was the night when me met, and the day I went into coma," she paused at that point and blew her nose really hard. "One theory," she continued, "is that I am in the coma and with a blocked nose, and it irritates me so much. But I can see no wake, and it causes my dream that I have a cold. I take Lemsip. I spent half my life blowing my nose, but it never quite clears, so it no is real."

"It's a better theory than I've got," I replied.

"There is more," she added. "These dreams gloss over some points."

"Such as?" I enquired.

"Smoking," she said bluntly. "I sometimes used to smoke whole packet of tobacco in one day, but in dream just gave up, just like that." She snapped her fingers. "I sure in reality that I fell off the wagon a few times, but you no say anything because you love me, and I got there in the end. I find it easier, because not really smoked in over two years."

Her theory did make a lot of sense if you could only see it from her point of view. We did seem to know each other very well from the start, despite never having met before. Seen from her side, I could see she might think that was all her dream and that I was just a vision of her husband.

I could also find logic in Kat's theory about the dreams, her constant colds, and the ease at which she gave up her heavy smoking habit.

"And this," she said, picking up the flask. "My favourite soup, and it refills. See?" She opened the flask to show it full again, even though we had been drinking it all night. "The time has stopped, because it no is real."

I cuddled her tightly, agreeing with her theory.

However, one thing that made me think Kat's theory was wrong was, if this was *her* dream, and she was in limbo, how come *I* was seeing all these visions? If this was *her* dream, then *I* would be sat in the hospital holding her hand

and not in a haystack.

I stretched my legs and sat up against the wall of hay while Kat, who had got to her knees when she blew her nose, shuffled over and laid in my arms just like she always did in the dreams when we sat in the chair.

I explained my thoughts to Kat. She listened intently as she always did without interruption. I could see in her eyes that although she saw my point, she wanted her theory to be correct.

I could see in the candlelight that there were tears in her eyes. I wiped them away with my finger and cuddled her.

"Rob, I know my theory might not be the answer to what going on," she sobbed, "but it's the best either of us has. Maybe we did just meet tonight, and strange things happened. If we did, then I do want to be with you always. But if my theory is right, I wake up soon."

"Okay," I told her, rubbing her head soothingly. "But what if waking up is just another one of these shared dreams?"

"I rather that than carry on, waiting to know," she sniffed, and then she let out a huge sob.

"What is it, sweetheart? I said, gently squeezing her as she cried into my shoulder.

It had suddenly dawned on me that although we were both still freezing, I was cuddling Kat out of love and compassion for her rather than just warmth.

"Rob," she sobbed, "I want just to wake up now, even if it hurts. I am mummy now, and I want to meet our baby. I am in coma, but I can feel your hand and hear baby crying. I just want to wake from this coma and meet our baby, so I can say mummy loves you both."

I felt terrible, both if she was right or wrong. It must have been horrible for Kat either way.

"Perhaps if we get some more sleep, we can resolve this," I told her gently.

"That's another thing," she said quietly. "If we really got hypothermia out here naked in the cold, and we vent sleep," she paused, "we would be dead, would we no?"

She was absolutely spot on right there, and I'd never questioned that. Neither of us should really have been sleeping here. We were, and we were still alive.

Suddenly, I became aware that Kat had come nose to nose with me, and to my dismay, she gently slipped her tongue into my mouth. She didn't taste the same as she did in the dreams.

There was the smell of cigarettes in her breath, proof that she had definitely smoked that evening. That wasn't a dream, but that didn't matter at all, because her kiss was full of magical love and passion, which I returned.

"Goodnight kiss always make me sleepy," Kat said, snuggling into me and laying her head on my shoulder.

"If we wake again, will you be wanting goodnight sex to send you to sleep?" I joked, thinking I was being funny.

Kat, however, took it literally as she became sleepy very quickly and as she nodded off, she whispered in my ear, "Of course we will."

Chapter 19

Five years later

I remembered the day Kat woke in detail. What she said often flashed back to me. On the five-year anniversary of the day, it came to mind as I walked home from work via the primary school, where I would pick up our beautiful eldest daughter Lydia May on my way home to Kat and the rest of the family.

On that day, Kat was woken up slowly by taking her off the drugs that had been keeping her asleep. The doctors told me that it would be several hours before she woke and that she might need space from her relatives to adjust to her situation. This being the case, Ela and Katie had both gone to work, but were coming in the evening. Kat's mum, sisters, and brother were coming with them after a day getting to know England and our hometown. So, it was just a sleeping Kat, and I with our bundle of joy, who would later be named Lydia May.

At just three days old, she slept in my arms while I held her mum's hand.

I sat there talking to Kat and waiting for her to open her eyes while the nurses popped in and out. It wasn't me talking to her that finally woke Kat from her sleep. It was only when Lydia whimpered that Kat began to stir.

At first, she mumbled in Czech. Even though she'd given me a lot of lessons, I was far from fluent enough in my wife's native language to understand. This was why I never laughed at her muddled English, which was far superior to my Czech. I could make out that she was saying something about not doing something.

She said it several times with her eyes closed, and then she changed to English and said quite clearly, "I am was no hoover the stairs." Then suddenly her eyes opened wide, and she repeated almost excitedly, "I am was no hoover stairs."

At that point, Lydia May responded to hearing her mother's voice for the first time since her birth by whimpering loudly.

Kat couldn't move her head because she wore a neck brace, so I stood up as she rolled her eyes sideways and mumbled, "Someone has a baby." She took a deep rattled breath. "I no see baby. I see? I love babies."

"She's here," I said, laying Lydia May down where her mother could see her. Tears formed in Kat's eyes as she made a cooing face and affectionate noises.

Then she said something that confused me. I could only put it down to her confusion at waking up from her coma. It was probably something she had read in a book or seen in a film.

"Once I was having my own baby, but God said I no could have it," she breathed sadly.

"What?" I mumbled. "She's here Kat. This is our baby," I reassured her.

She reacted as though she didn't hear me at all and

continued her worrying mumblings.

"My husband and I are having our baby, but I fell," she said looking terrified. "I no feel the baby move. I worry our baby went off with the other one. My husband and I so looked forward to being parents. If baby's gone, he might no love me."

"I'm your husband, and this is our baby. She's doing well, Kat," I said reassuring her again. "She's doing better than her mum."

Again, she didn't seem to hear me and continued weakly. "The baby them bad men made when I was fifteen," she mumbled. "My husband is no know about that baby, because if maybe I tell him he no will love me."

"Of course, I love you, Stilton lady," I laughed, still thinking it was a delusion.

Kat did not realise how injured she was. Though she was still in traction, she tried to sit up to cuddle Lydia. Katarzyna panicked and started to cry and shout when she realised she couldn't move. The nurses had then come to her aid.

When she saw that she was no longer pregnant, she began to scream, "Noo not again. Help! God took my baby again."

I often went through it in my mind. It was not the first time she had talked about losing a baby. She had said it in the hostel in in Hollywood after she woke up from her fit. But it was all more than five years ago and I woke from my daydream as I reached the school gates.

Our beautiful blonde bundle of fun, who only days after her fifth birthday was starting to look and sound like her gorgeous mother, came running across the playground shouting, "Daddy," in a happy voice. It was hard to believe that she was the same tiny bundle that had been cut out of her bleeding and broken mother on the day we thought we'd lost them both.

How many things had changed since then? Least importantly, no charges were made over the incident at the hotel. The only person to lose their job was my former boss Katherine. Katie escaped punishment for kicking Katherine, when several witnesses said they had seen Katherine fall on the steps. Not one of them could recall her being kicked by Katie and some said she had fallen down the steps. Vital CCTV images of the assault had also gone missing.

It turned out that Katie was totally honest when she said she was the head of Human Resources at Aricot International.

"So technically I'm your boss, Rob," she smiled, "so take as much time as you need. When you come back there I've promoted the gym manager to her job, so you'll be the natural replacement." She winked. "When you're ready, of course, but you're on paid leave until Kat is better."

More importantly, Kat's attitude after her fall was first class. She was in one hell of a bad way. With thirty-eight fractures and mild brain damage, she could not return home for some time.

There were a lot of tears when she first woke up and realised the enormity of her accident, but soon there was a steely determination in her eyes when she looked me in the face and said calmly, "Rob, I want to be the best mummy I can be to our little girl and with you beside me, my Broccoli, these nasty injuries will no do anything to stop that."

From that point, the real Katarzyna I knew and loved stood up and showed us all her fighting spirit.

People thought Kat was a cancer patient with her

bald head covered by the red scarf, but she was quick to correct them, explaining that she often wore the scarf before her head was shaved.

Kat was offered the chance to have her hair made into a wig, but being the kind, sweet lady she was, she offered to donate her hair to make wigs for people who were more ill. She said she was looking forward to trying new styles. But after growing it for ten years, it was like losing an old friend, and she did shed a few tears when nobody was looking.

The doctors told Kat it would be a year of hard work and physiotherapy before she could walk unaided again, but Kat just laughed and told them she would be running a marathon after six months. She didn't quite manage that.

As she was in a wheelchair for some time, we had to live in my parents' downstairs spare room. But as soon as the casts came off, she was pushing herself hard on my exercise bike to regain her strength. Three months short of the year estimate the doctors gave her, my brave and wonderful wife jogged on the treadmill during her physio session with a big smile across her face. I could not have been prouder.

Not only had Kat pushed herself beyond belief to get well, but she was also a first-class mum to our little Lydia. When she was a little more mobile, Kat and I scraped together enough money for ourselves and Lydia to spend two weeks at her parents' house on her granddad's farm in the Czech Republic. There I got to meet the whole family again, although her dad made himself scarce during our time on the farm.

I was blown away by the beauty and size of the place. The rolling mountains were covered with snow. The forests were big enough that you could lose yourself. There was even a back field that they rented out to local skiers. The farm seemed to me to be a big family with brothers, sisters, and cousins all doing their bit to pitch in with work while having their own jobs. It was a super friendly place.

I thought I had to ask again why Kat felt she needed to leave when she was sixteen.

"To find a new adventure," she had smiled.

"Did you find it?" I asked.

"Nope," she shook her head smiling. "No to start with, but then I meet my Broccoli, and I am live adventure every day."

Kat used her time away from work well. She had nearly finished her degree in business studies online.

When the time came, Kat didn't want to go back to work, but she insisted she had to give herself a month and see how it went. She felt it was her duty as a parent to be at least partly responsible for bringing income into our home, so we didn't starve.

She was also excited to hear that in her absence, my former boss Katherine had been employed as one of her cleaners by her temporary replacement. "Wait till she finds out I am her boss," Kat sniggered when she was told. She wagged her finger in the air and said in a very impressive impression of my former boss, "Hello, it's me. Have you been cleaning this caravan? Let me see." Then she pretended to run her finger along the skirting board as Katherine had often done to me when Kat was in the gym. "I no think been cleaning. I think you've been on the phone and eating chocolate. I think better get wriggle on, or you will work hour late unpaid, or I fire you." She smiled.

Fortunately, or unfortunately, it never happened. The Friday evening before Kat was due to start work after a year off, her uniform was already hung up on the bedroom door. I was feeding Lydia when Kat came out of the toilet on the phone to somebody, looking a little bemused and swearing quietly under her breath.

She took Lydia from me and sat down on my lap. We both fed our little girl together, and Kat didn't say anything. She gave me a kiss and cuddle, and smiled at Lydia as we took turns to feed her.

There was something not right with Kat. After a while, I asked, and she whispered in my ear, "I love you guys, and I am sorry."

"Is it something to do with the phone call?" I remembered asking her.

Kat said nothing, but just flicked the TV on and switched to the 6 o'clock local news where the headlines across the bottom of the screen read, "Caravan park to close with the loss of 100 jobs."

"Including mine obviously," Kat said with a twisted smile.

Even though she hated it, Kat was upset at the loss of her job. However, as head cleaner, she got a good payout for her redundancy. Less than an hour after becoming jobless, Kat was already hinting with a distinct lack of subtlety that now would be a great time to have another baby.

Things were hard for a while. Money was tight, but through it all, Kat and I stood together hand in hand always. There was never so much as the slightest cross word between us.

Another thing that had changed was Ela and Katie. In the beginning, Katarzyna supported them fully, even though she had wondered if it was just a passing phase and at some point, one of them might decide they were straight. On the contrary, we couldn't be happier for Ela and Katie when they announced their engagement as soon as the laws on gay marriage changed, but that wasn't the big shock.

Encouraged by the fact that Kat and I were trying for a second baby, Ela and Katie quite rightfully wanted to start their own family using a sperm donor. This wouldn't have been anything out of the ordinary, had they not both tried to get pregnant in the hope one of them would be successful. They never stopped to think that both attempts might be.

You could write a terrible movie, or a good sitcom about how this situation ended up. Three pregnant ladies, a toddler and an exhausted husband.

So, with little space and Katarzyna being the only one whose name was actually on the tenancy agreement for the flat, Ela and Katie had moved to a small house a few streets away from Kat and myself. Luckily, they were close enough that we could all help each other when the time came.

As if my life was not already dominated by females, my lovely Katarzyna gave birth to our little Zophia on a Monday morning in March of 2013. Katie followed by giving birth to her daughter Erin on the very next day. A miraculous week followed, with a very frustrated Ela who finally gave birth to her little one Alice on Sunday night of the same week, which coincidently, was her own 22nd birthday.

So, our lives were hectic, child orientated, and filled with pink clothes. Life was great, despite financial challenges and sleep being hard to come by at that time. We had lots of help between the four of us and Jenny, who was always happy to swap babysitting duties, and my now nine-year-old niece Jemima, who was constantly begging to come and help us with her baby cousins. We all managed to make it work one way or another.

Another thing that amazed us all was how well Katarzyna had adapted her work being a mum. We could have managed to survive with one wage, but Kat, being pig-headed as she was, refused to be a kept woman and used her degree in business studies to help her work from home as a web designer. She made good money too. I did everything I could to share the job of bringing up our family and didn't let Kat do it all like some fathers would.

Five-year-old Lydia was the spitting image of her mum with her dazzling blue eyes and blonde hair worn in a plait, just like her mum, who had spent years growing hers back. Lydia also spoke with a strong Czech accent and often muddled her words, just like her mum. This was to be expected from a child growing up bilingual, as all our children were.

On that May afternoon in 2016, little Lydia was chatting away excitedly about her day at school and was bursting to tell her mum about her painting project as we walked the short distance home, hand in hand with Jenny's daughter, Amy, now seven, in tow.

When we reached the top of the stairs to the flat and pushed the stair gate open, we walked in silently.

First, we saw Katie on the sofa between Erin and Alice, who had fallen fast asleep watching CBeebies on the TV. Zophia was also asleep on the arm of her mum's chair. Kat's arm held tightly around her, so she didn't fall.

Katie put her finger to her mouth to shush Lydia, who ran up to hug her.

Usually, Kat would have jumped straight up to see Lydia and I, but she was sat at her desk with her work computer on, talking to somebody on her Bluetooth headset and mopping beads of sweat from her forehead with her angry scarf—the same one she had used for several years. She gently pedaled on her armchair bike, which I got when she decided that working on a computer wasn't physically demanding enough to keep her in shape.

The poor woman was suffering terribly with her hay fever. Her face was puffy, and her eyes were streaming. She put down her scarf and started mopping her nose with a red handkerchief as she spoke.

"Yeah, so the solicitor has given me the keys, but I have no had a look yet. Rob is at work, and I no take either of girls, because we no know what state it was left in," she said, turning to me.

She mouthed that she would be finished in a minute and gave a smile to Lydia, while the person on the other end continued talking.

She took a pack of Maltesers on the desk, opened it, popped one in her mouth and pulled a very distasteful face, before discreetly spitting it in the bin next to her. She passed two each to Lydia and Zophia, and then lobbed the pack to Katie, so the other girls could share them knowing that I wouldn't want one. "Is okay, Carroll," she said into her ear piece, "no is point in you come all the way over here at the moment." Kat paused for a moment and picked up her extra-large red handkerchief—which was looking reasonably used—from her computer keyboard, and she sneezed into it twice in quick succession.

Little Lydia rubbed her mum on the shoulder on and said, "Bless you, Mumma."

Kat mouthed, "Thank you, sweetie," and blew her a kiss. "Hay fever," she said down the phone as I took Zophia, who was asking for a cuddle with her dad. "No is okay. I went while Zophia was nursery. Is no a problem. I am self-employed now. I can catch up work if client no complains, as day know I am working mum. Rob is home. I have got loads of explaining to do. Maybe Rob and I can help find tenants for you. You look after us, we look after you. Okay, Carroll, you have my word. Katarzyna is on the case. Get some sleep.

I talk to you later."

Kat took a deep breath, and as she let it out, the thing she was thinking accidentally slipped out in front of the five little girls. She put her head in her hands and clearly said, "Oh, fucky fucky fuckballs." Then suddenly remembering we were all there, she put her hand over her mouth in dismay at herself for swearing so blatantly in front of all the children.

Lydia's reaction made us all laugh. She took a dramatically shocked breath and bellowed, "Mummy, go and sit on the naughty step. *Now!*"

Kat laughed along with Katie and me. She lowered herself onto her knees and shuffled toward Lydia with her arms out. This exposed her belly, leaving nobody in doubt that she was pregnant with our third child in six years.

She put her arms around Lydia and hugged our girl as though she hadn't seen her in days. She had the look of a mother's adoring love in her eyes as she said quietly, "Mummy is very sorry. I will do twenty minutes on the step for each swear, yes? Deal?"

"And buy me sweets," Lydia smiled.

"No push it, young lady. It a school day."

"No mummy," Lydia teased, "It's *don't* push it young lady. *It's* a school day."

Although Kat hated being corrected, she smiled at Lydia's bluntness.

"Since when is it okay to correct your mummy?" I asked her gently.

"Since my teacher told me I would not learn to speak English properly until mummy learns."

I think we need to have meeting with Mrs. Partridge,"

Kat smiled. "Shall we speak Bohemian? Or Polski? Magyar? Deutsch? Francais?"

"I don't think my teacher can speak as many languages as you, mummy," Lydia smiled.

"Is mummy a better teacher than Mrs. Partridge?" I asked.

"Yeah," she said excitedly. "Mummy, the best teacher." She laid her head on her mum's pregnant tummy and cuddled her as I put Zophia on my shoulders. We all squeezed into our daily family hug. This was something we all did when we were reunited after a day apart.

Lydia was right. Her mum was an excellent teacher. In the evenings, we would cuddle up together, and Kat and I would assist Lydia with her homework. Not that she needed it. She was as bright as her mother, if not brighter. Kat had taught her several languages from a very young age so that she could speak to her non-English speaking relatives.

"Anyway," Kat said, as we all parted, "no forget mummy has to go to the naughty step for a long time."

"Off you go then. Quick march," I laughed, pointing at the door.

"Twenty minutes per F-word and I want you to sit and think about what you've done," Katie added, faking an authoritarian tone.

"No talking either," I added, "Or there'll be no pocket money."

"And it will be straight to bed with no dinner," Katie added, much to the amusement of Lydia.

"Can I appeal on grounds that it time for children feeding?" Kat asked, in a solemn voice.

"It's my turn though," I told her.

"But *I no want to!*" she smiled, stamping her foot and pretending to have a childlike tantrum.

"You're not cooking the kids' tea tonight. I am." Katie told us. "I'm babysitting tonight. You asked me to come over, so you and Rob could..."

"Oh yes, of course," Kat smiled. "Mummy will take her punishment," she said to Lydia. "In fact, I double it on three conditions. One, I get to go toilet, because of baby I need a wee. Two, I get to take a flask of tea. And three, Daddy comes too. And if you're good for Aunty Katie, you may get sweets as a one-off."

"What exactly is going on?" I asked in bewilderment, but Kat just kissed me and said, "You make flask of tea, I go to toilet, and then you come with me. I no tell you in front of girls."

The tea was made, and Kat came out of the loo and went into the bedroom. A few seconds later, she came out with a bundle of clean hankies, shoved them in her pockets, and put her nose drops in her nostrils. "For all the fucking good they do," she scowled.

"That's another twenty minutes on the naughty step for you, young lady."

"Sorry," she smiled, adding that she would extend her stay on the naughty step until she learnt her lesson.

"Come, boy," she teased taking my hand. "And no peeking at mummy, or no sweeties," she added to Lydia and Zophia.

~~*~*~*

Instead of going out onto the central staircase, she took me very slowly down the fire escape.

"So, what is this all about and why did you tell Carroll you'd been to the solicitors?" I begged.

"All in good time," she beamed, "but must tell you while we walk, a fairy tale." Kat turned, gave me her open-mouthed smile, and we kissed at the bottom of the stairs.

Kat gave her nose an almighty blow to help her talk through her hay fever. Then she took my hand and assured me, as we walked at a leisurely pace along the back of the building, that she didn't know the tale she was about to tell me until that morning.

"Once upon a time, there was a hotel in Cromer. No a one like where you work, but nice Victorian family hotel with big garden and dining area. It was nice place, class and style, but was no on the seafront or cliff. So is always second fiddle to big hotels."

"Okay," I smiled, knowing Kat loved to get to the point in most the dramatic long-winded way that she could.

She talked excitedly with big enthusiastic hand expressions that only my lovely wife could pull off.

"So, all is good in 1880s. There is railway nearby. Bring people from Norwich, London, Birmingham, and other places. There are in hotel sixty rooms, so is no too big, but nice friendly size. Hotel is doing okay. Then is first World War, and nobody is holiday. It shuts the first time, but reopens in 1920 and is all good. But in 1939, those…" she used a lot of swear words to describe the Nazi's, "…attacked my Polish great grandparents a second time. Europe then is World War, and hotel is shut. They use it to home evacuated children."

"So, are we going to an old hotel?" I asked.

Kat shook her head as she wiped her nose and told me, "No right now. Later if there is time. So is re-open in 1950s after big hotel on cliff burn down. Less competition. Is done when beach is back in favour as the 50s and 60s people holiday at home."

I realised that I had never been this far at the back of the flat before. I was gobsmacked at how much more of the building there was hidden from the road. There was a large open grassy area which was overgrown.

"I never been down here before either," Kat smiled. "Beautiful if looked after, isn't it?" I nodded. "Then," she continued, "the 70s come and people have money to travel." She rubbed her fingers together. "They take package holidays. Abroad business is slow, and by mid-1970s, is dark run area of town. Hotel's former glory gone, and now is cheap place for man to take his," she pulled a face disgusted as she said, "prostitute." She stopped and sneezed into her hanky twice. "I think we go this way," she said, pointing at a gap in a large hedge that revealed a patch of wall. In it was a small door, which she opened.

"That's somebody's garden, Kat," I told her.

"I know, but the owner knows we are here," she smiled.

I sighed. My crazy lovely super wife had finally lost the plot. Running her own business and being a stay-at-home mum had eventually worn her down. I went with the flow, but now she was breaking into people's gardens.

"So," she continued as I followed her through an arched hedge, "in 1982, hotel is closed for good. Is sold to local man. He put shops in the lower floors, and he built a flat in the attic. Plans to build more on other floors, but he ran out of money." She paused and had a little sneeze, before continuing as she pulled me by the hand into the garden. "The man died in 1985. His son is inheriting the building and is open his own shop. He and his wife lived in a house nearby, but they never quite had da time or know how to do anything with old hotel. He uses building to store stock for his antique shop, and never build any more flats."

"You're not talking about our old landlord, Mr Proctor, are you?" I asked.

"Rob, no try to guess the end," she frowned, and then smiled. "Anyway, you never guess end."

Kat stopped and sat down on a wooden bench at the end of the garden into which we had so rudely wandered. She sniffed and wiped her eyes, and then she took a cup from me as I poured her tea and mine.

Kat and I stopped and looked around at the garden we were sitting in. It was overgrown with colourful plants and trees, but it had the beauty of something created in the mind of Lewis Carol or Frances Hodgson Burnett. It looked as though the owner had once looked after the garden very well, but it seemed to have fallen into a slight state of disrepair. Despite the beautiful arrangement of flowers and trees, the grass was uncut, and the hedges were overgrown just as if the owner had left them suddenly.

"It beautiful," she said, cuddling up close to me with her mouth still open in awe. "I feel like Alice when she first stepped into Wonderland, or Mary when she opens the door to the secret garden. The Secret Garden, my favourite children story. I read over and over, amazing how the magic of a garden brings people together."

"I had the audiobook on cassette," I said, stroking her hair as she leaned back in my arms.

"You're lazy cheater," she laughed, slapping me playfully.

"It could also be Tom's," I looked at my watch, " 4:37 in the afternoon garden." We laughed at the stupid reference to another of our childhood books written in the early twentieth century.

"So," she began again, "for years, nice old man and his wife are owning the old hotel and run their shop. They rent out the flat to a few people over the years, but from about the year 2003, it sits empty and rundown. Then in 2005, this foreign teenager came and rented it out. She no speaks much English, is quiet and withdrawn, and pleasant, but no overly nice sometimes rude and stubborn. In fact, she not nice at all, but landlord needs money, and she is falling in love with the flat because of it first time she is have own home. Landlord happy that he has money coming in, but to start he no like the girl that much. She is often tired and grumpy. She is always swearing and smoking a lot and rude."

"Was the girl you, by any chance?" I asked Kat.

She sneezed heavily and nodded. "In time, though," she sniffed, "Mr. Proctor not like her to start with, but he starts to come around to her as she tries to better herself. Later she has boyfriend and her sister move in, and she is changed girl. They become friends. Later she is having children and brings them to see him in the shop. Now she is clean up her act, married, children, no smoking, has her degree and her own small business, the landlord realised he got her wrong all along."

She sneezed again as the pollen from the garden started to unsettle her allergies even more. She blew her nose and administered some more of her nose drops.

"Anyway," she said sniffing, "As you might remember, nice Mr Proctor died last year."

"You think I'd forget?" I laughed with sarcasm, as Kat mouthed a quick sorry.

It was me who had gone down to look for Alf Proctor

after his wife called to say he hadn't come home. I found him lifeless on the floor under his shop counter, where the poor old man had been dead for several hours. Katarzyna had been inconsolable at his death and funeral.

"Carroll is phone me from New Zealand this morning," Kat said, standing up and pulling me with her so that we walked hand in hand along the safest route through the garden. Carroll was Mr Proctor's wife and soul beneficiary of his estate. She was also our new landlady. They had no children, and after her husband's death, she had gone for an extended visit to her sister in New Zealand.

"Carroll is no coming home. She is old and wants to stay with her sister. She tells me the story about hotel and how she owns what's left of it, and she asked of me a favour."

"What sort of favour?" I asked, suddenly realising that Kat was about to drop something on me.

"She asks me to take care of her interests," she smiled. "Help her rent out the shops to new business."

"What do you get apart from thanks, considering we've got a third baby on the way?"

"We a get a cut of the rent from any tenants we get into shops or the hotel."

"That's not too shabby," I replied, but I still worried she was taking on too much.

"No only that," she smiled, pointing up the garden. I saw that she was pointing at a fair-sized ivy-covered cottage about a hundred metres or so away from where we stood. "This is Carroll's old house. I picked up spare keys from her solicitor this morning. Just say yes, and it ours for rent free if we agree to help sort out the flat, and look after the flat and the shops."

"But how has all this just come about?"

"I know the timing stinks," she smiled, "but we have needed a new home for a long time. This is the best opportunity. Just a little more work and we get all this free. We no have to do this all right away. Most of the building is standing empty for thirty years. We can just do a little at a time, starting by re-leasing the shops at the front and our flat to new tenants. Is no like she asks us to re-open the hotel. We can get on with our current jobs, and just collect the rent for her."

I nodded, seeing that Kat had thought it through well and not just jumped at it. She thought we could do this all quite easily.

"Just imagine our no so little family running around the garden, play football with the girls, and dis little boy," she pointed at her pregnant tummy.

I reminded myself that Katarzyna had never been wrong with her choices in the past, and if anyone knew what they were doing it was her.

"There is an alternative," she said bluntly.

"What's that?" I asked, although I was already on the verge of saying yes.

"Well," she said glumly, "Carroll could sell the place to building company and kick us out of flat. We have to find new home for us and the children, which will be nowhere near as good as this one."

"I think we know the answer then," I smiled.

"That's good," she smiled jumping up, "because I already tell Carroll we move in as soon as it ready."

"So, you've looked inside it?" I laughed, suspecting I knew the answer.

"No-oo-oo," she grinned, "but it got a garden. Is all that matter." She looked at her watch. "I am sitting on naughty step for thirty more minutes. Let's go look inside before we go get the kids and tell them."

As we got to the door, Kat reached into her bag and pulled out a rather heavy bunch of very old keys. Each of them had faded numbers on them. "For the hotel rooms," she said, smiling and nodding at them. From underneath, she took a smaller key for the door.

Inside the cottage, it was like a Tardis. I had expected it to be old and rundown, but Mr and Mrs. Proctor had either looked after it well or paid somebody else to.

It was a little dusty, but there was a large open kitchen and dining room. You could park a bus in the living room, which was already furnished. "We put office in the corner and our cuddle chair by the TV. So even when we are old and grumpy and hate each other, we can still have kiss and cuddle in our favourite chair." She laughed and grabbed me for a kiss.

~~*~*~*

Instead of going up to the flat when we got back we opened the door to Proctors' Antiques. The creepy old shop had been boarded up since Mr Proctor passed away. As a proud, if not overly successful dealer, Alf Proctor had kept his shop spotless, but now there was so much dust that both of us were sneezing.

I joked that we should add dusty old shops to the ever-growing list of things that made Kat sneeze. That was until she reminded me that I sneezed too, passing me one of a bagful of hankies she brought with her. She used the cheeky smile that she reserved for only me and said, "At least one of us is prepared, no?"

Kat was very sombre as we checked over the items that were left in the shop, looking through antiques that we knew nothing about, but clearly were worth something to somebody.

Apparently, Kat's sombre state was due to Mr Proctor's death hitting her all over again, which was understandable, because the lovely old man was her landlord for so many years.

As we went through the heavy wooden door that led through to the back, I turned to make sure it was shut and looked back around to find Kat with her mouth open as though she was about to sneeze again.

As it turned out, she was gawping in awe at the sight of what lay ahead of us.

The room in which we stood was three or maybe four times the size of the town hall. It was so big that when Kat did sneeze once more, the echo bounced around the room. To our left-hand side, there was a grand staircase that split two ways. The left staircase, I assumed, went up to the rooms, while the right-hand stairs led to a balcony.

"This must be the reception and dining area," Kat said, and smiled, wiping her nose impatiently as she gazed around the room.

"And the entertainment room," I added, nodding to the opposite side of the staircase where there was a small stage.

"It old dance floor," she shouted excitedly, "like Blackpool Tower. Only better, because it's right here and ours."

"We could create a ballroom dancing club," I laughed.

"No seriously, we could," Kat smiled. I saw that dangerous excited gleam in her eye. I could see she was already thinking of a way to make money out of this place. "We could cash in on Strictly Come Dancing," the very popular tv show in the UK, which involved celebrities dancing with professional dancers. "We could even contact the BBC and ask if we can host it here." She teased. "Imagine if either of us could actually dance without break each other toes," she grinned, taking hold of me in the pose of a waltz. "Imagine a band is playing, and we have hold of each other tight and waltz. It 1920s all over again."

It was one of those moments I loved, where Kat and myself would just do something spontaneous. We danced around the floor dodging between tables, chairs, and other antiques that had been stored there. We held each other tight and fooled around, pretending that we could actually dance, and we kissed and spun on the spot.

"We need to find a way to open this magical place back into the public," she sniffed, "even if it takes us twenty years to do it. Plus," she added, holding her face right against mine, "even though you my husband – a special man and I love you always, I hate you forever and ever if you no let me try." She gave me a big smile, knowing that I didn't dare say no.

I remembered hearing myself tell her, "You're the businesswoman. If you can make it happen, I'm right there with you."

She was already running through a business plan in her head. "If God forbid, Brexit actually happens, people will be forced to holiday closer to home. That could work our advantage, not that it would be a good thing." Obviously, this was just before Brexit actually happened, and we were unsure of the implications of Britain leaving the EU. "There no upgrade since 1955," she continued. "In 1980, people thought was old, but in 2016 it makes it a museum. So, we stay da 50s theme and maybe keep cost down."

"That's genius," I told her as her vision filled my brain.

"See?" she smiled. "No TV in rooms, no Wi-Fi, lock your mobile phone, laptop and iPad up in reception. People enjoy music and talking, and tea, and cake."

"We could park a DeLorean at the entrance," I joked.

"Why is that?" she smiled, with a confused look.

I fluffed up what hair I had, and gave her my best Doc Brown impression, "Marty, we have to take the DeLorean back to 1955."

She looked at me and burst out laughing, but said gently, "Rob, sweetheart, that is the worst Doc Brown impression I am hear in my life, but maybe you are on to something."

We were smiling and laughing as we carried on our little dance. Kat began to hum a gentle tune, which sounded something along the lines of *da da,da da, da de do*. She repeated it again and again, only pausing to sneeze. Then, she made me laugh by blowing her nose in time with the tune. She smiled and kept singing as we looked lovingly into each other's eyes. Then, lost in the moment, we drew closer and carried on spinning as we kissed as deeply and passionately as we had on the night out on the cold pavement when I first realised I would spend the rest of my life in the arms of this lovely crazy lady.

As we gazed into each other's eyes, I felt as though the world was spinning around us like a movie montage.

As we danced, I watched in my mind the moment I had first shaken hands with the figure I pulled out of the snow, the moment we greeted each other at the airport and later kissed in the snow outside the flat, our days having fun in the park, and the nights laying on the beach until sunrise.

Then there was our wedding day, and the big wheel on Santa Monica pier, the sun set over San Francisco, and the look on Kat's face when she told me she was pregnant with Lydia.

There was the shock and relief that I felt when I was told Kat had died, only to find it was not true, and the feeling of joy when she woke up from her coma and looked into Lydia's eyes as a first-time mum.

Then we were dancing with the girls in the garden, around our new home, and back on the dance floor. Things around us seemed to be taking shape. When baby Erica was born, we'd been sure she was a boy, but our third child was a cute little girl just like her sisters.

They lay on the floor playing with her as Kat and I worked together to clean the hotel rooms.

This hadn't passed, so how could it be when she wasn't born yet? Kat was six months pregnant when the dance started, and the hotel was a wreck, yet in only a few minutes our baby was born, and the hotel was taking shape already. But still we danced, and still, the future unravelled before our eyes as though our lives were in a movie.

We danced to a band as the hotel had its grand opening night, and the room was full for the first time. It was ready in only a year with the help of friends and family. Jenny and my dad kindly helped in the bar, while my sister Jeanette and her partner Charlie helped man reception. Ela and Katie supervised the children's party room away from the alcohol, while Kat and I mingled with the guests and handed out leaflets and web addresses. Invites included local business people, local MPs and town councillors, as well as ordinary locals such as ourselves.

Our first guests to stay in the hotel came all the way from the Czech Republic. It was Kat's family this time, including her dad and grandparents. My Nanna, now aged ninety-one, and my other grandparents, now in their seventies, were there, as was eleven-year-old Jemima and her little brother. Even our landlady Carroll broke her vow never to return to the UK and had come all the way from New Zealand, so she could be there to see the old place as her husband had always wanted it to be.

As the new proprietors, it was expected of Kat and I to have the first dance. We waltzed gently. We were joined on the floor by Ela and Katie, and then Jenny and Amy and my parents. Kat and I joined for a kiss in celebration of all our hard work coming together, and we closed our eyes to enjoy the moment with each other.

Suddenly, I was with Kat in the cold haystack with the candles alight. We were on our knees, cuddled together and waltzing to the same tune as Kat sang hauntingly. *Da da, da da, da de de de do do.*

"What's going on?" I asked, panicked, but Kat just kept waltzing and sang the haunting tune. I shook her, but I couldn't wake her from it.

I closed my eyes and opened them to find myself back on the dance floor with Kat. Only this time, we were joined by our girls, Lydia and Zophia, waltzing to the tune themselves while Kat and I held little one year old, Erica, between us.

The room was halfway decorated for Christmas, but this was a private party. There was a large picture of Kat up on the wall, and next to it Ela had written in letters that each took up an A4 sheet of paper, "Happy 30th Birthday Old Lady!"

Looking around, I saw dancing. In attendance were not only all of our friends and some of my family, but Kazia, Dusa, Dowid, and their families. After a few moments, we split apart, and Kat danced with her brother, which was something I never thought I'd see. Katie was in charge of music. She put on the song *Dance with My Father* by Luther Vandross, and Kat grabbed her father. Though she had previously hated and barely spoke to him, she now embraced him and danced with him for a good twenty minutes. It seemed all their differences had been put aside.

Closing my eyes again, I found myself back in the cold haystack. We were still waltzing on our knees, but Kat's tune had changed. She danced with her eyes closed as though she was still asleep, and she sang in full voice, "I would love, love, love to dance with my father again."

Again, I tried to wake her, but she just leaned on me and snuggled tightly into my shoulder. She said, "I love you, Rob," and then went back into her haunting tune. "Da da, da da, da de de de do do."

I closed my eyes again. When I reopened them, we were dancing in the hotel garden on a hot summer day. The place was full of guests relaxing in the heat of summer. With our three girls, we danced through the gate in the wall to our garden. When I looked down at Kat's tummy, she was apparently pregnant once more. "Maybe a boy this time," she smiled.

Soon after that, our fourth daughter was born. We named her Angelica. I could hear the doctor's words ringing in my ears. "Your daughter has Down's Syndrome. She will never live a normal life."

Kat had an answer for that. It was, "You just watch her."

We waltzed in the fields in front of Kat's parents' farm. We danced through several family birthdays, Christmases, and funerals of my Nanna and Kat's grandparents. Each time, we looked around at the kids growing up way too fast. Before

I knew it, my little niece who had cuddled up to us to watch Bambi the first night Kat and I were together was a woman, and we were hosting her wedding reception at the hotel. She already had her own little one cooking in her tummy.

As we continued to dance, I smiled lovingly at Kat. She smiled, but not the same way. She looked a little scared but kept humming the tune to us both.

"Are you seeing these things?" I asked in a panicking tone. Kat nodded and seemed frightened, but kept singing.

I began to realise as it went on, that this crazy montage of visions might actually be our real lives passing us by as we danced in our daydream. So I closed my eyes tight in the hope that when I opened them, the world would stop spinning so fast.

Each time I closed my eyes and tried to stop, we were back in the haystack. Every time we opened them, we had both aged at least six months.

Suddenly, Kat in the hay spoke without opening her eyes. "Rob I dink this mean we are waltzing through our lives. Need to stop before they are over."

"How do we stop it?" I asked hurriedly.

"I no know," she panicked. "Just kiss me passionately one more dime before we no get another chance."

Chapter 20

The family get together

N ot knowing which world or time I was in, or whether it would help, I threw myself into Kat and felt her lock lips. Suddenly, we were pushing into each other and kissed as though we would never get another chance.

Kat's face was all that filled my vision. I wasn't sure whether we were in the haystack, or the dance hall, or even what time we were in, but it didn't matter as long as we had each other.

Suddenly there was a voice behind us that said, "Ewww."

Kat and I almost jumped out of our skins. We'd been in the hall, dancing and thinking we were alone after clearing away the plates from breakfast. The hotel was half full, which was very good considering that we lived in a summer town, and it was currently November and raining.

This time of year, we seemed to be booked by old retired couples or young couples with either preschool age children or none.

Anywhere over a quarter full in the run before the

Christmas holidays was good business. This meant there were only about forty breakfast bowls to wash up and the same number of guests to check on before the whole family got together and started decorating for Christmas.

Kat and I had taken a moment between the busy times for a quick dance. We looked around to see who it was, but it couldn't have been anyone but our Angelica with a grimace on her cute face.

"What is it Angel?" her sister Erica called through from reception where she was checking guests out. Seconds later, she walked through to the back brandishing one of her mother's pretty homemade hankies as though she had just stepped out of reception to use it.

"Mum and dad were kissing," Angel replied, pulling the most disgusted face.

Our third oldest daughter Erica was only six weeks or so past her seventeenth birthday. She was a little older than her mother was when she came to the UK, but she was going on about thirty.

Despite being the only one of our now five daughters who didn't look even slightly like her mother, she was more like her than she knew in attitude. She wasn't quite as tall as the others, and she had my eyes, with bobbed dark hair and glasses, causing her sister to tease her by saying that she was Meg Griffin from the animated TV show family guy, the ugly one who the others picked on, although she was far from ugly.

However, she pulled faces just like her mum and also had her mum's tendency to come into work even if she was ill. Just that morning, she had come to work with a heavy cold despite her position being voluntary.

She had been quietly spoken, but since her elder sisters had gone to university, she had come out of herself much more. She had a lot of energy and enthusiasm, and a lot to say for herself when her more dominant sister Zophia was not around.

Erica was at college during the week studying catering, but rather than resting at weekends, she insisted on coming to us in the hotel. This was because, like her mum, she was incapable of relaxing, but she also just loved the place.

However, Erica stood there in the doorway giving us a look Kat had given her when she was a naughty little girl. "Mum and dad, don't be so gross. Old people over forty shouldn't be kissing," she laughed, speaking through her blocked nose and giving us a wink.

It was clear from Erica's voice that she was suffering badly, but just like her mother, telling her to rest and take it easy was like throwing a personal insult at her. This was why we didn't even try to stop her coming to help anymore, apart from the fact she was a great worker.

"Seriously though, mum and dad," she grinned, "I'm sick, and I've been hard at work all morning. You had one job. I get thirty seconds to come out here for a break, and catch you kissing like naughty teenagers."

"I remind you of that when you forty, young lady. It's only twenty-two years and eleven months away, missy, and you have no even got boyfriend," Kat told her with a smile.

Erica turned away and sneezed heavily. You'll all be dead by then, mum," she sniffed, while Angelica and I just giggled.

"I will be sixty-nine. No dead, young lady," she laughed.

Erica put her hands over her sister's ears and pretended to vomit, saying, "Angel and I don't want to know what you guys will be getting up to in the bedroom on my fortieth, thanks, mum. And get the maths right, mum. Your birthday is two weeks after mine. You'll still be sixty-eight, but you'll be sixty-nining."

Kat and I were holding on to each other, trying to keep our faces straight at our third daughter's fast wit. "Do you even know what you're making jokes about?" I asked, knowing that Erica probably had no idea.

Erica sneezed again and shook her head smiling, "Honestly, my chastity belt and I really haven't got a clue about stuff like that."

"You no should talk about what you no know about then," Kat teased.

"You know I'm a party girl mum. Always out on the pull, me," she laughed.

"Ah, so that's reason I tucked you in bed every night because you felled asleep doing you homework at 10 pm after being at college all day, because you work too hard."

"Only following your example mum," she grinned before sneezing again.

"Well don't," Kat teased.

"Seriously though sweetheart, no be embarrassed," Kat told her. "You pretty and you're old enough. So if you want, bring home boyfriend or girlfriend and use your own bed where you are safe and comfortable."

Erica went bright red. "I'm definitely not doing it now that the old people have said it's okay," she said with a smile. "Love you, mum and dad," she added, and blew her nose with a cringe-worthy noise.

"Love you too, young lady," Kat said warmly. Then

she added more sternly, "Is why you are going home to bed until you feeling better."

Erica protested, saying that she was fine and that her mum never took a sick day.

"All right, I give you that," Kat conceded. "But one more sneeze out of you, and you'll be..." Kat stopped dead, drew a short breath, and sneezed very heavily herself, causing Erica, Angel and I to laugh.

Kat smiled too seeing the funny side of it.

"One more sneeze from you, old lady," Erica teased, putting her arms out to give her mum a friendly hug.

Kat backed off, saying, "No give me your illness, young lady!" There ensued a chase in which Erica chased her mother around the hall trying to hug her, while Angelica and I just laughed at the pair of them as they ran.

Everyone knew that Kat would never send Erica home, knowing how much work meant to her. Angelica left them to it, and I went to make tea.

Angelica was nearly fifteen. Despite her Downs Syndrome, we didn't treat her different from any of our other children. She went to a special needs school in Norwich, but other than that, Kat and I, and her other siblings did our best to treat her the same as everyone else.

That said, she did need a little extra help with things, and she had a very close bond with Erica especially, who loved to take her younger sisters under her wing, just like Lydia and Zophia had done with her. Angel was very close with all her siblings and loved to cuddle her little brothers, Charlie and Roger. Yes, Charlie and Roger were named after the cat, who was still somehow alive, and the rabbit who was no longer with us, and little sister Jenny Ela-Kate.

If you have been concentrating, you'd realise that seventeen years and a few months had gone by in a flash, but to us, it actually seemed like we had lived those years. The baby Kat had been pregnant with when we started waltzing was seventeen-year-old Erica. We now had seven children in all, five girls and two boys. We had no real plans to add to our brood after reaching forty. Though Kat had spoken in passing about her desire to round it off to eight, no plans had been made.

Going back to Angel, she did come out with some strange and funny things at the best of times. One of these moments came only a few minutes later as the whole family of over thirty people sat around the table drinking tea and planning who was going to do what.

As I sat and looked over around the table, it still amazed me at the size of not only our family, but the extended family who had come to help. Who would have thought that when I met Kat all those years ago that we would end up with seven children and five of them would be girls, with three now grown up? There were also several of our nieces and nephews.

What made me feel really old was seeing my niece, Jemima, now nearly with her own growing family.

"I blame you two for this," Jemima smiled, pointing from her baby bump to her three children. "I was certainly influenced by spending time with your lot. Especially this one. She was such a cute baby." She grabbed her cousin Lydia for a hug.

"Love you too, Cousin Jem, and I can't wait to have cuddles with this one," Lydia told her, having not seen her cousin since the summer. She kissed her on both cheeks and then bent down and kissed the baby bump.

"It your fault we had big family," Kat smiled at Jemima. "I no want children before I met you. Remember dose times when you and your uncle and I babysat, and we watched Bambi and cried together?"

"Good times," Jemima grinned, teasing that we could do it again for old times' sake. "I don't think you can fit me on your knees, Uncle Rob and Aunty Kat," she laughed.

"You could try, but no break the chair," Kat teased. "You were such a cute little girl I had to have my own."

"But you didn't get a cute one straight away," Lydia laughed, saying, "You had me, Zophia, and..." she stopped and gave her sister, Erica, a teasing smile before adding, "Meg Griffin from Family Guy. All before you got a cute one." She pointed at her sister Angel.

She gave her mum and I a hug as she went to sit down, insisting that Jemima put her down for babysitting when she was back from university for Christmas.

I was humbled by how many people had turned out to lend a hand free of charge.

Even my mum and dad came. A surprise visitor was Charlie the cat, who somehow made it into the hotel and kept trying to fuss people. This was the same cat that Kat had rescued three years before she met me twenty-five years earlier. He wasn't young then, so he must have been the oldest cat in history.

Getting the hotel ready for Christmas was such a big family event that Lydia and Zophia had both come back from university to help.

We were all older than the year before, but what scared me was how frail and ill Katie looked. She was forty-nine now. While that was no great age, Katie was suffering badly in a tough battle with cancer. Even so, she was putting a brave face on it, and there was no talk of her giving in.

Kat and I were sharing a chair as always. Though we were in our mid forties and parents of seven children, we still loved up like a pair of randy teenagers as Zophia had pointed out affectionately.

It was when we'd finished our tea and were about to crack on with the job at hand, that Angelica, who had been cuddling her six-year-old brother, Charlie, and eight-year-old sister, Jenny Ela-Kate, suddenly said rather loudly across the table to Erica. "When are you going to pay me not to tell Mum and Dad about that pregnancy test?"

Suddenly all conversation stopped. You could have heard a pin drop. Every eye in the room was on Lady Erica. She calmly poured herself a second cup of tea, took off her glasses and cleaned them, then put them back on and gave everyone a bemused and frightened look. I felt shocked and sorry for poor Erica as she wasn't exactly comfortable with an audience at the best of times.

Stunned, I tried to say something, but Kat was first to react. Her voice boomed down the table, enough to scare us all. "*Erica Irenka Susana Brownlow*, is this true?" she said in a loud, but calm voice.

Erica nodded calmly glaring sideways at her sister.

"Sweetheart, do you know who the father is?" Kat asked more quietly, as many of the other people including her sisters looked away awkwardly.

Erica just shrugged her shoulders and took a sip of tea. Then she looked around at everyone as she sanitised her hands like her mother always did and said, bemused, "Why is everyone looking at me?"

I couldn't believe what I was hearing, but still, I was not surprised that one of our lovely daughters was making

Kat and I grandparents. I had to admit that I was very surprised at which one it was. Lydia was twenty-two and had
a steady boyfriend, and Zophia was twenty and no Virgin
Mary from what I'd heard. But I thought seventeen-year-old
Erica had more sense, because she was a squeaky-clean, good
girl. I loved the friendly banter we had with her. I'd never had
to tell her off as a child, and she was the one who told us she
had sworn off men until she was older.

"Well maybe," I responded calmly, "it's because we've
just found out you're making us grandparents, you don't
have a boyfriend, and you don't know who the father is."

Erica looked back at me across the table, turned a
deep shade of red, and laughed nervously. She covered her
face with her arms as she giggled out of control, while people
looked on in awkward silence. Finally, she came up laughing
all over her face to say, "Dad... I don't know who the father is,
because it's not mine. Angel found it while we were cleaning
the loos and asked me what it was."

"It's not yours?" I breathed.

Erica sniffed and shook her head, saying, "Last time I
checked, I was single and about a million miles from ready
to mingle." Then she looked down at her legs, smiled, and
added, "My chastity belt is well secured, and I'm not open for
business anytime soon."

There was a burst of relieved laughter around the
room and a bemused look from all the younger kids, who
had no idea what Erica was talking about. My heart rate
calmed. I felt Kat breathe a sigh of relief as she sat back down
on my lap. The funniest part of it was that we all knew Erica
wasn't joking about her chastity belt, and she did indeed
wear one.

The relief, however, was short-lived, because Ela
stood from the next table and said boldly, "Okay, girls,

whose is it?"

Everyone looked round at each other and silence fell, but it was quickly replaced by murmuring. It was Zophia who spoke loudest. *"All right, everyone, stand up,"* she ordered, and strangely everyone did, because everyone always listened to Zophia.

"Okay," she said, once we were all standing. "This is simple. Everyone who's not pregnant sit down."

Jemima clearly was, and we all knew she was about to pop for the fourth time.

Not only that, neither had Lydia, and they were staring at each other confused and gob-smacked.

I was even more gob-smacked to see Ela and Katie's two girls, Alice and Erin, still standing and giving each other a different, but similar look to that of Zophia and Lydia.

"Erm, ladies jokes over," Eric called to the other girls. "Angel wanted to play wind-up, so I helped and we never found anything in the toilet. Errrm, got you." She added.

The room had gone dead silent again, and I felt like somebody was going to jump out with a TV camera and tell us it had all been a TV prank. Zophia looked confused as though she had been expecting to be the only one standing, and Lydia was smiling.

In a touching act of solidarity all four of the young ladies who were all either sisters or cousins and had grown up together, walked up to each other, all with shocked looks on their faces and hugged each other without daring to look their parents in the face.

It was Lydia who stepped forward first and said nervously "Hi guys… erm… my partner Tom and I have been together two years and I'm only a year younger than mum was when she had me. Love you mum and dad, so we were going to wait and tell you when we got to three months. Well, erm... *surprise*."

Eric ran up and hugged both her sisters overeagerly and both tried to keep her at arm's length to avoid catching the illness.

I sat with my arm around Kat, and she stood with her hand on my shoulder. We smiled at each other with that kind of smile that says, *Oh my god we are so excited to be grand-parents,* but at the same time says, *That's our little girl. Where in hell did the time go?*

As Lydia came over to hug us both, it was Katie's birth daughter, Erin, who was a very shy girl who just looked at her sister Alice, who spoke briefly and just said, "Erm... Erin and I although we're only twenty, we've both been with our boyfriends since school and wanted children young while everyone is here to enjoy them and," she looked at her sister. "Apparently, we are both having one."

She didn't say it in words, but the look on her face said it all. What she was saying, was that both girls had chosen to become young mothers to give their mother Katie a chance to become a grandmother while there was still a chance of beating her cancer.

Then there was a moment's pause as they both turned and hugged both their mums. It was one of those moments where your heart went out to them, all because there was nothing more special, after Katie had fought her cancer for two years, than for her to find out she was going to live be a double grandmother. The announcement had a great effect, because only a month later we got the news that Katie's cancer was in remission and she was going to live.

Zophia was at the end of the line, and she stood there awkwardly breathing hard saying, "I know what you think.

You're right, I'm a slag. I had several one nights stands. I don't know who the father is and... I'm going to throw up." She turned and ran towards the toilet.

"Well, I don't think anyone's surprised about me." Jemima smiled, showing off her huge belly, she sat down.

Kat and I were just in shock, I stood up silently and gave her a kiss and cuddle. Both of us were in tears. I wasn't sure if it was happiness or shock or becoming grandparents. Both of us were a little shocked and upset at Zophia's revelation that she had been sleeping around and didn't know who the father was.

However, the overwhelming thought was that she was our daughter, and we would support her whatever happened and that the most important thing was her baby. We were shocked, but happy grandparents twice.

Not that it was unusual to become grandparents in your forties, but Kat and I both still saw ourselves as middle-aged parents, because of the age gap of sixteen years between Lydia and Charlie who was six.

However, you saw just how much time had flown when you realised, that little girl you held in your arms and rocked to sleep as a baby was now a twenty-two-year-old lady expecting a little baby of her own, and only a moment later to find our second little girl was now twenty and expecting too.

Katie and Ela must have been thinking the same thing. I then began to realise just how much life had moved on, as I looked at our youngest son and it just hit me that it had been a little over six years since Kat had given birth to him at the age of thirty-nine.

Kat and I had talked a year or so ago about the possibility of having one last baby, but I looked at her now with a couple of wrinkles starting to show on her forehead and the single streak of grey in her hair which she wore proudly. I realised it was time for the younger generation to take over baby-raising duties. You could love them and play with them and give them back when they cried, I had thought to myself, but I wasn't ready for what came next.

"Mum didn't sit down," Angel suddenly said rather loudly causing everyone to look at her, "Mum didn't sit down," she repeated.

Then everyone, including me, looked at Kat who smiled back at me nervously. "Mum, sit down," Erica told her, "you're confusing Angel. She thinks you're pregnant," she grinned. The grin, however, left Erica's face when Kat stood perfectly still, calmly mopping her eyes and nose and looking bemused.

"Is dare something interesting, or has my epic noseblowing become so famous that I need an audience," she laughed nervously, looking around the room.

Erica sneezed again before telling her mother clearly again to, "*Sit down*, Mum, and stop confusing the kids. They think you're pregnant." It was Ela who got to her feet and gave her sister a hug.

Just then, General Zophia came back into the room, gulping a glass of water, and she looked around at the silence.

"It was a joke, guys. I have really got a boyfriend. His name's James, and we've been together for about eight months, and I love him to bits," she was smiling. "We found out last week. He's coming down later to meet you all and we were going to tell Mum and Dad." The room was still in shocked silence at all the pregnancies that had just been announced. "Guess what?" Zophia added, holding something in the air, "there really is a positive pregnancy test in the bogs."

"O bugger, that where I dropped it," Kat said suddenly, walking over and grabbing it from her. "Rob I'm sorry," she said, looking a little as though she thought I might be angry, as if I could ever be angry at Kat. "I was going to tell you when we dancing, but I got interrupted and then this is all happens."

I just shook my head at Kat and kissed her as hard as humanly possible, then whispered in her ear that it was one of her best wind-ups in years and that she almost had me fooled. I added that it would have been nice to have one more while we were just about young enough.

"Vell that good really," she smiled, "Everyone," she said to those people still staring at us, "Has anyone seen Father of the Bride 2?" Most of the people in the room just stared at us. "Mother and daughter pregnant at the same time, no? Anyway," she smiled nervously, "I been pregnant eight times before. Why you no stare at one of the first-timers."

"Mum there are only seven of us, not eight," Lydia corrected quietly as she hugged her mum, "Old and pregnant baby brain," she laughed, tapping herself on the head. "Are you sure you didn't have another one before me," Lydia teased.

"I no have made love to anyone but you father," Kat said firmly, and the look she gave Lydia said, *"I know you're teasing but it's not funny."*

I thought about her wording, *not made love*. You could have meaningless sex without making love, or you could be raped without making love. Both could get you pregnant without love.

At that moment, I flashed back, remembering this was not the only time Kat had spoken about a further pregnancy. I remembered the look in her eyes when she awoke from her coma twenty-two years ago and said, "God wouldn't let me be a mum. He took the baby the bad men made." Then there was when she had that fit in the hostel in Hollywood. When she awoke she had asked about the baby, and we'd question whether Kat had been pregnant before. Now for a third time, she had mentioned another pregnancy.

Whatever it meant didn't matter, twenty-five years together and soon to be eight children later, if Kat did have a secret from me, it clearly caused her a lot of pain and was irrelevant and never would I bring up the subject. Anyway, it could well have been all in her head from when she was in the coma, and as she said, baby brain and age causing her to miscount. I was probably putting two and two together and getting five.

In the shocked silence, it was Erica who jumped up next to hug her mum and me, with Kat still halfheartedly trying to push her away, telling her to keep her germs to herself, but as soon as the shock was over, we were getting hugs from everywhere. Soon we found each other dancing again and time once more began to pass.

Chapter 21

Goodbyes

After another eight months at the age of forty-seven, Kat gave birth to twins. A boy and a girl, a fitting end to our lives as new parents. Zophia was our second child, but she gave birth first to a son who was born a week before our twins. Kat called her a lucky bitch for getting a son the first attempt while Zophie moaned that she had wanted a girl.

Lydia and her partner brought another little girl into the world.

However, things were not all Rosie away from the main core of the family. News from the Czech Republic was not good. Kat's mum was ill, and she wanted to see her daughters together.

Lady Erica, who was still not quite nineteen, tried to convince us both that she could run the hotel if I went with Kat, because she was a second-year hospitality and catering student, and a qualified gym instructor, and trainee chef.

Kat pointed out that on paper, our third daughter was more qualified to run the hotel than either of us. But she also mentioned that Erica didn't have the qualifications to run licensed premises, and that she wouldn't pass her course if she took time off to help us.

Kat wasn't well either, and that was by her standards. I was used to her having a cold most of the time, but she was really quite ill. She had coughed and sneezed very heavily for the last three nights, and her throat was so sore she could barely talk. We'd been up all night with the twins, and I was really worried that Kat was now starting to feel her age more than she was letting on.

Things got worse early that morning when the phone rang with the worst news. It was Ela crying hysterically with news that their mother had passed away during that night.

Kat had taken this news in her own way. She didn't talk about it. Instead, she sat up watching the twins as they slept. We didn't say anything to each other, but just stayed together. It was only as the sun had come up, and the realisation hit Kat, that she started to cry silently.

It was left to me to break the news to all the children. After early calls to Lydia and Zophia, I got around to telling the younger kids who still lived with us. I went to knock on Erica's door, but she was already standing outside her room, mopping her damp eyes with a hankie. I realised that being a bright girl, she had heard the phone ringing and guessed what had happened. She just put her arms out and held her dad. Then she offered to come and help me break the news to Angelica, Charlie, Roger and Jenny, Ela and Kate.

In the circumstances, we couldn't have asked for better daughters. Erica, having forgiven us for refusing her offer to run the hotel, took up her mother's, *I'm going to be as helpful as I can whether you like it or not*, attitude.

While I helped Kat with her packing, Erica had not only phoned her college and explained the situation, but phoned around all the non-family staff, as well as Jenny.

She made sure the younger kids were ready for school and placed herself at the front desk where her mother or I would have been, so that she could start checking out guests.

We strolled to the entrance hall to meet Ela's daughter, Alice, who was driving them both to the airport. Kat hadn't said a word for a couple of hours, and I was really very worried about her. She was suffering from a fever and coughing and sneezing very heavily. All of this was on top of dealing with her mother's death and travelling with two babies. She insisted on taking them because she wanted to keep busy. I wondered if I should let her go, or even if she should be allowed on a plane with other people, but it wasn't the time to say anything.

Kat stopped just in front of the doors to reception and mopped her face with her angry scarf, the same quite pretty purple scarf she'd kept for over thirty years. She gave me a weak smile, threw her arms around me, and said in a shaky voice, "In all these years, Stilton has always loved and appreciated Broccoli with all her heart, but never more than she does right now."

I smiled weakly and told her, "Broccoli loves Stilton always, and will be here for Stilton as long as we both live." Her face began to crumble. She buried her face in my shoulder, and the poor heartbroken woman howled with tears, so strongly her cries bounced around the room and grabbed the attention of everyone who was stood in reception.

Suddenly, I felt more arms grip Kat from the other side. I realised Ela had come through from the front and joined our embrace. Then more arms came around from the side in the shape of Lydia, who had just arrived, and then Zophia, and Erica.

I became aware that all our children were joining in along with others. Jenny, Amy, Jeanette, Jemima, and my parents, had all come to see her off. Even Charlie, the cat, had come to say goodbye to his mum as if he knew she was going.

"I must have done something right as a mother to get family like you guys," Kat said nervously.

"Well obviously... You're only like the best mum ever in the entire universe, "Erica grinned weakly, as she kissed her mum on the cheek.

Kat and Ela said their goodbyes, but just as they were about to get in the car, Kat grabbed me tightly, and explained that although she was devastated at her mother's death, the real reason she was crying was that she had to leave her family. I knew her pain. It hit me now that I had been with Kat seven years longer than I'd been alive on the night we met.

We had not been apart for even a day, and she was going to be away now until however long it took for her mum's funeral to be arranged. That could be weeks away, and neither of us knew how to function without each other. I, at least, had the kids to keep me busy. My heart worried for her health as the car disappeared.

Chapter 22

WAKING UP

K at was there with her face into me and sobbing. My obvious reaction to this was to pull her into me and kiss her gently, but Kat backed off somewhat surprised. She then pulled herself back towards me and said gently, "Rob, just so you know before you kiss me again, we are no dreaming anymore. But no would mind another lovely nice kiss."

At that point in the night, after all that we had done and seen, it didn't matter that she rolled over and kissed me some more. I thought both of us had come to realise that if what we were seeing was the future, then at some point we would forget everything anyway and start again.

Who knew how that was going to happen? But I no longer believed that showing each other some affection would do any harm.

There were two possibilities. One, if the dream wasn't the actual future, then there was no harm in getting intimate. Two, if we were really man and wife twenty-five years into the future and only dreaming of the past, the damage had already been done.

Getting my bearings, I became aware that we were right back in the cold haystack again. "Are you okay, Kat?" I asked. "Why were you crying?"

"Cos that was so sweet," she sighed. "I love every one of those kids of ours. They no real here, but seem so real."

"I know, I love them too," I heard myself say.

We lay there in the dark, just talking through the memories of the dream and about our future children. "Lydia," Kat was saying, "what a super little girl she vas. All of them, everything I ever wanted in children."

"They all got their brains from their mum," I smiled.

"All of them must have been swapped at hospital, cos they all more intelligent than me," she laughed.

"They were an awesome set of kids, every one of them."

"You know, until tonight I never have any ambition to be a girlfriend or a mum," she said, with a rattling breath. "But now, I just want husband and baby, so I wish dream was real."

"You would rather be forty-seven than twenty-one?"

"Certainly, I would rather be that forty-seven than this twenty-one," she sniffed.

I could see her point. Indeed, when I thought about it, now she was twenty-one, single and alone in her flat, while I was nineteen and living with my parents. Even if we did get together and had all the fun times we'd dreamed of, we still had the hard times to come. We had long hours at work away from each other, after which we'd come home so tired that we'd have no energy to have fun and just fall asleep.

Yet in our forties, we were still young enough to have fun and travel to places. We also had enough money and luck behind us after years of hard work that we were comfortable.

When I told her my thoughts were the same as hers, Kat just rubbed her hand on me and told me that she wished she had been with me all of those years.

"If we are here though," I told her, pausing as she coughed and sneezed once more, "and not dreaming in the future, we could make the future better."

"How we make it better?" she sniffed. "Is already perfect. Perfect husband, perfect children, lovely home, and best jobs ever. I no could ask for more."

"Well, you could not fall down the stairs when you're pregnant and break thirty-seven bones."

"You are never let me forget that, are you?" she said sharply.

"Of course, I won't," was my reply.

"Good. Thank you," she giggled. "I need you to keep telling me, because I am a stubborn bitch. It's good advice, because between you and me, it fucking hurt and no want to do that again." After a few moments of silence, Kat spoke to me softly and gently, "Rob, you really want this like me, don't you?"

"It would be the most amazing thing," I replied, "but even though we're both here, I'm still sceptical over whether a girl like you would really want to be with me."

Suddenly out of nowhere, Kat clicked her lighter and spread light throughout the haystack for dramatic effect. As she tried to speak, she coughed really severely. It was so bad, in fact, that I had to bang hard on her back to help her settle. She finished her massive coughing fit with a big sneeze.

"Rob," she breathed, when she got her breath back, "Why think a girl like me no want you? We had this conversation in..." She paused. "Actually, we won't have it for another year, but you need more confidence. Yes, I am brainy, and I know a few more things like languages, but you not stupid yourself. Just low self-esteem, because of I nothing special really."

"You're special to me," I added.

"I turn it around," she said smiling, "and ask you what a girl like me actually is?"

"That's a hard question," I thought, as the wind outside the haystack whistled. There wasn't another girl I knew of like Kat to compare her to. Then it hit me that it was the conclusion she was looking for.

"There isn't another girl like you," I told her.

"Correct," she grinned. "Everyone is different, and you should no put people in boxes."

"So, you're saying that's what I should learn from tonight?"

"No," she laughed, "that what I learned, but I guess you learned it too." She coughed some more and swallowed.

"Do you think we are a having these dreams, because someone or something is trying to show us we should be together?"

"I'm not sure what to believe, because whatever it is, it's really fucked up."

"Can I speak, truthfully?" she asked.

"Have you not been speaking the truth all night?" I teased.

"After you rescue me, I invite you to my home for dinner, and I say as 'friend' before we ended up here."

"Which was really kind of you," I added, causing her to smile again.

She gave me a nervous look. "I had already begun to change my mind about things, but I no want to say date, because I dink you no want me. So, you see it vas me who wanted to ask you out, but get cold feet because I scared of you say no."

My heart had gone out to her right from the moment I met her. It now made a funny beat. Despite the dreams—whatever they were for—Kat and I might well have got together anyway.

"I would have said yes," I said, putting my arms around her tighter.

"Rob," she choked, "I respect your theory, but if we were getting together anyway, no point in waiting for two weeks to start being in love when we can start be in love now."

"You want to?" I asked. My mind was lost as would be the mind of anyone who was reading this right now.

"Yes," she said, very positively. "I am see three situations. One – we are just alive and well. In twenty-six or more years from now, we are dreaming in our cosy warm bed of when we first met. We have big hotel and lovely awesome kids. Two –"

"We are here dreaming of a possible future for unknown reasons," I added.

"Correct, but shut up you lovely man. I am talking," she told me with a cheeky grin. "But if this is the case, then we have to wait two weeks, and we are know our whole future, which is boring."

"Something makes us forget like we did in the dream,"

I added.

"True," she nodded.

"But situation three is we just forget the dreams and be together anyway and have any future." She paused, sneezed heavily, and coughed several times, before continuing to elaborate that even if we did just get together, we still might forget. The dreams might be the future.

So basically, what she was saying was, it was an all-around winning situation. The only thing that could go wrong was if we didn't make it out. Situation one meant we got out, made it home, lived to have a family. Situation two meant that we hadn't done all those things yet, but could look forward to that life. Situation three meant that if we officially got together now, it wouldn't necessarily stop the other two situations from being real.

So, weighing the options, Kat was right. Getting together now wouldn't affect either of the first two situations. That would be the case, especially if we were just dreaming, or there was something else to come that would wipe our memories.

"You get my point?" Kat asked, mopping her nose vigorously. I nodded, and Kat reinforced her grip on me as we kissed passionately to confirm that we had decided to start our relationship then and there.

"We need to get out now if I going to be on that flight," she said, going over to the end of the stack to check on the snow once more. I glanced at my watch again in the hope that it would have changed, but to my horror, it still read 2 am. It seriously must just have been broken.

"Rob," Kat called from a few feet away.

"Has it stopped?" I asked.

Her reply scared me. "There is no way out! It is just hay."

"You're at the wrong end," I laughed, crawling to the opposite side of the stack and hoping that I was right. But I wasn't right. There was just solid hay.

I didn't need to shout as Kat was already behind me with her lighter, shining it all around. We pushed and pulled at every hay bale we could find, searching for the way out, but all we could find was more hay.

"Rob, we must stand and push the roof off," Kat told me in a panicked voice. Both of us combined our strength to try to lift off the top bales, but they would not shift.

"I think," Kat breathed heavily, "we maybe need change theory again."

"We must be dreaming," I agreed.

Shakily, she said, "Maybe we are, but maybe no. I know this is fucked and crazy, but maybe who or what is show us dreams no is finish. Maybe if has the power to show us these things, perhaps it has the power to make us stay and has more to show us."

I believed she was right again. "What if whatever it was put us here in the first place?" I wondered.

"One thing is true. We are no get out of here this way," she said shakily, "so dreaming is our only way out."

It was almost like we both knew that we had to see what the dreams had to show us. We both wanted to get out and be together the rest of our lives, but it seemed like the only way to find out what that would be, or how to get out would be to curl up and go back to sleep.

"Are you still cold?" Kat asked, as we snuggled up.

Come to think of it, I wasn't at all cold for someone who was naked and wet in a freezing haystack in mid-winter. "No," I told her.

"Nor me, and that worries me," she breathed, "because we should be cold."

We poured some more of the never-ending soup into the cups, and then suddenly it hit me. What if we were dead? It all fit. We were cold when we fell in that water. Nobody could have survived that cold, even if we did try every means possible. They said when you died, your life flashed in front of you. But what if we died and it was the future flashing in front of us to show us what we could have had together if we had lived?

When I whispered my theory to Kat, she began to softly cry. "That's what I'm scared of, Rob," she sobbed, holding me tighter than ever. "I no did want to say it, but I terrified that you are right."

"Well there's not much we can do," I sighed, lost in the thought that this might actually be the end of my life before it had really begun. I would do anything to live out the rest of my days with Kat, but it seemed maybe that had already happened.

"Is one more thing," Kat said softly, reaching down between my legs. "If we are dying, it is no over yet. There is still time for us to make love while we still can." She breathed, "Make love me now please, Rob."

I didn't need a second invitation. If we were to die there and then, we would not be virgins.

~~*~*~*

If Kat and I were dying, it was a very easy pleasurable death. After making love gently and passionately, for a period of time which we hoped would never end. When it did, Kat and I continued to kiss and cuddle each other to sleep. Kat laid her head on me. Gradually, we drifted away in the dark and the cold, smiling happily as we passed into another warmer world.

Even the longest day of summer couldn't last forever. As the sun faded down under the horizon, everything went into the night.

Sometimes it was possible to live too long. It wasn't just a quote from Dr Who, an old TV show that we watched in our younger days that in fact was still going strong over one hundred years on. It was the bare-faced truth of the matter.

Over the years, we had done so many things in our lives beyond what we expected. When the children were young, and our businesses were new, it was tough for a while, but we got through it with hard work and love.

We finally made it back to the pier at Santa Monica with Ela, Katie, and Jenny. This time, we rode the big wheel with our two youngest in tow. Being fair parents we paid for our older children and grandchildren to go on their own holidays together with their own families without the old people.

Kat's dream of running a hotel turned out better than we could ever have imagined. When the owner Carroll passed away, she left it all to us. By that time, we had taken over the running of three more themed hotels in other towns with the help of our children and extended family.

We ran the business well into our seventies, when we semi-retired and passed control of the company to Erica, who had lived around the hotel since her birth. She lived and breathed the place, and worked her backside off for many years to earn the job.

We didn't really retire and still helped her with the day-to-day running of the businesses well into our nineties. Erica, herself, was semi-retired when she was seventy, but generations of our descendants kept the running of the businesses in the family. We still helped run the place on occasion before we both got too old and sick.

Katarzyna and I didn't spend all our years working. In our seventies, we used our savings to travel the world. We spent time in India, China, Australia, and Europe before settling down back home in our cottage.

You wondered if you'd lived too long when you saw the people around you dropping one by one, while you seemed to go on forever. It wasn't fair. So many faces had come and gone. After Kat's mum, her dad followed not long after. I lost my parents about five or six years later.

Katie had been the first of our generation to leave us. She never truly recovered from her cancer. Although she beat it twice, it had been over thirty years since it came back and killed her. Her funeral was like an episode of East Enders, which she would have loved. Her sister Katherine had turned up, pretending that they had been friends. She was forcibly ejected by Katie's daughters, sons, nieces, and nephews.

Ela found life without Katie terribly hard. She moved back in with Kat and myself, and just like the old days, joined us wherever we went in an effort to keep her mind away from her loss. However, one morning, we found her motionless in bed with a picture of herself with Katie, their children and grandchildren against her chest. We said goodbye to Ela at the age of seventy-six.

We put her ashes together with Katie's and scattered them in the fields of the family farm in the Czech Republic. Kat and I joked to our children that when we passed, they should just put us in the bin with the other old crap and save the cost of a funeral.

It was okay for old people to die, because they had their life and opportunities that those who died young would never have. This was much the case of our poor daughter Angelica Rose, who was without the things most of us took for granted. She gave the world all the love she could only for a short time. She lived life to the best of her ability, and despite her Downs Syndrome, she always tried to laugh. Our Angel gained her wings due to health complications.

Although always a child in her mind, she was thirty-two in body when she passed away.

Even if you had known real pain, you didn't know how much it hurt until you lost a child of your own. Angelica's death had the most profound effect on her big sister, Erica.

Erica had adored her little sister and insisted on being her main carer to help her become more independent. The two of them lived together in our old flat at the time that Angelica passed. It was the only time I'd seen Erica lost for words. We all cried silently on each other's shoulders.

We lost our bossy child General Zoph in her sixties to cancer. That was an incredibly hard time. Kat had lost all of her sisters and little brother on top of losing our two girls. She pined for every one of them. All we had was each other and our remaining children, grandchildren, and their families, all of whom we loved with all our hearts.

It was horrible watching our children grow as old and doddery as we had become ourselves. The love and youth of our grandchildren and great-grandchildren was uplifting. There wasn't one of them who was not lovely.

Even Lady Erica surprised us. After insisting she

wanted to remain single, the loss of her favourite sister inspired her to change her outlook on life. Finally, she unlocked her bedroom, took her chastity belt off, and married at the age of... you guessed it – forty. The age when she told us we should stop kissing.

Showing what we already knew that love knew no age or race, her husband was a twenty-two-year-old man from South Africa. On the day she had teased us about our love life, her husband was still yet to be conceived. She gave birth to her first child at forty-one. They went on to have three more. She was now a seventy-one-year-old grandmother of six herself.

Charlie, Roger, Jenny Ela-Kate, and the twins, Katarzyna and Robert Junior, all went on to follow our example and have successful, hard-working lives and big families. Jenny Ela-Kate was the only one of our children to have her family with two different men after her first marriage broke down. While Roger and Kat Junior both followed their auntie's example of marrying a person of the same sex with our full blessing.

Now, even our unexpected, but much-loved twins were grandparents. In fact, unless I'd miscounted, eight of our nine children had given us at least thirty-five grandchildren. I was too old and tired to count how many great-grandchildren and great-great-grandchildren we had.

My niece Jemima went on to have seven kids too. She was now eighty-five and still going strong.

I found myself sitting on a bench in front of the sea with an oxygen mask helping me breathe more easily. There was an old lady who sat next to me very closely. The wind was blowing through her hair, and she also had a breathing mask. She struggled to take off her mask.

Her breathing was laboured as she spoke, and it was

only when she did that I remembered who she was. "Once upon a time my husband and I came to this place to watch the sun come up over the sea."

I couldn't blame her for thinking I was a stranger, especially with my own mind the way it was.

"Katarzyna, I am your husband," I told her gently.

"Who is Katarzyna?" she asked, looking confused. Then she looked at me and tried to give me her open-mouthed smile. She put her mask back on for a moment, and then said breathlessly, "After all these... years. I get you still... wind-up."

I smiled. "Do you know the score?"

"Does it matter?" she smiled.

She was about to put her mask back on when she sneezed suddenly. She didn't have the reflexes she had in her youth when she would have caught it in her handkerchief.

"Let me get that for you, Nanna," said someone from behind us. A girl came into view and took Kat's handkerchief. She helped her to wipe herself, and Kat thanked her, but wore a look of frustration.

"I swear I know that young lady from somewhere."

"Zophia," I said slowly.

"Well remembered," she smiled.

I wondered if I'd just seen a ghost. We lost our Zophia to cancer nearly twenty years ago, but here she stood in front of us, looking as fresh and healthy as she did when she was eighteen.

"I was named after my great-grandmother who died just before I was born," she told us, quietly adding "I wish I'd known her."

"She was a bossy cow," Kat said suddenly, to the shock of young Zophia, "but we wouldn't have had her any other way. Such a lovely person... at... heart. I miss her... b-bossing us a-about." Kat smiled, and did a very accurate impression of our late daughter, "Mum and dad, don't be so lazy. Stop drinking tea and get your butts to work."

Young Zophia laughed, backing away to wherever she had come from, and saying, "I love you Nanna and Gramps. Happy anniversary."

"Thank you for wiping my nose, you sweet girl," Kat said. Reaching into her bag, she tried to pass young Zophia a £50 note. (£50 in 2090 was not worth much)

"Nanna, put your money away," she smiled. She hugged both of us and then disappeared.

"That vas Zophia?" Kat asked breathlessly.

"Apparently, she's our great-granddaughter," I replied.

"No," she breathed, "that was Zophia... standing next... next that young lady who too is also called Zophia."

Maybe it was her mind again, but maybe just perhaps it was our lost daughter coming back to visit the parents who loved her and the great-granddaughter she never met.

Getting a proper look at her, she was still my Katarzyna like she'd always been. But even with all the healthy eating and exercise, it couldn't stop age in its tracks when a person was nearly one hundred and three years old. I probably looked much worse. Her hair now was still thick, but all the blonde had turned a ghostly white. She still had the glint in her big eyes that she had almost eighty-two years ago, when she came running downstairs on that cold January night, and we sealed our unlikely love with our first kiss.

After all these years, that tired and sometimes doddery old lady was still and always would be the same much younger woman who I fell head over heels in love with all those years age. My love for her had never for even a millisecond changed.

"This bench is new," she said breathing hard. She pressed a button, and suddenly a massive hologram shot out in front of us causing us both to jump and grip hands.

The hologram projected words a foot tall in front of us and played a video clip, which read the words in a loud advertising tone.

"This park bench is brought to you via sponsorship of the Bobal Brownlow historic Hotel Cromer. This bench was erected on September 12th 2090 to mark the 80th wedding anniversary celebration of Katarzyna Bobal Brownlow and her husband Robert Bobal Brownlow, married in Las Vegas September 12th, 2010. May they spend many more happy years together."

Both of us sat there shocked for several minutes until Kat took a deep breath on her oxygen mask, looked at me, and said, "Who? Who the fuck put this piece of crap here... God... help me... I... will... strangle them."

Suddenly there was a loud roar of *"Surprise!"* from behind us. Both of us jumped out of our skin. Slowly, we looked at each other in fright, and then looked around behind us to see a crowd of people gathered around us.

There was a large tent, and there were tables with lots of old people sat at them. In front of them was a group of young men women and children sat on the floor. In the middle of it all, there was a massive banner which said, HAPPY ANIVERSARY.

Kat looked over at me, took another deep breath from her mask and said, "I dink we have... gatecrashed... a party."

"I think... It's ours," I breathed.

"Who are you again?" she said, quietly smiled, and gave me a little wink to say she was kidding.

"I tell them," she breathed, "no to make big thing."

It was only then that it hit me that the old people sitting at the tables were not just random old people. There was Lydia, who would be eighty next year, and Lady Erica, Jenny Ela-Kate and their husbands, alongside Charlie, Roger with Kat and Rob Junior. Alice and Erin were there too, and everyone had brought their families.

The young people who sat closer were not just some people. The middle-aged people were our grandchildren, the younger adults were our great-grandchildren, and the floods of children ranging from one to eighteen were our great-great-grandchildren.

Kat and I glanced at each other with that look that said, "How did our love for each other create all this?"

Before we could say anything to each other, the younger generation was already helping us into our wheel-chairs. We were then being wheeled around to meet and greet our army of descendants. I thought we even spoke to the local press, and probably ended up on the Holovision news, Holovision being the hologram replacement for TV. Kat, being a very private person, still wanted to know why anyone would want to know about us.

Somebody had gone to the trouble of creating a large feast, and there was a big bouncy castle for the children all set up next to the play area.

The celebrations went on all day and into the night. We were treated to a very expensive-looking concert performed by a combination of our favourite bands and performers including Bon Jovi, Meatloaf, Simon and Garfunkel,

Eric Clapton, Rod Stewart, David Bowie, Cliff Richard, The Rolling Stones, and The Beatles. They finished with sets from Kat's very favourite performers. Bob Dylan sang *Forever Young* and Abba who finished the night with *Thank You for the Music*.

Of course, these performers had all been dead for many years, but were brought to us via a very expensive-looking holographic virtual reality stage. With modern technology, it was only us and our party that heard and saw it.

I hoped it didn't cost too much money.

The young children went home to bed, and so had many of the old people, but the hardy souls, including ourselves, some of our children, and some of the younger adult members of the family, stayed.

Kat and I sat up all night on our park bench and watched the sparkling waves glistening as the sun rose over the sea, just like we did in our early twenties before the patter of little feet came along.

After breakfast, we sat in our seat again for a while. Then we were taken back home in a car by two lovely young ladies. I recognised one of them as our great-granddaughter Zophia and another young lady. Kat asked Zophia to remind us what her sister's name was. She laughed and replied, "Nanna Kat, she's not my sister. This is my cousin, Katarzyna. She's named after you."

Kat took a deep breath of her oxygen, then smiled and laughed, "How original."

When we got back to our cottage, the ladies struggled to push us through the garden in our wheelchairs. I was very tired, but Kat seemed to be using the last of her energy to ask questions that she had probably asked a thousand times before.

"How much... do you get paid... for look after us?" she asked, as we got inside the house.

"Nanna Kat, you know your family takes it in turns to help look after you," the younger Katarzyna smiled. "We do it out of love for you."

"We love you, girls, too," I told them gently.

"Do you have... jobs?" Kat asked, and both ladies nodded. Zophia explained that her cousin was a nurse and that she was a personal trainer. "You take after you great-grandpa" Kat smiled.

Kat and I asked that we be helped into our reclining chair rather than be put to bed. It was the same chair that we sat in together on the night I first went back to the flat. However, it had the cover changed a few times in eighty-two years.

Young Zophia and Katarzyna helped us into the chair. Kat laid herself on me carefully, making sure we didn't sit on each other's catheter bags. After the effort of getting up into the chair, we sat breathing hard into our masks.

Since when did just sitting in a chair with the lady I loved become such a struggle? We gave each other a knowing look that said, "This isn't as fun as it was in our nineties, let alone the decades that came before." However still in my heart, she was that same wide-eyed young woman who sat in that chair smiling and laughing with me the night when I brought her home from the airport. That was the night we fell in our deep love that had never ended.

"Are you sure you want to stay in the chair?" the young Katarzyna asked.

I looked at Kat. She looked at me. Finally, she said, "I

think the bedroom... would be too... much effort."

"Okay," young Katarzyna smiled. "I never knew how you shared a single bed all these years."

"No... the same one," Kat breathed hard, looking at her, then at me and back to her smiling. "We broke... at least three... creating your great-grandparents."

"You crack me up, Nanna Kat" Zophia laughed. She brought us a pot of tea and lemon with two straws. She picked up a handkerchief to help Kat wipe her nose, before throwing it in the wash and washing her hands at the sink.

"Do you ladies... have men in your lives?" I asked.

Young Kat lifted her finger and smiled, saying, "Oh granddad, you came to my wedding last year, and you hosted it at the hotel."

I couldn't for the life of me remember having done such a thing. "What... about you?" I asked Zophia.

"Single and not ready to mingle," she grinned.

"I knew... a girl... like that... once," Kat struggled. "No, leave it... too long... young... lady."

"I won't," she replied softly.

Kat looked at me and turned to the ladies, "You... girls must be... dying for a cigarette."

They looked at each other and Zophia said quietly, "Nanna we don't smoke. I'm a personal trainer, remember."

"Good girls... for no... smoking," Kat looked at me wearily.

"Ladies" I breathed, "Would you... mind popping to the shop for... some more tea?"

"There's plenty of tea in the cupboard, Gramps,"

Young Kat replied.

"Maybe... you like to go... and see you... husband?" I asked young Katarzyna.

"It's okay. He's at work. We're fine here," she smiled.

It was young Zophia who cottoned on to what we were trying to say. "I think Nanna and Gramps want to be alone," she said, gently touching her cousin's arm.

Both ladies came over and kissed us on the cheeks as they covered us with a blanket. We thanked them for everything they'd done and told them we would always love them and the rest of the family.

"Do you think... they know?" Kat struggled to ask me.

"I think... the younger... does," I breathed.

"Our Zophia is... here," she struggled, her breathing seemed even weaker than normal.

"She's gone now," I said gently, suddenly feeling how tight my own breath was.

"No," she said, almost in a whisper, "our little girl... who left us too soon. Her sister is too... poor Angelica... Our Angel is an angel... with wings."

"What... you... saying?" I breathed.

"They here with... baby," she mumbled, and took a deep breath from her mask.

"What baby?" I gasped, feeling sleepier than ever.

She looked at me sadly. "The baby... bad men made who died, when I was a child myself."

I thought she was delirious, but I wouldn't tell her so. Then she looked at me and smiled with what strength she had left and said, "I will always love my Broccoli."

"I can't... be without my... Stilton."

We took our masks off and touched lips as best we could with old broken bodies. She might have tasted a little different, but this battle-scarred old lady was my Kat, right down to her last breath.

"My sisters... all... here with us," she said, turning her eyes to something behind us in a voice so weak that it suddenly hit me what she was saying. My wife's time on earth was closer to the end than I thought it had been. We both struggled for breath and looked into each other's eyes. Then I saw something that both scared and comforted me at the same time.

Behind Katarzyna stood somebody I'd only ever seen in pictures – my great-grandfather who died before I was born. He stood with his arm around my grandmother, Maggie, who had supported us in our youth, paying for our holiday to America.

In front of them were the rest of my family – my mum, my dad, and sister Jeanette, and all of my grandparents. To one side of the room was a plump young Jenny and her father and a lady who must have been her long-dead mother. I guessed Kat's sisters were behind me, but I couldn't turn my head.

In the middle of the room stood our two lost daughters. General Zoph was looking like her mum in her young days, and Angelica was a little lady with big wings and a big smile. In the middle, was a smiling boy I didn't recognise.

Both of us sat staring at the ever-growing number of people in the room. We both got more breathless as neither of us had breathed from our masks in several minutes, but we didn't put our masks back on.

As we had sat watching the sun rise over the water

that morning, I wondered when would be the last time, but I hadn't expected that to be our final day. It seemed Kat's time had come, and I was not letting her go alone.

As Kat and I slowly put our heads together, I said to her with my penultimate breath, "Ladies first... like you always said."

Kat closed her eyes, and her head dropped. I thought she was gone, until she moved her lips and said, "Always... the gentleman... Broccoli and Stilton."

Then we both spoke our last word, which was, "Together," our eyes closed. Kat fell on me so that our legs linked together and the two parts of the old tattoo we got in our twenties connected. It still read, "Kat and Rob, in love always."

Chapter 23

<u>Flashbacks</u>

The first nineteen years of my life passed by in a flash. I saw things from my childhood fly by from the haystack, my first birthday, the day I first rode my bike, my first time in a swimming pool, the first time I got on a plane, and my eighteenth birthday party. From then on, my life became one thing. From the moment I touched hands with the figure that came out of the snow, it was her.

In a moment, I relived our first kiss, the first time we shared a bed, those hours I spent teaching Kat to swim and ride a bike, and when she tried to teach me languages. The times we climbed mountains and ran marathons, when we walked on the beach as the sun went down and carried on until it came up again. The times we laughed so hard that we cried, like the time Kat accidentally answered the door to my family in the nude, and the times that we loved so hard that we couldn't let go.

Then there were the births of each and every one of our children and grandchildren. Then there was the rise and continued success of our hotel, before the twilight years when we clung to our love to get us through the pain of our losses. Then came the love for the ones we were leaving behind, and the joy at being back with old friends.

There may have been pain in the illnesses that caused us to die, but actually passing caused us none.

I opened my eyes to Kat's eyes looking right back into mine with new brightness. Her hair had gone from white to sandy blonde, and the cracks were gone from her face with pink cheeks. For a moment, we stared in shock at each other, but the throes of passion took over. We kissed with energy that we hadn't had in years.

A blazing round of applause made me jump out of my skin.

Slowly and in shock, Kat and I stood up and looked each other up and down. We were both back in the bodies we had in our early years. Kat was how she was at her healthiest weight, which meant basically she wasn't skinny like she had often been. We were both in the athletic shape we were from our marathon running days.

I began to realise that in death, how a person looked was down to the perception of the person who saw them, and how that person remembered them at their best. If that had not been the case, my grandparents and parents would have been young, like Kat and I. But they were how I remembered them before their health went downhill. However, to themselves, I suspected they too had regressed to their younger selves.

The first to break the line was Ela. She came barging in and hugged her sister before I could get a look in. Seconds later, she grabbed me for a hug and strangled me so hard I thought I was going to die again.

"How on earth did you pull off dying right at the same time?" Ela begged to know.

Kat smiled and said loudly, "I poisoned our drinks."

"What the? I didn't drink any," I said in disbelief.

She just laughed and said, "Wind-up in afterlife score is one nil to me."

We couldn't stop hugging our girls for at least ten minutes. Everyone was just hugging both of us and chatting away to each other. I remembered joking with Katie and asking why her sister Katherine had not come to greet us, knowing how much we all hated her.

"Haven't seen her since I died," she smiled, adding, "I think she went somewhere else." She pointed downwards and frowned.

Suddenly we all became aware of a light in the centre of the room that was steadily growing stronger.

"Mum and Dad, it is time to follow," Angelica told us in a bold, strong voice that she never had in her short life. Everybody walked through the back door quite literally. Nervously, Kat and I held hands preparing to walk through after the light.

As we took a last look back at the crumbled and broken piles of skin and bones that were once our physical homes for so many years, the door opened.

Our great-great-granddaughter, Kat, was creeping back in to check on us. We would have left quickly if she had screamed, but quietly as a church mouse in realisation of our fate, the brave girl kissed us goodbye and covered us while shedding tears.

Our many welcome party members stood either side of the back door to the garden, forming an arch for us to walk under. The numbers of people had grown, and we were joined in the garden by all the pets, all the dogs, cats, rabbits and other animals we had owned over the years. Katarzyna picked up Charlie, her cat, which she had the day we met, and Roger, the rabbit, who she had cuddled at night when she was alone.

We followed the light at a steady pace as it headed through our beautiful garden and through the door in the two hundred and fify-year-old brick wall. As Kat and I reached the wooden door, knowing that our fate was on the other side, we stopped and looked each other in the eye, gave each other a squeeze, and together we said, "Love you always, beyond death do us part, and after the stars go out, and the earth stops spinning, and our souls are blowing on the wind." With that, we stepped through.

~~*~*~*

Heaven seemed to be made of hay. The others were gone, but Kat and I were naked and back inside the haystack where we first met. We were no longer cold, but we were no longer cuddled up to each other. Kat and I were on our knees staring at each other with terrified eyes.

The light in which we could see each other was not the light from the candles that had long since burned out. In fact, it seemed to be the same light which had been in the dream as we made our way towards our fate.

In the light, I could see things so much more clearly. Kat and I might have been kneeling there looking at each other, but it was what was between us that terrified us both. The reason we were looking at each other in horror, was that the thing on the floor between us was, well, it was us.

Our nineteen and twenty-one-year-old bodies from the night we met were tightly wrapped around each other for warmth, but it wasn't enough. We were blue with cold, and there was not a beat in either heart or breath of air in either set of lungs.

"Kat?" I shuddered.

"Rob," she shivered.

We looked at each other and said, "Eeerrr..."

"Rob," Kat said slowly, "I no think these dreams can come true now."

"The final dreams of dying," I heard myself say.

"The life we could have had, wasted," she said sadly, "but at least we enjoyed thinking it was real."

"That buggered my theory of what was going on."

"I think we need new theory," she smiled awkwardly.

I thought for a minute. I heard that when you died, your life flashed before your eyes. That was one way it could have been, but surely you would only see a life you had lived and not one you didn't.

"My theory," Kat said, "is exactly as I say. What we saw is life we were meant to have. We never figured out how we get out of here..."

"Because we never did get out," I finished.

"But nobody this time is come to meet us," she said sadly.

"Only because they're not dead," I told her gently.

"Are you upset that you died so young and never got to live?" I asked softly, feeling more than a bit angry at our deaths. The anger was more for the people who it would upset, like my parent and grandparents.

Kat, however, shook her head and sniffed, saying, "Na, because I already had a nice life with you. My family might miss me, but I see them again. I do miss our children though."

"We'll never have them now," I breathed.

"Sad," she said in a whisper. "I loved every one of those kids, and they never will live."

"Me too," I told her, "and I loved you most of all."

Kat reached her hand out to me and smiled. Softly, she said, "Do you still love me now we strangers again? And ghosts?" she added.

"I couldn't not love you," I told her, giving her a big tight hug which she returned.

She took a deep rattling sniff. "I still have a cold," she said with a puzzled look. "I no supposed to still be ill after I die, and my naked ghost is no have a hanky."

"Maybe there's a clean one waiting in heaven," I smiled.

"I really do hope so. I need a good blow," she sniffed, smiling. We watched as the light made its way out of the stack. "Let us follow it together," she smiled, adding, "We may not have that life, but I still want you."

Holding hands, we crawled towards the shimmering light and were about to exit the hay together. As we did, we stopped to look at each other sadly, and then kissed as though the whole thing had been real. Then, we turned to get out of the haystack and followed the glowing beacon of light, to jump or float or fly away, whatever newly departed souls would do. No matter what we were doing, one thing was certain – we would always be together.

The story could have ended there, but that would have made it even more complicated and confusing than the ending that about to be told. How could a ghost manage to type all that?

When we jumped down, rather than flying away I fell and lost sight of Katarzyna completely. I felt as though the pits of hell had opened up to pull me in, and she was gone up to heaven without me.

Part 3 Real Life

Chapter 24

After death

I fell far beneath the earth, being sucked down until suddenly I hit the bottom with a thud and landed on something soft.

Unhurt, I called out in the dark for any sign of Kat. There was no answer, just a red light in the dark. When the red light came gently into focus, it formed numbers 04:00.

I wondered to myself why Hell would have these numbers in the darkness to greet new inductees. Surely if this was Hell, then I'd have been dragged away by a monster, but there were only numbers. I could hear the beasts of Hell roaring below me with a fearsome growl that made me shudder. The number changed to 04:01, and as I took a closer look, it seemed familiar.

It was then that it hit me that I was in my bedroom looking at my radio alarm clock from when I was a teenager. I was a teenager, that was my radio, and that terrible noise was my dog, Narla, at the foot of my bed snoring.

I was in bed. After all that, it was *all* just a dream. But would life do something like that to me?

Well, that was the kind of life I had. Nice girls like Kat only spoke to me in dreams, as if any girl would speak to me in reality. Even if Kat was real, the chances of me plucking up the courage to talk to her without making an idiot of myself were slim.

I was on the middle shift at work and not due in until 9 am, so I tried to sleep again for a while. But the dream was so much in my head. It felt like I'd been with Kat in the same bed forever. I didn't feel that I could ever be comfortable enough to sleep again without her in my arms, which was pretty tragic, as she was only a figment of my imagination. Why did my brain taunt me with illusions of love and happiness? It should just accept that I was a nobody, worth nothing, and with no chance of meeting somebody special.

It was no good trying to sleep, so I got up, made breakfast, and sat in front of the TV, trying to get it all out of my head. Unlike one of my usual dreams, this seemed to stay in my head as though it had all been real.

Even at work that day, all I could think of was Kat and what she would have had to say about the mood my boss was in and so on. By the end of the afternoon, my lifeguard colleague, Chloe, had begun arguing with Katherine just like in the dream.

It had been Chloe who had walked out in the dream, which had meant I had to stay on late. That was how I later found Kat on my way home. In the dream after leaving, Chloe had been given her job back by the area manager who sided with her against Katherine.

To be fair, I wasn't exactly concentrating on work and spent time talking to my clients about the strange but happy dream, that was stuck in my head. I wondered how or why my brain could have made up these situations, all the lovely people I'd encountered, and all their details.

The stereo was playing ABBA's *I Have a Dream* as I came back from cleaning the toilets. It was one of Kat and my favourite songs. I glanced over at the treadmill and thought I saw Jenny there.

"Come on brain, stop it," I said to myself, blinking, but when I opened my eyes, Jenny was really there walking on the treadmill. Of course, Jenny Hughes was a real person, but it had been a while since Jenny had been in the gym. I had wondered if she had given up coming, so why had my brain added her to the story?

She was a very nice friendly girl. I could talk to her, because she was a client and it was my job, and because she had a long-term boyfriend, I wasn't worried about trying to pull her.

She was, as in the dream, a very big girl having been on medication for back pain that increased her weight. Her back pain was the reason she was limited to gentle exercises, such as walking cycling and swimming. Despite her appearance, she had been my most dedicated client until she just stopped coming about nine months earlier.

After dreaming about her the night before, here she was. She saw me and shouted over, "Hey Rob!"

I slowly made my way over to her. I didn't want to put her off coming back by telling her that she was in a dream I had, because that was just a little freaky, especially because in my dream she had been nine months pregnant.

"Hey Jenny, how are you?" I asked, looking up and down. I was unable to tell if she was pregnant, because poor Jenny was so fat because of her health problems.

"Never better now I'm single again," she said with a

smile.

"That's a good thing?" I asked.

"Yes," she said brightly, adding, "Turns out my ex was cheating, and I was the other woman, so I dumped his backside and told him to go back to wife his wife."

"Well you seem happy to be free," I told her.

"I'm freer than you know," she smiled, adding, "I loved him though, more than his wife ever will."

"I wish I liked being single," I laughed.

Jenny smiled. "Do you remember my Czech friend, Zee Zee? I think you met her when we bumped into you a while back and you had tea with us."

"Oh my god, I do," I remembered out loud. I had seen Jenny out somewhere a while back and she invited me to join her and her friend for tea. Her friend, like Kat, struggled with English, but she was kind and very nice and I liked her a lot, but we never saw each other again.

Had my crazy brain made up Kat based on a very brief meeting with Jenny's sweet, but hard to understand friend? I couldn't even remember where it was that I had met them, but now that she mentioned it, I remembered that I had a chance encounter with Jenny and her friend some time ago

"I remember her briefly" I smiled.

She smiled back saying, "I told her she needs to join the gym and get some help from you."

"Cool," I said, "It will be nice to meet her again."

"She has the opposite problem to me," she laughed,

rubbing her big belly. "Lovely girl she is, but too skinny. Doesn't eat enough and has an awful smoking habit which she wants help with. So, I thought you'd be great for her."

"I never turn down a challenge," I laughed.

"She's a challenge alright" Jenny grinned, adding, "She's a tough girl with a bit of attitude, but a heart of gold when you get to know her."

"You should have brought her along tonight," I said brightly.

"She's off on holiday tonight," Jenny continued, "I was supposed to give her a lift, but my car doesn't go far these days."

I laughed, "It sounds like you need a good mechanic."

"If only that was the case," She smiled shaking her head.

"Nothing wrong with the car, just the driver I'm afraid."

"Anyway," Jenny smirked, "Zee Zee is looking forward to seeing you at some point, and she's... you know," she winked at me, "Single and ready to mingle, if you know what I mean, but don't call her Zee Zee, she doesn't like me doing it her real name is..."

"Katarzyna," I blurted out, without suddenly interrupting her.

We gazed at each other for a moment.

So, Kat was a real person, *Bloody hell*, I thought to myself. She must have told me her name when we met, and my brain had made up this silly dream because I was a fantasist.

I was going to ask Jenny more about her friend, but just then Chloe the lifeguard came out, shouting at Katherine.

"You're being unfair," she was thundering. "I was told by Lucy…" the leisure centre manager, "…that I could book holiday next weekend because of my daughter's first birthday."

Katherine's make-up-covered face leered at Chloe, "Well, if you didn't want to work on her birthday, you shouldn't have given birth to the brat."

Chloe just stood there, stunned. Jenny looked at me, then at them, and at me again. "You need to stand up to the bitch, and tell her you to know Katie Barns, and you're going to call her."

Before I'd even thought about what Jenny had said, I became enraged with how Katherine had spoken to poor Chloe, who looked like she was going to cry.

I was only nineteen and had little self-confidence. However, I had changed since having that dream. Having seen her get what she deserved once in the dream, which somehow made it easier for me to just walk up to her and risk being fired to give her a piece of my mind.

Amazed at my own bravery, I explained that I was friends with the area manager, her sister, and I knew her secret—I didn't know any secret really—and that I would tell Katie about her behaviour if she didn't apologise to Chloe. Then, I reminded Katherine that family and children were the most important thing in the world and that she would never understand that. Finally, I offered to do the shift myself, so Chloe got to be with her daughter.

Having said all this to her, I suddenly realised that what I'd said was a load of rubbish. One, because Katie was just a random dream character, and even with a slim possibility that she did exist, I could not follow through my threat as I didn't actually know her.

I wasn't sure what I was thinking, but didn't Jenny say, "Tell her you know Katie"? Did Jenny know her?

Katherine, however, looked at me in shock that I'd stood up to her, and stuttered, "Erm, okay, Rob... yeah if you want to take over her shift, then arrange it between you two." With that, she walked off in a bit of a huff.

"Cheers Rob, you're a star," Chloe said, giving me a friendly pat on the back. "It's the second Saturday morning in January, by the way."

"No worries. You enjoy her birthday," I smiled.

"Who were you talking to out here?" she smiled awkwardly.

"It was just Jenny Hugh's," I told her. Chloe looked around. I noticed that Jenny was no longer on the treadmill. "She must have gone down to the pool," I reasoned.

"Really? I thought she quit the gym when she got pregnant and I she had... I must have got her confused with somebody else." Chloe shrugged, "Anyway it's five past five. You were supposed to go home five minutes ago." Then she smiled, and added, "Lucky you waded in when you did. I was going to walk out, and then she would have made you do my shift tonight." Chloe turned to go, and said, "See you next week. Enjoy your day off tomorrow, if you get one."

I got that strange feeling that this had happened before, but in a different way. Then it hit me that in my dream, it had been *Chloe* who quit her job, causing me to have to work late.

Okay, I thought to myself. It was time to go home, so it was very unlikely that my dream would come true. At least I was going to beat the worst of the snow, so I could sit at home alone and play my Xbox.

As I passed the changing rooms, Jenny came out with a bottle of water. "You off, mate?" she smiled.

"Yep, I'm off to get an early night," I yawned. "I had a mad dream last night that made me very tired."

"Was it good one?" she laughed.

"The best ever," I smiled.

"Well, have a good sleep," she smiled as she passed. "Oh, and watch yourself in the snow. You don't want to crash your car and end up spending the night in a blizzard." She gave me a massive wink.

Seriously? I thought to myself as I walked out the door. Did Jenny know she played a massive part in my dream? If so how?

Fresh from having stood up to Katherine and with the dream still running in my head, I was in quite a state as I walked down the slope to the car park. How could you explain your emotions to anybody in that state? They'd say it was just a dream, and you should live in the real world. That was all true, but I missed Kat terribly, to the point that I'd almost expected to find her waiting in reception, like she had done time and time again.

I thought it more than a little weird that Jenny had

been Kat's best friend in the dream, and there was Jenny, who had been away from the gym for quite a while, still trying to pair me with her very best friend. Could her friend actually really be the Kat from my dream? If so, why was it that I had a dream about her and was it co-incidence that Jenny had appeared after so long.

The biggest thing by far was my shot in the dark about Katie. I'd lost myself back in the dream for a minute. I thought Katherine would have laughed and called me an idiot. However, she had backed down right away as though she was terrified. Did that mean that Katie from my dream was a real person? If she was a real person, then maybe Kat and Ela were real too.

In reality, what were the chances of Kat and I ever meeting, let alone having a relationship?

I'd parked my car out on the road due to the ice on the slope when I got to the hotel that morning. The snow was driving into my face as I struggled to unlock the iced-over door. In frustration, I took a small step back in order to kick the car when something hit me from the side with a thump. I jumped back in surprise to see a figure in a dark coat carrying a rucksack. The person had crashed into me so hard that they had fallen on the floor and dropped their possessions.

"Are you okay?" I asked bending down to help.

The person's face was covered in a scarf, but a very sharp angry female voice cried out in pain from behind it, and when I reached down to help her she screamed, *"Kavur,"* Then breathing quickly she added, "Dobře, nepotřebuju, abys pomohl, ale měl bys ti otevřít kurva oči, ty pitomče."

"Sorry," I said, picking up her handbag and passing it

to her.

"I give you sorry," she snapped. "I have worst day of my life. I am just saying goodbye to my best friend. I have a stinking cold, and I am in a hurry to catch bus. Then some random nobody prick knocks me over, hurt my leg, and spill all my tobacco in the snow." She pointed at a pack of Golden Virginia lying on the floor, its contents scattered in the snow.

I was still not sure how this mad, possibly hormonal woman thought it was my fault. Although I had taken a small step back, she would have walked into me anyway. "I-I-I, I stuttered, trying to help her.

But she screamed at me, " Jsem zima, unavená, nemocná a rozrušená... křičela... Měl jsem strašný den a chtěl jsem jen ten malý luxus, kdy jsem mohl kouřit cigaretu před autobusem. Teď to nemůžu mít."

I remember hearing her accent and thinking she was German. The first thing I thought to myself was, *Bloody foreigners,* but instead I apologised again. "Sorry," I said again as I helped to her feet.

"Yeah whatever," she said angrily, not accepting my apology and retorting, "Maybe if you opened your eyes more, you could see well enough no to knock over innocent people and hurt them. You could write an apology, then go shove it up you ass and go fuck you self with it."

"Merry fucking Christmas to you too, season of goodwill and all that, bloody German," I heard myself shout back at her.

Her response was to shout back at me, " *I no am German,* you fucking retard!" With that, she limped off towards the bus shelter, having clearly hurt herself when she fell. I felt bad, and I would have helped her if she hadn't been so rude. I saw her pause and take some sort of scarf out of her pocket to wipe her face as I turned back to the car door.

I thought to myself that there was something very familiar about this rude, aggressive, foul-mouthed lady with the rucksack, but I couldn't quite remember where we had met before. As I finally got the door open, I looked over and saw that she was still stood under a street lamp only a few metres away, but she had turned around and was limping back towards me.

I was about to jump in the car and leave before I got more abuse, but suddenly I heard a more solemn and tearful voice from under her headscarf.

"I sorry. It was my fault," she sobbed. "It dark, and I have shades on. It no easy to see. I was rolling myself a cigarette, and no look where I was walking. I sorry I swore at you and called you names. I have a horrible day. Lots of stress and upset. I just wanted to sit down and chill with a cigarette, but it my fault." She sniffed. "I no should have snapped. No excuse. I am a rude horrible and very sorry lady."

Her voice reminded me of Kat from my dream, but of course, she could have been any foreign lady with a rucksack catching a bus. There were quite a few people from Eastern Europe working in the crab factory at this time of year. Plus, the Kat I knew would never have reacted like that, even if she was hurt. Would she? The fact was, that whoever she was, she had been big enough to apologise for her outburst.

If I had learnt anything in the long life I'd dreamed, then it was that everyone deserved an opportunity to apologise. Plus, the poor lady whoever she might be, was sobbing and clearly injured in her fall. Her instant reaction might have been because of the shock.

"Please don't cry. There are no hard feelings," I said. I offered my hand for her to shake as proof. She quickly took off the small pair of shades she was wearing. We looked and saw each other's faces in the light of the street lamp for the first time.

There was a solitary tear dripping from her eye. She had apparently been crying, probably because she really had hurt herself when she fell, but didn't want to show weakness. I felt terrible about this as she wiped the tears on her arm, and then she pulled off her glove to shake my hand.

"My friends, if I had any left," she said quietly, "call me ZeeZee, but my real name is..."

She suddenly had a big sneeze, and in the time, it took her to recover I said, "Katarzyna."
I saw her eyes opened wider in shock as they adjusted to the light. When she saw me clearly? I heard her gasp, "Rob? Oh my god, Rob, it's really you."

We stood in the snow and looked at each other without a word for several seconds.

"That wasn't the reaction I was expecting," I smiled, "I think I met you before, but don't remember where or when."

She smiled, "But I know you work in the gym and are big strong man, but you give awesome cuddles. You are good teacher of sports and health."

"You're Katarzyna. You have a sister called Ela, and you work at the caravan park. But you are amazing at cooking, sewing clothes and so many things that I can't name them all. You're going home to the Czech Republic on holiday."

She nodded. "Well that's almost correct, and later tonight, you found me out on the road after taxi driver... umm..." She looked uneasy.

"Then we ended in the haystack in the nude," I added.

"Maybe you no take that turn this time," she smiled.

"Is this weird to you that we know each other?" I asked quietly.

"That is ultimate question," she sniffed, rubbing her nose with a very well-used handkerchief. "I think maybe." She stopped suddenly and sneezed heavily twice. "Excuse me," she shuddered, before continuing, "I think you have had a dream as I did."

"So, you had a dream too?" I asked, now stunned.

She turned her head slightly for a third sneeze. Then she nodded, mouthing, "Sorry about my awful cold," very quietly and nervously as if having a cold was a crime. I just smiled as she continued. She spoke much clearer after. "It was in some ways," she said quietly, "best dream ever, apart from having nasty fit, fall downstairs, and died of hypothermia. But the rest was heaven." She looked at me sadly as though she was reminiscing about her dream.

"Maybe we're still dreaming," I smiled.

"No, I no think we are," she told me softly.

"Well I'm not staying late at work tonight," I told her, adding that if she did indeed end up getting into trouble, I wouldn't be driving along that road at the right time to find her.

She grimaced in pain. "That leg is worse than you want me to think, isn't it?" I asked her concerned.

"It bloody sore," she admitted. "I no know if I have power in to fight taxi driver if he attacks me."

It seemed like a perfect time to break the ice and wind her up. "Sounds to me like you're pretty screwed," I told her, as I sat down on the driver's side.

She looked quite shocked as I sat down and pretended I was going to leave her there. "Rob," she stammered, touching my shoulder, "would you... erm... please you help me?"

"You only had to ask," I told her, getting out and taking her rucksack from her. I gently placed her backpack in the back seat and joked that I'd leave it at the hotel reception for her to collect when she arrived on the bus.

Kat pulled a face at me as I put an arm around her for support as she hobbled into the passenger seat.

"I know you no leave injured girl out in the snow," she smiled quietly.

"It's you, Kat," I replied. "Of course, I was going to offer you a lift, injured or not."

"You're a good guy, and you would have helped anyone whether it was me or not." She grinned. "Rob," she said softly as I sat down before. "We met three minutes ago. We are no even friends." She must have seen the sad look on my face, because she quietly added, "Yet, I hope soon we are. I am still pay for dinner at the hotel like I said I would in dream."

"We're having dinner?"

"Yep," she nodded, "I pay for dinner, or you leave me here."

"Okay, "I replied. "So, we're having dinner. Does this mean we are friends now?"

"Think of it as a, 'Sorry for my horrible nasty, shameful little outburst just now' and 'Thank you for your kind help of lift' dinner, in which I want to discuss what happened in our dream."

"Okay," I smiled.
"And yes," she said.

"Yes, what?" I asked.

"Yes, we friends," she grinned.

I turned the ignition on my Mini, and the car sputtered, but did not start. The second time I tried it the same thing happened. I looked over at Kat to apologise for the fact that we seemed to be going nowhere. However, she smiled at me, then leaned down and pulled the choke out causing the car to start on the third go.

She laughed, "You always forget the choke."

Chapter 25

The real Katarzyna Bobal

I had written this part of our story many times, but due to the many things happened I chose to speed the story along.

Kat's English was audibly spoken much slower than in the dream, but just like in the dream, her accent was very thick and hard to grasp when you first spoke to her. She pronounced her Ws as Vs and Ts as Ds examples of this were, vas, vere, vair, dhis and dhat.

"Rob," she said softly as I got in the car. "You are understand brain is no work right today. Because last night I am..." She looked at me and started to shake violently. "Brian no recovered well."

"You had a fit? Was it a bad one?"

She nodded speaking slowing, "Normally my English very... good. Today is bad and slow because of seizure. And left is well... you know?"

It was really strange for both of us seeing each other. Neither of us knew what to say to each other on the way out of the town. Kat kept looking at me as though she wanted to talk, but then she went quiet again.

I had to stop at the fuel station and while there I thought it would be fair to replace Kat's spilt tobacco. The cashier called me a hypocrite for buying the tobacco in my fitness instructor uniform and called me a liar when I said it wasn't for me, but I refused to stay and argue. I also bought her some painkillers for her leg and some bandages because she said it was bleeding.   However, I should have known she already had paracetamol and ibuprofen in her handbag.

Kat both kissed my cheek and slapped my leg at the same time when I gave the tobacco. Her reasoning for this was that I'd been very naughty and very kind at the same time.

"Good job I got rolling machine in my pocket." She smiled awkwardly, nodding at her left hand hanging limp.

The next shock came when I offered to look at her leg for her and see how hurt she was, so I could help bandage any cuts.

She gave me teasing look. "When... I was... child, when cut is knee, my teacher is teased that they will cut it off."

"My mum used to say that too," I laughed.

"But you still have legs though." She smiled weakly.

"Well," I smiled, "I guess your mother never cut your leg off either."

"No." She shrugged, casually dropping a bomb shell, "The surgeon at the hospital in Prague did instead."

She pulled up her left trouser leg to reveal nothing but a stump above the knee.

I sat there with my mouth open for about thirty seconds, until Kat spoke to tell me that she had put her prosthetic leg on the back seat if I wanted to see.

"Other leg is hurt though bad." She grimaced. "Maybe we are look at in hotel room under light. Need to go. I quite like to smoke soon if you mind.

"Are we going to talk about what happened to your leg?" I soothed, "Or is that one of the questions where you suddenly need to blow you nose until I stop asking?"

It might not have been mentioned, but she did that throughout the dream when she didn't want to answer something.

"Honestly," she shrugged, "I have smelly cold and need to blow my nose. But am tell you story my leg another time."

"Do you mean a stinking cold, not a smelly one?" I teased, and she nodded.

As I began the drive, silence fell between us again.

There was a somewhat nervous tension between us to start with, but it soon came to an end when Kat asked quietly if she could put the radio on. Just as she did our favourite, *A Winter's Tale* by David Essex came on. The song itself was terribly sad about failed love, but in the dream Kat and I had rewritten the words for our own situation, after a moment of us both humming quietly we just broke out into song and smiled at each other.

We quietly agreed not to talk to about the dream we shared until we made it to the pub, this was so that we could talk over dinner.

It was the weirdest feeling seeing Kat there with me knowing she was real. This version of Kat was a different kettle of fish from either of the two versions of her that I met in the dream. She was quiet and nervous, and she very politely asked my permission to do everything apart from breathe. Just like the Kat in the dream, however, she seemed to have a very heavy cold.

When we got to the hotel, Kat screwed her prosthetic leg on with one hand. It was clear that Kat's other leg was hurt more than she had originally let on, so I had to help her walk as she winced and yelped in pain. I felt awful for my small part in knocking her over.

I took Kat's rucksack for her and let her hold on to me as she walked to the car park to the hotel. Kat sat on a bench outside and smoked her cigarette while insisting that I stood ten metres away, so I didn't inhale the fumes. Another observation I picked up on was that Kat did not hang about with her smoking. In fact, she sucked up her hand-rolled cigarette in a matter of only less than ten breaths before saying, "Okay, in we go."

She was booked in by a red-headed girl around our own age who said asked her if we wanted to change the room for one with a double bed, saying they had been expecting two single girls. Kat explained that Jenny had been supposed to stay with her for the night, but it was no longer possible.

Chapter 26

Kat's decision

When we got to the room, we just sat on the beds opposite each other, looking at each other and not saying much. In the light this version of Kat looked like she did in the dream with her smiley face her and her thick blonde plait wrapped around her.

The difference was that she looked exhausted and very ill. She was so skinny that she had a gaunt look to her and there were black rings under her eyes as she mopped her face with her hanky.

"We can talk about this another time if you want to stay in the warm. Maybe meet up when you come back." I said gently.

"No" She replied rather sharply. Then in a softer tone. "No is because..." She paused and looked at my face as she spoke softly, "No is because I woke up this morning and when I found, I was I decided that when I leave tomorrow, I am no coming back. I am quit my job and give my landlord a month notice."

"You... you, you're not." I stuttered in disbelief. I just had her back. She couldn't be leaving.

Kat leaned over and touched my leg with a smile, and said quietly. "That was the decision I made this morning when I woke up. After the dream, realised how badly my life is sucks donkey dick. I quit my job and gave my notice to my landlord."

"So that's it then. You're going," I said plainly.

"Well," she said, with a little grin, "I didn't think I'd be meeting you, and by the look on your face and tone of your voice, you don't want me to go so…"

"But about your cat and your rabbit. Who'll look after them?" I protested. She smiled at me and looked the floor and said that I must have had exactly the same dream as her if I knew about Charlie and Roger. Then she looked up with a tear in her eye and said bluntly, "I never had a rabbit, the pet shop wouldn't let me have one, because I live in a flat and didn't have a car to take one home in. Charlie doesn't need looking after, because somebody ran him over three weeks ago and killed him."

"Well that sucks," was all I could manage to say, and when Kat looked at me, there was a tear in her eye. She quickly wiped it away with her hanky and gave her nose a loud honk. Then she stood up gingerly wincing in pain, switched the kettle on and plonked herself down next to me on the bed. To my surprise, she put her arm around my shoulders as she dug around in her handbag and pulled out a set of plane tickets.

Kat smiled at me and when I asked why she was smiling she simply said, "The plane leaves at 9 am tomorrow morning, and it's still only five past seven in the evening." She picked up a second ticket and showed it to me to reveal the return date and told me she had not yet cancelled it, then with a cheeky smile, said, "You have thirteen hours and fifty-four minutes to talk about our dreams, and for you to convince me that England isn't done with this girl yet."

Kat suggested that we order room service and then hit herself on the forehead and made a noise like Homer Simpson when I explained that Travelodges didn't even have restaurants, let alone room service.

So, I helped Kat hobble across the road to the Oaks pub where we had eaten in the dream. She was in so much pain that I had ended up carrying her the last few metres to the smoking area where she apologised for puffing on another roll-up before we went in.

We found a room right at the back of the pub where we looked at the menu and had fun guessing what each other was going to eat. Astonishingly, we both guessed correctly, and while we waited for the food, we began to discuss the dream. Kat tore a piece of paper from her notepad for me to write on, and laughed as she told me she was writing her own note in her own language, so I couldn't copy her.

From my early exchanges with Kat, she seemed as lovely as she was in the dream. However, in the beginning, I did get the feeling that she was on edge, and that two wrong sentences from me might cause her to get up and leave, but after a while, she seemed to relax.

Earlier that evening when we had collided, Kat had reacted like an angry snake. But that venom-spitting cobra had now been replaced by a playful Labrador puppy.

She was also easily as ill as she had been in the dream, in fact, I'd go far as to say her cold was much worse. Just like in the dream, Kat was extremely polite in dealing with her coughs and sneezes. She actually laughed at it all and told me that her theory for the reason she was often full of cold in our dream was that she really was full of it.

I didn't have a better theory, so I agreed with her. I saw

a lot more colour on her face as we talked about our lives in the world of sleep. In fact, we had both gone back to the all you can eat extra carvery and veg and had pudding of chocolate cake. We washed down three pints of orange juice each and were on our second pot of tea. That was before we finished talking about the dream.

After a quick break for the toilet, Kat hobbled outside for a quick smoke while I got us more tea. I helped Kat stumble back to the corner seat where she had been sat all evening. As I tried to take my place opposite her at the table, Kat grabbed my arm in both hands and instructed me to sit next to her.

"Sit with me I don't bite," she said, grinning and adding, "Although I did bark like a Jack Russell when I spilt the tobacco, but I calmed down quick enough. "

When I sat next to her, she opened up her handbag and took out a pair of glasses, then put them on and smiled. Other than her shades, she had never once worn glasses in the dream.

"You have glasses," I said, confused. Kat just nodded and told me she had to take out her contact lens, because it was itching, but I had no idea that she wore them.

Then she shocked me again by pointing at her left eye and saying, "I only need one lens, because left eye prosthetic since my sister Dusa poked me with a knitting needle when she was two years old."

My mouth dropped open, and I was about to say, "Fuck that shit, one eye and one leg missing, fucking hell." When Kat offered me her hand to shake.

"Hello, I am Katarzyna Zophka Bobal, please forget everything you think you know about me, so I can tell you about the real me."

"Hi back. I'm Rob, and I'd love to know the real you," I said, shaking her hand gently. To my surprise, Kat was quite hesitant to let go of my hand. In fact, she then took my left hand to her right and gripped it tightly.

Kat wanted to know my differences from the dream first, because she said she had a lot to tell me about. The only difference that came to my mind was my Nanna who had given us the money to go on holiday in the dream, actually died from cancer when I was a baby and left me the money in her will. I told Kat that I kept the money for a rainy day. Kat actually shed a tear at this news, and she leaned over and hugged me.

When I told her, I didn't want a hug because my nanna died, she whispered, "No, I need a hug because you nanna died, because I was look forward to meet her."

Kat's analogy was that I must have kept the money and not spent it because I didn't care about it and would have given all of it back to have my nanna for just one day. I couldn't have agreed with her more.

I couldn't think of anything else different from the dream, so Kat started on her list and went through putting marks on things.

"I'm not a farmer's daughter." She bluntly added, "I grew up in big house, the grounds of my granddad's farm, but my father is no a farmer, he is a professional asshole."

I laughed as I asked how he could be a professional asshole, and her reply was to tell me that her father was a big city banker. "And given he often works in London and is part of the cause the current credit crunch in this country, I can call him worse than an asshole."

"He works in London?" I asked, stunned.

She nodded, "London is one of many places he works,

but it's only two hours away on the train, and he knows where I live and hasn't visited me once. That makes him super mega asshole."

My reply was, "I have to agree with that." What father worked in the same country his daughter moved to and didn't arrange to meet up?

Kat, however, seemed both sarcastic and philosophical about the situation. She thought that it could be because she stole her mother's credit card, and used it to set herself up with a cheap hotel, so she could look for work and accommodation when she got to England.

"Did you pay it all back?" I asked, when I realised she wasn't joking.

"Every single Koruna." She nodded, "But it was wrong to steal, given that my father is rich and would have given it to me if I asked. No look at me through rose tinted spectacles, Rob," she said, suddenly looking at my eyes. "Like forget the sweet innocent happy-go-lucky Kat that you think you know and meet the one who ruins other people lives."

I didn't want Kat to confess everything to me, because the past was the past. Kat, however, threatened to walk in the door if I did not let her confess the things she'd done.

The root of Kat's perceived guilt came from early on in her time in England, when she was working as a farm labourer in Thetford living in a small cramped house with other women.

"See Kat in the dream said bullied horribly living there. In the dream, she really was bullied, and it really affected her, and I believed in what I was saying and felt the pain in it all." She took a long gulp of tea and wiped her lips on her hand the wiped her hand on her napkin. "It's a dog eat dog in those places," She told me quietly.

As single women, they were lucky enough to be offered temporary accommodation while they worked for the company while male workers slept in tents. The conditions of the accommodation were not good, rotting floors and no hot water in return for a cut of their already low pay.

Five girls living in a two-bedroom house. In the dream Kat had opened to me and told me about the girl who bullied her and humiliated her.

"Everything I told you in the dream that girl did to me." She told me a hushed voice, shaking her head and not even able to look at me. "I did them all to her and worse."

Kat explained how she was fully aware of her fiery temper and her tendency to assume control of everything in her life. She told me that her housemates were scared of her temper and that she assumed control and bossed them around.

It was Kat and not her roommate who was the sharp-tempered bully. She had done everything she could to work her way to the top of the pecking order, including blackmailing her roommate. One evening while moving her roommate's bed against the wall she found lesbian porn stashed away under it.

The girl was young, nervous, scared of coming out in case it brought shame on her family back in Lithuania. Rather than be sympathetic, Kat had picked on the girl and teased her, and even blackmailed her demanding money for her not to tell. When the girl ran out of money and failed to pay up, Kat in a temper had outed her to the other women the house. The housemates, when they heard what Kat had done, had sided against her and forced her to leave the house.

"I was right little bitch was no?" She asked quietly,

still looking at the floor.

"Yes, you were," I replied bluntly. "But we all do things we regret when we are young and learning, don't we."

Kat replied to this by saying she didn't want forgiveness or excuses made for what she had done, and that she got what she deserved.

"And what was that?" I probed.

"Several hard slaps to the face and sacked from my job."

"You learned you're lesson then."

"I did for a while," she nodded. Kat went on to explain that she thought our dream might been trying to teach her a lesson. "In the dream, I was the one who got bullied so that I knew how it felt, and it was my sister who came out. I know how angry I would be if somebody treated my little sister how I treated that girl."

I tried to reassure her, "Remember, as I said you were young and learning. We all do things we're not proud of, and we learn from our mistakes."

"Yes," she retorted "but I still do these things, and I'm not twenty-one years old."

"Still young and learning then," I grinned.

She laughed, "I'll still be young and learning when I'm eighty."

When I asked if Kat had apologised for her behaviour, she nodded and smiled. "Apparently phoning her randomly to apologise for something I did four years ago was mistake. She told me go fuck myself."

In a moment of seriousness, I couldn't keep my mouth from saying, "And did you go fuck yourself?"

I thought for a moment that the night was over there and then.

However, Kat took the joke in good humour as she laughed her head off, and said, "No my vibrator is out of batteries." Then she followed with, "No, I mean I no have a vibrator."

When I assured her that her secret was safe with me and I wasn't going write a book about it, Kat began to open up to me further.

"Bringing the subject back to sex," She smiled, "You remember our dream daughter Erica was misguided on sexual contact?"

"Lovely girl but she did have strange views and habits."

Kat told me bluntly that everything Erica had said on the matter in the dream were her own views, and they sounded stupid coming from somebody else.

Intending it as a joke, I asked Kat if she also wore a chastity belt, but rather than laugh, she went silent.

After my question, Kat sat in silence for several minutes in which she kept looking down, then up at me and opening her mouth without speaking.

"Have I said something wrong?" I asked after a few moments, but Kat smiled weakly and shook her head.

She looked at me as though she was going say something, then she shied away. I assured her that whatever it was she wanted to tell me, I wouldn't judge her.

"Pretend I'm still your husband and you can tell me anything."

Kat smiled awkwardly, before telling me it would be

a lot easier to talk about if I *was* her husband. Instead of answering me directly, Kat looked around the room to check that there was nobody looking and quickly lifted the elastic waistband of her jogging bottoms and gestured that I should look at something.

Not wanting to look too hard out of courtesy to Kat, seeing as she was not even my girlfriend, I only needed the briefest of glances at what she was showing me.

My joke had been in poor taste. Kat was showing me that she did indeed have her own chastity belt, well and truly locked onto her.

"Why?" I asked simply.

"Because I'm scared," was her reply.

"Of sex?" I asked gently, but she shook her head.

She looked away from me and said softly, "Although I never have, I no am scared of making love with a person I love but…" She paused to cough heavily, and allowed me to rub her back until the coughing fit calmed, then she turned to look me dead in the eye and said, "Until I met you, I am terrified of men and their intentions."

This didn't sound like the Kat I had known. Kat in my dream was very naïve in the beginning, and looking at everything in life with the intention of finding good in it. This admission that she was terrified, rocked me slightly. What could have happened to a young woman to make her so scared that felt she needed to wear the belt to protect her when she had intended to ride a bus.

I thought this was something I needed to ask more about, so I gently asked Kat if I scared her, and if so why? Kat looked at me uneasily once more, and quietly told me, "I no am scared of you, Rob, but if I am no have the dream, I would have been very uneasy."

When I asked her gently, "Can I ask why?" Kat covered her face with both hands and rubbed her face, before letting out a long breath that made her lips vibrate like a fart effect.

After a moment of consideration and looking around to check that nobody was listening, she spoke in a tiny voice, "I suppose now the subject has come up, it is better to tell you now rather than let it fester."

"You don't have to—"

"Yes, I do have to tell you." She interrupted, adding that if we were to have a future together that we needed to be honest from the start.

Kat told me that she knew her fears were mainly irrational, but she refused to take any chances or trust anyone. I instantly wondered, as Kat told about her lack of trust in men, if there must be some big reason for all her hatred and fear.

"Fear is the reason I sleep with the light on every night," She shivered, "and the reason I lock bedroom every night, and I wake up screaming every night. The reason I fly off the handle at the slightest touch."

As she was saying these things, my mind suddenly went back to the dream in the haystack. When Kat had told me about her fight with the taxi driver, she had said, "It was terrifying especially for a person who has been raped before." But when I had questioned her over what she meant, she had told me that she was talking hypothetically. However, from the way she was now talking, I was concerned that she might well have been talking from her own experience.

"Kat," I said, holding my hand up apologetically to stop her talking, "Are you scared of men because you've been raped?"

It was very bold question for me to ask and Kat stopped in her tracks, then gave me a long look, before deciding to blow her nose again. It was clear to me, though, that she was only doing this to stall while she considered her answer.

After a moment, she looked me dead in the eye and said, "I told you I want to be honest from the start, but it's difficult."

I reminded her that she didn't have to tell me everything, but Kat being Kat actually smiled, and said. "It's difficult to tell when you have got to know somebody well enough to trust them with your secrets. We only just met, but I already trust you with my life, and I will tell you because I trust, but it's hard to know the time."

I nodded in agreement, as Kat did something that caught me by surprise. Having said she was scared of men, she totally contradicted herself by sliding over towards me, and lifted my arm over her shoulder that made her feel safer like old times.

Old times that hadn't happened yet, but she fitted me like a glove and she was able to talk quietly in my ear. This was how that poor lady told me her story so that she couldn't be overheard.

~~*~*~*

Kat began her story in the school summer holidays of 2003 on her grandfather's farm when she was fifteen.

I was going to be a star athlete," she reminisced, "Under 16 girls 5k, I came second in my country, went to the Junior European championships and made the final. I should have been on the plane to Beijing last for the Olympics last year."

She reached in her bag and took out a picture to prove

what she was saying was true. The photo showed a pretty young Kat dressed in her country's colours, with a silver medal around her neck. She beaming all over her face with pride.

"You were amazing," I gasped, shaking her hand out of a new found respect.

"Was" she sighed. "Until live went to shit."

"Your leg?" I soothed.

"Partly" she smiled sadly. "It was harvest." She smiled, reminiscing as though she could see it in her mind, "Those few days when all the local farming families get together and help each other gather up the hay into bales for storage. My favourite time, because although we no are live on the farm, my father, mother and siblings and I would always offer our help to my grandfather, uncle and cousins."

She continued after a sip of tea, telling me that she loved the days when the family got together and worked hard on the land. "It kept me grounded." She smiled, "and it made sure that I no did become a spoilt little rich girl that I could have done while getting to spend quality time with my father. Plus I love getting fresh air, exercise and banter with my cousins who joke with me that a girl's place is in the kitchen while I run rings around them with my hard work."

I could imagine she did from what I'd seen of her in the dream.

So, Kat was looking forward to harvest, but the night before that day came to join her family in the fields under the mountains and the burning sun, Kat was struck down with anepileptic seizure.

"Parents told me to stay in bed for a couple of days," She said sadly, "But I told them I go help anyway, even though exhausted, aching all over, limping, dazed, not myself, apart from being pig-headed."

When I told her it sounded to me like her parents were right to tell her to stay inside, she just laughed, saying, "I was a teenager remember, it's every teenage girl's ambition in life to do the opposite to what their parents tell them."

So, Kat had forced herself to go out and work in the field with her family. The way she explained it was that in her part of the world at that time, the farming machinery was old and primitive. Not to say that this was the case in the whole of the Czech Republic, but this was the case on her granddad's farm and those surrounding it. What would be a two person job here in Norfolk with a tractor, a trailer and a combine harvester. No tractors or combines, just a small cutting machine and baler with lots of people using pitchforks, throwing the bales into a truck.

"I wanted so much to work hard to prove that the seizure had no affected my ability, do my bit for the family, but when I was already suffering after an hour in the working heat, it was clear to everyone I was not myself. The heat added to the after-effects of the seizure and I was slow and dizzy. My father asked Kazia to take me home to lie down, but I didn't want to, so I refused Kazia's help and went off in a huff."

Kat continued to tell me how she stormed off crying, not because she was in trouble because she wasn't, but because she was upset and frustrated with herself. She was angry that her epilepsy stopped her from being able to do what she wanted.

On her way back up to the house, Kat had become dizzy and lightheaded, and realised she could be about to faint. She had sat down on a small pile of hay bales that had been left outside ready to be stacked inside of the barns. It was a hot day, and she found she was drenched in sweat and probably suffering from sunstroke as well as her other problems. When she tried to drink from her bottle of homemade iced tea, she found it empty.

Kat had soon become aware that there were other people around her, familiar faces who she thought had seen her looking unwell and come.

"They were four middle-aged men," she told me, looking down at her tea as she continued to explain that she knew them, because they were builders. "They had been recently worked on a side extension to her family home. A new changing room for the family swimming pool," which was ironic seeing that she couldn't swim.

Kat told me how she had been happy to supply the men with tea while they worked and how she had become friends with them, but was surprised to see them back as the work had been finished four weeks earlier.

All seemed innocent to start with. The men sat with Kat and offered her some of their drink.

I was horrified at where this conversation was seeming to be going, even though I had known from the beginning that Kat was telling me about a sexual assault. When I asked her why the men were there, she replied sharply.

"I didn't know at the time father paid them a deposit for the work they did, but my farther wasn't happy and refused to pay final bill, and left them short of a huge sum of money."

"They were there to have it out with him." I breathed, and Kat nodded.

"That was the original aim I think," she sighed. "Only changed, they changed plans and decided that beating the shit out of his daughter as payback might make him listen."

"Which daughter did they take?" I asked stupidly.

Kat, quite rightly, looked me up and down as though I had just asked the dumbest thing she had ever heard, and she told me

"Rob, I think you're a lovely guy, but you're not the sharpest pencil in the tin are you?"

Kat continued to tell how the men had given her drink and she had taken it thinking they were being kind and helping her. She told me how the water had tasted awful, but due to her seemingly unquenchable thirst, she continued drinking until she felt like she was going to vomit.

"No was water, it fucking vodka" She scoffed, "I was fifteen and came from a very Christian family. I never even drank more than the tiniest mouthful of the communion wine."

An ill and now drunken teenaged girl was no match for the four men. She was so sick and drunk that she couldn't even scream as they bundled her into the barn which was half full of hay bales. They had dragged her on to a small gap in the bale of hay.

I put my hand over my mouth as she told me how they had shoved her head scarf, which she wore to keep sweat out her eyes, into her mouth to stop her screaming, and beat her around the face.

As Kat told me this, she lifted up the arm of the woollen jumper she was wearing and showed me a long scar on her arm. Before I could gasp, she just told me casually that it was one of many they caused. I asked her gently if she had been truthful when she had told me that her sister had been the one who poked her eye out.

She prodded her eye to prove to me that it was prosthetic, then shook her head saying, "No, I made that up.

Those men did that too. I try stand, but I fell to ground, and they just laughed horribly. That's when I realise they are drunk. They pick me up between them. I thought they were trying to help me, but they put me down inside barn on hay bales out of sight from the house or fields. I was fifteen. No old enough anyway, but they no care." She sighed. "I am already no feel well as it is, and with shock of vodka, I have no strength to fight them."

I sat in horror at what Kat was telling me. What kind of monster could do that to anyone, let alone to a poor, innocent, ill teenage girl?

"I was dizzy drunk. I no could move," she sniffed. "They picked me up. I thought they were being kind and take me to the farmhouse but…" She paused. "They take my sweaty headscarf and put it in my mouth, so I no can scream. They push me into the haystack, bales falling everywhere. When I try run one of them hit me with spade and is my leg above the knee. Then they tied me up and gagged me. They then shut the door and left me crying and bleeding. They then sent a ransom note to my father. After two days the whole town was out looking for me."

She paused, blew her nose and sipped some tea, as I just sat silent and gobsmacked.

"Nobody suspect that kidnaped girl is in barn in the sight of her own bedroom. After three days of starving, feeding only alcohol to quench my thirst and keep me too drunk. They told me my father had not paid the ransom they asked for. Then two of them held me while one reached up my skirt, pulled my knickers off, and put his erm, in my erm."

She pointed between my legs and then between hers as though she couldn't say the words. I felt sick. No wonder she hadn't trusted men. No wonder she had problems with her temper and addictions to cigarettes and tea. It also explained why the poor sweet lady was very defensive and unorthodox in her ways and didn't wear the dresses she so lovingly made. I couldn't begin to believe how terrible poor Kat's life must have been from that moment.

For a while, I held her in my arms and said nothing. I simply gave her time as she wept. I didn't have to hear anymore, but to my horror, she continued.

"All four of them had a go on me," she told me in a hushed, tearful voice as I sat shocked and speechless. "My leg was in so much pain hanging off. I no could fight or scream, and I could barely breathe, but I had the strength to look them in the eyes as they held me there, with silent tears rolling down my face."

Anger pulsed through me as Kat stopped to dry her tears. Still, she gave me a sad smile. I thought it was to show her appreciation for the physical closeness and for me listening to her shocking tale.

"It gets worse," she sighed.

"How can it be worse?" I whispered.

"Ela was eleven, and she was in kitchen helping my aunty and my mother make huge afternoon tea to feed family who are now out searching. Mum sent Ela to tell them it time for tea break."

Having just cleaned herself, poor Kat sneezed again. Then for a moment, she just sat there staring at the floor and talking in a whisper, even though we were the only two in the room. There was a reminiscence in her look as she told me how the siblings had all been very close, how she worshipped Kazia, Dusa, Ela, and Dowid.

"Ela was my little shadow," she breathed. "She followed me everywhere, just like Dusa and I did with Kazia when were younger. She saw my water bottle and pink handkerchief lying on floor by the barn and come to see what is going on."

"She saw you getting raped?" I heard myself finish.

"For the second time," Kat nodded. "She no understand tries help, but they are big strong men, and she is little girl. They tell her if she says a word, they will do the same to her."

I was speechless. What an ordeal this poor girl had been through! I didn't know quite what to say to her.

Kat seemed to realise this and continued hesitantly, saying, "I tell you this, because you need to know why I am sometimes how I am. You understand?"

"It's why you're very defensive and strong-willed, yet terrified of strange men."

Kat nodded gently and added, "Is also partly why shout, swear a lot, and smoke too much. Also, why I clean myself all of time. Is why I sleep in tiny boxroom in flat when I have a bigger room. It makes the world small. Is why I hate big public places and of being alone with man." She paused for a second and then added, "Well, apart from one particular man I met this evening."

She stopped, and another tear rolled down her face. I instinctively took her angry scarf, which she had been twisting in her hands and wiped them away.

She gave me a little grin and said, "You know after all

these years I think these are the first tears I've cried over this. Even when it hit me what happened, I never shed a tear until now when I realise just how much it affected me."

When I suggested that Kat must have been the bravest woman in the world to stay so mentally strong she just said in a clear voice. "I was broken inside, but I tell myself that I can't let it rule my life when it was only a few minutes of it, but still it does. I see them in my sleep every night, laughing my face and mocking my screams."

She stopped for a moment screwed the purple scarf tightly in her hands, then took a breath, "You know why I use this particular scarf to stretch when I get angry or sad?" she asked, looking up at me, so I could see that she had already stopped crying.

I shook my head in reply and Kat continued, "Because this the same one they put in my mouth to stop me screaming."

"You keep it as a reminder, so that you never forget and remember never to trust anyone." She gave me a little nod. "And what happened to the men who did it to you, if you don't mind me asking?

"Ela was one brave little girl," she said simply. "Despite their threats, as the fourth man was got on top of me, she bit the man who was holding her, so hard that he had to let go. Then she ran screaming to my father, uncle, and cousins. When they hear her, they come they running? The men leave faster than... I no know the word," she said weakly. "Something fast, but no superman, because they fat and drunk."

She paused and took a huge gulp of tea. "I remember Ela and Kazia came back to find me, while my father, uncles, and cousins chase the men. I never sawed my big sister cry like that before or after. I was numb and shaking. My head banging from the alcohol and broken bones everywhere. I am bruised, bleeding, ache all over, but so numb I couldn't even cry. Kazia held Ela and me in her arms, while Dusa called the police."

I just sat there in shock, not knowing what to say to Kat, but finding even further admiration for her bravery.

She took another sip of tea and said, "The police and ambulance came. They take me to hospital and do DNA for records, but no match found. Look for fingerprints on my granddad's farm and from the areas of the house that they worked, and look for their van."

"Did the police get them?" I asked gently.

She looked up from the floor and showed me those lovely big eyes of hers, before she shook her head with a hint of a smile. "No sorry about what happened to them. They no hurt anyone else," she said, with a hint of a smile in her eyes again. "My family no told me what day did. Only they never left the farm, and I no want to know more." After a pause, she added, "Just remember though, never ever piss off my cousins, and you will be fine. You understand?"

~~*~*~*

So I in hospital for week maybe three," She sighed, "They no could save my leg. Bye bye Olympics. Hospital are given to me the morning after pill, so I no have but..."

I wondered what she was going to say, but suddenly I thought I knew. In my head and heart, I guessed what Kat was going to tell me. If my guess was correct, then it mattered not, because I already knew that night that I wanted to spend the rest of my life with Katarzyna. Something from the dream was coming back to me. It was something we hadn't discussed that evening, something I had nearly forgotten.

I waited silently and gave her a friendly squeeze while she finished her tea. I poured us both another cup as she wiped her nose. Then she put both arms around me in a hug before she sat up with her arm around my neck and spoke softly.

"I wanted not say anything at all and hope it would all just go away but..." she paused and sipped more tea. "...the pill is no work, because my medication blocked it just like in our dream when we had Lydia. I started to get sick in the morning, and my tummy gets fat, so I have to tell my mother I'm pregnant."

"You're a mum?" I said quietly, thinking about the sort of hell it must have been carrying her rapists' baby. I found even deeper respect for her now that my guess had been confirmed. But Kat shook her head and quietly said, "Would it have made a difference to the chance of us together if I was a mummy?"

I weighed it up briefly in my mind, but nothing changed. If I was going to be with Kat, then her having another man's child would not make a difference to me. However, I could quite understand if she had chosen to terminate the pregnancy under the cruel circumstances.

I shook my head, and Kat smiled at me. "You would have made a great stepdaddy, but I no want to keep my baby," she breathed.

"That's understandable. You don't have to explain to me," I told her.

"I want to be honest always," she smiled. "Just because I no want keep my baby, it no means I no love my baby. You know what I mean?" I nodded.

Kat went on to explain how she wanted to give her baby to a loving home. Although her family would have helped bring up the child, she didn't feel she could bring up her rapists' baby.

So, she had found a married couple in her town who could not conceive. That was such a brave choice to make for somebody so young and innocent. If my respect for Kat could get any higher, it was now glowing.

"I breaked two arms, a leg all in two places, as well as my pelvis," she said sadly, as I cringed. "With that, my fits, and the baby, I am never go back to school. They send me work, and I am doing at home like a good girl. Other than to hospital and meet the baby's new parents, I am never come out of my room apart from go to toilet."

"Too scared of the world?" I asked gently.

She nodded slowly. "I am happy that my baby is going to have loving home and family," she smiled, "but each day, fits are getting out of control. I try hard to be careful. I was sixteen years old and eight months pregnant with the baby when..." She stopped dead, and made a high pitch squeal and put her hand to eye and took deep breaths say, "I... refuse... to... cry."

I looked around the pub in case anyone mistakenly thought I was hurting her. Instinctively I kissed her head. She took a deep breath and looked around at me. Her face was red, crumpled, but not tear-stained. She clasped her arms behind my head, so we stayed face to face.

She kept looking away as she said tearfully, "One morning I have a horrible fit like in the dream. I remember it, but I fitted so hard I fall out of bed and..." She paused and screwed up kind eyes once more but no tears. "That was that. I fell on baby," she told me bluntly.

It didn't quite sink in. As she fell onto my shoulder still trying not to cry, I held her skinny body as she shook all over. It finally hit me as she weakly said, "Rob, my fit killed the baby."

I was struggling to take it all in. If the dream was an ideal world, then of course, none of this would have happened. Kat would not have told me, because it hadn't happened. No wonder the poor, sweet, lovely Kat had confessed to being off the rails and out of control at times. I didn't know a single person who had ever gone through so much shit in a whole lifetime, let alone at such a young age.

Despite this, she still had the strength and the balls to bounce back. She'd also had the guts and courage to try to make a good thing out of a bad situation by giving her baby to someone who could love it, despite her pain. All this only to be left with the pain of losing that baby.

No wonder she had come all this way and never been home before tonight. No wonder she, in her own words, lost control of herself and her temper. No wonder she had run from her home, whatever her background, rich or poor. I couldn't say I would have done the same thing, but I didn't have her strength.

Kat was tearful and shaking, and seemed to have gone numb after pouring her heart out to me about it all. As if I didn't already know I loved this lady within minutes of meeting her, this just confirmed that I had to do everything I could to make sure this girl never hurt again as she did now.

"Do you want me to help you out for another smoke?" I asked gently.

Her reaction was to give me a guilty look and nod, saying she was disgusted in herself after all her confessions.

~~*~*~*

Despite Kat saying she would pay for dinner, she let me agree to pay when I pointed out she had just spent a lot of money on her flights and quit her job.

"The worst thing about it all," She told me as we sat on a bench outside the hotel, struggling to light her cigarette in the icy wind. "Is that my father is not an unreasonable man, and all he wanted was a few things fixing before he paid those builders. It was the amount, sixty thousand Koruna, about twenty-three thousand pounds including materials. Pocket change to a rich banker like my father. He's not unreasonable, wasn't going to let their families go without money."

"It sounds like they went very quickly from going to speak to him about the money to raping his daughter," I said quietly, sitting next to her causing her to hold her lit cigarette and tell me off for getting too close.

Kat kept expressing her guilt at the fact that the men who raped her had been taken from their families. Saying that although they should not be allowed to do it to anyone else, their children did not deserve to lose their fathers and end up in poverty due to the loss of income.

Officially it was still an ongoing case, and the police

were still looking for them. Unofficially, Kat told me that her father was good friends with the chief of police, who knew exactly what had happened to the men.

I asked her if she knew herself what happened to the men. She sighed and told me that she knew that her father, her uncle, her grandad and her two teenage male cousins had caught up with the men. A gun was involved, but they were taken alive, but she was not told where they were.

"I have my suspicions though," She told me with a grin on her face. "There's an old outdoor toilet on the farm with a deep pit under it. I think at least one of them is down there, because I can see it from my bedroom, and many of my family started walking down there to use the toilet, which is extremely odd when our house had seven bathrooms. There must be some in the cellar under the barn as I saw mother take the leftovers from dinner after it had a few days mould on it."

"Seven bathrooms? Your poor cleaner!" I queried.

She laughed, "We may be rich, but we no are posh. My mother no had five children to employ a cleaner, and I like cleaning. Where you think I get my love for cleaning. It may be why I dream of cleaning caravans. Rob where do you think we really go when we die?"

I had to think for a moment, about my answer, and I told her that I wanted to believe in heaven, but saw no evidence to convince me that we did anything but rot in our graves.

She had a little laugh and told me that despite being brought up to believe in heaven, she agreed with my views, and rotting away actually sounded quite fun and romantic if you had someone to rot away with.

"But just for a minute, suppose heaven did exist." She smiled up at the sky, "I want to think that my unborn child is up there looking us, and I want to make him proud of his mummy."

"I'm sure you'll make him proud if you haven't already," I told her putting an arm on her shoulder.

"Not if I keep bloody smoking," She laughed, before taking a last drag on her fag and stubbing it out in the snow, then she put her arm around my shoulder, so I could help her stand.

"I wonder," She said out loud, but didn't elaborate on what she wondered, so I asked her gently.

She took a long breath and coughed several times before answering. "What if people do go on after they die and with all the people who died recently, including the person we can't talk about. What if one of them, or my unborn baby sent the dream to us, help us be happy and stop me leaving for good?"

I could not rubbish her theory or ignore it, and I told her that even though I didn't believe in life after death, I didn't have a better idea as to who sent the dream. I also didn't know who this person we were not talking about was, but apparently from what Kat had just said, this person had recently passed away. I chose not to ask who she was talking about, because I didn't want to seem stupid.

Chapter 27

The hotel

Once in reception, the young redhead behind the desk smiled at us and asked if we had a nice dinner.

We both smiled and told her we feeling very full.

As I guided Kat towards the stairs the redhead called to us. "Good night guys. Have sweet dreams."

"You too!" we both called back to her.

Once upstairs, we sat down together on one of the beds. There I asked Kat if I had been successful in persuading her to return to the UK.

A big smile grew like a flower on her face as she revealed, "Of course I am coming back. Now give me your phone, and I'll put my number in it."

When I passed Kat my phone, she took it and quickly started to type in her number, when all of a sudden she stopped. She stared at the phone with her mouth open, and when I asked her what the matter was, she passed the phone to me.

She had only typed in the first four digits of her number, yet the phone had come up with a suggested contact, and it was there clear as day. It read **Kat Bobal**.

"How you have got my phone already when no have given it to you?" She demanded.

I was lost for any clue as to how on earth I got her number on my phone. The only thing I could think of was that she had given it to me at the time we met previously that neither of us remembered.

Kat smiled and added that she thought Jenny must have stolen my phone one day in the gym and put it in there in an attempt to make me call her.

Kat told me she wanted me to stay with her, so I took it from there and didn't try to build expectations.

Kat had a very quick shower and got into her PJs, then we sat in a chair talking a while about various things, while we paid limited attention to a movie on TV. We just talked like close friends who were so very comfortable with each other's company that Kat had laid her legs across me as she lay on the sofa sleepily.

She had taken out her prosthetic eye and put it in a glass with cleaning fluid and just lay there rolling up the rest of her tobacco into about twenty very skinny cigarettes which she put in her handbag.

When I commented on how organised she was, rolling her cigarettes for next day, she laughed and told me that they were just for the morning. She then smiled, gave my leg a small tug and told me she was kidding, and that she was trying to make them last in an effort to cut her smoking down, with a view to giving up when she got home. I smiled as she joked about planning her addiction with military precision, including finding the best times and places to hide it from her family, concluding that the best way not to get caught smoking was to stop smoking.

"Kat, where do we go from here?" I asked tentatively. Kat looked me up and down with her one eye, then glanced at her watch saying, "It passed midnight and have to be at the airport by 8 am, so probably bed." She didn't realise that I meant it metaphorically, but she continued sleepily, "If you meant our future, you remember all those times I pretend I have to do something to stall the conversation until I worked out what I wanna say?"

Wondering what on earth she was getting at I played along, listing things that I remembered her doing when she was stalling the conversation to have good think. These things included undoing her hair then redoing it, suddenly deciding to do the washing up by banging pots and pans that were already clean, or suddenly having to run to the toilet.

"Or refolding my hanky about twenty-two times until it perfect, then changing the conversation because I no can think of a response." She added, in a voice that sounded absolutely exhausted.

She then made me smile by telling me to pretend she was doing one of those things, because she was too sleepy to do any of them. Then she grinned, told me to take the fact that she was falling asleep on me to mean she wasn't going anywhere.

The next thing out of her mouth was a big snore. I took the fact she felt comfortable falling asleep in my arms, meant that my life, which that morning had been dull, had just become an adventure once more. An adventure that was looking forward despite there being actual talk of Kat and I starting a romance, but figured she was fragile and confused like me. If this was going to happen, it would need time and only time for the future.

I carried Kat over to the bed and tucked her into one of the single beds. I set a glass of water on the bedside table, laid out her morning pills and her hankies, just like she had always done in our dream. Then I crept away leaving my new friend to get some sleep, intending to phone her in the morning to make sure she was okay, and offer further assistance to get her to the airport.

"Oi, Oi, sneaking off and leaving, are you?" said a familiar voice, and I turned to see the redheaded receptionist coming out of a doorway to my left. "I didn't pay for the room, and I'm not on the booking."

Looking at this woman, she seemed so familiar, yet I couldn't put my finger on where we had met before.

"Well, I'm the manager of this hotel," She said proudly, "and I don't give a shit whose name is in the booking. So, what should I tell your friend in the morning when she wakes up and wonders where you are?

I thought about this hard for a moment, then I replied, "I'll call her in the morning, but if she asks, tell her I left to get some good sleep and give her time to herself to have a proper think about things. She'll know what you mean."

"Of course, I will," she smiled with a wink.

I smiled and thanked her, then I added, "Oh, and please if you would be kind enough, tell her that I don't know her very well, but she's the most special human being in my life, and I'm going to pick her up and take her out for breakfast in the morning before she leaves."

"Well that sounds like the plan of a good guy," she smiled, adding that she wished she had a boyfriend who said things like that about her.

I smiled and told her that there was somebody for everyone, that I worshipped Kat and wanted to give her all my love, and hoped she would choose to give me the honour of spending the rest of my life with her.

"Well, I think she knows exactly how you feel," She smiled, looking over my shoulder as though she had seen a friend.

"How do you know she knows that stuff?" I queried in interest. But all she did was nod to the person behind, and my question was answered by a loud sneeze.

I spun around to see Kat, inches from me with her face buried in one of her hankies.

The red-headed hotel manager walked over and patted Kat on the shoulder, then smiled, saying to me, "She did well, the poor girl was trying to hold that sneeze in the whole time we were talking." The manager walked on smiling and continued checking the corridor and left Kat and I to it.

"Kat... erm..." I stuttered.

"Erm, what?" she replied, somewhat coolly.

"Erm, bless you for sneezing and... erm, how much of that conversation did you hear?"

She looked at me with her single eye scanning me all

over. "I heard enough to know you were leaving me on my own." She replied quite snappily. Surely if she heard that part and the rest, she had no reason to be angry, but she sounded fuming like she had been when her tobacco spilt.

"Kat I—"

"You know what Rob?" She interrupted, "No bother coming back in morning, because there will be no point."

Feeling slightly hurt by this unexpected outburst, I decided I couldn't let Kat see me break down from having unintentionally upset her. I turned to walk away and leave as requested.

Kat, however, saw me about to turn my back on her and she leapt forward, grabbed my hand, and grinned all over her face laughing, "Wind-up. As if I let you go home after all those nice things you said about me. You right. I do need time to think." She told me after a deep breath as I calmed down and she took my arm to help her limp back the room. "I have thought, and I think you'd be silly to waste time and fuel driving home in the snow for two hours' sleep at most, when there is a nice warm, cosy bed right next to mine."

Back in the room, I thanked her for letting me use the bed as we settled down to sleep, and she replied, "There are conditions attached to the use of the bed though."

"Really what are they?"

All of a sudden, I felt the cover lift slightly and Kat climbed in with me in the dark. She whispered in my ear, "You have to share it."

Chapter 28

Waking up

Nothing happened between Kat and I that night, other than her wrapping her arms and legs around me and going to sleep with her head on the pillow.

I strongly liked it that way, because it showed what we had was not about sex and more about the need for closeness to each other.

Kat had even taken off her chastity belt, stating that it was not an invitation to go there, but it was a sign that she trusted me not to try my luck.

"I do understand why you left me to sleep, but was hurt and scared you weren't coming back." she had yawned sleepily, adding, "This tired Stilton can't sleep without her Broccoli,"

I explained to Kat that I felt the same, but she would have to cope when she was away for two weeks.

"That if," she breathed, "if I don't just choose to stay here."

Wearily she pulled me closer as if she was trying a

last-ditch attempt to kiss me before she fell asleep. Our lips barely touched, however, before the poor exhausted lady began to snore gently.

The rhythm of Kat's gentle snoring in my ear sent me off into a deep sleep.

Half of me had suspected that we would wake up again in that cold haystack. Considering how strange life had been, I would not have been at all surprised if this was all just another twist in the tale. However, what followed was a night of the deepest and most peaceful sleep I'd had in a long time. Any dreams I had were flashes of that day gone past and not as vivid as the mammoth dream of the night before.

In the morning, I woke up slowly, opened my eyes, and found darkness. I stretched and reached out for Kat, to find that I was alone in the dark.

The radio alarm was playing the same tune from the previous morning, *A Winter's Tale* by David Essex. "Yes, a winter's tale is all it was," I said aloud to myself.

It was cruel how my brain could play that trick twice. I had that fantastic dream only to find that it wasn't real. Then I met that lovely lady again thinking it was real, only to wake up in my own bed and find it was another dream.

I didn't even want to lift the cover, because I didn't want to see that I was back home alone in my bedroom once more. As I lay there trying to keep control of my emotions, I heard two noises. One of them sounded like a kettle boiling, and the other sounded distinctly like a toilet flushing, but still half asleep, I thought it must be the next-door neighbour.

I had for a long time hated my bedroom being the

other side of the wall from the neighbour's toilet. I even thought I heard a girl's voice humming along to the radio. My neighbour was an old man, so it must have been one of his relatives singing along or something.

Suddenly, as I stretched my legs, about to roll over and get some more sleep, I felt the cover lift gently. It was still dark outside, but the bedside lamp was on.

As my eyes adjusted to the light, I saw a painfully skinny Kat standing there in nothing but bra and knickers, grinning.

"Kat, you're here?" I breathed.

She gave me that cheeky grin of hers and looked around the room, and said quietly. "I think so. Sorry woke you, I had to go for a wee wee, but I make us both cup of tea."

"I love you," I said sleepily.

She smiled and said, "No expect me make tea in bed every morning. Next time is you turn. Now," she sniffed, "give me moment to sort myself, and then we have thirty-seven minutes and nineteen seconds of tea and snuggles before we have to be up for breakfast."

Her leg was obviously still hurting her, but as she hobbled back to the kettle, she gave me that look that acknowledged my desire to help her, but begged me not to so she could do it herself.

So, I just watched as she shuffled over and placed two cups of tea on the bedside table. She took a sip and smiled without speaking. Then she picked up the handkerchief I'd left by her bed and blew her nose until she was satisfied it was clear. She then apologised softly for being gross and just stood there smiling nervously.

I expected her to get back into her PJs before getting back into bed, considering Kat had told me about her phobia of being naked, or having skin anywhere below her neck touched. So, it was to my surprise that she smiled at me uneasily all of a sudden, removed her bra and knickers, and looked down at her dreadfully skinny stomach.

She smiled and said, "I think a big, high calorie, fat woman breakfast is required if I going to convince my mum I eating properly."

"Are you eating properly?" I asked.

She looked down at me, sheepishly moving her eyes from side to side. Finally, she answered, "I will eating proper as of today breakfast." She looked at herself again, and I asked if she was okay. In response, she just smiled and whispered, "This my first time I been naked with anyone except my mother."

"I dread to think what you and your mother got up to," I teased.

As she flicked on the main light, I saw her fully for the first time. I saw scars on her arms and legs where she had been put back together after her bones were broken. More worryingly, there was a line of crosses scratched into her arm, which showed me she had been self-harming.

"I'm damaged goods am I no?" She smiled nervously.

"Damaged and battlescarred, but not beyond repair," I smiled, lifting the cover so she could get into bed.

"Uh er..." She smiled at me, refusing to get in bed. "I got naked now you turn, Rob. Get out of bed and get those shorts off," she said with a cheeky grin.

Kat had totally put me on the spot, and she had done it because she was bright enough to realise that I was just as uncomfortable about baring everything as she had been. So, the lovely, brave lady had taken the bull by the horns and faced her own demons first to make me feel at ease.

This meant I had no trouble doing what she asked. We just stood there looking at each other and smiling awkwardly. It was only when Kat sneezed, that I ordered her cheekily to get back in bed and get warm before she made her cold worse.

In a strange way, it was nice that all we did was lie there innocently with each other, drinking tea, and talking about what to do for breakfast, and how best to spend the short time we had together. The conversation slowly became a mature discussion about when would be a comfortable time to take our relationship further, and we were both in agreement that we should wait until we both were comfortable.

Suddenly, Kat reached down the bed and smiled, "Well somebody no is thinking about Margaret Thatcher on a cold day anymore, no?" I laughed, and Kat gave me a serious look. "Why are you get aroused by this horrible, yucky, skinny thing I call my body?" she asked.

The smile on her face was priceless when I told her it was the person inside the body that attracted me, and then she rolled over and picked up her tea, laughing that neither of us had come prepared.

I nearly gagged on my drink when Kat looked up to the ceiling and announced that she wished whoever had used magic to get us together, had the thought to magic up a pack of rubber protection.

After a while, she began to sing along with the radio, and I told her I couldn't wait to hear her play her guitar.

"Not possible," She said quietly. "After all the shit that's happened in the last month. When I found my cat Charlie squashed like a pancake, I loosed my shit big time. I went all rock and roll, but it turns out that smashing guitar against wall like Jim Steinman, no make it sound better, did destroy it."

"Well, least I don't need to worry about what you need me to buy you for Christmas."

Kat leaned closer, smiling and teasing, "Rob, time I looked you couldn't buy common sense in a shop, but failing that, a new guitar is the sweetest thing ever."

Kat, having left her phone, used mine to make an apologetic call to her landlord to cancel the notice she had given him the previous day. The old man seemed relieved that she was staying.

Minutes later, we checked out of the hotel and set off for the terminal. I wanted to drive Kat the quarter of a mile, as she was hobbling on that badly bruised leg. She, however, wanted to confess quietly that most of her limp was indeed caused by a long-standing leg injury from the rape. "The real reason I never made it to the Olympics," she added.

I agreed to this on condition that I carried her bags to take the weight off her legs. It seemed that the real Katarzyna, although exhausted in the evenings, had a hyperactive nature in the mornings, just like in the dream.

She was telling me as we walked that she hated to sit still on long journeys due to hyperactivity. I could certainly see that the reason she enjoyed hard work was to get rid of the excess energy she always had in the mornings, so I could sympathise that sitting on a plane all day with little exercise was her idea of hell just like it was mine.

I stood with Kat at the luggage check-in desk. The lady smiled and asked me why I wasn't going with her. When I explained that we were a new couple, she smiled and told us how sweet we looked together.

We sat in the cafe waiting for the plane boarding to be called, and Kat used up some of her nervous energy throwing punches at my hands. We chatted, just like we had done in our dream when she invited me in. Time ran away when you're having fun.

Kat was sat on my lap eating a huge breakfast of American style pancakes smothered in chocolate. When she finished she asked, "You still love me and let me sit on you if I get big fatty bum bum right?" I nodded and grinned, "Good because I want pudding. Happiness an contentment make Katarzyna hungry."

With that, for the first time, she instinctively turned to face me and pressed her lips against mine and gave me big chocolatey kiss.

"We should have done that last night." She grinned, gasping for air when we finally gave up kissing due to lack of oxygen.

"Still want pudding?" I smiled.

Kat looked at her watch and shook her head saying,

"Fuck pudding. More kisses are required," adding that she would get some in the airport when she landed in Holland before the connecting flight.

Chapter 29

A familiar face at the airport

All too soon, it was 8:45, and after Kat had a quick smoke and went to the shop. We stood outside the entrance to the small departure lounge, just looking at each other and taking in everything that had happened in the last few days. My heart was hurting at having to leave her so soon, and I didn't want her to go anywhere.

Kat stopped at the security gate, and she clung to me shaking like a leaf, as she whispered. "Rob, fuck the holiday, please take me home."

I looked at her face and was surprised to see tears running down her face. When I asked her what was wrong, she replied, "Rob, I can't be brave anymore. I tried, but too terrified to get on the plane in case crashes."

I squeezed her tight and tried to tell her it would be okay. As she leaned into me, I saw a familiar-looking lady watching us. She was not very tall, and was smartly dressed, with dark hair down to her shoulders.

"Can we help you?" I asked the woman, quite annoyed that her staring was interrupting a tender moment.

The woman stepped forward and offered me her hand, smiling said, "I was going to ask you guys the same. I couldn't help noticing your uniform, seeing as it seems we both work for Aricot International and I just wondered if your girlfriend is okay."

"She's just scared because it's her first time and she's going on her own," I told her, looking down at Kat who was still quivering with fright.

The lady smiled awkwardly and put her hand on Kat's shoulder and smiling, said, "It's okay, sweetheart. I've flown out of this airport more times than I can remember and I'm still alive to tell the tale."

Kat looked down at the lady who was much shorter than her and stopped crying and nodded. As she did so, the lady got a look at the ticket, and her mouth fell open,

"What are the chances of that?" She exclaimed, holding her ticket to Kat's, "We're going to the same place and sitting next to each other on both flights, so I can look after you."

Kat nodded slowly and took the lady's arm, saying, "Hi, I am Kat"

"Katie Barns."

It was too. She looked a little different from when we met her in the dream, which was not for another year, so no wonder she looked different.

Kat turned back to me with the tears replaced by a sense of wonder on her face, and she breathed, "Rob, it's Ela's Katie. I have to go with her. Whatever is happening is still going on and it has brought us together. Maybe no is done, and it need our help to bring Ela and Katie together too."

With that, she gave me a gigantic kiss and promised to call me when she landed, shouting, "I love," as she followed Katie through security.

Part 4

After

Chapter 30

Back to being lonely

It was my day off, but all there was to do was go home to an empty house and walk the dog, go for a run or something, and wait for Kat to call me. The flight to Schiphol was only an hour, and she had a two-hour stopover between flights where she had promised she would eat a good dinner. She would call to let me know she was safe before flying on to Dresden in Germany, which was is the closest airport to her family's home despite being in the next country. Then she would call me again to confirm that Kazia had picked her up.

After two hours, there was no call from Kat, and I started to worry that something had happened to her. Of course, I told myself she was a strong woman. As a teenager, she had sat in a minibus with a rucksack, halfway across Europe and fought for everything she had built up. She had the strength to rebuild her life after the horror of her past.

As line supervisor, even though she had quit her job, she had been further up the career ladder than me. Then there was her temper. Her outburst the previous night showed that she could look after herself verbally if needed, but it worried me that she was physically weak from lack of eating, and her leg injury was hurting her more than she was letting me think it was.

In truth, the probability that something had happened to her was small. It was entirely possible that she didn't have any phone signal in Schiphol, or that her phone was out of credit or not working due to roaming conditions. I was hoping she wasn't getting frustrated or upset if that was the case. It was also true that if Katie was going to the same place, Kat had busied herself making friends and trying to get Katie's phone number for Ela.

Later that morning I got a call, but it was not from Kat. It was a receptionist at work asking if I could go in, because the gym manager's daughter was unwell. Rather than say no like I wanted to, I thought it would take my mind off worrying about Kat, so I agreed. I sent Kat a text to explain, and said I would call her from work on my break to check she was okay.

I called the number she had given me. It rang for a while, but then it stopped. There were two messages in Kat's voice – one in English and one in Czech, both presumably asking to leave a message, which I did.

Still, there was no call from Kat. In fact, days went by with no word from her at all. I called her at the times we agreed, and her phone rang, but she never picked it up. I began to realise that maybe she had changed her mind about everything and was too scared to tell me. My parents were away for Christmas, and I never saw my friends anymore.

So, I volunteered to work every day which earned me lots of brownie points with Katherine as I tried to get Katarzyna out of my head.

On the morning of the day I was supposed to pick her up from the airport, I had a change of heart. I thought to myself that despite all the pain she had put me through, I would give her one last chance to answer, in case she had a good reason for not responding and still wanted me to meet her from the plane.

I knew she was on an early flight and would be up and about, but I planned to leave a message to say I'd come anyway. It would also give her a chance to explain her reason for blanking me. So, I sat in the car outside the hotel and dialled her contact. It started to ring as it always had.

Clearly, she kept it charged, because it always rang. It was only as I sat there in the car that I heard a weird buzzing noise coming from under the passenger seat. As soon as Kat's phone went to voicemail, the buzzing stopped. I stopped the call and started again, and as I did, the buzzing came back.

My heart skipped a beat, and I reached down under the seat. Looking down, I saw lights flashing, and there it was. I felt bad for thinking Kat would ever have ignored my calls.

Unnoticed by me, the poor, daft woman had left her phone in my car. It was plugged into the charger, giving me an illusion that she had been charging it, but it had been there all the time. I'd written my number down for her, but she could easily have lost it in a rush.

There were over a hundred missed calls and several texts on the phone. Several of them were from me, but a few from other numbers. I wasn't somebody to go through people's phones, but I thought going through Kat's phone to find a number would be the only possible way of getting hold of her.

I unlocked the phone by typing in her birth year (1987) and opened her voicemail. The intention was not to snoop on her, but to look for something to help me contact her. There were several messages from me begging her to call, and one from her former boss at the seafood company asking Kat to call him on his mobile for a chat. There was another from a nice sounding lady from the caravan park, asking Kat to call her before the end of work that day regarding a job.

Finally, something interesting came up. There was a quiet, tense voice, and it said, "This Kat. Rob, please, if you have found my phone, I am so sorry! I remembered where I left my phone when it was too late. I so sorry. I miss you and love you. If you get this message, you are no in any trouble for listening. Please call me on Kazia's contact number. She doesn't mind. Please call if you get this. I am so sorry. I think I remember you address. I will write you. I love you."

At the end of the message her voice cracked, and I heard her sob. My heart nearly stopped. That message had been sent two weeks ago, the night I'd gone to work after dropping her off. She must have realised I hadn't found her phone, but there had been no letter from her. Immediately, I dialled her sister Kazia's number into my phone and called, but I was answered by a message that sounded like the Czech equivalent of, "This person's phone is switched off. Please try later or send a text."

I scrolled through and found her mum's number, but there was no answer. There was no contact for Ela or Kat's dad, but I found her younger sister, Dusa, and called, hoping she wasn't still at home in bed and that she could speak English. To my surprise she answered straight away.

"Hello, do you speak English?" I asked. There was a long wait for a response. I thought she was going to hang up, but suddenly a man spoke.

He told me that he was Dusa's partner and that she couldn't speak English well enough to explain. He knew who I was and that I was trying to reach Katarzyna. He told me she'd just been to say goodbye to Dusa and left for the airport only fifteen minutes ago. He said that she was in sombre mood and upset that I hadn't replied to her letter. She was not expecting me to meet her, but she was pained to say she was not breaking up with me over it, because she should have taken her phone. When I explained I had only just found her phone, and there hadn't been a letter, he just laughed.

"That is woman for you," he said, and wished me luck in making up with Kat. He was sure she would understand.

Chapter 31

Back in the airport

So, there I stood outside arrivals, waiting for her as the people piled in off the flight from Schiphol. I waited, looking at every person that passed, trying to catch Kat. Nobody who passed me even slightly resembled her. I went back to the seated area in case she had been held up in baggage, but she never came, and I started to worry that I'd missed her.

I was about to check the smoking area, the shop, the bus stop and the taxi rank, but when I turned to get up, I saw Jenny standing so close I almost jumped.

"Quick message – I can't stay," she said. "Zee Zee is coming, and Ela is with her, but their flight was late, and they missed the connection. They're stuck in Holland at Schiphol until the 8 pm flight. They'll get here at 9 pm, so go home, have dinner, and come back to meet them. Zee Zee will be exhausted and very grumpy, but she doesn't blame you in any way because she knows she lost her phone and put the wrong house number on the letter she sent you. She plans to come and find you, but as I said, she's tired and very grumpy and needs her Rob."

"But how? What?" I asked.

"It's not like last time we sat here Rob," she smiled.

"What? When?" I stuttered.

But she continued, "You and Zee Zee will be together and have a very, very good, long life together."

I looked over at the exit gate. "What do you mean last time?" I asked Jenny. "How did Kat tell you what was happening?" But when I turned back to Jenny, she was already several feet away and walking towards the door.

I went home to an empty house again and walked the dog, had some food, and watched TV. So, Ela was coming too. Kat must have made up with her sister. Perhaps she didn't need me.
She had sounded so upset, but neither of us was really at fault. It seemed we'd both done our best to get a hold of each other. If she'd called Jenny to come and find me, she couldn't be mad at me for not replying to a letter which I never received.

However, if she knew Jenny's number, why had she not just got Jenny to come and find me at the gym to get my number or tell me she had lost her phone?

At the airport, I was again running late because of traffic. I parked the car as close as I could and jogged over, but people were already filing out of the arrivals lounge. I could have missed them already.

Several people passed, but I didn't see them. I stood there for a few minutes wondering to myself what I'd even bothered coming for. I was about to go and check the smoking area, the bus stop, and the taxi rank for the second time when I heard the sound of arguing foreign voices coming from the arrivals door.

Two women with rucksacks were both dragging wheeled bags. They were arguing about something in a foreign language. They were both tall. The nearest one was walking sideways with her back to me. Although she was blonde, when she turned around it was not Kat. However, just recognisable behind her, was Kat.

"What's the argument about, ladies?" I asked calmly walking over while holding Kat's phone. Kat was glaring at Ela, and she didn't look at me. She just answered, "We have been stuck in Holland all day, and my sister lost her rucksack because missed it going around on belt four times. Now we have to go ask security for it. No, what I needed when I tired. I have to go find the love of my life and give grovelling apology for no speak in two weeks."

Ela then looked back at her and said, "I didn't mean to. It's your fault, because I kept sneezing because you gave me your cold." Ela stopped dead. Neither of us was listening to her. We were just standing there, looking each other up and down. Kat wore her ripped jeans and white coat. Her dark shades were pushed up into her hair, and there was something different about her, but I couldn't put my finger on it.

Slowly, she put her rucksack down with a bump and walked towards me. "Robert Brownlow," she said, turning her mood on me, and taking her phone from my hand. "I spent whole day with my nephew making you Christmas card with a letter to say that I sorry for loosed phone and no call you, and you no reply!"

She gave me a vicious, red-faced look, drew her hand back, and brought it crashing towards my face, only to stop at the last second and place her hand on my cheek. Then she burst out into a smile.

"And I sent it number 5 Noringsham High Street when you live at number 25." She pretended to slap her own head. "And still you are here, even though we are on wrong flight and you could no have known."

Her working eye was crying, and I guessed mine were too because after we had stood there for several minutes kissing, she pulled out her hanky and started rubbing my eyes.

"How's your cold sweetheart?" I asked once we'd stepped back. I'd taken her rucksack remembering how unwell she had been when I last saw her, and practically every time I'd met her.
Kat looked at me, took a sniff, and a sharp intake of breath. Then she put her head back with her eyes closed and spread her hanky in front of her in both hands, building up to a big sneeze. Then she put her hands down to show a big smile across her face. "I'm fine," she laughed, walking toward me for another kiss.

She hinted heavily by holding the clean hanky out to Ela, who took it with a begrudged look as Kat said something in Czech, to which Ela replied sharply.

"I tell her stop bloody sniffing and blow her nose before I slap her," she smirked "And she says, 'Okay mum.'" After Ela had obeyed, she smiled and tried to give me a pleased-to-meet-you hug, but Kat blocked her and said, "No you give my boyfriend your cold, you yucky ill girl."

"I gave you my cold, did I no?" she said with an apologetic smile as I nodded.

The banter carried on in English as we walked

through the airport. Kat held one of Ela's bags as I now had her rucksack. The girls were bickering about who gave the cold to who. Ela was blaming Kat—who was eating an apple a she walked—for the fact she felt so ill, and Kat was saying it was their mum who had given it to Ela and Dusa, who had given it to her after catching from Kazia.

"And who gave to her?" Ela grinned.

"I no know. Anyone apart from me," Kat laughed.

"So, you infected your whole family?" I grinned.

"Would I?" she laughed as we reached the car.

We started driving with the intention of going straight to the flat, as the ladies had eaten dinner in Schiphol and Ela had asked us to take her straight home to bed. The poor girl was as sick as Kat had been weeks earlier.

Despite her illness, Ela was still talking in reasonably good English, though it was not as good as in the dream. Ela told me she had only stopped speaking to her sister because she was upset that Kat had not let her come to England with her when she was twelve, but as a nearly official adult, she could now understand why.

On the way home, Kat called the lady from the caravan site. I had phoned her back on Kat's behalf to explain that she had left her phone, and explained that she could call back that evening. The lady had been very gracious about it. Kat was chatting on the phone with her all the way back. It sounded quite like this might well have been a late reply to the job Kat had been interviewed for. When she put the phone down, she had no time to discuss it as we got to the flat and started taking Ela's stuff in.

We took Kat and Ela's stuff upstairs. Kat made up some of her cold relief drink and gave it to Ela with some of her home-made hankies as they went into Ela's new room and made the bed. Kat's flat was exactly how it had been in the dream, with two bedrooms, a combined lounge, and kitchen.

She came out after a few minutes, telling me Ela was sparked out on the bed. She confessed she felt terrible for passing her illness to her little sister when she'd been so excited about coming to England.

Kat had been keeping her hood up ever since she arrived home, but she now unzipped her coat, took out her arms, and said she had something to show me.

She smiled, throwing her coat on the floor. She stood there in her jeans and t-shirt and pointed at her hair with one hand and her tummy with the other. Then she gave me twirl and sung, "Da da."

Her golden Rapunzel plait was all gone. Her thick blonde hair, which had been down to her knees having not been cut for several years, was cut in line with her mouth, and swinging as she in the air as she spun.

"What you think?" she asked, smiling and leaning forward, so her reading glasses that had been perched on her head fell over her eyes. "Be honest," she grinned.

I thought it suited her brilliantly. "I liked it how it was," I teased her bluntly and walked up to her as she stuck her tongue out at me in reply. "And love it the way it is," I added.

"New start," she smiled removing her glasses. "New

hair, new future husband, partly new me. And," she smiled proudly, tapping her tummy, "I am put on two pounds." Just as she said it, the t-shirt she had stuffed down her trousers popped out and fell on the floor. "And I lost one of them," she added sadly. "But I am trying now. I get my man back. I am hungry girl and I want you take me get food."

"Well done you for gaining what you did," I said, putting an arm around her. As a personal trainer, it was far from often that I congratulated weight gain, but Kat's eating disorder, however mild it was, concerned me. Any gain she made was a good thing.

"There is more," she told me, grinning all over her face.

"More good news?" I smiled.

She nodded. "That phone call to caravan site," she said and beamed, "It's not what you know it's who you know. When I sat with Katie on the plane, I explained that I was unemployed, and she told me her brother's wife is the owner of Aricot International who also who owns caravan site, and she pulled some strings, and I start work Monday. That lady remembers me from interview and says I didn't get the cleaning because I have too much experience for it, she is leaving for bigger things and wants to train me up as her replacement as HR manager." My mouth dropped. "I totally know, right?" she beamed. "I in shock. Is no is my sort of job, but I will no say no to the extra money. Enough for us go on a nice holiday, and 9 am starts, so I have in the mornings with man I love."

I didn't know what to say to her to tell how proud I was, but I didn't get the chance because, without warning, Kat flung herself at me. She sobbed into my shoulder, telling me how much she missed me and how sorry she was for losing her phone and my number and for sending the card to the wrong address. I just held her tightly, congratulated her on her new job, and told her how much I loved her. I told her it wasn't her fault--although we both knew it was—but she was more than forgiven.

We stood there for a while just holding each other and kissing until Kat reminded me we still had stuff to do. She put £20 in my hand, saying it was for fuel and that we were going out.

I tried to give it back, but she pulled a frumpy face at me and insisted that I take it. I gave in because she was getting paid more than I was now.

"Me main breadwinner in this house now although I never did get that term." She teased, "Prize for going to work is money to live on no a big loaf brown of Kingsmill extra thick. How I going to pay bills with."

"Well," I teased, "Give half to the landlord and two slices to the council, then one each to the water, gas, and electric companies then save one, and we'll eat the rest. So where are we actually going?" I asked as we got to the top of the stairs.

"You have to pack you stuff and come and live here with us, and I want go meet your doggy," she grinned.

"Of course, you do," I grinned, remembering in our dream how much Kat loved my mum's Alsatian Narla.

As we walked down the steep and very dangerous winding stairs, Kat reminded me that we needed to bring Narla back to the flat with us, so I didn't have to keep going home to feed her before my parents got home.

"I am so look forward to new start," she smiled happily as we reached the bottom of the stairs. "New forever boyfriend, new job, new hair, and my sister back being best friends."

"I can't wait to spend the rest of my days with you, "I grinned.

"Just one thing dough," she sighed.

"What is it, honeybun?"

She pulled a face, took a hand-rolled cigarette out of her pocket, and popped it in her mouth with an ashamed look on her face. I reminded her of what I had said before about it not making a difference in my feelings for her. She smiled and told me proudly that although she hadn't stopped, she had cut down to five a day. She was still angry at herself, but I just told her how proud I was that she was trying.

"Were your parents hard on you for smoking? I asked, assuming she'd had quite a telling off. But Kat shook her head, smiling and taking her cigarette out of her mouth without lighting it as we stepped outside. "My dad caught me behind the barn at my uncle's," she smirked, going a little red.

"Did he go nuts?" I asked.

She shook her head. "He said it's okay. I am twenty-one, grown up, my choice, and can he have one?" she said, bursting out laughing and turning red as a beetroot under the street lamp. "You know," she said, after we composed ourselves, "after all this time, I actually got something in common with my father – we both hiding cigarettes from my mum."

She was about to light up when she took her unlit cigarette out and started telling about how this meeting had prompted a father-daughter heart to heart.

"We made our peace with each other, sat and had tea and father-daughter chat," she breathed. "Poor man blames himself for for not paying those men and sending me back when I wasn't well when I got raped. Is why no is talk me, cos he blames himself. I told him I no hate him. No his fault what happened to me or Ela."

She went on to tell me that she'd told her dad all about me and how we were a new couple, but not how we got together or that we only got together the day before she left.

"He is want come over and meet the man who stole the heart of his little angel," she smiled, adding, "He's working in London, then coming to spend the weekend here with us."

As we talked, she kept putting the unlit cigarette in her mouth and then taking it out again. Finally, I gave her a gentle squeeze and asked her if she was actually going to smoke it. She lit it and took two drags and then stubbed it out, saying it was too cold to be standing around smoking, so we got in the car.

Chapter 32

<u>Remembering the Harsh Truth</u>

T wo hours later, after having been back to the city, we found a 24-hour Tesco. Here I expected Kat to spend ages looking at different clothes and trying them, which was something Ela would have been more help with. However, Kat just ran around the clothes department, picking up clothes and knowing which ones suited her without even needing to try them on. She even got them all two sizes too big, saying she was planning to grow into them by starting to work out.

We stopped off at my parents' house to pick up Narla, as my parents were away until the next day. I took Kat out into the garden telling her I had to get something from the shed, but when I switched on the outside light, her mouth fell open at the sight of two white Rabbits in a run on the grass.

"You got Roger bunnies," She screamed excitedly.

"No," I told her shaking my head, "This is their temporary home until their owner get a house with a garden.

"Who is lucky owner?" She asked, disappointedly as she knelt by the pen on the cold grass.

"She's a lovely blonde lady who currently lives in a flat

Cromer," I told her smiling.

"Hang on, I am a blonde lady who lives in... *oh.*"

"A belated Merry Christmas, sweetheart," was what I tried to say through the barrage of kisses I was being smothered with.

We sat on the sofa having a midnight snack of pasta pots. Kat ate noisily because she was hungry and enjoying her food. I went upstairs to pack some of my clothes while Kat was in the loo.

As I was packing, I heard her creep up the stairs, but she didn't come into my room. I didn't mind her having a snout around the place, because I knew Kat just wanted to check out her new surroundings.

After a few moments, I heard her sneezing somewhere the other side of the stairs. I realised something had set off her allergies, so off I went to see if she was okay. I found her across the hall in my parents' dark bedroom with her back to me, mopping her nose silently. She jumped back with fright when I asked her if she was okay.

"I no was meaning to snoop," she said, in a sudden frightened voice. "I forgot I given Ela my hanky. When I sneezed, I come in here to borrow a tissue."

"It's okay darling. I'm not angry. You can borrow as many tissues as you like. But don't put them back in the box," I teased. Then I put my arms out to her, and she rushed forward and cuddled me tight. She took a step back and looked down at the floor but kept hold of my hands.

"When I was away, I had horrible nasty dream," she said, without looking at me.

"Did I do something to you in that dream?" I asked, hoping the dream version of me hadn't done something to hurt my lovely Kat.

She shook her head and sniffed. "I thought it was a horrible, horrible dream until I came in here and realised it was all real. I no blame you one bit for no want to talk about it."

"I don't know what you..." I stopped when I saw that she was looking up at me with her eyes flooding with tears.

Quietly, she said, "I know where we met before, and why we are not end up together then."

She was scaring me now, I could have sworn I hadn't ever met her before that night two weeks earlier outside work when she called me a prick, but then somewhere deep down in my soul I felt she was right.

"I hope this doesn't end up like one of the horror movies where it turns out I'm a serial killer with memory problems. If that's the case, I would run if I was you," I teased nervously, and Kat smiled weakly. "If there's a reason for us not to be together, tell me now before I finish packing," I told her nervously. Rather than back away, she kissed me gently, yet passionately enough to show that breaking up was not on her agenda.

We sat down side by side on my parents' bed with our arms around each other. Kat reached into her jeans and took out her purple angry scarf, but rather then hold it herself, she put it in my hand and told me I might need it.

"I blocked it out of my mind because I was so upset and traumatised," she sobbed.

"Blocked what out?"

"About a year ago Jenny's dad and his girlfriend went on holiday for Christmas. She stayed with me while they were away, so I came with her to airport to meet them off the flight." She paused for breath, and I gave her a squeeze, which she returned with double strength. "We were waiting in the arrivals lounge because plane was delayed. Lovely man, who knew Jenny, came over to say hello to her. He was really nice, and we get talking, and then we all go for cup of tea together while we wait for plane. I was really surprised that I really liked this guy because really no like that many people, but he got me." She smiled. "He clearly likes me too, but was too nervous to say so. I went push out boat and ask him to swap numbers. Then I tell him I go to toilet."

I gave a little laugh, I didn't mind Kat admitting she had a brief crush on somebody else. "By toilet, you mean a cigarette, don't you?" I laughed.

"Nooo," she lied with a cheeky smile. "I go to toilet and then have cigarette, so I no was quite lying to him. But no going to tell him I smoke before we have been on date when he likes me."

"So, I wasn't the first man you were attracted to?" I smiled, giving her a squeeze to let her know it was okay.

"I would no quite say that," she told me, looking down and smiling. Her working eye was full of tears for some reason that I still wasn't sure of, but I dabbed at her eye with her scarf, and she smiled harder. "So why are you here with me and not with him?" I asked gently.

"When I went back," she sniffed, "the place was crawling with transport police. They have closed the arrivals lounge, and there was pain and sadness everywhere." She paused and took a deep rattling breath before continuing. "The connecting flight from Schiphol – the very same route Ela and I took this evening – containing Jenny's dad, his girl-friend, and that young man's whole family, is hit by some-thing in the air and is fell into the sea, killing everyone on board."

Holy bloody hell, I thought to myself. No wonder she'd been terrified of getting on her first flight when I left her at the airport two weeks earlier. I remembered seeing it on the news now and thinking that it was a horrible way to die. Many local people lost relatives when it came down. Air crash investigators were still working on it a year later.

"No bloody wonder you're not a fan of flying," I soothed.

She shook her head and said, "You are right, but is no about me dough. Jenny lost her dad and the woman she called mum. That poor young man who swapped numbers with me? His whole family were on that plane."

"I can't imagine how horrible that must have been," I tried to soothe.

"Was awful for me and a million time worse for every-one else," she sobbed. "My best friend was crying hysteric-ally, and dis poor young man all on his own lying face down. He not crying, but just banging his head on the floor in shock. I can't cuddle them both. I no have enough arms, and I have to give priority to Jenny as my best friend."

As Kat cuddled into me and took a moment to clean herself up, I could picture it in my mind. The hysteria, people everywhere crying, and me not knowing where to go or what to do, just wanting the ground to swallow me whole.

"You didn't call that guy, because you didn't know what to say to a man who lost his family, and he didn't call you because the last thing on his mind was love." She sniffed and nodded in reply. "If I were him, I would have forgiven you for not calling him," I reassured her.

"My brain blocked it out and forget. Something clicked the night we met, but I was no sure. That's why I said you and I had more to talk about when you ready. Then last night, I have dreamed it all again. Then just think was dreaming, but being in here, it all fits."

"What fits?" I asked, unaware of what she was implying.

She looked at me with big, knowing eyes. "You parents' room is much dusty compared to rest of house." She picked some of the dust off the bed with her finger and blew it into the darkness, making herself sneeze again.

"I don't clean my parents' room while they're on holiday," I smiled, but Kat didn't laugh or even smile.

"When did they go away?" she whispered so softly I almost thought she didn't want to hear the answer.

"About a week before Christmas. They come home tomorrow morning," I replied, still confused. Kat cuddled me, and I caressed her back and breathed her in, knowing what I thought she was going to say next.

Softly, she asked, "A week before which Christmas, Rob? How many tomorrows have they been coming home?"

After a few moments of looking for answers, she swung her legs over, so they were either side of me. Then she sat on my lap with her arms tightly around me. Our eyes stared directly into each other's gazes.

Kat swiftly wiped her eyes dry and looked at me with the sort of face that told me there no more screwing about, because we had to get to the point, in the nicest, loveliest possible way she could.

"Rob," she said softly, "the dream was of an ideal world." She took a deep breath. "In the dream, your parents came home the Friday night when you met me from airport. They no did catch a plane."

"And if they were coming, they would be here right now," I finished.

"You have to realise I would have said earlier if I had no shut it from my own mind," she trembled.

"The dream made you believe so hard you actually thought they went away just before I did and were coming home. Just like me, you forgot all about what happened before." She paused before finishing with, "Because everything else came true, you hoped this would too."

I nodded and held her close without words. "I was a mess, Rob, and you were my knight in shining Armor. When I told you about my past, you took me in your arms and began to heal me."

"I love you to pieces, Katarzyna," I trembled.

"I love you equally, Rob," she returned. "And is why, as you girlfriend, it is time for me to stand up and be you leaning post and be strong for you like you have been and always will be for me in the way that I no was strong enough to be on the first time we met."

As she looked into my eyes, we held each other so

tight I thought I would choke as it flooded back to me. When we swapped numbers the night we met, Kat's contact detail had already been in my phone and mine in hers.

In the airport, Jenny had said to me, "Don't be worried. It's not like last time we sat here."

Kat was right about the dust on the bed. It had not been slept in for over a year, and that horrible day my mind had been shut away. In the dream, my parents had gone on a two-week holiday, and I was so wrapped up in everything else being true that I didn't realise that my family's absence did not mean they were on holiday like in the dream.

"My sister Jeanette and her husband moved to Australia years ago, and they had a baby," I told Kat.

"Lovely little Jemima," Kat added.

"All the family went to visit them for Christmas, apart from me, because Katherine at work said I hadn't been there long enough to take two weeks off. So I had to stay."

"No get me started on that cow bitch," Kat grunted, as I found myself pulling on her angry scarf behind her back.

Kat listened quietly as I explained that my sister Jeanette wasn't getting on with her husband. It turned out that he was hitting her, so she and Jemima had got on the flight back to England with the rest of my family.

At this, Kat put her hand over her mouth in shock as if to say she didn't realise that Jeanette and Jemima were on the fight too. In the dream, little Jemima had been very close to her Aunty Kat way into adulthood.

"Jemima," she cried as I continued.

"Four grandparents, two aunties, one uncle, two parents, one big sister, and one lovely little niece, who I had only ever seen on Skype".

As I shook, Kat embraced me quietly. It was a moment quite like the critical scene in Sixth Sense, where it turns out what you believed was happening was not true at all. The goings on in the dream really had warped my mind enough to make me forget the horrors that had destroyed my life.

The realism of the dream had rubbed off on Kat too. Though she never knew them, it was so real that she'd grown to love my family like her own. It was her loss now as much as mine.

"Sweetheart," she said to me, "whenever you need talk about this, the good and the bad times, or just have a good cry, my ears will always listen, and my shoulder is yours to cry on."

"My grandparents I can take. You expect them to die," I said, crying into Kat's shoulder, "but not all at once. Parents you know you will lose one day, but not till you're middle-aged. My sister and I argued like cats and dogs as kids, but despite the fact she moved to Australia, we talked on Skype every week. She was a good mum with a brilliant sense of humour and never hurt anyone."

Kat squeezed me tight, telling me that she would lose the plot even more than she already had done if she lost a single one of her three sisters or her brother.

"It is easier to pretend every day that they will come home because you no have to face reality. You go to work every day and work all the hours you can, no because your boss is an incompetent cow—although she is—but because you no want be here in this place."

I nodded. "Worst of all," I sobbed, "is my poor little three-year-old niece. Not only is it not fair to kill a child, but how scared must she have been?"

I could see her face in my mind, excited about her first trip by plane and only thirty minutes from landing. The terror that must have been in her eyes as the plane—from what I'd heard—powered nose down into the English Channel like a stone. Those who didn't die on impact, drowned in the minutes that followed. In the dream, she had grown into that charming funny lady with a loving husband and lots of children. But in reality, she died a terrified child.

Kat just sat there trembling. "I no did know was all of them," she shuddered. "I no did know Jeanette and Jemima died too. How does God get away with this shit?" she said quietly. Then suddenly she flew into a red-faced, tearful rage. "Every Sunday, I am going to church a pray for the soul of my little boy who he took away from me and from two amazing adopted parents." Her rage was scaring me. Even as I tried to calm her, she continued yelling towards the sky.

"I pray for an end to third world hunger, and even give all I can and a start to world peace, and for what? If God was really good, then why would bad things even exist? He let things like this happen to good nice caring people like you and you family. His is make pregnant ladies fall down the stairs and break their necks and die like my poor like poor Jenny. And he is letting sweet, innocent, little girls die in plane crashes, and children born starving and dying in the third world, and all over the world, while rich politicians are robbing from them. He no is looked after the world. He laugh at it."

She reached into her top so suddenly that I nearly dropped her from my lap. Then she screamed, "Fuck you!"

At first, I thought she was screaming at me for nearly dropping her, until I saw that she had pulled her large silver crucifix from around her neck and was frantically trying to break the chain.

Suddenly it snapped, and she threw it to the floor. Then she stood up and stamped on the cross shouting and screaming at the ceiling, "God, if you actually exist, then go fuck yourself. I have all my life been a good little Catholic, confessed all my sins to an old fat drunk."

She hadn't finished. She went on to tell her god that he'd better hope she wasn't going to die anytime soon, because when she did, she was coming to kick him in the balls.

Had it been funny, I would have laughed, but Kat and I were both in emotional turmoil and needed the only thing we both had, which was each other.

I stood up took and hold of her to try and calm her down, but both of us fell onto the bed in a tangle. We lay there sobbing and cuddling each other without talking.

Kat's little outburst might have put some people off, but not me. Even as a sceptic, I would have been the first to support her in her love of Christianity, which she lost in the dream. But I also had to support her when she fell out of love with her god. I loved the fact she cared so passionately about getting rid of bad from the world, and that she had the guts to stand up and shout at her god and question him when things went wrong.

I was never sure how long we both lay crying in each

other's arms. I thought of my mum and dad. I wondered what they would have thought of Kat and me if they could see us together. My sister would have welcomed her to the family, and so would little Jemima.

After what could have been an hour or a day, or just a minute, we both suddenly stopped crying and edged closer towards each other. We kissed and sat up together. There weren't many words spoken between us as we drove back, other than Kat apologising for her outburst.

After getting out of the car Kat asked if I was okay to take the stuff up, "That is job for a strong man," she grinned. "While you do that, I will take doggy out the back for toilet, because a weak skinny girl job where I can sneak a quick smoke without you seeing me." Then she quickly added, "Apart from I just told you what I was doing so I expect a good telling off."

So, with that, I kissed her and made sure I gave her bottom a tap and told her she was naughty, but I loved her, and I would see her in a moment.

After four trips up the stairs, one with my stuff and two with Kat's new clothes, there was still no sign of Kat until I came down the fourth time and found her sat on the tiled floor at the bottom of the steep spiral stairs. She had her arms around a bemused looking dog.

When she saw me, she quickly sat up and wiped her eyes on her angry scarf. "I wasn't crying." Kat crawled over to the bottom step and sat there waiting for me to join her. When she looked at me, there were tears her eyes. "Going away and coming back again to this place brings back all the pain and bad memories."

I hadn't got the foggiest why the bottom of the stairs would bring back memories of her rape, but then I realised she might have been talking about the memories of her heavy fall in the dream when she had tumbled down the stairs.

"It must have bloody hurt," I said soothingly.

"No, Rob, no that." She sobbed, "I tried to save her. I done everything I could, but even the paramedics and doctor no could save her, but no want to think her in pain." She pulled me close to her saying, "I don't know how you stay so brave when you lost your whole family? I managed no to cry the first time I came back but couldn't help myself a second time."

I was really confused now, so I had to stop her and ask her to explain, "Kat, what happened? Who are you talking about?"

Kat stopped in her tracks and looked me dead in the eye, but she pushed away from me so that she could get a better look at my face to make sure my question was genuine, then she clammed up and couldn't speak about whatever it was.

It must have been ten minutes that she just sat there dumbstruck and trying to say something to me. When I finally plucked up the courage to ask if I'd done something wrong, she reached for my hand and shook her head.

"Two weeks ago when we got together there was a thing we were not talking about." She said in a tiny voice and asked, "What you think the thing we no talk about was?"

At this point, I had to confess that I didn't know what

she was talking about that night.

I shook my head as she said, "You don't have time to read papers or what news, and you knew nothing about Jenny's accident?" She said in a much harder angry tone, but giving me a look and squeeze because I was not person she was angry at. "I went up to the hotel, and I asked you boss tell everyone what had happened."

"But Kat sweetheart," I said, pulling her into me, "Whatever happened to her, she seemed okay when I saw her when she came to airport this afternoon to tell me you were delayed. Which was really good of her by the way. How did you contact her?"

Kat just looked at me blank for a minute unable to speak, and then she rummaged in her handbag for something and took out two things, one which she put behind her back, and the other was her wallet from which she took a small picture and passed it to me. It was picture of Kat and Jenny together arm in arm with straws in their mouths, pulling faces at the camera as they shared what looked the biggest glass of ice cream I had ever seen.

"Is this the Jenny Hughs you know from the gym and saw today?" She asked me in a sombre tone.

"Yes, that's her." I nodded.

"Okay," Kat replied, looking somewhat shell-shocked as she brought the other item out from behind her and revealed a larger picture of Jenny, "And what about this one? Is this her too?"

As I nodded, Kat muttered something under her breath, which sounded like some sort of apology and took out the broken crucifix from her handbag and held it to her chest saying that she should have known.

"I should have known all along who it was that sent us our dream. She just wanted us to be happy."

"I'm really confused, Kat, what's going on?"

Kat took a moment to breathe, then stopped crying and kissed me gently and smiled asking, "Rob, do you believe in ghosts?"

I replied shakily that I wasn't sure, and I was terrified at what Kat was about to tell me.

She shook her head gently and turned over the picture of Jenny for me to see the other side. As she did so, in a tiny voice she mumbled, "I think we both need to accept that ghosts exist.
It was not a picture she handed me, it was booklet with another picture of Jenny on the front, with big smile on her face.

The writing underneath made my blood run cold.

In loving memory of Jenifer Alexandria Hughs
14th of April 1984 – 29th November 2008

Chapter 33

<u>Kat explains</u>

After a few minutes of letting the shock set in, I told Kat where and when I had seen Jenny – in the gym and again the airport that afternoon.

As we made our way, Kat told me in a whisper that she hadn't believed in ghosts, but she did believe me, so by default she now believed.

After making some cocoa and changing into our bedtime clothes in the chair where Kat—who seemed to be a little bit taller than she was in the dream—had to spread her legs out on the arm, laughing as she told me. "I told you I was smaller in the dream."

So I couldn't begin to explain the surrealness and Kat settled down to explain how a person I had seen and spoken to that day had died five weeks earlier.

I was still expecting that this was a hoax and that any second now, Jenny was going to burst out of the bedroom laughing, and that she and Kat would shout, "Wind-up." That Jenny had moved in with her after the plane crash took her family like it did mine.

Jenny had been beside herself with grief and unable to

cover the rent on her own. She had been struggling with her emotions and her long-standing back injury which was the reason I had not seen her in the gym.

"Two best friends looking after each other," Kat said quietly. After about two months, Jenny had met a man and got into a rather quick relationship, rather like Kat and myself. Only Jenny's boyfriend never moved in. Her relationship had ended after a few months when she had found out that he was married.

Kat said she was torn, because to her personally, she hated the idea of anybody cheating, but the guy's marriage was already all but over, and he apparently loved Jenny. Jenny didn't see it like that though, and her attitude was that if he cheated on his wife, he would cheat on her. She not only kicked him out, but took Kat with her and found his wife and told her everything.

"You know who his wife was turned out to be?" She asked, but when I shook my head, she grinned and pretended to smother her face in make-up, then put on a big false smile and, "Hello it's meeeee." In an eerily good impression of my boss Katherine.

"No fucking way? She's really married?" I gasped, gobsmacked as she nodded.

"It's hard to believe, I know," She smiled, "But apparently, miracles do happen, because I got man in my life now and no an oil painting, and I more fucked in some ways than she is."

"You're right, you're not an oil painting" I teased to which she pretended to be greatly offended, telling me that I was supposed to lie and say that she was. Then, I added that she wasn't a painting, she was a smart, pretty and engaging lovely young woman.

Back to the conversation, Kat told me that Jenny had told Katherine everything when she ended the relationship. Two weeks later she realised that she had fallen pregnant with Katherine's husband's baby.

In this situation, neither woman had done anything wrong, and Jenny had done the right thing when she had found out she was the other woman.

Katherine, however, had taken her husband back and chosen to forgive him and blame Jenny for everything. However, when she found out about the baby, she was fuming.

Kat, on the other hand, had supported Jenny by supporting her with her physical and mental health, and her job, while not charging her half of the rent so she could afford things for the baby.

"I was no going be just Aunty Kat, I was going to be mummy number two," she said proudly, yet with a sad look.

"You felt that by helping through her pregnancy, so that hers didn't end the ways yours did?"

She nodded and took a such a big gulp of her cocoa that she left a big brown stain around her mouth. Then she told me that she had not wanted give up her baby and she felt pain every day.

"Whether or no I gave him up I always be his mummy. He would have been five soon. I still dream about him every night and wonder every day what kind of little man he would grown into."

I already knew Jenny wasn't a well person after a

childhood accident left her with damage to her spine and legs, meaning that she was heavily medicated which contributed to her weight gain. I had to be very careful when I designed her workout plan, to use equipment that would help her lose weight without putting pressure on her injuries.

Kat also admitted struggling her own mobilities at times, never fully recovered from her injuries. I had to say that I had noticed that her limp had not improved much from two weeks ago. I did wonder if it had been like that before I had accidentally tripped her.

Kat had taken her role of looking after Jenny very seriously. She even put her hand on her heart and told me it was the honest truth that she had given up smoking the moment she found out Jenny was having a baby. She had been smoke-free for six months until things went wrong, then she had turned back to her addiction with a vengeance.

It didn't escape my thoughts, the date of Jenny's death was a familiar one. It was Kat's birthday, the one she claimed in the dream that she had forgotten.

It was a Saturday, and both ladies were off work and had spent the morning together watching a new DVD that Jenny got Kat for her birthday. "My favourite movie ever, *Mamma Mia*." She sighed.

After the movie, Jenny had fallen asleep in the chair, but Kat with her hyperactivity disorder couldn't sit still, so she had to go and do something and felt that with the baby due soon the stairwell of death—as she aptly called it —needed a good hoover. I remembered in the dream Kat was the one who had fallen while doing this and nearly killed herself.

So, after hoovering the stairwell from bottom to top, Kat had taken the hoover to the top of the stairs while she took the bag down to the bin. At the bin she had bumped into her landlord, Mr Proctor, who had invited her into his shop. She had a cup of tea with him and his wife while they gave her a birthday present.

She'd been there about half an hour when there was suddenly a blood-curdling scream from above. This was followed by several loud thumps as though something heavy was falling down the stairs. Kat had gone red in the face, but was willing herself not to cry as she told me that she had run to see what had happened.

She had found Jenny lying at the bottom of the stairs in a horrible way with blood everwhere and broken bones. She had been awake and tried to speak, as though she was warning Kat about something while Mr Proctor called 999.

However, in the moments that followed, she had slipped away. Kat had carried out CPR on Jenny, but even when the ambulance arrived, the paramedics couldn't bring her back.

"No air ambulance for Jenny." she whispered, shaking her head, "She and her baby are died of multiple injuries, covered in blood on that cold floor right where we sat this evening.

I sat there in silence, rubbing Kat's shoulders while she buried her face into my chest, rising after a few moments to confess that after her best efforts to stay strong, she had, in fact, shed a couple of tears. However, now she was smiling and I thought it strange that she could be smiling after such a sad conversation, and I wondered again if Jenny was going to jump out of the bedroom and shout, "Wind-up."

She went on to say that say she had been up to the hotel to inform the gym staff of Jenny's passing, but my boss turned her away.

Kat, however, explained her smile, saying there were a few theories as to what happened there, but she really believed I'd seen Jenny.

"It all fits," she said excitedly, "Even before that day in the airport, Jenny is say to me, Zee Zee, you have put out that filthy cigarette and come to gym with me and meet Rob before less suited woman snaps him up."

I grinned at Kat and smiled back as I told her Jenny must be playing Cupid from beyond the grave. Kat, who had by now taken out her prosthetic eye, leaned her face against mine so that our noses touched.

"I wish I acted sooner while she was alive." she breathed. To which I replied that it takes two, but she shook her head and said that any effort I made would have been pushed away by her. "Wrongly," she added quickly.

The conversation moved on to how things had changed now that we were sure there was an afterlife.

Kat said with a glint in her eye, "I can keep smoking, knowing that death when it finally kills me is not the end, and I can come back haunt you and the kids." She then backtracked and said that she contradicted herself, because if she wanted a baby, she would have to stop.

Despite me telling her I thought she was wrong, Kat seemed to believe that she was somehow to blame for Jenny falling down the stairs. She believed that Jenny had tripped on the hoover, and that maybe Jenny had sent the part of the dream where she fell down the stairs to get back at her for it.

I was just trying to tell Kat that Jenny would not have done that to her best friend, when all of the sudden there was knock at the door which made us both turn and look at other.

Chapter 34

A visit from oldest friend.

W ho on earth would be knocking on her door at 4:30 am.

"That bloody sister of mine has been out in the night," she said, stomping off to the door of the flat with a look like thunder on her face.

She was ready to give Ela the telling off of her life, thinking that she had been for one of her night time walks, but as Kat unlocked the door, I heard a snore from Ela's room.

Realising it was not her sister, I was concerned for Kat opening the door to anyone at this strange time of the morning. It might have been a neighbour, angry that we had woken them. If so, Kat needed some backup.

However, as the door opened, there stood a tall hooded figure. It was a scene reminiscent of how Kat had looked that night in the dream when I found her frozen and dying on the road.

We grabbed each other in fright as the hooded figure stepped forward into the room uninvited. It pulled down the hood to reveal that it was not the grim reaper of death. In fact, just like the night I had picked Kat up out of the road, it turned out that under the hood was a young woman with shocking red hair.

We looked from one to another for a moment. Kat and I naturally grabbed each other for comfort, not because this woman seemed at all dangerous. In fact, she seemed to be around our age and a little nervous herself. We waited for her to speak and explain what on earth she was doing in Kat's home.

"Hey, Kat. Hey, Rob," she said nervously after a moment.

Kat and I looked at each other and then back at the strange, but weirdly beautiful redhead.

"Erm have we met, young lady?" Kat asked.

"Yes," she smiled awkwardly. "Rob and I know each other very well."

Kat looked accusingly at me as if there was something I wasn't telling her, like this was some jilted ex-girlfriend of mine who had come to seek her revenge.

"I don't recognise..." but I *did* recognise her. It was the manager of the hotel we stayed in two weeks ago. "She was the hotel manager," I said out loud.

The redheaded woman spoke directly to Kat and said, "Yes, I was, but I knew before that he remembers me, but he doesn't recognise me apart from being the hotel manager. It's been too long, and we are too different."

"I'm dumb. I don't get it," I told them both.

"Typical bloke," the redhead smiled, "either doesn't recognise me, or doesn't want to admit to his new girlfriend that, as a child, his best friend was a girl."

In the confusion of everything that had gone on that day and at that late hour, I was slow to respond.

Kat, however, was on the ball. "Actually, Rob told me all about you," she smiled, offering her hand to the young lady. It was my turn to look at her in a way that said "*I did??*"

"Rob, this is Sally," she smiled. "Your best friend from when you were little a boy."

"It has been ten years, in his defence," Sally said, with a grin.

After her mum and dad both passed away within a short time, her teenaged sister was left to look after her. Sally had been the only girl in our class at school and was just seen as one of the boys. She'd been my friend since play school. Even before her parents died, we had often played together, or she had her tea at our house.

I'd always seen Sally as an extra sister. When she and her sister moved back up north where their family was from, she had promised to stay in touch. However, they seemed to disappear. I never saw her again.

So apart from being very happy to see her and knowing she was okay, after ten years apart, I was baffled as to how she knew where my girlfriend lived and why she had chosen 4:30 am to come and visit. I also wondered how on earth she got through the locked door at the bottom.

We all stared at each other for a moment. Finally, it was Kat who went to Sally with her arms wide open and gave her a big hug, telling her it was a pleasure to meet her. "However," she said, stepping back as I stood there in shock, "Why you here now? We were about to go and get some sleep. What can we do for you at this time?"

"Well," she said said rather nervously, "I am so sorry it's so late. I was hoping that it was me that could explain things to you guys about what's been going on."

"Okay," Kat smiled, coming back to put her arms around me. "Well as long as you no here to steal my boyfriend, you stay for a drink with us."

"Don't you worry, love," Sally smiled, "I have no intention of stealing Rob. Believe me, he is so blindly in love with you that I wouldn't stand a chance even if I wanted one."

Kat gave a little laugh. We kissed and then she gave me a little shove towards Sally saying, "Give you friend a hug while I make her a drink." Sally and I just sort of stood there awkwardly. "Go on; you hug her. She has come a very long way," Kat said, giving me another push. "And," she added, "you have special girlfriend permission, so if you no cuddle her for more than twenty seconds, I make you apologise and do again."

"What happened to you? Where have you been? Why are you here? And why now?" I asked, stepping towards Sally as she put her arms to me. Kat stayed to make sure I did as I was told and then went off to put the kettle on.

Cuddling Sally didn't feel like it did with Kat. It was just like feeling the love of a long-lost sister with none of the sexual spark I shared with Kat. She was strangely warm for someone who had been out in the cold, and the heat seemed to radiate from her along with emotions. In some ways, she seemed upbeat and happy, but still a drained shell of the happy little girl I knew before she lost her family. The emotions I felt from her were of sisterly love, which didn't surprise me as she had always said I was her brother from another mother.

However, the love and happiness coming out of her seemed to be on several different levels, like she was telling me a story through her emotions that I couldn't quite translate.

I had no idea how she was doing it, but in the twenty seconds or so of hugging, I could tell so much.

I could feel that Sally had felt both anger and longing. Maybe it was for her parents' untimely deaths, but it seemed to be much greater. She showed pain and remorse for something she had done, which was not her fault. I could tell there were things about Sally that she wanted sincerely to talk about, but for some reason, she could not say. Her overwhelming emotion was her desire to put the world to rights and spread happiness.

That was the Sally I had known as a little girl. However, to me, what made her happiest was seeing Kat and me together.

"So, Sally," Kat said calmly, coming back from putting the kettle on, "how long have you not been human, sweetheart?"

I looked at Kat in shock that she could say such a thing. What a rude and horrible thing to say to someone you'd just met, even if they had just invited themselves into your home in the early hours. Having said that, though, she had a point. Sally seemed somehow different.

It was not just that she was just ten years older, and with that thing with emotions leaking out, who knew? With strange dreams connecting people, Jenny's ghost floating about, and Sally coming back from years away in the middle of the night, Kat might well have been right.

Sally just replied calmly, "I knew it wouldn't take you long to work it out, you bright spark."

"Well," Kat said, showing Sally to a dining chair at the little table, "A few dings gave it away. One, there is no way you know where to find us, even if you asked somebody, because we no tell anyone where we are. Two, who visit an old friend after nearly ten years at 4:30 in da morning? Three, we no hear you come upstairs. And four, the downstairs door is locked, so how you get in? Five, what the hell happened when you hugged me?"

"Are you a ghost?" I heard myself ask.

"Not quite buddy," was her reply. She was about to sit down, but suddenly, she stopped. For a moment, it looked like she was thinking hard, and then she smiled at us both, and said, "You won't tell?"

"We promise," Kat and I both said together.

"No, you really won't, because the men in white coats might want a word with you if you do," she said, looking at us rather nervously. Sally turned to Kat with a grin, and said, "Also, if you tell the police, they may want to know what you're rolling in those horrible cigarettes that you're not going to smoke any more of."

"I agree. They horrible, yucky, and I have to stop, but I never put weed in... apart from that one time," she pleaded. "It was one time for a dare when I was eighteen," she said to me apologetically, as if she thought I was going to tell her off, but I just laughed.

"Anyone you tell about this will think you're full-time stoners," Sally said, with a nervous laugh. She moved into the middle of the living room and slipped off her big long coat, leaving us speechless.

Folded up tightly and hidden under her coat was something that made Kat and I cling to each other in both fear and awe of Sally. She had a pair of dazzling golden wings, which spanned at least ten feet when she spread them out. She popped a big golden ring over her head where it just floated.

"I bet you no get those out in public very often," Kat said in a hushed voice, after what seemed like hours of staring in amazement.

"Only at fancy dress parties," she smiled, flapping them lightly while we gawked. "They're bloody annoying actually. It's tough to shop for clothes. You don't see many people go into a clothes shop and ask for tops with a four-foot zip in the back."

"Well, I am glad I am never stop praying and believing in God. Also glad that I never have said rude things to him," Kat smiled very nervously.

"Pinocchio's nose grew when he told lies," Sally teased, reaching out and touching the tip of Kat's nose. "Would you like me to make yours grow each time you fib?"

"I no know what you mean," Kat replied.

Sally smiled and asked her, "So this wasn't you at 1:13 am this morning?" Sally proceeded to do a very accurate impression of Kat ripping off her crucifix and yelling at God to fuck himself.

"Nooooo," Kat lied in an unconvincing tone. To our

shock, Kat's nose grew by a few millimetres.

Sally then grinned and told Kat that she had no problem with her calling God names. She added that she shared Kat's opinion and anger. She was about to put Kat's nose back, when Kat asked if she could leave it that size, saying a small nose was hell during hay fever season, and Sally agreed, saying that she had the same problem.

"You hid those very well when we were kids," I told her. nodding to her shocking yet stunning wings.

Sally smiled at Kat and said, "You'll find Rob, a lovely bloke, but he isn't always quick to cotton on to things, like the fact I was still alive when we were young, and I'm dead now." She winked at me as if to say she meant it as a joke between old friends and not in an unkind way.

"I no am sure I am understanding myself completely," Kat said, shakily putting Sally's tea down on the table. "I am only start believing in ghost when Rob told me he saw Jenny, and then a beautiful angel comes to have tea with us?"

Sally gave her wings a good stretch as though she hadn't had them out in a while. Then she tucked them back behind her as she perched awkwardly on the little dining chair and took a big sniff.

Kat and I sat on the opposite dining chair, of which there were only two. Kat sat on my knees with her arms tightly around my shoulders, so she didn't fall off.

"So, what happened to you?" I asked Sally, squeezing Kat.

"Well, it's a very long and interesting story, but I can't explain it all now because it would take hours," she beamed, adding, "Please be assured it was not my intention to bugger off without saying a word and not contact my friends."

"It must have been you who send us our lovely dream," Kat said overly excited.

Sally nodded and smiled. "Got it in one, Sherlock," she said, but added, "There were lots of us involved. It wasn't my idea. I was just able to use my powers to channel it. Rob's a really special mate to me. He was my only true friend, who was always there for me when my mum and dad passed away. Kat, the more I get to know you, the more I love you."

Sally smiled broadly at both of us as though it gladdened her heart to see us so close.

"Well the story isn't about me, but that's how it starts," she said, and smiled awkwardly before going into a brief fast-spoken rant which Kat and I barely understood.

Sally looked up at us with tired eyes. "The world is not what we think it is during our lives on earth," she sniffed. "What we believe to be God, if you believe in religion, is not what happens? God is everywhere, yet nowhere. He can't hear your prayers, because there are over a billion planets out there and the struggle between good and evil going on all the time. So life and death don't really matter when you see it in the grand scheme of things. Although, it hurts those left, it doesn't hurt those of us who have died half as much... I died about a year ago," she sighed. "But my death is another story, so that I won't tell it all, but it was a fascinating story. However, I'll tell you over a beer in a few years when you're dead. It was one of our new angels, who only died recently, that brought you both to my attention. She explained the situation and how she felt you two should be together, which I definitely agree with. Unfortunately, although I love a good love story as much as the next person, and I want my friends to have the best life they can, fixing love can't be a priority when there's so much shit going on the world to fix."

"Like children starving in Africa," Kat added.

"That's your favourite comparison, isn't it?" I smiled and kissed the side of her head.

"That is an area of great concern," Sally added, "but humankind needs to help itself in some cases. There is so much more going on than I can ever explain."

"I no would want to be you anytime soon," Kat sympathised.

"It's not all doom and gloom," Sally said, with a smile. "You two got fortunate, because you were a mistake that needed fixing."

"I'm a sort of team leader of angels," she smiled. "When Jenny came to me for help, your case would have been left to her to sort out and given low priority. But she insisted I give it a second look and wouldn't leave me alone until I did. Thank the stars I did because it's so important."

She took another sip of tea and Kat, and I exchanged looks of worry, wondering what on earth made our love so important.

"You mean Jenny as in, my best friend Jenny, do you no?" Kat trembled, and Sally nodded.

That must have had something to do with the reason I saw Jenny after she had died.

"The plane crash wasn't meant to happen," Sally sighed. "Collateral damage from something else you don't need to worry about, but the gist of it is that you too need to be together."

"So why have you helped us?" Kat and I asked together.

"Fate," Sally said, simply and took a deep breath. "I wanted to help my best friend if I could anyway." She smiled, and I knew she meant it because the Sally I knew was a kind, loving girl like Kat who could not let a friend go by without helping them if she felt they were in need.

She looked at Kat, who whispered, "Rape and miscarriage," under her breath.

"I cried when I read it on your file," Sally added. "The thing is though," she said in desperation, "you two are part of fate. Without you getting together, the entire fate of the world would change forever, and that's why we had to butt in quickly."

"Because I was no coming back," Kat stammered suddenly.

"That's it exactly," Sally smiled. "If Jenny was alive, she would have got you to meet Rob again very soon. But Jenny's murder left you friendless."

"What murder?" Kat asked, "It was an accident, not a murder."

"No, she was most definitely murdered. You intended to go on holiday with a view to staying, so we had to come up with a plan to make you stay with very short notice."

"So, you lovely people made us dream of each other?" Kat beamed all over her face and squeezed me. "So, I have reason to come home."

"It was very short notice, and even angels can't really

stop time, so we only had a couple of hours to work out what to do before you would have been gone with no way to get you back," she told us as Kat nodded.

"We basically got everyone on the other side who knew either of you to brainstorm a story in a couple of hours. We put it into practice while you were both asleep."

My heart jumped several beats as Sally reeled off a list of relatives, mainly from my family, including my mum and dad, my grandparents and Jeanette and Jemima. Then she listed some of Kat's distant relatives, whom Kat smiled but shrugged at as though she wasn't even sure who they were.

"But lastly," she smiled, "your unnamed little one was most insistent on helping."

Kat and I stared at each other, and then at Sally in wonder, gasping in pure appreciation for all of those people who joined together to help. I think we were flabbergasted at the lengths they had gone to. Kat and I were both driven once more to tears by this news, and Sally smiled as we wiped away each other's tears.

Sally told us how they had discussed various aspects of both of us and our lives and how to best put us together.

"Things didn't quite go to plan, though, like they never do," she said with a laugh, adding to me, "You sat next to me at school, so you know I never could make up a story. We made up some of the things that went into the story, but your minds worked a lot of it. They wanted you to live with people you wanted there, even if they couldn't really be there. Basically, it was meant to be a perfect world where the bad things didn't happen to you both. You found love, and you would know what to do when you did meet each other. Your first meeting was meant to be at Jenny's funeral, but we didn't know until the last minute that Rob didn't know she was dead."

"Things from the real world broke through," Kat said bluntly, adding that she had nearly died in very similar circumstances to Jenny, and that maybe Jenny had put that bit in to get back at her for causing her death.

Sally shook her head vigorously, "That was all you. You are punishing yourself with your free will," Sally sighed. "Jenny was in tears seeing you do that to yourself."

"And there was the bit where Kat told me about her rape without me cottoning on to it," I added.

"I am a strong-willed lady," Kat smiled at me, adding that she would've wanted me to know the truth.

"Rob would have been a really good stepdaddy," she added to Sally, who agreed.

"You actually pretty much bossed the dream, even when you nearly blew the whole thing," she told Kat. Kat looked bemused, so she explained. "Do you remember when you went outside to poo, and you collapsed and thought you were hallucinating about using your toilet at home? Then you didn't want a cigarette afterwards?"

"That was very strange indeed," Kat replied, nodding heavily.

"That's because while we were panicking for time, you actually woke up for a comfort break," Sally laughed, seeing the funny side in hindsight. "We were having kittens over the timing, while you were having a poo, making a cup of tea, and having a smoke, taking painkillers you didn't even know it was real. You filled up your nicotine levels and didn't want a fag for the rest of the dream."

"I am so sorry," Kat giggled. "I often wake up for quick cup of tea and smoke when have an early night."

"There's early nights, and then there's you," Sally teased. "I mean, we were expecting you to turn in early, but who really goes to bed at 3 pm with no dinner?"

"A very cold, tired, depressed, broken-hearted, worn out lady, who is ill with stinking cold and chest infection," Kat retorted grinning. Sally immediately raised both hands and apologised, saying she'd not intended to be so judgmental.

"So, basically, it was a bit of a balls-up, but it worked." Sally beamed at us both. "The point of it was to show you guys how you would like each other if you met, because you wouldn't have done so willingly. You're both too shy. We wanted to show you the type of couple you could be and the lovely family life you could have together, regardless of friends and family, but obviously, you wanted them around. I'm sorry I can't do something to bring them back. Once someone is recorded as dead, they have to stay dead, because people would notice if someone who died in a plane crash suddenly got up and started walking around."

"So Jenny was in the dream, but you weren't, Sally?" Kat probed.

Sally considered her answer. "The Jenny in your dream was in your head, sweetheart," She told her calmly. "You wanted her and her baby to live and be happy, so you cancelled their deaths and made up a fitting happy future where..." Sally looked at me and grinned before continuing. "Rob didn't put me in the dream, because I'd been out of touch for such a long time that he assumed I moved on to a new life away from here and wanted no part in his life."

"You would be welcome to be our friend, wouldn't she, Rob?" Kat said looking.

"Always," I replied looking back at Sally.

"But I was there keeping an eye on you all along." She beamed, adding that Kat hadn't met her and I hadn't seen her since she was since her tenth birthday, so neither of us recognised her as an adult.

"You caught me watching you when you met Kat and Ela from the airport first time around, and I was working behind the bar at your birthday party to name a few."

I wracked my brain going back over anywhere else where I could remember seeing her, and then there was the moment in the movie *The Sixth Sense* when you saw all the bits where you should have picked up on the fact that Bruce Willis was a ghost. There were times that had not even entered my mind until I looked at it again. It was Kat who spoke.

"You were the lady weeping on the back row at our wedding who was crying," She breathed. Sally nodded.

"And you were the nurse who was feeding Lydia when I walked into the room after thinking Kat was dead," I added hastily.

"Guilty," she smiled, adding that she couldn't resist a cute baby and that the major downside to dying so young was that she would never have a child of her own.

"You were my doctor when I went to ask my cold." Kat grinned.

"Congratulations on your new job by the way." She grinned at Kat who looked a little down.

"I thought I got that job on my own back."

"Oh you did, sweetheart. I didn't do anything at all, Kat." Sally added quickly, making Kat's face light up. "Although, it might well have had something to do with you making friends with Katie on the plane, seeing as her brother is married to the owner of a lot of the caravan sites. She also owns the Aricot hotel chain where you work, Rob."

"So getting back to the dream" Sally continued. "Basically, we wanted to show you the whole of our story we wrote, because we were kind of proud of our little ending. So we shut you in the haystack to finish the story, and well... nobody expects you guys to just get on and..." She made the gesture Ela had first made in the dream, as Kat and I looked at each other red-faced, and we all laughed a little.

"I can't die without making love to a gorgeous man at least once," Kat laughed.

"Well, you'd better go and find one before you die" I teased before kissing her.

"And all those colds," Sally added to Kat, "You guessed that well. It was only because you were so ill that night that you kept having them and couldn't get anyone else ill."

Kat just smiled and announced, "I never want to get ill ever again," then asked if Sally could help her get rid of her hay fever.

Sally smiled and explained to Kat that she would if she could, having suffered heavily from the condition herself—something which I remembered well about her.

"There were things in the dream that showed you guys that you can do what you want." She smiled, looking at me as she said, "You learned to come out of yourself and be confident and stand up to people like Katherine McNallty. And Kat?" she said, turning to her. "You gave up smoking. You did that all your own because you wanted to. You learned about computers and went and did your degrees, all because you wanted to, and you got your rewards." She added, "If I know you guys like I think I do, you will do those things all over again."

"I no am sure about the smoking dough," Kat sighed. "I given it up three times, only seriously once for so long and then start again."

"Addiction," Sally said simply. "The oldest joke of the devil's spawn driving you to want more. They laugh while it slowly kills you, but it's a waste of time. It doesn't hurt the soul, just the body you're in at the time. If you want to live a long healthy life, it's a pretty crap thing to do. Thankfully, you're young and strong-willed so you can reverse the effects on your health," she beamed at Kat. Sally suddenly stood up and touched Kat on the forehead, saying, "Think of that as an everlasting nicotine patch."

Kat's face was a picture as she breathed a heartfelt, "thank you."

"Strict rules prevent me from fixing your eye or your epilepsy," Sally added kindly, "but your neurologist is not helping. That's why you're still fitting regularly. That volatile temper of yours that feels like it's somebody else?"

Kat nodded. "I hate myself when I am short temper. I shout and scream at people who no deserve it."

"You're on the wrong pills," Sally said simply. "Cheap and substandard drugs. The NHS has no money. Your doctor is racist and won't give you the good stuff because you're not British. They cause your temper problems without curing your real problem." She advised that when Kat requested a change of doctor, the results would surprise all of us.

We all worked out that the end of the dream was just the logical ending. In reality, we were naked in subzero temperatures, so of course, we were going to die. It made the whole thing seem rather silly, because neither of us had even wondered why we didn't die of hypothermia within minutes.

"You two were actually a lot less difficult than we imagined." Sally smiled, passing us a piece of paper with handwriting all over it. It appeared to be a list of points about Kat and myself as individuals and then together. This was done by circling our names and lines coming outwards with points on different subjects and how to overcome them. The names Ela and Katie were also circled with lines coming out.

Two of the things listed for both of us were a fear of opposite sex and nakedness. This was circled in red with the words, "Force them to get their clothes off within an hour of meeting each other."

There was also an observation about how we were both very nervous and shy people who wanted to come out of ourselves, but felt repressed by life in general. We were scared to show our emotions to another human, but afraid of this being exposed.

I noticed that Kat looked very impressed and yet a bit annoyed as she was skimming through.

"Dis is fucking amazing that you wrote dis in my language, but that no is right," she sounded somewhat irritated by what she had read.

"What do you mean it's written in your language?" I asked in complete confusion, as it was clear to me that it was English.

"These things are written in multi-language," Sally explained, "so everyone in the world can read."

"That is very clever," Kat smiled, uneasily pointing to sentence on the of paper regarding herself and read it aloud. *"Hates all parents because she is jealous because of losing her baby.* That no is me," she said a little grumpily. "What I hate no is people who have children, but people who no appreciate what they have. People on low income who put alcohol and cigarettes before children, people who shout at and hit their children, parents who are split up and use children as a weapon. People who don't worship their little ones every minute of every day and show their children the love they deserve, because they are no know how hard it is to want to have children and no have them."

Sally looked like she was going to cry at Kat's statement. Her response was to apologise for that remark and admit that she had quite quickly realised she'd made a mistake about Kat. In turn, Kat got up and went to hug Sally and apologised for getting grumpy at her. She even went as far as to kiss her on the cheek.

With this act, she handed the paper back to Sally, saying we didn't want to read anymore. Sally accepted Kat's apology with open arms and beamed, saying she could see why we didn't want to read all the details they had on us.

"Is there anything you guys want to know while I'm here?" Sally asked, adding that we were never likely to get a second chance to see an angel, so we should ask away now. Kat and I looked at each other. Kat seemed like she was thinking what best to ask, so she kissed me gently and told me to ask first.
I turned to Sally to ask about the first thing that had stuck in my head and cuddled Kat as hard as I could, in case she didn't like the answer.

"Why did Jenny come to see me, but not her best friend?"

Kat gave her a little smile. "I was going to ask that," she said softly.

"And I'm sorry I didn't make that clear," Sally told us awkwardly and looked Kat straight. "You were holding her hand when she died," she smiled. "I couldn't have shown my-self, because Rob didn't know me after all these years, you wouldn't have had a clue who I was and would have thought I was a stranger. Rob didn't know Jenny was dead, and if she had just showed up if front of you, you would have gone crazy and run a mile."

"Me run a mile? That's optimistic with my fitness and my smoking habit and that cough and cold I had, along with me hopping everywhere?" Kat replied with a half-smile. I think she was a little relieved at the reasoning.

"You were not to blame for her death," Sally told her. "You thought she tripped over the hoover you left out, but she didn't."

"Then what did happen?" Kat demanded in a soft voice so that Sally realised she was not being pushy or having a go. She was desperate to know what happened, having blamed herself for Jenny's death.

Sally looked at the floor, gathering her thoughts, and then looked up at us as she spoke. "The death of a person who was not supposed die doesn't have as much effect on the world as somebody who was not supposed to live."

"Jenny no was supposed live?" Kat stuttered.

"Not Jenny," Sally told us shakily. "Her baby."

Kat breathed sharply. "If her dad no had died on the plane, he would have put a stop to her relationship with that man and baby would never be born."

"I don't agree with what was done," she sighed. "I don't deal with things like the murder of unborn babies. That's not my department, and I don't think I could look myself in the face if it were."

Obviously, after Kat's rape and the death of her unborn child, this was something close to our hearts. Sally knew this, because she explained something that made so much sense despite not seeming right. She explained that in certain cases, if an unborn baby died, it did not mean it will never be born. Often the soul of the one you lost gets another chance in a new body. Sometimes with a different parent, but in most cases with the same parents.

"Your little boy isn't gone," she smiled at Kat. "He just went back into the queue behind his four big sisters."

At this, Kat was sobbing and smiling through her tears. "Five babies!" she cried, smiling and kissed me.

"You had nine in the dream," Sally reminded us.

"I have ten this time," Kat teased.

"The other thing you are both dying to know is why?" she said softly.

"Why?" we asked together.

"Why you guys being together was so important to the world," she added.

"Okay," we both said, eager to hear her explanation.

"In five thousand years, a descendant of your third daughter will commit a very important murder that will change the world."

Kat and I exchanged looks of terror at the thought an ancestor of ours could do such a thing.

"We are stopping at two children," Kat told me bluntly. "No descendant of mine is killing anyone."

"No, this is a good murder," Sally protested. "The fate of the entire planet rests on this murder. This may save the planet and life as we know it."

"Really," Kat asked leaving her mouth open.

"Nah I'm just winding you up." Sally laughed, "That plot has been so overdone in the movies already."

"Oh well, that's okay then, I suppose," Kat smiled awkwardly.

"Honestly," Sally said, standing up and placing a hand on each of our shoulders, "The most important thing is that you two love and look after each other always. Your love will spread to your children, and your children's children, and your children's children's children's children. Get the point?" Her smile radiated over to us, filling us with warmth.

Kat, however, looked back sadly at Sally.

"What is it, sweetheart?" I asked her gently, but in reply, she spoke to Sally.

Sally replied, "And you will use what you have in you to bring joy to others. Just because it didn't work out before it happen many times in the future."

"You are talking about babies. Aren't you?" Kat beamed,
"Rob, she is. I can use what have. I might not be able to help the couple in my home town, but I can be a surrogate for people here who no have their children."

"I love you for the thing you just said alone" I grinned, holding her in my arms.

"You are a kind, sweet, amazing, lovely, very beautiful angel, and we love you so much for that. Don't we Rob?" Kat smiled awkwardly and I nodded vigorously in agreement. "The thing is who is help you? You look tired and stressed. Who is help you when need a friend to just sit and talk with over cup of tea."

Sally looked shocked, and yet not surprised as she turned to me. "See" she smiled, "haven't you got the most awesome future wife right here? Everything that's going on right now, and all she wants to do is look after an angel whose job it is to look after her. Which is an honour, not a chore by the way."

"Well answer me!" Kat demanded. "Because you might be strong, super angel, but everyone needs friend. If you ever need come sit and eat chocolate, drink tea, and watch crappy TV, you welcome here anytime."

"Trust me, that sounds like something I'd love," she smiled. "Unfortunately with so many people in the world, we are limited and only able to show ourselves twice in a lifetime. So, as much as I'd like to stay, even I don't get to change the rules. But I will be popping in from time to time to spy on my favourite lovebirds... Oh by the way," she said, suddenly looking behind us to the armchair, "you've got another visitor."

Kat's mouth dropped open, and she stared at the large figure sitting back in the chair who had just appeared out of thin air with big smile on her face. She nearly deafened me as she sprang up, knocking me over with the chair, and screaming with pure delight. "*Jenny!*"

As I picked myself up, I saw Kat mouthing an apology for knocking me over as she clung with disbelief to her friend as tears of joy rolled down her face.

"Whooooooooooo?" Jenny boomed as Kat flung herself at her, "Whooooo I am?"

We all looked at each other as suddenly Ela's bedroom door opened, and she stumbled out sleepily in her onesie. Her eyes were only open a crack to see why her sister had screamed. As she opened her eyes, she stared blankly at Sally, whose wings were clearly showing, and a look of fright spread across her face.

"It's all right, sweetie," Sally and Kat both told her at the same time.

"It's a dream," I said, quickly taking her by the shoulders and steering her back towards her room.

"But Rob, those ladies had wings?"

"Don't worry," I teased, "it's common in England. She's just had a lot of Red Bull tonight, and that gives you wings."

Sally and Jenny tried not to burst out laughing, but Kat either didn't understand the joke or was still in too much shock from seeing Jenny to think about laughing.

As I coaxed Ela back towards her bed, she turned to me and said, "That lovely fat girl, Jenny, was in my dream before Katarzyna came home."

"It's not nice to call people fat," I reminded her gently.

"Sorry, I didn't mean it rude," she whispered sleepily, a little confused considering Ela and Jenny had never met, I asked, "Who else was there?"

"Super best sister ever, Katarzyna," she smiled with her eyes closed. "Best brother-in-law Rob, and lots and lots of nieces and nephews and..." She paused as if the memory caused her pain. "Alice, Erin and mummy Katie. I like girls, and I realised it's okay to be me."

"It's always okay to be you, Ela," I told her gently.

Ela was back in a deep sleep by the time her head hit the pillow. As I shut the door, I looked over at Sally.

"You gave Ela and Katie dreams to get them together too, didn't you?" I smiled.

"Rules say I can only talk to you regarding your own situation," she told me in a very official sounding voice with a nod and a big wink.

Jenny and Kat were still crying silently into each other's shoulders, so Sally pulled me aside as she fussed Narla by rubbing her on the head.

"I am to believe we did a good job in repairing what should have been?" she asked, quietly looking lovingly over at Kat and Jenny who now whispering to each other.

"I already just love Kat more than I can ever express, all thanks to you guys," I told her, shakily putting my arm around her too. "I don't think I could ever thank you enough," I said, squeezing her shoulders and getting that odd feeling of emotion.

"You were there for me when dad died and then my mum," she said, putting an arm around me. "I repaid you by disappearing for years and not being able to save your family, even though I saved the rest of the planet."

"Tell me more about what happened to you," I asked, hoping she would spill the beans, but she shook her head.

"Maybe over a lot of drinks in eighty years or so, when you guys are as dead as I am." She smiled then, pushing me towards Kat who was beckoning me over.

"Come say bye bye to Jenny," she beamed, throwing herself into my arms. As she did, Jenny stepped forward for a cuddle, putting her arms around us both, squeezing Kat into the middle, and kissing me on the cheek.

When I thanked Jenny for her help, she just smiled and said, "Just look after Kat for me." Then she poked Kat on the shoulder and said forcefully, "You young lady," she grinned, "stop telling people you were a bully to me just because you called me fat a few times. You were only being honest."

Jenny clearly had Kat's cold as well, and took such a big sniff that made Kat dig into her pocket and pass her a clean hanky.

"You don't change, do you?" Jenny smiled, taking it.

"Neither do you," Kat smiled with tears in her eyes.

Suddenly there was another knock at the door. It was odd having another one at nearly five in the morning, but Sally seemed to know who it was, so she opened the door to let them in.

The sweetest little dark-headed girl stood there in the doorway. We looked her up and down as she spoke in her Australian accent, which she didn't have in our dream. "G'day guys! Hey Uncle Rob and Aunty Kat. I am an angel now."

"I think you know one of our youngest recruits," Sally beamed, as Jemima came running into my arms.

I cried at that point. I never ever met my niece when she was alive, yet from thousands of miles away I loved that little girl with all my heart. Of all the family I lost, I missed my Skype calls with her the most. I picked her up in my arms and just squeezed her. That lovely little girl squeezed back so hard her face went red and we both cried. Kat grabbed her from the other side, and the three of us held each other for what again seemed like an eternity.

"What happened to you, little lady? You were supposed to meet me here twenty-five minutes ago," Sally asked with a teasing smile.

"I'm sorry guys. I met someone on the way," Jemima said. She turned to me quite innocently, and asked, "Do you want to stroke Aunty Kat's pussy Uncle Rob?"

For a moment, there was silence, until Jenny came out with, "I used to love watching *Kids Say the Funniest Things* on TV." Then Sally and I both laughed a little.

Kat kept a straight face and said, "But sweetheart, my pussy is died." There was another silence.

"But Aunty Kat," Jemima said in a matter of fact tone, "Sally, Jenny and I are all dead, but we are here. He's just hiding behind the door because he's scared of Narla."

I lowered Jemima to the ground, and she ran over to stroke Narla, who she had always wanted to meet when she saw her on Skype.

Just then, there was a hell of a screech from the door, sort of a, "meeeaaaawwwww," and Charlie poked his head round the door.

Kat was there in a flash, tears of happiness streaming down her face.

"Never separate crazy Kat from her crazy cat," Jenny laughed. Kat was already picking him up kissing his head and making faces at him.

"This is all just another dream, isn't it?" I said, out of earshot of Kat, so only Jenny and Sally could hear me.

"It may seem like it in the morning," Sally said, shaking her head in a definite no as Kat came back to us with Charlie purring loudly.

There was only time for a quick chat to Jemima, who proudly told us that she didn't cry when she died. We both told her we were proud of her.

There was an awkward moment when Kat asked if it hurt to die and got three different answers. Sally said she died too quickly to notice, Jemima remembered feeling cold, and Jenny went into a rant saying, "Of course it bloody fucking did. I fell down four floors and took an hour in the agony from hell trying to hang in there and keep my baby alive before my heart finally stopped."

"We were trying to play that bit down," Sally said nodding to Jemima with a smile.

"Can you guys promise me one more thing before we go?" Jenny said, starting to cry as Kat turned and wrapped her arms around her best friend and wept.

"Anything for my Jen sweetheart," Kat soothed.

Jenny took a big sniff and asked quietly, "Could you check the CCTV and find out who pushed me?"

After we exchanged shocked looks at each other, Jenny explained that she had not tripped as she fell to her death. Instead, she had answered a knock at the door to find nobody there. Sally stood with us, saying nothing and blowing her nose quietly. Jenny demonstrated how she had come to answer the door. Seeing nobody there, she had gone to the landing to call out, when somebody jumped out from behind the door and pushed her down the spiral stairs.

"There are several cameras belonging to the antique shop," Sally said, stepping out onto the landing in her coat as if to leave.

"You no going stay for more tea?" Kat sobbed.

"We'd love to stay forever," Sally said earnestly, telling us that her contacts had picked up on something bad that could be about to go down. She and Jenny needed to go and investigate, in case the world was in danger. The look in her eye as she said it told me she was one hundred per cent genuine.

"We're not going to see any of you again in this life, are we?" I asked, taking Kat in my arms. She dissolved into tears and grabbed hold of both me and Jenny, as if to say Jenny was going nowhere. Sally shook her head, teasing that she would only come back to bang our heads together if we ever argued. The next time we saw them, we would be dead.

Gently, Sally added, "But that does not mean we don't check in on you when you can't see us."

"If you ever watch Bambi, save an empty seat for me," Jemima grinned, passing Charlie to Kat.

"Kat sweetheart," Jenny said quietly, "pray whenever you need, but there's no need to drag yourself to church on Sunday. It makes no difference where you pray. God can't hear you because he's far too busy."

"But we hear you. We care, and we do what we can," Sally added.

We all hugged each other as if none of us wanted to be parted.

"We love you guys, and we'll see you guys in about eight years", Jenny sniffed.

"She means eighty years," Sally laughed. When she saw the shock on our faces, she explained that time for them moved ten times faster than on Earth.

Sally stepped back and wiped away tears as Kat passed Charlie to Jenny, but Jenny gave him back to her saying, "We can't bring a person back for obvious reasons, but nobody's going to miss a cat."

"Look at you? You bring cats back from the dead, who are you? Andrew Lloyd Webber?" she smiled.

"One final thing," Sally told us, putting her hands on Kat and I, and turning us to face each other. Charlie went back into the flat. "Us angels cry magic dust which charms the lives of those it touches and seals relationships forever."

"As if that's real," Kat and I both laughed as we looked lovingly at each other.

"I wasn't really kidding," Sally smiled. Stepping back she took her handkerchief which she had cried into at our wedding. She dropped the contents over Kat and me.

The room was filled with golden particles. I could see nothing but gold, and feel nothing but Kat in my arms. We kissed more passionately than ever, until a most fitting end when the dust caused Kat to sneeze.

After that, I teased her, saying she should add magic angel dust to her allergy list, but she just smiled and wiped her nose on her sleeve having given Jenny her hanky. We carried on kissing, for neither of us knew how much time had passed.

When we finally went parted and went to bed, Sally, Jenny, and Jemima had long disappeared and left us to our future.

Chapter 35

Final Word

Whether or not there were really angels in Kat's flat, or whether they were just another strange shared dream in which it had all been explained, it all fit. We had been about to go off to sleep when the door went. If it had all been a dream, then that made sense. Angels didn't just walk into your home and tell these things. Maybe they did it through form of another dream.

However, dream or not, Charlie the dead cat was alive and well and asking for his breakfast when we woke up snuggled to each other the next morning.

True to her word, the next morning, Kat flushed her tobacco down the loo. With support from me and the help Sally gave her along with her own strong will, she never touched another cigarette again.

So, what did the dream do for me, you might ask? Through the love of friends and family who had now passed, it showed me, the lonely young man who was never comfortable when it came to trying to attract girls, that he had the potential to blossom with the right person. I had just been looking in the wrong places. I was in complete turmoil over the deaths of my family, but in the dream, I saw them live the lives I wanted for them. That gave me some solace. The same with Jenny, who I didn't know was dead.

It also changed my pre-conceptions of people from other countries and helped give me strength to stand up to people who used my lack of confidence to walk all over me. It got me over my fear of conversing with women outside of work and showed me that my future could be different from the one I envisioned for myself. It introduced me to one of the loveliest human beings I had ever come across and showed me how to find her.

For Kat, she already knew she was outwardly a strong, confident lady despite everything, but inwardly, she was awkward, lonely, running from her past and left frustrated at her inability to convert her potential into success. She was left broken by the loss of Jenny and hated herself for things she'd done. She was kidding herself that she didn't want the things she wanted most because she was lost and scared.

Her everyday life and struggles and that horrifying experience were always on her mind. She was always on the defensive, causing her to be sharp-tongued and short tempered. This made her good at her job, but terrible for making friends. She was scared of being touched, let alone being naked. She was terrified that if she ever let herself settle down with a man and get pregnant again, the pregnancy would end in the same way.

The dream showed Kat that despite her depression and fears, her true self-was still there alive and well. It just needed time. She didn't need to let horrible experiences ruin her life, and not every man she met had indecent thoughts and intentions. It taught her that she was a smart, funny lady, capable of so much more than the life she felt limited to and the love she didn't think she could give anyone. It showed her that she had a future as an amazing, wife and mother, businesswoman, and role model.

We both needed fixing in our own ways, but the dream led each of us to the only person who possessed the tools to help us face our demons, reach our potentials, move on with our lives, find the love we needed, and be the happiest we could be. The people we needed were each other.

On Sunday, we went to see Mr. Proctor who owned the antique shop and asked to view the footage from the cameras on Kat's birthday.

We sat in shock and tears when we saw that Jenny had not been alone in the flat. While Kat left the door open, another person had crept into the flat less than three minutes before Kat came running to Jenny's aid. A second shot from the back of the flat showed a clear view of a woman, very familiar to all of us, running from the scene via the fire escape, chased by a big tabby cat, Charlie, who tripped her. She fell to the floor, but then she got up and kicked Charlie several times, leaving him still on the ground. Seconds later, her car reversed over the lifeless cat as she sped away.

Kat was interviewed and told the police everything she knew about Jenny's relationship, how she had not known she was dating a married man, and how she had come clean to Katherine when she found out.

I was at work when the police showed up to arrest Katherine McNallty for the murder of Jenny Hughs. The staff all gawped and jeered at her as she was taken away.

As for Kat and myself, over the weeks that followed, despite us being close initially, things changed rather quickly. I know that in a lot of cases after the event, real life kicks in, things get tough and arguments start, especially with the stress that was going on from Jenny's murder, but that wasn't the case for Kat and me.

As time went on, we helped each other get over our individual sadness. By each other's side always, we learnt to smile and laugh again, and get each other through the hard times.

Kat excelled at her new job. She was loving life, and more often than not, was a happy and smiley lady who showed no signs of the constant illness that plagued her in the dream—until hay fever season hit again.

With Katherine fired and awaiting trial, I was promoted to gym manager, meaning Kat and I both got to work 9-5 shifts and spend more time together.

It was after only a few weeks together that Kat and I, along with Ela, decided to give up the flat and move into a small house not far from both our jobs. It had a garden for Narla and Charlie to run around with any future children and was cheap to rent too.

Despite Kat having formerly been the black sheep of the family, our house became a holiday home for Kat's close or extended family, who were always popping over for their holidays. Her mum and dad stayed over for two weeks at least twice a year, and they got on better than ever these days. The rest of the year, the spare room was filled by her brother, sisters and cousins who were all welcome, as long we got our privacy.

With the help of a solicitor, we got on top of the mess of the rather dauntingly sized inheritance I unintentionally gained from the loss of my whole family.

I inherited several properties owned by my grandparents, which they had been renting out. I had never known they existed. With a lot of help from Kat, who was very good with numbers, we ended up renting out the buildings, including seven houses and three shops. We were running our own property rental company as well as doing our own jobs. To be honest, I'd rather have my family than the properties they left to me.

After a short engagement, Kat and I married in what was meant to be a small ceremony with a few friends. But when her family got wind of our plans, the venues soon changed to her grandfather's farm in the Czech Republic.

The reception was held in a large barn behind the main house. As we had our first dance on the makeshift dance floor, Kat grinned at me from under the veil of the wedding dress she said she would never wear. She whispered in my ear, "I always wanted to dance on the grave of the men who raped me." She looked down at the floor and then to a trap door in the corner and smiled, "What a shame they still alive down there." She giggled eerily. That was the moment I learned not to piss off my wife's family at any cost.

After consulting with the hospital, Kat changed neurologists and was put on better drugs. She was free from fitting for over a year and given clearance to learn to drive. Hats off to her, she booked herself straight for a week's driving crash course and passed first time. She was nine months pregnant with our first child at the time and gave birth days later.

For two years, the whole town was speculating about Jenny's murder. Kat was already three months pregnant with baby number two when she stood in the witness box.

The defence tried to claim that Jenny had fallen while attempting to attack Katherine who, in her words, had come to settle things. The jury, however, was having none of it. There was evidence from the prosecution, including statements from both Kat and others. It included rather harrowing tales of violence against Katherine's now former husband, who she would beat.

The court was silent as he told how she beat him and cut him and made his life a living hell. He broke down as he talked of his intentions to end his marriage to Katherine and start a family with Jenny, who he said was the love of his life.

Other witnesses for the prosecution included Katherine's sister, who described her childhood as one where she was terrified and repressed by her bullying from her older sister. She had only got away when her parents had split up. She had begged to live with whichever parent didn't have her sister. Having later become the European manager for the same hotel company that had recently taken over where her sister managed, Katherine was at the point of losing her job before the murder.

On the 12th of June 2011, more than two years later, there were cheers in court as Katherine McNallty was sentenced to life in prison for the premeditated murder of Jenifer Alexandria Hughs. The sister who gave the statement, as you may have guessed, was a lady called Katie Barns. She was the very same lady who, in our dream, had married Ela and was the same one who took the flight with Kat

Katie met Ela after Kat introduced them. Soon after they met, they had fallen deeply in love. They were married as soon as the laws on gay marriage changed, and were currently living in their own place with a daughter each, just like we dreamed.

The hotel we dreamed about might not have existed, but it mattered not. The dream showed what could be done, and as of this year, Kat and I put the savings made from the rent on our inherited properties into renovating a similar building not far from the one we dreamed of. Bookings were already being taken for summer 2017.

Until now (2016), we had not seen either Sally, Jenny, or Jemima again, but we always knew when they were watching us. We could feel their presences through little things, like a smell or an emotion, that little breath on the back of your neck, or a whisper in your ear.

The picture of Kat and Jenny eating ice cream still takes pride of place along with one of myself and Sally as children. Each sit above the fireplace in our second new home, by the side of our wedding picture and a picture of us with our two little girls, Lydia and Zophia, just like in the dream.

As her manager, Kat used her position to start up a free employee nursery, so that staff could have their children with them at work and not have to leave. That was how she managed to keep her job when we had two little ones of our own.

Kat looked a little different now. She laughed so hard earlier when I teased that she looked like a fat bald man. I was joking of course. The reason Kat was bald was that she had very recently raised thousands for cancer charities by shaving her head along with Ela and Katie.

The fat big tummy was baby number three. Number three for us in all Kat's fifth pregnancy with two surrogate pregnancies that made local couples as happy as we were, and more planned—I'm so proud of my wife.

My dog Narla was twelve when we got together and was no longer with us. But we have a great pair of four-year-old female Labradors called Topsy and Turvy lying on the rug by the fire. Stretched out between them was Charlie, the cat who came back from the dead.

It's late November and Kat's twenty-ninth birthday. Ela and Katie took her to the theatre, and the girls and I—including Ela and Katie's two kids—stayed home, and with me we made her a big birthday tea. There were lots of happy tears, and Kat called for several family hugs.

Ela and Katie took their girls home to bed. We let our girls stay up after their bedtime, and Lydia fell asleep cuddling her little sister who also sparked out.

~~*~*~*

Sitting here now in our chair, I think it's a good place to finish our tale. My lovely, amazing wife is snuggled up to me under a blanket by the fire, dozing quietly with a pretty smile on her face, a half-drunk cup of tea on the table, her hand resting on her tummy, out of which our third daughter is due to pop out of very soon.

Ironically, she has a bit a of a cold. However, after all those colds she had in our dream, I can assure you, apart from her hay fever, it's the first time in eight years since I met her that she has had as much as sniffle. After eight years, I still love my wife like I did that day I left her at the airport, and of course, the day I married her.

Every so often she wakes up from her snooze, looks over at our girls, gives me a big kiss, and drifts back to sleep with a big smile on her face. As I watch her sleep, a thought crosses my mind.

What if it was all a double bluff? What if we were right from the start? What if we really were dying and Sally just told us what we wanted to hear? I have a theory that maybe it was not my family that died, and that our naked bodies were discovered in the haystack in the days that followed.

I reason that, despite everything that went on before, our lives could not be much better than they are right now. This leads me to believe that we may actually have died and that this is our heaven.

When I tell Kat my theory, she gives me that smile of hers. We kiss, and she tells me that it's a lovely theory. We both have one opinion that's the same. Dead or alive does not matter either way, because no matter what happened or where we are, we always have one thing... each other.

One more final thought crosses my mind, what if this is all just in the head of dying teenager, whose final dreams are of living a life with a lady he met only for minutes one time. The reality could be that I crashed my car after sliding on the ice and died alone.

So, the final message is this. To all those people, young or old, who live without love, keep in mind that there is reason for everything. There is someone out there for everyone, no matter their gender or country of birth, or how many you got wrong before. There is a person waiting for when you least expect it—in the middle of a snowy road for example—and it doesn't matter if it's not who you wanted or who you expected, as long as it's who you need in your life.

THE END
Or maybe just the beginning

Also by Samuel J. White

Derailed and Dispersed Series

The survivors of a train derailment on a remote line in East Anglia have come together to tell their story years later. They tell of heroism and true friendship in the face of a great evil hiding in the dark marshes. This is a story of bloods, guts, gore and dark magic, with monsters, vampires and werewolves.

Not for the faint of heart
Reviewed in the United States on 15 October 2020
Verified Purchase
The tension and horror builds slowly, catching the reader by surprise. Prepare yourself for plot twists and surprises-there's even a dash of romance. Might wanna make sure the electric bill is paid up as you'll want to sleep with the lights on for a while.

Buy it at this link http://mybook.to/DADSeries
Recurring Characters in this series from A Mid-winter Night's dream, include a young Katie Barns and Katherine McNallty, and Sally the before she became an angel.

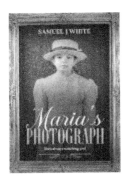

Maria's Photograph

After being widowed in the second world war, Young School teacher Judith moves to start a new life in a remote Norfolk village. Finding herself alone in her remote cottage for long evenings she often finds herself talking to an old photograph of a young girl which came with the house. When the girl begins to haunt her dreams Judith becomes involved in a terrifying and jumpy ghost story.

5.0 out of 5 stars Must read
Reviewed in the United States on 25 March 2020
Verified Purchase
Maria's Photograph was everything I expected it to be and so much better.
Every time I think I knew what is going to happen, it wasn't.
I read this in one setting and this spooked me a lot, but it was well worth reading. I really enjoyed this one.
If you enjoy Thrillers you need to read this.
This was better than a thriller movie by far.
Must read!!!

Reviewed in the United States on 24 November 2019
Verified Purchase
Maria's Photograph is creepy, gripping, surprisingly loving, and difficult to put down.

It is one of those books that takes hold of you and makes you think you know how things are going to go, but you are oh so wrong. Samuel J White has woven a masterful tale and doesn't leave you disappointed.

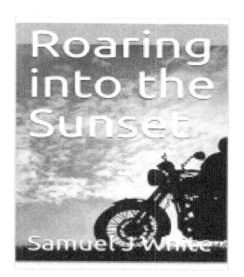

Roaring into the Sunset

Told from both points of view. The complicated lives of young biker couple Dave and Sarah flash before their eyes as they hurtle towards almost certain catastrophe. Will they come out alive to tell the tale of their winding deep and winding passionate love story? Or will the many twist of fate that led them there course an untimely demise.

Pre order for November 2021 mybook.to/sunset

About the Author

Born in Norwich England in 1985 I grew up in the Norfolk broads.

I'm a qualified personal trainer, I've also worked at three petrol stations and in catering at Norwich City FC, but now working as a carer for disabled family members and writing in my spare time.

I have a sporting background, I won the English lightweight indoor rowing championship five times between 2005 and 2009 before having to retire through illness.

I grew up as a sea scout leader's son and have been a Seascout leader since I was sixteen. I teach both Kayaking and Sailing.

I am married and I have stepchildren all in their teens.

I'm currently a season ticket holder at my boyhood club Norwich City.

Printed in Great Britain
by Amazon

25507784R00294